ANGUS PETER CAMPBELL is from South Uist. He has worked as a lemonade factory bottle-washer, kitchen-porter, labourer, forester, lobster-fisherman, journalist, broadcaster, actor and writer. He graduated from the University of Edinburgh with Double Honours in Politics and History. His Gaelic novel *An Oidhche Mus Do Sheòl Sinn* was voted by the public into the Top 10 of the Best Ever Books from Scotland in The List/Orange Awards of 2007. His poetry collection *Aibisidh* won the Scottish Poetry Book of the Year Award in 2011 and his novel *Memory and Straw* the Saltire Scottish Fiction Book of the Year in 2017. *Tuathanas nan Creutairean* (George Orwell's *Animal Farm* in Campbell's Gaelic translation) appeared in 2021. *Constabal Murdo 2: Murdo ann am Marseille* won the Gaelic Literature Awards Fiction Book of the Year Prize for 2022. In 2023 he was named as the Gaelic Writer of the Year at the Highlands and Islands Press Ball Media Awards.

LIONDSAIDH CHAIMBEUL, who made the drawings in this story, is an Honours graduate of Edinburgh College of Art. She works as a sculptor, designer and school bus driver. Her art work is on display in public places from Benbecula to Irvine and in several private collections. She represented Scotland at the first ever Scottish International Sculpture Symposium in 1986.

Electricity

a novel by

ANGUS PETER CAMPBELL

Luath Press Limited

EDINBURGH

www.luath.co.uk

First published 2023

ISBN: 978-1-80425-050-1

Printed and bound by
Clays Ltd., Bungay

Typeset in 10.5 point Sabon by
Main Point Books, Edinburgh

Images © Liondsaidh Chaimbeul
Text © Angus Peter Campbell 2023

One can always exaggerate in the direction of truth
Matisse

Contents

Acknowledgements

MY THANKS TO everyone who helped make this book. To Louis de Bernieres, Catherine Deveney, Professor James Hunter, Fr Colin MacInnes, Karen Matheson and Selina Scott for their generous endorsements. To Peter Ferguson for the cover photograph. To my wife Liondsaidh Chaimbeul for the beautiful map and hand-drawings as Annie, and to my daughter Ciorstaidh for the drawing of the yellow on the broom. To Jennie Renton, Maddie Mankey, Amy Turnbull and Gavin MacDougall at Luath Press for their work and support. My special thanks to Gwyneth Findlay who edited the novel with grace and precision. She said on first reading the novel that it was like getting a big hug. I hope that you also feel the same, warmly welcomed into this community by Annie, Mùgan, Niall Cuagach, Lisa, Sgliugan, Hazel, Dolina, Mrs MacPherson and all their pals. *Taing dhaibh, agus tapadh leibh uile.* Enjoy!

√

My Dear Emily,

I hope you're well. And may Gran's adventures make you feel even better! Remember that time we camped out for the night? I know it was just the back garden, but you said it was like being in the middle of the forest, because you could hear the wind blowing through the trees and the owls hooting far off. We were at the centre of everything. And how we both snuggled into the sleeping bags and lit our wee torches and then played shadows on the canvas, and you said it was an elephant when it was a mouse and then when we put the torches together yours was the sun and mine the moon! In the morning, I was the only one who heard the birds singing, for you were fast asleep in my arms. Said you were cold during the night though we both knew it was just an excuse and I was so pleased when you snuggled in and slept, breathing warm as toast, while the wind whispered outside. All that mattered was that we were alive and together.

I wish I could go over and see you, or that you could fly over here. If I were with you I'd hug you long and close, and I know I'd want you to hold on and never let me go. I've written down my story for you, as promised. As a sort of tent in which we can coorie in! Everything has kind of raced by, and all I want to do is to tell everyone I ever met how beautiful and strange they all were.

Once upon a time, it seemed as if change came from the outside, like a gale-force wind, when all the time it was ourselves. But you can shelter from the wind. I look in the mirror and see the changes. Those lines on my forehead when I deliberately frown, and the way my mouth purses when I put on my lipstick. Inside, I am forever the girl I was, running across the machair in the middle of May inhaling the sweet smell of the clover while the larks sing overhead.

I had wee headaches at first and didn't think anything of them.

*Though Mam said she'd also had them when she was my age
and that they would go after a while. Which they did. There were
some things we didn't talk about in those days. You just found
out about it by magic, as it were. Like finding an unknown object
on the shore and by handling it discover it was light and made
of plastic, and that if the bit at the end was fixed (which Dad
repaired) it could fly! It was a toy plane. Things can surprise us.*

*The thing that happened was that I grew up the same time
electricity arrived. It was as if the two were directly connected.
The way the bulbs sizzled when they were first lit was the way
I felt. Crackling and fusing together and then illuminating
everything with that soft, flickering light.*

*But we also feared it. Sensed that nothing would ever be the
same again. Dad feared the loss of the hearth and the fire. Mam
knew what speed meant. It spoilt the making of things. She
always did things slowly. Carved the bread as if it felt every cut.
Milked the cow gently, because it made the milk creamier. Folded
the tablecloth ever so softly, because the linen remembered all
her kindness. In the midst of it all I met Antoine, and it was as if
the whole place was lit up by will-o'-the-wisp, with my bike and
the grass and the seashells all shining! It's all that matters, those
moments. Remember how the moths all hovered outside the
tent that night, vainly trying to get in? They never did, and once
we turned the torches off, all was silent, except for your quiet
breathing, and me trying not to breathe in case I woke you.*

*Everything will pass, my darling. That's all. The bad too,
so hold on to the good, for its day will come again. And
just to remind you of the shadow-shapes we made with our
hands in the torchlight, I've done a few drawings to chum all
these words I've written. They are in memory of dear Mrs
MacPherson, who made the best cup of tea and the nicest
scones in the whole world, even though you think Gran does!*

*I learned the recipes from her, so really it's always been her
scones. As is everything else, sort of hand-me-downs which*

arrived like lightning and quiver on like a candle. You know fine I can work a computer, but I've written all this out by hand because you once told me that you liked my hand-writing since it was like those white swans we saw swimming in Inverleith pond! Remember, a dog barked suddenly, and the swans looked at each other, as if wondering whether to fly away, but then just dipped their heads into the water and carried on fishing.

Isn't it amazing how we remember all the details of some things, and can't remember a thing about others? Bet you remember the name of your first pet and infant teacher! Flora the Frog and Miss MacIsaac! It's a beautiful starlit night here in Edinburgh. I was down the bottom of the garden earlier, just as the sun set. The maple and cherry trees were red and orange, and Hector the Hedgehog, my daily evening visitor, was trundling along as usual between the gate and the hedge. He loves the apple cuts I leave for him there every night. When you next come over, bring some of those Fujis with you, which he likes so much! They're impossible to get over here. Poor old Hector has got such a sweet tooth!

I know it's daft, but you know what I've done, Emily? The reason I was down the bottom of the garden was not just to feed Hector, but to set up the tent! It's a warm night and I'm going to sleep out there for old times' sake. Don't worry – I've got three hot water bottles ready and those fluffy pyjamas that you said make me look like Paddington Bear! Come out with me and if you take your torch we can once again make the sun and the moon and the elephant and the mouse. And if I get cold, can I just snuggle in beside you so that I get nice and warm, like toast? Let's, Emily!

Oh, and I got a large packet of the Liquorice Allsorts we both like we can share with everyone. I promise I'll keep the yellow ones for you and the stripey white and black and orange ones for myself, and folk like Campbell will just have to make do with the plain sticky black ones, so there!

Love, Gran xxx

I

Silver Morning

IT'S BEEN GOOD. When I was wee we used to play a game. Dolina and me. As we cycled along, she counted the things to her left, and I counted the things to my right. The houses and the people and the stones and the walls and the sheep and everything. Without cheating, because that spoilt the game. You couldn't just say that you saw five starlings when there were only three. We made up stories about everything we saw.

The big rock as we turned northwards by the machair track was Helen Carnegie who'd been turned to stone by the wicked witch, and the river that ran into the sea was the Mississippi for me and the Amazon for Dolina. Mine had swamps we had to swim through, and hers had crocodiles we had to wrestle with to get to the other side. They always took big bites out of our legs.

We also played houses. Pebbles were little cottages and we made long and winding sandy roads up to them and kings and queens and princes and princesses and witches and goblins and magicians lived in them. Smoke always curled out of the chimneys, and I still can't draw a house without putting a wee road up to the door and two matching windows and a curl of smoke rising up to the blue air. The door is always open and the kettle forever on the boil.

There was a small cave down by the shore that was our first castle. Duncan and Fearchar helped us pull an old cupboard door down to the castle, and if anyone wanted to enter they had to knock three times on the door with this special white stone before they were allowed in. Inside, we had sticks and a kettle and a cupboard and shelves and everything where we held big feasts. In the summer when the days were long and there was hardly any night we lit a fire and roasted marshmallows on sticks and then ran and danced until the sun shone orange.

I'm writing with a pencil because that's how I learned to write at school, and I know that if I make a mistake I can rub it out and start again. We used to rub things out with the heel of the white loaf, but these days I use Jamieson's round erasers. I get them from Simpson's round the corner. Thing is, with the loaf you could still see the smudge, as if writing and sums had as much to do with rubbing out as putting in!

Same with everything. Mam was forever washing things and Dad always clearing fields so that the potatoes would grow. It was as if nothing could happen without something else being removed. When Niall Cuagach divined for water he never knew where the exact spot was, or whether it was a trickle or a well. We watched him following his stick ever so carefully and then came that remarkable moment when the twig twitched, and there it was. Water. It was as if the stick was alive in his hands. He gave us the stick to try, but though we waved it about everywhere we never found water. It only ever worked for him.

The first time Mam gave me a pencil when I was about two or three she cupped her hand round mine and made this amazing shape which she said was an 'a', and then she cupped my hand and made a different shape and said 'And that's a capital A'. It was like the difference between a lamb and a sheep, I thought. I got it right first time and didn't even have to rub it out and that's been my aim all my life.

The birds are singing outside. They are always at their best at this time, first thing in the morning, as if every new dawn is a surprise to them, needing a song. Goodness, the way Claudia my neighbour moans, as if it's a trial being alive. I'm lucky, because I have trees in my garden, so all the birds gather there, summer and winter. They've grown since you last climbed them! I sleep well enough, though I wake early. But no matter how early, the goldfinches are always up before me. The gowdspinks. On spring and summer and autumn mornings they are in full song by six or seven, but even in winter, because I put seed out for them, there they are as soon as the sun rises. Maybe the sun himself rises when he hears their songs?

I've had my breakfast. Today, fruit and yoghurt. And black decaffeinated Earl Grey. The one with the blue cornflower blossoms and bergamot you thought was a perfume the first time you were here! I add orchid petals. For the antioxidants, I tell myself! Though it's really for the colour which matches that gorgeous Japanese pot you bought me from the charity shop.

Oh, and did I tell you I bought a stove? The man installed it a while back, but it wasn't working properly. Then he came back and fixed the flue. Blamed the flue of course, saying it was faulty! And you know what? The local garage down the road sells those bags of peat, and once the fire gets going good and proper with wood and a handful of coal I add the peat so that the fragrance of my childhood fills the air. Forgive an old woman adding her bit to global warming, my dear child!

It's a silver morning here. The sun is shining in through the kitchen window and the percolator is already bubbling. Wasn't it lovely being outside on a clear and starry winter's night? We might have been eaten by moths or frogs! Or been invaded by those starships you said you saw flying between the moon and the horizon! And isn't it nice too to be back inside, the stove cosy and warm, and the smell of coffee in the air, and this new day and the chance to tell you all those other things I forgot to tell you about after the man in the moon fell asleep when the clouds covered him! Remember?

2

Home

WHEN I WAS your age I often felt as if everyone else was smarter and better and prettier, and could run and do sums and all kinds of things better than me. Now it doesn't matter so much. Who cares if Mrs MacPhee next door can still play 18 holes of golf every day when it's enough for me to walk down to the local shop? It's not a competition.

At first, the world was Mam and Dad and Duncan and Fearchar and me. The boys shared a bedroom, and I had one for myself.

Your great-uncle Duncan is three years older than Fearchar who is two years older than me. I don't suppose it matters much now, though it did then. Duncan the big boy, then Fearchar in the middle, then me. Like steps on a stair. Though it was more like a triangle. Duncan at the top tip and Fearchar and I at the angles at the bottom. Otherwise it wouldn't be a triangle, as our maths teacher always said. With Mam and Dad I suppose it was a pentagon! And once we add the rest of the family we have an apeirogon where we all hold one another together! Or maybe it's all a circle?

Everything in the world is a different shape, Niall Cuagach used to say. A round wheel can be bent, but a circle is a circle forever. Old Gillies the blacksmith used to put the wheels in the forge and make different shapes of them. He would thin out and thin out a bit of iron until it was like chewing gum. It was amazing how far he could stretch it and how long he could make it.

Strange to think that time itself is like that, and that now I'm seventy, I'm still ten as well. Like a piece of stretched iron where the longer you pull the thinner it gets, though still tied together like an elastic string. The same as playing shadows. Your shadow is sometimes ahead of you and sometimes behind you or to the side, depending on where the sun is shining from. And strange how it's always longer or shorter than you are. You jump to try and catch it, and you never do! I remember being a baby and lying in my cot watching sunbeams dancing in the air. I tried to catch them but they always floated away. Upwards and out the skylight window. I mind the time you were here and because the sun was obscured by the tree where I stood your shadow was longer than mine. And then you asked me to stand where you were and you stood where I had been and you were so pleased that Gran was back to her normal bigger size!

I've been thinking about how we all dress up. Ministers in their collars and football players in their strips and pop singers in their outrageous costumes! Duncan took to wearing a cap when he was in Primary Seven. He could already lift the old stone by the gate shoulder-high and soon managed to raise it above his head and became a proper man. Because that was the sign, all the boys said. He imagined he had grown-up things to do. Planting the potatoes in spring. Keeping an eye out for the shaws appearing. Harvesting them at autumn. Cutting the peats, gathering tangle from the shore, driving the tractor when Dad was busy with other stuff. I think he lost his childhood being big. For a while he took to walking backwards whenever he could, claiming that strengthened his leg muscles so he'd be able to run faster than anyone else and win all the races at the annual games.

When he drove the tractor he pretended he was Captain Cook and Daniel Boone, his eyes forever on the horizon, conquering the world. There was no end to it, he said, for beyond our fields were more fields and the moor and the mountains and then the mainland. On the other side the machair and the sea all the way west to America. The blue and gold history school book said it was the land of the free, so you could do whatever you wanted there and it wouldn't cost a thing, unlike here where even a penny caramel cost tuppence out in MacLean's shop, because by time it got here, old MacLean said, he had to pay the man who made it as well as the train-driver who carried it to Oban and then the ferry workers who took it all the way across the Minch as well as the porter who carried it up in his barrow from the pier.

Our house was the last one in the village, next to the machair. We had a green door. A kitchen to the left and a sitting room to the right and Mam and Dad's bedroom at the back. Duncan and Fearchar and I had the two rooms upstairs. From the windows we could see the sea at the back and the whole village from the front stretching out towards the wide moor. There was endless talk of putting an airstrip out there by the old cattle-fold which we looked forward to so much because we could then fly off quickly to the mainland. But we knew it would never happen, because grown-ups were always talking about things they wouldn't do. Unless the fairies themselves built it and why would they because they liked the peace and quiet and the long flat green space where they could run and play all night long.

I was the first to discover the Arctic. I found it the day after Christmas in a dark crevice under the wee stone bridge – a heavy block of ice which neither Duncan nor Fearchar had noticed. I was smart enough not to take it home because I knew it would melt. And I never told them. Even though it lasted through till the beginning of summer. By then it had diminished into a thin sliver of ice. Then it disappeared. It never came back. I know because I looked for it for years. Next time you come over to visit during your summer we'll go down to the Lothian Burn which always gets frozen over in January. I bet you won't believe how well your granny can still skate. But only as long as you hold my hand!

We had hardly any books when I was growing up. Most people had none. Written words aren't everything, after all. Old Murdo brought back from sea hundreds of yellow magazines called the *National Geographic* and whenever Duncan and Fearchar and I called in to give him a loaf Mam had made, we'd watch him reading the magazine. He was forever talking about The Plantations, saying that was why everyone smoked so much.

We weren't allowed candles in our bedrooms in case we knocked them over and set fire to things. We would peer out and follow the trail of candlelight on the other side of the road as Mrs MacPherson moved from the kitchen where she spent her evenings and slowly climbed the ten steps to her bedroom where she threw fascinating shadows behind the curtains for a while until it went completely dark. She never jumped steps like we did.

When the electric came, folk always said it must have been so dark *before*. Well, it never seemed that way to us, we had as much light as the seasons gave us. Light all day and all night in the summer time. Besides, in the dark you hear everything, like when you're cuddled up in bed and can hear your own heart beating. I remember you telling me that's part of the reason you go camping. To hear your own heart thumping while the owl hoots and the stars crackle. Some say it only reminds them of how alone they are, but when I hear my heart beating as I lie awake at night it makes me smile with the joy of still being alive.

I talked to the birds. They were my friends. They listened, and had so much to sing about too. Their songs were all learned ages ago. The little robins perching on the window-sills in the winter, waiting for crumbs. The owls crooning to one another in the eaves of the old barn. The peewits – peesweeps we called them – always inviting us to play high up in the skies. The swallows whooping in every spring, telling Dolina and me about Africa, where they couldn't even land on the burning desert.

Mrs MacPherson told us that the swallow was the spirit of a young woman who got lost out on the moor years ago and now spent her time travelling the world crying for her Mam. Everything meant something. The best games I had were with the oystercatchers and curlews. I ran after them, along the shore, and allowed me to get near, then ran away again. I liked watching the cormorants and wild ducks and swans running across the water, flapping their wings and taking off into the blue sky.

Like Dolina and Peggy and Katie and myself when we played. The ancient standing stone was home. Katie had a scarf we used, tight over the eyes and tied with two knots at the back.

'Else you'll all cheat,' Katie always said.

Then we counted, the numbers getting louder. It's always the best part, isn't it? One to TEN! Sometimes to ONE HUNDRED, when you could go off and hide at the end of the world. *Here I come*! And everyone was invisible. Nothing moved.

Sometimes the boys asked the girls to play 'soldiers' with them – knocking the heads off stalks of ribwort. If any boy found a toad or a frog, or even a mouse, they cut it into pieces with their pocket-knives. Except for wee Davie MacNeil, who they pushed away and called a jessie. I liked him, for he always shared his pieces with us and offered to carry our bags without it meaning that we'd have to give him a shot of our bikes or anything. Cycling through mud and holes and puddles was never good enough for the boys, they also always had to do wheelies. Show offs!

They were always scratching their names on the school desks and dinner tables and even on the rocks outside, leaving their marks wherever they were. And every playtime we could see them standing in a row seeing who could pee highest, as if the mark they reached on the wall meant something! To us, the boys smelt. Or maybe it was just that we girls smelt differently. Whenever anyone lost a jersey all you had to do was sniff it and you knew instantly whose it was.

Dolina and I wished we were in an all-girls school like they had in the comics and on the mainland. But we had no choice. There was just the one school, so we had to put up with Sgliugan and his green snotters and the cow-dung smell off Roderick MacPherson. Why couldn't he clean his boots in the stream on the way, like everyone else? Snurfy Smith smelt of fried onions, so we all avoided him. We noticed that boys would never take their jumpers off. Not even on

ANGUS PETER CAMPBELL

the hottest summer day. Or when they were soaked wet with rain on the way to school, they'd just sit shivering and sweating in their woollen jerseys, steam rising off them like cattle in a byre. As if they had something to guard.

At home, Duncan and Fearchar were like that too. Mam had to battle to get them to use soap morning and night. It was as if the smellier they were the more manly and grown-up they thought they'd be. There was one boy called Murdo MacInnes who was different. He smelt okay and spoke nicely to me and Dolina. All he was really interested in was the fishing, so whenever we asked him to play with us it had to be a game involving boats. He'd have to be the skipper with a cap on his head (one of his socks) and we'd be the crew hauling in endless lobster-creels. According to Murdo, if you didn't know fishing you didn't know anything. He had a Swiss Army Knife which he was always trying to impress us with, all blades and daft screw things. When he grew up he became a renowned trawlerman working out west as far as Rockall.

Some of the older girls were chasing each other across the playground; some standing, looking around, waiting for someone to be their friend, which never happened just like that, because friends are long made and forever, and if you didn't have a friend by the time you were in Primary Seven you never would. So they said, though it wasn't true. There's nothing in the world like having true friends. Ones that like you and aren't just pals because their parents told them to pity you or admire you or because they're related to you or something. Someone you can tell your worst things to and they won't correct you. It took me ages just to listen.

Bets Dolina will be behind the shelter again, I always thought. And Peggy, crouching behind the bicycle-shed. Katie was unpredictable. And unfair. She always needed to be first. Talk about cheating! She could be anywhere. Even inside the school, which was out of bounds during playtime. Well, she could stay there. I wasn't going to get into any trouble going inside looking for her. She would just lie anyway, saying she'd gone inside to use the toilet

24

or get a book or some other excuse. The lying toad, because lying was cheating and almost as bad as stealing. And she had no shame! When she did cartwheels she went round and round and round, not caring that everyone – even the boys – were seeing her knickers and bum. At least we did it over in the girls area. You just tuck your skirt into your bloomers and you can then cartwheel across the world if you want to!

And besides, she thought she was cleverer than all the rest of us. Told us one day she was writing a story.

'A proper story,' she said. 'For grown-ups. Lots of words with no pictures, cos they're just for babies who can't read.'

Smartypants. What was the point of a story without pictures? Even where there were no pictures, weren't the words themselves, words like 'sea' and 'blue', pictures? She wasn't half as smart as she thought. Katie ended up 'writing' sure enough, as a secretary in some lawyer's office in Fort William. And then the bell rang and the game was broken.

But the game with the birds never broke. I always wanted to be a bird, but they never wanted to be me. I couldn't hop long enough or jump high enough or sing like them or make a nest up high or anything. They pecked in the little sandy pools while I tried various ways of getting near them, though they were reluctant to come near me, even when I put crumbs into the open palm of my hands and sat still as a stone. They might think I wasn't a danger then. Which I wasn't. But I never convinced them. Because, at the end of the day, I wasn't one of them, and they didn't care for me as much as I cared for them.

So at first I ran as fast as I could, but they always ran faster and rose and wheeled off into the air. I tried doing the same but could only jump about a foot. So then I tried creeping up ever so slowly and silently, but they just raised their little heads and hopped off as far again as I had come. The distance never got any smaller. It never does, which is why you need to persevere. Because one day a little robin sat on the palm of my hand, and I've never forgotten it. He had such brown eyes. Usually they perched for no more than seconds on a bit of wire or on top of a fence-post. Staying still was boring for them, I suppose. Fearchar told me that pigeons could travel at 90 miles an hour when they were delivering post, which was really fast. Much faster than Roddy our postman who pushed his parcels along on his old rickety bike. Honestly, the snails on the road were faster than him!

Mam moved slowly, like the summer stream, yet everything she did happened quickly. I'd spend ages with her mixing dough or threading wool on to the spool, yet next thing the loaf was steaming warm and a scarf made. I loved her more than anyone and anything else in the whole world. I miss her terribly. She never flew off like the birds. It was the sacred way she did everything, whether washing her hair or sewing a button onto Dad's shirt. It's as if she wasn't doing them but unveiling them. She handled things as if they could vanish at any moment. Loosely, so that they had freedom to disappear if they wanted. I see that in you too, in the way you speak, without any malice. Mam always said that spite was like a knot in the thread. It spoilt the best work.

Mam loved combing my hair and always sang as she did it. When she mixed dough for bread, the flour rose into the air in clouds and I tried to catch the specks as they slowly tumbled back down into the bowl. I never could. She cooked everything slowly, saying the food was like the sun, needing time to rise, shine and set.

'That way it gives you all its strength. Speed only extracts the goodness out of it.'

We never held hands, yet we were always touching.

'Hold it this way, Annie,' she'd say as she guided me through the stitches. I always loved the way she said my name. Annie, with her tongue caressing the letters *nn*. 'Purl the wool on here, then loop the needle round this way. Look, Annie – see,' her palm resting lightly on the back of my hand, guiding the needle as if it was a fish diving for worms and rising for air. Her hands were scarred and rough from work.

> *Mach's a-steach.*
> *Leum am breac.*
> *(In and out,*
> *Leapt the trout.)*

Later on, when I was teaching my own children how to knit, I also used the old trick of turning a chore into a chant:

> *In through the front door,*
> *Go round the back,*
> *Out through the window,*
> *Off jumps Jack!*

I wonder if Aonghas can still knit, or whether he's put that behind him as a childish activity, like all other things? Though everything clings on, the way the mist lingers in the glens though the sun is shining and the skies are all spotless and blue.

I listened to the smooth click-clacking of her needles downstairs as I drifted off to sleep every night. I always knew when things were going well because the sound was soft and smooth. When a stitch was dropped or a mistake made, the needles made a sharper, quicker sound.

Mam birthed the lambs in spring and after a while I was allowed to help. It all happened naturally. Sheep know how to give birth, but sometimes Mam sensed a difficulty, so she kept an eye on some of the expectant mothers. It's a fine thing to be doing, caressing the mother sheep as the new-born lamb comes into the world. The trembling foot, and the little head first, and the lamb and mother's tongue flicking in anticipation, then the mother licking every inch of the bloody lamb who struggles to get to its feet, reaching all the time towards the teats for food and life. The perfect training for me when I did my stint later on in the maternity ward!

Mam treasured everything she'd been given. Because of the givers. Her own mam's wedding ring and silver brooch with a dove engraved in the middle. The letters and postcards Dad had sent her from these mythic, faraway places. Bahia Blanca. Buenos Aires. Vancouver. The white stone I gave her from the beach the day we had a picnic there and I learned to paddle. She kept them all by her bedside, and sometimes when I wasn't well and slept curled in beside her I watched her hold them and smile. She liked brushing my hair, and as I snuggled in she ran her bony fingers through, unsnagging all the little tangles I'd made during the day. There was no end to them.

She also kept beautiful things in the sitting room, where people could see them. A painting of the hills made by the local vet, a lovely clock the Royal Hotel in Oban gave her when she left, and some of my shells and other odds-and-ends she'd gathered here and there. If Dad had his way, there would have been no ornaments or anything like that in the house – just the beds, a few chairs and a table, and he would have filled the rest of the space with spades and sickles and scythes and ropes and saws and scraps of wood and bits of engines. It's as well Mam was there. She wasn't fussy about things, but couldn't bear them to be shabby. Folk's houses and furniture could be untidy and messy, unkempt, old, rickety, even dusty and dirty – as long as they weren't cheap and shabby. That was simply a lack of taste and unforgiveable.

The thing I enjoyed most was making butter with Mam. The two of us skimmed the cream from the milk into the wooden pail, then into the churn. We had two churns. One you turned with a handle, and one had a stick you pushed up and down. I liked the one with the handle best. You turned it ever so slowly at first, then faster and faster until your arms got sore. The more I turned the handle the thicker and creamier the butter became. I was allowed to stick my finger in and lick the thickening cream. The best bit was when our hands got all mixed up as we rolled the butter on the baking paper so that sometimes I didn't know which were my fingers and which were hers.

Mam always sang as we churned the butter together and then moulded it into shape with the butter-pats. I liked the squishy sounds they made. You could make all kinds of patterns on the top of the butter so that it looked nice and fancy. I liked making swirls which were like flower heads. The butter always tasted better when it was a snowdrop or a primrose, which were Mam's favourite flowers. She told me that the snowdrops had made themselves white because they'd seen the snow fall and wanted to be part of it while the primroses had seen the rising sun and made themselves golden yellow.

Mam was always working. She got things done. If not cooking, sewing, and if not sewing or stitching or patching, then feeding the animals, or milking the cows, or cutting the hay, or making sure our shoes were clean for school. She once made a lovely wee jacket for me from Dad's old green corduroy trousers. When I pass old-fashioned clothes shops I think I see her in the window tidying up the display, checking the jacket lapel here, the proper crease of the suit-trousers there. So many things that need put right.

Songs were sung to pass the time, though the words and the melodies made magic happen. For what's the point of words if they don't change anything? You bless and curse and wish and hope and cry in songs. You wish for the impossible and make it happen by weaving a daisy-chain which ties everything together. Milking songs and herding songs and waulking songs and ploughing songs made work easier. As soon as the work was finished, the song ceased. Except it kept going round and round in our heads. Beautiful ringleted lovers appeared – and heartbroken women wept – as the milk squeezed out of the udder or as the cloth shrunk under pounding arms. I learned all the songs by singing them, again and again, with Mam. It was part of things, as natural as drawing breath, as necessary as walking to the well for water or to the shore for sticks. Amazing how you learn things better when you're moving. Rhythm helps you remember. I tried yoga once, which taught me the very opposite. It never worked for me. I've known too many still, silent people, weeping inside. We could hear the dead crying down in the cemetery on quiet winter nights.

Some people liked working in silence, building small stone walls slowly and quietly as if they were asleep or in church. A noise might make the wall fall. Not even whistling. Which was odd, because whistling was one of the privileges of working outside. No one ever whistled inside. That was the work of the devil himself. James Thomson had whistled and next thing had two bumps on his forehead which disappeared as soon as he stopped. The boatbuilder Angus MacIsaac worked in an old wooden hut which smelt of candle-wax and paraffin-oil and whenever I passed I was almost lulled to sleep by the smooth sound of sawing and the soft blow of a mallet on wood, beating like a faraway lullaby. You never heard him, just his work tools. One day I saw him chasing after the postman, and it struck me he was the only grown-up I ever saw running.

I tried to tell Duncan and Fearchar about the songs.

'Boring old things,' Duncan said. 'I hear far better ones on my transistor.'

Though I knew he secretly envied what I was learning. Thing is, I spent far more time with Mam. Duncan and Fearchar spent more time with Dad, who never sang. Hardly spoke really, apart from giving instructions or directions. As if words couldn't say thoughts and needed to be grown like potatoes before they could be peeled or said. For it is one thing to think a thing and quite another thing to say it.

'You move the handle that way.'

'No. Not like that. The other way round.' Sometimes we only understood what he said by working out what he didn't say.

And yet Dad transformed when he told his stories at the cèilidh. It was as if he never then had enough time to tell everything he knew. His words ran like Thorro's River in full flow, bubbling over with actions and descriptions. Each story was always told in the same way. He never used hand gestures. Just the words and pauses, that was enough to tell everything. As if the story was in the telling.

I don't know how much that had to do with the fear of the unknown, as in the books I read, where strange lands were marked with the words 'Here Be Dragons!' Maybe the words and phrases in Dad's stories were like ancient markings telling him which way to go, like one of those walks you can do in your sleep. I always try and find new walks to go on so that I can be surprised at every turning like when I was wee. Don't believe it when they tell you that old people don't want surprises too!

It's best when you make your own markings. Like when you reach the bottom of the road from our old house the track turns rightwards towards the machair and then there's a fork leading you down to the cemetery. But just before you reach it there's an old broken plough and if you follow the furrow line, that will take you on down the familiar path to the shore. If you didn't know to turn at the old broken plough you'd go in the other direction and end up in the bog, and sink. Dad's words were like the immovable mountains after all, rather than like the tumbling waters. Outside the story, he was almost mute, in the same way that water is silent until it moves over a rock or weir. The ocean itself looks calm and quiet until you're near it, when you sense its might.

So the boys became stilted too in public conversation, as if saying anything more than four words was burdensome, like writing a school essay about 'My Favourite Thing.' What a cheek! Imagine. That was a private matter between us and our best pals, not to be told to a teacher for approval and correction. As if Dolina or I would tell any grown-up what we were thinking. Perish the thought! Why should I tell a teacher or any other nosey adult what my favourite thing was, or what I did on my holidays? The boys were not quite monosyllabic, but their three commonest public words were Aye, No and Maybe.

'How are you today Duncan?'

'Fine.'

'How's school, Fearchar?'

'All right.'

'Are you coming out to play this afternoon?'

'Maybe.'

Yet when they were together they talked endlessly. About football and puppets. The puppets only worked properly if you could suss out from the shape what they were about to do. Fearchar made football players out of them. The best goalkeeper ever was Lev Yashin who once saved three penalties in a European Cup match against Dinamo Zagreb, even though his own team, Dynamo Moscow, still lost 2-0. I heard it so often from them that the teams and scores remain there like a poem learned by heart. I find myself wandering down the road reciting 'I must go down to the seas again to the lonely seas and the sky' and the best of it is that I don't care anymore who hears. You reach an age where any sound is welcome.

And the most important thing about making a puppet are the proportions, Fearchar said. If you're making a human figure, the best way is to divide the body into eight equal sections, a head itself measuring from the crown to the chin. The next section takes you from the chin to a line drawn across the nipples, and from there to just above the navel, then to the hips, the middle of the thighs, to just a little below the bend of the knee, to a point a little below the calf and from there to the base of the heel. It was like some kind of magic formula, or the Hail Mary. It only worked if the words were right.

'But everybody is not the same size,' Duncan argued.

'Doesn't matter,' said Fearchar. 'I'm not talking size, I'm talking proportions.'

'Huh!' mocked Duncan. 'Proportions! That's a big word for you. You don't even know what it means. It's just something you read in that booklet.'

But Fearchar knew so many other strange things. That if you kneel down you are a quarter of the height you are when standing up. That the face from the hair-line on the forehead to the point of the chin is equal to three nose lengths!

'How do you know?' Duncan asked. 'Have you measured every nose in the world? Pah! You haven't even measured my nose.'

'Can I?' asked Fearchar.

And it was true. The length of Duncan's face from the hair-line on the forehead to the point of the chin was equal to three times his nose length!

'But what if I had longer hair? Or shorter?' said Duncan. 'Or a bigger nose. Like that corker Robert has. It wouldn't work then, would it?'

'Would so. It's nothing to do with the length of your hair, but with the hair-line. Where the hair starts on your head. Any old idiot would know that.'

Duncan was lying on his bed and flung a shoe at him to shut him up. If he said anything else Duncan would hit him. But Fearchar went quiet. He knew the signals. And anyway, surrender would hurt Duncan more. Everyone liked Fearchar because he was pals with you even when he had nothing to gain by it.

I could hear the boys talking next door from my own room, though I couldn't exactly make out what they were saying. Well, I could if I really wanted to, which I didn't. Why would I? Everything is much more interesting imagined than spoken. But I knew the tone of their voices so well. Duncan's had suddenly grown lower, like the drone of a bagpipe, while Fearchar's voice was still that of a boy. Without hearing any words I could fathom it all. The silences, and the length of the silences, told most. Agreement. Disdain. Peace. Anger.

My own voice was changeable. I could make it go high or low whenever I wanted. My best voice was being a bird: I could do them all. Up and down like a swallow, whistle like the oyster-catcher and my all-time favourite, wheeping like a peewit. Curracagan we called them, because that sounds like the song they make when they cry out in the heather. *Kak-a-ka-kaa*. Four syllables. It wasn't that difficult really – I just turned their cries into vocables as my mother did with the songs she had about the swans and the seals. Everything can be imitated, even though you don't often then turn into the thing you pretend to be. Though Dolina could, folding herself into a swan. You need to be careful, however. So many people had turned into crows and toads from singing deliberately out of tune and slithering along the ground instead of walking properly. Dolina said crows and toads were just enchanted people doing penance and would become good and kind people again after a thousand years.

It's an amazing thing to listen before you speak. Then you're hearing for the first time. They say the dog yaps and the kitten meows and the cow moos and the sheep goes baaaa, although that's not what I heard. Maybe our animals made noises in Gaelic? Ha! Sometimes I'd còorie in with Dìleas the collie, and he breathed ever so slowly, making a noise that sounded like *capooh*, and when I stroked the cat he purred, and the cow grunted and the sheep made a clacking noise as they munched away at the grass. For you need to tell someone what you've seen or heard, even if you're only a sheep.

I asked Mrs MacPherson about it once.

'Do the birds speak to one another like we do?'

'Of course they do. Just watch the swallows – how they warn one another if someone is approaching, and how the doves sit in pairs. For company. It's obvious they have their own language, to tell things to each other. Swallows speak to swallows and eagles to eagles, but eagles never speak to swallows and swallows never speak to eagles. Otherwise there would be no secrets, and the smaller birds would be in terrible danger from the bigger birds, and from us. You must have ways of telling and keeping secrets. And only the small birds sing. No bird of prey was ever given the gift of song.'

I liked Mrs MacPherson because she was interested in me as a person. In what I liked or didn't like and what I felt. Most of the other older people only ever asked me how Mam and Dad were, as if I was just something, like a watch, that told about something else. Maybe that's why I've never worn a wrist-watch. I just carry Dad's old pocket-watch in my bag. It's got a beautiful carving of a griffin on the face. It doesn't work, so it doesn't tell the time, which is even better. Mrs MacPherson looked after Hazel, who was a special girl. Her Mam was always unwell and no one knew who her Dad was, so she spent a lot of time near us at Mrs MacPherson's. She sometimes danced out in the moonlight singing happy songs as she moved about the garden. 'First the heel, then to the toe, that's the way the polka goes.'

James Campbell was the man who made the dream of the airport come true. Which may have been why he was regarded by some as the bad fairy who had spoilt things by changing them. When old people died he bought their houses and did them up and sold them. I'm not sure if I ever told you about him. He was much older than us but not as old as Mam and Dad. I was afraid he would silence the birds, because he couldn't speak or understand their language and disliked everything he wasn't in charge of. Even though he used such sweet melodic words himself, comparing planes to the elegance of the golden plover in flight and to the power of the eagle in its ascent and descent! I suppose he might have been a bird-catcher in the bad old days. Those guys who used to go round the place snaring larks and linnets to sell to gentry to put in cages. Sometimes it's hard to believe how wicked people can be.

'Aeroplanes are mere birds with the power to carry humans,' he said. 'Just an extension of nature. There are beings, and I count myself among them, to whom the skies matter more than the land and the earth. They even make the same sound. Wee-ah-wee!'

'Don't worry,' Mrs MacPherson told me, 'he's not God. And though devils can fly, Campbell's got no wings. And even if they did, they would be clipped. And remember, darling, that if the cows and birds are all evicted by him, they will find other places to graze and sing. You'll hear them all your life, Annie, because you're hearing them now.'

It was as if everything was still to be learnt, rather than already known. It took me ages, for example, to realise that birds fly by the wind as much as by their wings.

Strange to think now that electricity and aeroplanes were regarded then by some people as great dangers. Of course they were – we could all see that, in a way – but then again so was everything. You might fall into the well. A bull could gore you as you crossed a field. If you went up the hill the water-horse might get you. Lachlan MacIntosh had been drowned swimming in the sea because he refused to listen to anyone who told him it was dangerous. People fell into ditches all the time, stumbling their way home from the pub in the dark. They went there for company, to find someone to talk to. It was strange to want to be in company, and even stranger to want to be alone, so no one ever won.

Sometimes the more beautiful a thing was, the more dangerous it was. Martha in the next village was drowned trying to pluck one of the lovely purple water-lilies from Loch Challainn. She was so stupid, because we'd all been warned so often not to crawl out through the rushes to try and get them. They were so tempting though, floating ever so gracefully in the water. There were white and yellow ones as well as purple ones. We plucked the ones along the water's edge and then took the sticky bits off and put the blossoms in our hair or sometimes in a vase in the house, even though Dad said that was unlucky. Maybe things should be left where they are anyway. We were brought up believing we should always leave things as we found them. Maybe the owners haven't gone far – just popped out for a walk over the river a hundred years ago and will be back before evening.

Truth was that danger lay everywhere, and the arrival of electricity and the development of the local airstrip seemed to me no more dangerous than cycling downhill or when the first horse and cart or car arrived, or when the first steam boat sailed between the islands, billowing smoke out and up into the heavens. And besides, it was exciting: who didn't want light at the flick of a switch, and who didn't want to fly high in the skies like a beautiful bird? We could do everything instantly. When *we* wanted. Not when someone else decided. Be immediately on the other side of the globe, faster than on any imaginary magic carpet or any wick of straw that these daft old people at the time talked about. Who knew anything about an energy crisis as the pot bubbled on the peat stove? You can't fathom the future by what you don't know.

You only fear it if you haven't bothered to cut enough peats to last you through the whole winter.

Old Murdo said that the electric was just like sheep and had to be controlled.

'It's to do with electrons,' he declared, 'which stray about all over the place like sheep. But when a stick is applied to them, you can steer them along just fine. That's just the same thing a good dog does when you whistle him to lead the sheep to the fank.' He imagined everything worked the way sheep did.

Sometimes it looked as if the sheep were running around playing chase-and-catch in the fields, but it was just Murdo and his dog gathering them all in. Despite his daft opinions, Murdo was thought very highly of because he had the best collie in the village. Intelligent, lovely to look at, with a perfect white diamond patch just above her nose, and a joy to watch working as she sat and crept and gathered without even a whistle from Murdo. I think Murdo was in love with his dog and his dog was in love with him. She was called Polly. We called her Pretty Polly and used to sing 'Polly put the kettle on' as we walked with her to school. As soon as we arrived at the school gate and finished the song, she barked once and then ran back home to Murdo.

We were conscious of a discontent, especially among some of the older folk, who feared that the imminent arrival of electricity would change everything and that the little they had would be taken from them. Things would be different, and not as they had been anymore. Already, things were getting faster and bigger and stronger and better. Old Murdo proved it by telling everyone that while a cart only had two wheels the new cars had four, so they could obviously go twice as fast. Though Mùgan reminded him that he'd seen kangaroos in Australia which, though they only had two legs, could still run faster than any four-legged sheep or cows he'd seen ambling lazily around our fields.

Who cared at the time? For life was all change, and Dolina and

Morag and Katie and Duncan and Fearchar and I liked fast things. Even as they stood still, in those long, endless days. We all dreamt of going fastest downhill without any brakes. Angela Smith held the record, though we all knew she'd cheated by taking off her outdoor clothing and shoes and doing it in just her vest and pants so that she'd be really light. There was no rule against that, but it wasn't really fair because no one else was daft enough to go next to naked in public.

Every day brought something new – Peggy making a new doll out of a wooden clothes-peg or Dolina who always picked the nicest flowers on the way to school and stuck them in a different way in her hair every day. Some days in a bunch, some days one above each ear, some days in a sort of hoop round her head. And then it was the best time of year again – time to pick the daisies and make chains. Dolina was always the best at it, splitting the stalks with her teeth and then weaving them into each other until they were just the perfect size to hang round our necks as decorations, though sometimes we all ganged up together and made one long chain that went on and on forever. Once, we made one that stretched from the school gate all the way across the playground, right over the wall and on over on the other side to the pond, and though the boys wanted to break it, none of them dared, for they knew that was bad luck and whoever broke it would die.

And we realised that seasons came and went and always looked forward to the lambs being born and then quickly forgot them in early spring time as they grew bigger when it was time in school again to play rounders, and we saw the hay and corn grow all summer long, and watched the older boys and girls grow big and tall and strong, and wondered as they suddenly sailed away to make their fortune. Milk became cream and cream became butter and corn became bread and peat became fire and flames and boys and girls became men and women.

Sometimes we got a shilling for keeping the birds off the corn. But as soon as we left, there they were again, gleaning away to their heart's content.

3

Mam

MAM'S NAME WAS Cairistìona, though we never called her by her first name. That was for others. Cairistìona Nic Dhùghaill NicNeill. Cairistìona nighean Dhùghaill 'ic Sheumais 'ic Nìll 'ic Alasdair 'ic Dhòmhnaill an Tàilleir. Cairistìona daughter of Dugald son of James son of Neil son of Alasdair son of Donald the Tailor. Though I can also name her genealogy through her mother's side – Ciorstaidh nighean Sheònaid nic Ealasaid nic Oighrig nic Chatriona nic Chiorstaidh Bhig. Ciorstaidh daughter of Janet daughter of Elizabeth daughter of Euphemia daughter of Catrìona daughter of Little Ciorstaidh. Usually, children were only taught their father's genealogy, but Mam made sure we also knew her side of the family on both sides. All these women who stood around her day and night showing her how they'd sheared sheep and baked bread and gleaned the fields and made beds and nursed the living and the dead, telling her what to do and how to do it and what to sing and how to sing it.

Her birth certificate told her differently. There, she was Christina MacNeil. Mr MacLeod the old registrar insisted on the English-language version. Otherwise, he told her parents, it would lead to trouble later on.

'If she ever goes to the mainland, people will not be able to say her name. And besides, when it comes time for her to register for a job or even get a passport, it will be better in English, in a normal language that everyone understands.'

'Why on earth would she ever need a passport?' Grampa said. 'We never got one when we went to Gallipoli.'

When Mam went to school her teachers verified that her proper name was Christina MacNeil, though her own family and all the local people called her variants according to who they were and where they met her. I still have some of her old school jotters with that lovely name on it. It was as if everyone went to school so that they could write their names properly. The priest called her Cairistìona. Her parents, Curstag. Her friends, Chrissie. Mam.

When she left school, aged fourteen, she went to the Domestic Science College on the mainland where she registered herself as Christine MacNeil. Some of her friends there called her Chris, though she told me she always despised that, as a man's name. She enjoyed the college and the course. It was situated on beautiful grounds in Kintyre. There was an orchard, and when the girls picked the apples in autumn they made all kinds of things from them. Pies and pickles, sauces and strudels. Her favourite was the caramel apple pie oatmeal that they could have for breakfast or supper.

> One tbsp of butter, one diced apple
> one tspn. of ground cinnamon
> half pint milk/water
> one carton rolled oats
> one tbsp. brown sugar
> sprinkling salt
> drizzle caramel

The ingredients were really simple – one tablespoon of butter, one diced apple, one teaspoon of ground cinnamon, half a pint of milk or water, one carton of rolled oats, one tablespoon of brown sugar, a sprinkling of salt and some caramel for drizzling. When she brought the recipe home, her own mother dismissed it.

'Where on earth would we get any of these things here? Cinnamon and caramel?'

Mam simply said, 'It tastes equally as good without those two things.' And it did.

She then worked in the hotels for a while. Not as a cook, but as a cleaner and maid. Those big white-washed hotels that used to be full all summer long. The best thing, she told me, was the friendship and fun with the other girls and the one day off when they all went shopping or to the pictures or to a dance together. She served a season in the Imperial Hotel in Fort William, then three seasons in the Great Western and the Regent hotels in Oban, before going further south to work in the old Adelphi Hotel in Liverpool. Her friend Marion got a job there as Head Housekeeper and pleaded with Mam to join her.

She was glad she did, for she met Dad there. He was a bosun in the Merchant Navy, sailing regularly out of Liverpool on one of the cargo ships run by the Palm Line. Curstag met him in church. The Sunday 7am Mass. She needed to be at work at eight, and Seumas had just arrived overnight from Panama. She recognised him when he entered the church, crossing himself and genuflecting before sitting over on the other side. He hadn't seen her. She looked at him when everyone bowed their heads.

Curstag knew him from childhood, though he was older. Primary Seven when she was in Primary One. By the time she was on Primary Seven he'd already left school and gone to sea. But she'd see him occasionally when he was home on leave. He used to hang around with a group of young men who had scooters. Such unsuitable things for the place. Noisy and flimsy machines which blew half over in any wind. That was probably the challenge and the joy for them – trying to hold these small fragile bikes upright against the north-westerly storms. Isn't it wonderful how nothing is dangerous when we're young and daring? You don't have enough memories yet to hold you back.

The scooters were beautiful looking things. Full of colour. Red mostly, though Dad and his best friend Angus had silver ones. They glittered and shone in the rain and sun. He once gave Mam a lift home on it. Sat her on the pillion while he stood and steered all the way down the hill, leaning sideways to counteract the wind. She was terrified and thrilled. She was nine then and he was sixteen. She noticed that one of his ears was slightly bigger than the other. The left one.

She met him in the aisle as folk filtered out of church. Nodded to him. He smiled back. It's what we remember. It's what she best remembered in her final days.

'That smile,' she said. 'As if he was seeing an angel!'

'Curstag,' he said outside, shaking her hand. 'What a surprise to see you here.'

He had slim, exquisite hands. Always did, no matter how many bales of seaweed or how many scythes or spades he handled.

'And you.'

'What...'

'Working. At the Adelphi. Started a month ago. You?'

'Same. Here today, Panama tomorrow. Or Glasgow. Or wherever. Have you had breakfast?'

'No. But I'm on shift at eight.'

They both looked up at the church clock.

'Lunch then?'

'I'm finished at two for the afternoon.' she said. 'Back on again at six.'

'Right. Two it is then. At the Adelphi? Main door?'

'Aye.' She smiled.

They went to a tearoom. She had an omelette and orange juice. He had chops and chips and cabbage and tea. Mam had such remarkable memory of those early days, even to the very end. All the little details of long ago. It's what she always talked about then. Living it all again. She'd hand Dad the knife and fork as if he was still there. 'Here,' she said. 'Thanks,' he said.

'I've stopped drinking,' Seumas said. 'It was beating me. Too many nights in cells in strange ports. Feel all the better for it.'

'You're looking well,' she said. 'Though you should maybe lose a pound or two. Too many chops?'

'Curries. We have these wonderful Indian cooks on the ship. Amazing curries. I eat too many chicken masalas. Even for breakfast.'

'Porridge is better, a Sheumais. You know that.'

'I know.'

Afterwards they went for a walk.

'Not by the Mersey,' he said. 'See too much water every day as it is.'

So they walked to the Botanic Gardens where they sat on a wooden bench next to one of the water fountains by the conservatory.

'There's the bench over there,' she told me, pointing to the wooden chair in the corner where her dressing-gown lay. Things become what we imagine they once were. The older Mam got, the more she lived in a magnified past. We walked the same familiar road again and again, each of us gracefully astonished by every old surprise.

'I don't know anything about trees,' he said. 'Can't distinguish one from the other.'

'That's ash,' Curstag said. 'And those over there are willows. The Chinese used to break off a willow branch and give it to a departing friend. They grew in the grounds of the Domestic College, though we weren't allowed to break any branches. Argyll is full of trees. Less sheep maybe? The branches are soft and bendy. Make wonderful baskets. Weave together like fingers.'

Seumas was holding her hand. Racking his brain for something to say about trees.

'There are stories about the rowan,' he said. 'The sacred tree. If you have one by the door no evil can enter. Rowan tree and red thread make the witches lose their dread.'

'But more songs about the apple tree,' she said. 'About love.'

'Hah!'

'I remember you singing,' he said. 'At the school concert.'

She laughed. For singing wasn't the same as saying. She couldn't know if he loved her if he was just singing about it. Maybe he was afraid to say it. Just as she was.

'Ha! That nonsense? What was it? "Heart of Oak"? Or maybe "Shenandoah" that old witch MacAllister made us sing every year?'

'No. I think it was "The Gypsy Rover".'

'Who came over the hill, down through the valley so shady...?'

They both hummed it for a while and then fell silent.

He squeezed her hand ever so slightly, so she sang. The old great song about the apple tree. Craobh nan Ubhal – 'Oh, apple tree. Know the tree that is mine. The tallest with the sweetest apples. Its trunk strikes downward, its top is bending. Apple tree, may God be with you. May the east and west be with you. May every sun and moon be with you. May every element be with you.' It's an ancient song which tells people are like trees, dependent on so many environmental factors for survival and flourishing. Some grow big and tall and strong and last centuries, others are frail and slender and sway with every passing breeze. The silver birch and the hazel and the rowan, for example.

Better to bend with the elements than to stand firm and be broken in two. To warp and shrink and bend and twist rather than break. The wind was always stronger than the flimsy shelters and sheds and walls we erected, even though the old story claimed that the sun was stronger than the wind. There was a war between the sun and the wind. The wind bet the sun that he would make the boy take off his coat, but the harder he blew the tighter the boy clung on to it until the wind was exhausted. Then the sun shone and he didn't need it anymore. Love triumphs. The wind was always there, pushing us or pulling us this way and that all the way to school. Dolina and I made a den down by the fank which fell in the first gust and Duncan and Fearchar were forever putting up goalposts which clattered down in every gale.

They met again after her Monday shift. Went to a jeweller on Lord Street where he bought her a silver engagement ring.

'We didn't see the point in waiting,' Mam said. 'If something's right, Annie, just do it.'

'Matches the scooter,' Mam said when she tried the ring on.

'The scooter! Goodness, I'd forgotten all about that.'

'I haven't. Bet you couldn't lean into the wind like that now.'

He laughed.

'Just wait and see.'

He patted his tummy.

'This is going to go. On this next voyage. Hard labour and no masalas.'

She touched his ears.

'These are still the same, though. This one ever so slightly longer than the other. Bigger.'

They kissed outside the shop as he slipped the ring onto her finger properly.

'Yes,' she said.

'A couple walked by, clapped and shouted "Congratulations!"' Mam said. Dad held her small waist in his hands and until the day he died he remembered that as the happiest moment of his life.

'I'm sailing again on Wednesday,' he said. 'On the West African route. I wouldn't normally do two trips back to back but half the crew are sick and they're short. And it's double time for six months. I'll write. Even though I'm not very good at it,' he added.

'I'm a good reader,' she said. 'I can read in between the lines, even if there's only one line.'

'I'll manage that,' he said. 'I'll certainly manage that, if you can fill in the spaces.'

4

Dad

DAD WAS NEVER half as much fun as Mam. Too serious, as if a thing could only be done one way. This way, and not that way. And he didn't really listen. Just sort of half-listened so that he would get the gist of what I was trying to say to him and then say something before I ever finished what I had to say, with the important thing maybe still left unspoken. Even though that shouldn't matter, because I can always make out what someone is feeling even as they stumble half their words out. It matters to them. And yet he must have listened well as a child, because he had all the old traditional stories off by heart. Unless there was a different way of listening and remembering then.

It's probably easier to tell a story than tell what you feel, though. I know Duncan remembers most of Dad's stories, Fearchar some of them, and I only remember bits of them because the parts I don't remember had nothing to do with me. All about big strong men carrying swords and setting fire to castles and killing their enemies and carrying off their wives and cows. If the cows were lowing it was not because they were happy but because they were sad. They'd been stolen from another clan and were weeping for their familiar glen and grass and people.

Like Mam with her Mam, Dad heard the stories from his Dad and other men who came visiting. Stories about wars and boats and sheep and a man called Gladstone, but also nicer ones about magic lanterns and swords, and how you could travel across the world on a wisp of straw if you knew the secret word. Often the secret word was simply the name of your home village. It released most power. The devil was afraid of home because he had been exiled from it, and though he wanted to go back he knew he couldn't, so he hated it because it was so near and yet so far.

If you spoke the word you could be delivered instantly from the Tower of London and from death itself. The name of your home village carried infinite power. But only if you loved it. Being in a city far away was obviously a dangerous thing. Full of strangers and unknown and sly and wicked people. There was the story of Captain Joe MacCormick with the noose round his neck on the gallows who shouted 'Boisdale', and that very instant he was back herding his black cows through the heather on Easabhal. Forever afterwards he was seen wandering the shore looking for messages in a bottle and stopping folk to tell them that the truth of a single word is always better than ten cows. That's why places had names. If you got lost you could always ask someone the way to Linsiadair and they'd tell you. By the way, if you're ever herding cows always use three different sticks. One made from birch to help them birth, one from hazel to find them when lost, and an oaken stick to calm them when in heat. And never strike them with an angry hand. They're blessed animals.

It took a while for Dad to realise that all the stories were essentially the same ones, told over and over again. For they seemed new every time they were told, as if every teller was making it up on the spur of the moment, watching the action unfolding in front of his eyes. The better storytellers made the action happen rather than watched it. Conjuring up the man with the bow-and-arrow, placing the apple on the boy's head, then drawing back the string to aim. It was not what they said but how they said it. For neither the boy nor the man were described, though you could see them. The man was tall and thin and the boy was small and fair, though no one ever said so.

But he began to recognise common things. There were always three apples and seven swords and twelve rivers, and every time the hero was in trouble, his hound and the King of Greece's daughter was on hand to rescue him from the Saracens. The best thing was to die a hero. The worst thing was to be a coward. Dad said that when Alasdair Mòr spoke about the Boer War he could literally see the gun-smoke on Talana Hill.

'A terrible war,' he said, 'but at least better than no war at all. Kept the lads from mischief. And they got paid for it. With a smart uniform and pension too, if they survived.'

You believed every word he said.

Later, when out herding the cows, Dad's old neighbour Archie sat on a rock and told him that giants lived beneath the earth. Archie played a whistle made of an oat-stem. He played reels in the morning and slow airs in the afternoon and evening because you needed to calm down before you slept. If you played the tunes the other way round and rattled out the reels as darkness fell, the fairies would hear and take you away dancing all night long, which was forever, because by the time you returned your beard was white and hoary and frost-ridden and everyone you knew was dead and no one recognised you as they travelled through space on wheel-less carriages and spoke a strange and different language with machines in their hands showing them all the kingdoms of the world in all their splendour and glory.

The rock was covered with lichen, which in spring was the colour of silver and in autumn the colour of gold, so that it was called Creag an Airgid 's an Òir (the Rock of Silver and Gold), though some people claimed that was because some Spaniards had hidden doubloons deep inside when they were fleeing north after the wrecking of the Armada.

'If you put your mouth to that crevice in the rock and call your name, he and all his giant friends will call you back,' Archie told him.

And so they did. Giant after giant. Every time. They called back his name, again and again and again and again. *Seumas Seumas Seumas Seuma Seuma Seum Seum S S S* growing ever fainter and further away, and when their voices finally faded into silence, you shouted your name once more, and they'd call it back as long as you kept calling them. If you were silent, they too were silent. Listening to your silence as long as you listened to theirs. They had such good manners, and they never spoke without being spoken to.

'Why does my name get fainter and fainter?' Dad asked, and Archie replied, 'Because every time they call back your name they step further and further into the hill to tell their friends deep inside that you're here, and then when they can't hear you anymore they come back out again with their friends and listen to see if you'll call once more.'

'Why are they in there? Are they trapped, or being punished or something?'

Archie smiled.

'No. The very opposite, son. They are great warriors rewarded with their own vast underground kingdom, where there is no rain or wind. They can sleep or fight or eat or play all day if they want to. Imagine that, Seumas. They have a house built of rock which will withstand time itself, my boy. Wherever you are in the world they will magnify your voice. Did you know that your eyes as well as your ears get bigger in the dark?'

The biggest giant was called Mac-Talla-nan-Creag, a direct descendent of Fionn. He had put all the rocks where they were in the first place when the whole world was just one land without any sea. Mac-Talla-nan-Creag was out hunting one day when the wild boars turned on him and chased him. In his anger he lifted huge lumps of earth to throw at them, which landed with such force that they became rocks. Eventually he threw such a large clump of earth that it broke the land into smithereens and divided Ireland from England and Scotland from Iceland and he was safe because the boars hadn't yet learned to swim.

'What about the fish?' Dad asked Archie. 'Where did they come from?'

'From the air,' Archie said. 'They were originally birds that flew very high, too near the sun where it was so hot they got tired and almost fried and fell all the way into the sea. That's why they have fins, which are the same as wings. And that's why fish can swim as fast as birds can fly. In fact, fish and birds are the same thing.'

'Do you think I could fly?' Dad asked him.

'No. But you can do something neither birds nor fish can do.'

'What's that?'

'Ride a bicycle.'

Dad loved his bike. He assembled it himself. He loved making things. Two spindly wheels he found on an old wooden cart, a frame he found at the dump, and other bits-and-bobs he collected from byres and ditches and friends and outhouses. Chains and threaded bolts and plugs and wire and even a half-full can of glue someone had thrown out. His pride and joy were the saddle and the handlebars which he made out of the side of a discarded settee covered with tweed, and the two bars from thin rods of iron he found on the shore which he welded together with a blowtorch borrowed from Old Gillies the blacksmith. The best thing in the world is making things.

Old Gillies built hand-made carts and ploughs and wheels to last, as if they were the final technology to change the world. They were beautiful things. Mostly he painted them green and red, with yellow trims, and if you sat in his cart you could be sure that no stray splinter of wood had been left to stick into your backside! They were lovely, whether trundling along the road carrying bags of peat or sand or Mùgan himself lying flat snoring in the cart after his latest spree. The horse knew his way. When I go to heaven I want to travel there in that cart.

Nothing Old Gillies made could be improved upon. Everything was invented. The whole purpose of life was to make things that would last forever so that you could stay where you were, as you were, forever. We could hear his carts and ploughs and wooden wheels and trailers and barrows filled with sand and stones and sea-weed click-clacking down the machair road on quiet mornings.

He made the world as he went along. Always talked about building the carts with bottom-boards that ran longwise rather than crosswise, because you could then shovel the load more easily without any ridges getting in the way. He gave Fearchar and me a sweeping-brush and we swept the cart and it was true. Nothing got stuck.

The carts were beautiful because they were necessary, he said, and I suppose he believed that necessity would never change. It's always like that. The thing that we most fear losing is the thing we make eternal. I sometimes went with Dad and watched Old Gillies working and it was as if his hands always remembered how to do things by themselves, because he never looked at what he was doing and was always busy blethering away about Captain Scott and how he'd died in the terrible cold, while he sawed or planed or chiselled something. He always tidied up after him so that nothing was wasted.

'It's what the Master did,' he said. 'Gathered the spare bits of bread in the basket and then fed another five thousand. With his bare hands. Amazing what you can do with your hands.'

No one else could ride Dad's bike. The handlebars were too stiff for them to steer and the wheels too large, but Dad mastered them after a while, and said he could even do wheelies as he raced through the village, blowing the powder horn that old MacFarlane claimed to have carried back from the Boer War. Mam used to watch him from their house up on the hill.

When Dad went to school he heard different stories. That if you multiplied six and ten you had sixty, and that an octopus has three hearts.

'And that's a fact,' said MacIver, the Schoolmaster. Which is what Archie also said about his stories.

'Nise, sin an fhìrinn, a Sheumais,' he said. 'Now, that's the truth, Seumas.'

Things were repeated in school too, just as in the old stories, for repetition itself made them true. You couldn't just change two plus two to make five any more than you could change a story to give it a different ending.

Though Dad realised it was not a matter of proof but of possibility. For anything was possible, and you needed courage to believe in that. If he closed his eyes, for example, he could be anywhere. In a country called Assam with a boy called Sami he read about in the school book. Sami could walk for miles through the forest carrying a large chest of loose tea on top of his head while yellow and red-beaked birds flew all around him. We didn't have any of these amazing birds, but if Sami could do it, Dad could. Or he could be playing alongside Roy Race at Mel Park, or running alongside Alf Tupper down by the canal. Best of all would be going on that great adventure across seas and oceans with Ralph Rover and his pals, building shelters and fighting pirates in Polynesia. The pictures in the book were amazing, he said: white sands and palm trees, where you could easily build your own den. Everything was in colour. The grass so green, the skies so blue, the sand so white, whereas around here it was always raining and windy and grey and dull and wet. Even the sea was grey most days. The pictures gave him the idea that things didn't need to be as they were here. That's why he went to sea in the first place.

His favourite story in school was the one the teacher read to him one day when he was in Primary One. It was called 'Ivan and the Birch Tree', and the best part of the story was when Ivan cut the tree down and found the hidden treasure inside and became a very rich man. He found 20,000 roubles, which was an awful lot of money and could buy him anything in the world. Even a pair of St Crispin Wings football boots with white laces and everything.

Other lands were always green and pleasant compared with this bare rocky windswept land of his. Though they didn't have Fionn. Bets he would have won all the heavy events at the Olympics, for he could throw the javelin for miles and miles and throw the heavy stone from Ireland to Scotland as if it was just a pebble. He'd once pulled up a fir tree, and after lopping off the roots and branches, used it as a walking-stick. Then grabbed hold of lightning, squeezed it into the shape of a pancake, and kept it in his pocket. Nothing had come into being on its own. Someone must have made it or carved it or moved it or put it there, otherwise it wouldn't be as it was where it was how it was. Dad's best friend Angus was strong too – the only lad in the district who could raise the old millstone high above his head. Dad could only manage it to his chest at that time, but one day he would. He would. If he practised and worked hard at it. He could already lift the crossing stone down by the river above his head, which no one else his age could manage. The ambition of all the boys was to be able to lift a weight greater than themselves.

Archie's best story was about the young man who asked a girl he fancied, as she stood at an open window, when she would go out with him. And she said,

'When I have lifted the linen, lowered the glass and put the dead to bury the living.'

So because she was only promising the future and not the present he gave up hope, left and sailed to foreign parts. Returning after a three-year voyage he heard she was now married to another, but was very unhappy. This grieved him, and on going to see her she told him he'd simply misunderstood her words.

'All I said was that I would go out with you as soon as I would have removed the tablecloth from the table, shut the window and smoored the fire. By which time you had disappeared.'

Dad vowed never to misunderstand words, because they were life and death. So when the priest said 'God be with you,' he answered along with everyone, 'And also with you,' knowing that words needed to be said to work properly. It was like playing football. Everyone played and no one was allowed to just be a spectator. It was a team game. A promise was a promise. It was important that Mam had said 'Yes' without pause or hesitation. And his own life-long sobriety was guaranteed, because he'd made a vow, if only quietly and to himself.

For words had meaning. 'Let there be light' and there was light. 'Hurrah for Kintail,' and the prisoner was immediately back in Kintail. Dad had a collie dog called Rover, and whenever he shouted 'Rover!' the dog appeared. Later, as bosun on the ship, he gave orders and whatever he said happened. Not because he was a tyrant but because he was trusted. It was good to work together as a team, everyone dependent on one another. He himself was under orders from the skipper. Though he had refused orders once. They were sailing down the east coast of Africa when he noticed a green tinge in the water as he was coming off watch at 4am. The Captain had ordered them to sail five degrees to port. They would end up on the rocks. He changed the order to starboard to save the ship and their lives. Sometimes a faint light to port was a lamp hanging in a farm byre. Sometimes it was a native boy lighting a fire in the bush. Sometimes it was the moon illuminating a reef.

Mam met him at the Seaforth Dock on his return from Freetown. They got a taxi into town and had lunch together at The Bluecoat. Steak and chips for both of them. Mam told me all about it when nothing else mattered.

'Eat up,' she said. 'You've lost too much weight.'

'Means I can have pudding?'

'Me too.'

'You finished?'

'Aye. Last tourists of the season left on Saturday. Hotel more or less closes down for the winter. Except for the pub bit.'

'So?'

'So I'm going back home. You too?'

'Me too.'

They took the train north next morning. To Glasgow, then the slow one to Oban. They had plenty of time. The ferry out west, past Kerrera and Mull and Coll and Tiree out into the wide open Minch. They sat side-by-side upstairs.

'This will be nothing like your journeys?' she said.

'No. Because being with you is an adventure, not a journey.'

She pinched him on the arm.

'Though the sea is the sea wherever you are. All voyages are the same and different. Bigger waves, mind you. It's just that in a calm sea every man is a pilot, and the best skippers are always sitting on the quay telling how it should be. And anyway I'm working when at sea, not sitting watching the sunset over the Bahamas. Doesn't compare to this. With you.'

'This adventure!'

They snuggled into one another.

He took three more voyages out and back before they got married. One to South Africa and two to Australia. A year and a half. He phoned one night from Adelaide.

'They've given me the job. I can start next time I get ashore. In a month's time.'

For a moment, she feared.

'Which one?'

'The one with the Fisheries' vessel. Home every night.'

So it was, all these years. Ones they could readily spare because there seemed to be so many of them, like showers of rain. Up and down the Minch looking for illegal fishing catches. And there were plenty of them. Large east-coast trawlers fishing inshore where they ought not to be. Nets adjusted to catch stocks that were protected. Undercounting the catch so the extra cash would go into their own back pockets and not into that of the exchequer. Dredging all the goodness out of the seas. Though the sea was big, it was emptying every day.

And everyone had a story to fit the occasion. They'd

misunderstood the rules. The previous owner had left the small-mesh nets by mistake. The counting machine had broken down halfway through the trawl. It was not that they told lies, just that they rarely told the truth, so that the gap between the two magnified the more they explained. As if explaining something made it true. For once you start lying nothing needs to be true. Just as a bicycle wheel which is ever so slightly off at the hub never quite runs true no matter how fast or slow you move. It simply needs to be replaced. It was like the time Maghach Colghar tried to cheat Fionn. No good came of it but his own ultimate destruction. And it was such a mean thing too, enticing Fionn, who had taught him every skill he had, to Fionn's possible death. Cowards always tell lies.

On their wedding night Dad and Mam went sailing on a yawl he'd renovated over the previous months. They sailed south lit by a ribbon of stars on midsummer's eve in calm seas towards Mingulay. They spent their honeymoon in a tent where their firstborn, my eldest brother Duncan, was conceived. There, on an island filled with birdsong and cleared of people, our family began.

5

Niall Cuagach

SO, THERE WAS Mam and Dad and Duncan and Fearchar. And my best friends Dolina and Morag and Peggy. And my sometimes-friend Katie though I could never trust her completely because she was so changeable from day to day. And Hazel. Then there was Dìleas the collie with a beautiful white patch just above his nose which I used to kiss every morning and night as he snuggled close into me, and Rosie the cow who gave us milk every day and then there were the birds standing perfectly balanced on stones or fences when they weren't flying and the daft sheep in the fields and the rabbits we hunted by moonlight just after Halloween, when we girls were allowed not just to blind them with the torches but also to smack them over the skull with the mallet and take them home for stew. Then there were all these other people who were big people at the time but now that I am older than they were then I realise they were just children too if only they had been allowed to stay like that which some of them did, and not act as if they were important and all grown up. Somewhere along the way they were persuaded to become adults. Thing is, as with the birds who all sing different songs, everyone sees things differently. I suppose some birds sing because they're glad and others because they're alarmed.

Niall Cuagach, for instance, who lived up the hill from us and was my Dad's second-cousin on his mother's side. Some thought of him as a solitary eagle up there on the mountainside, but I felt he was more like a swallow, coming and going from territories of its own. He always wore a big green storm-coat, summer and winter, as if it might rain any time, even indoors. It had huge deep pockets with things in them. We'd call by to see him sometimes, and other times he called in to see us. He spoke slowly as if he was unsure what word might come out next and surprise him and let folk know something that he didn't want them to know. So he was very careful.

It didn't seem to matter to him if a thing was true or not as long he believed it to be true. When a cow stopped giving milk, he believed it was because someone had given her the evil eye and had drawn the goodness out of the beast. The thief will be fat with the produce and is easily recognisable, he said, so keep an eye out for anyone waddling through the village like a duck. But Niall Cuagach knew that the thief could also be thin like a heron, for the devil has a thousand ways to disguise himself. He told us that you needed to find things out for yourself and reach your own conclusions, for everyone just made things up, fat or thin. It was as if he believed he could wish things into being, for once you stopped hoping for things you were as good as dead. Or it may just have been that he had thoughts which nothing could bring to life. You couldn't think of nothing anyway, because the moment you tried to think of nothing you always thought of something. I tried it out and it was true, for after a few seconds I always thought of something while I was trying so hard to think of nothing.

He called in one evening when we were doing our arithmetic homework and told us that addition was always better than subtraction. As if that was news to any of us, for who didn't know it was better to have two lollipops and then get another two rather than have two which you ate and then you had none? And when Mam made our porridge in the morning she always added things to it to make it better. Raisins and almond nuts and cream. You'll know that from cooking – flour by itself is not much use, but add baking powder and butter and a dollop of milk and a sprinkling of salt and pepper and you're on your way to a loaf or a scone or a pancake or a nan. That's how things happen.

So we knew fine that anything – even a thing that is thin and weak and small and bland – can be added to and made fat and strong and large and tasty. That's also how we reared our pigs and sheep and cows. They were born like wisps of air and left us like mounds of compost filled with steam and life and goodness. The more they passed wind the healthier they were! For we were taught that animals had eternal value, unlike money, which fluctuated. Always wool for your back and mutton for your dinner and broth for your supper, unlike a pound note which is worth twenty shillings today and just as likely ten tomorrow. Especially if you kept it in a tureen under your bed alongside your urine-pot like Niall Cuagach did! I now have one for myself, just in case. I call it my Goesunder.

He kept the best ram in the place and called him Crock of Gold because he used to rent him out to the others at half-a-crown per sheep. Just to remind myself that capitalism wasn't invented yesterday in Inverness! His greatest ambition was to have a byreful of good manure, and if he saw a good ploughed field he always started whistling. I think that manuring the soil was the greatest thing he could imagine. It made him a wizard. Gave him power over the earth itself. I suppose it was kind of like baking for him, taking one thing and turning it into another. Mrs MacPherson always said that he was the only man in the place who knew how to work horse and cow dung properly.

'The dung and the urine need to be kept in a pit or covered in a dark place,' she told me, 'so that all the power is retained when it's spread and dug into the ground rather than being left outside in a dung-hill to be bleached and wasted in the sun. It's the foundation of all good husbandry.'

And so it is.

Niall Cuagach also knew that doing a thing was stronger than just saying it. So when he wanted to injure someone he made a clay effigy of that person and then stuck needles into the effigy. Into an arm for dropsy, into both eyes for blindness, into the ears for deafness, into his genitals for barrenness, into his legs for incapacity.

Thread was also good: tying up red and green with black mixed the victim's mind up, so that he would begin to forget things, and tying up the effigy's legs with string meant that any plans he had became entangled and confused. It worked the other way round as well. If a demon attacked you and you managed to make a drawing or stick-likeness of him and cursed him to his face he lost all his power, because the things they hated were the names of Jesus and Mary and Joseph and all the saints and the sight of their own faces. It reminded them that they were the same as others. But the drawing had to be accurate: no use making a stick of a dwarf if the man was a giant, or of a man if she was a woman.

Because so many things could go wrong at any time. Big Roddy caught a cold and next thing he was shivering and sweating on his death-bed and would have gone had they not opened all the doors and windows and chinks in the thatch and the gaps in between the stones to let the demons out. And then there was Janet MacInnes who started fainting everywhere until she returned to carrying the rosary all the time, for you couldn't just let things take their course, especially with that new young drunken doctor in charge. Though you couldn't control the wind, still you could put up a drystone wall and shelter behind it when the storm blew. You were always safer protected by a beautiful thing. Her rosary was made of olive wood, smoothed into hollows by her prayers.

'Thread works on the mind, needles on the body,' Cuagach confessed to me later when he was ill. It wasn't that he was stupid or primitive. He knew fine that the thread and needles in themselves were powerless. Only the wishes and hopes and dreams and curses he spoke as he handled and spun and pushed and pressed them gave them any power. In the same way a song is useless until you sing it. Like I knew a ball didn't move on its own. It only moved if Duncan or Fearchar or I kicked or threw it, or unless it was out in the open and blown along by the wind. It never moved of its own accord. Which is why if you left something – a bike say – at the end of the house and found it somewhere else next morning the fairies must have moved it during the night.

Cuagach could also bless. When he heard Mrs MacTavish was ill, he took soiled water from the basin down to the stream and added seven clean handfuls of running water from the stream, and she became well. Seven and three were the eternal holy numbers, he said. His prayers in the name of the Trinity always worked – when rain was required, he prayed for it and it came, just as when good dry weather with an easterly wind was needed, that also arrived. He prayed simply, like a child, believing that what was asked for would be given. I used to hear him in church when he forgot to pray quietly like everyone else. I tried to shut my ears because the things he asked for were so intimate and it was like listening in to someone's best hopes and secrets. All the winds had colour. When he prayed for a warm west wind he asked for the green one. The cold east wind was purple, which he prayed fervently against because it blighted the potatoes. He must have saved so many people from starving through the winters.

Other things seemed equally straightforward to him. Folk moaned constantly about the weather, as if it controlled them.

'Can't do much today in all that rain.'

Or wind, or sleet or snow or burning sunshine. When all they had to do, really, was to deal with it. Build good round walls against the wind, face their door to the south, tilting towards the sun and opposite the prevailing rain, plant their potatoes on the upper side of the stream. The slower a stream ran the older it was. They'd forgotten that too, as if it didn't matter anymore. Build storm porches instead of leaving their homes open to the elements. It was their own fault for being stupid and ignorant and lazy. Always victims. Never in charge of their lives.

Even the stars had their storms. He'd seen them, hurtling across the sky, sending sparks flying. You learned to know the value of things in a storm, for they could be destroyed in a moment. And if they were – so what? They could be replaced. A storm was a great thing. It shook and destroyed and renewed everything. Surely by this time the sluggards around him ought to be used to four seasons in a day? Nature was always their friend, not their enemy. And rain always made the world bright and shiny afterwards. No matter how heavy the downpour, it always stopped at some point. Same with the wind and the sun. Wait, and things would change.

I realise now that Niall Cuagach read nature like a book. Every wisp of wind was like a letter in the alphabet, every blink of sun a word, every cloud in the sky a sentence. Or maybe it was more like a painting to him. Or like music, where he could hear the ending of the song from the first line. Because a good song is always inevitable. The joy or tragedy is always in that first note. As soon as he heard the word *Adeste*, there he was by the manger in Bethlehem. A white cloud thinner than a silk scarf can hold no rain. A cloud the shape of a fist in the north-west will be a storm within forty-eight hours; the way the hares cower behind the hillocks signals the distant presence of a fox; the flecks of white on the waters signify the rising tide. Everything indicated its own future. None of it was concealed. He knew where the best fishing grounds were simply by looking at the birds. That was surely something? They always followed ploughs and fishing boats, remembering from centuries before where food could be found.

'If a bird has a fish in its mouth it's heading for land; if its beak is empty it's heading for the fishing grounds. But that's also a sure sign of a coming west wind.'

He seemed certain of it, though he must have had moments of doubt, like the rest of us.

We watched the arrival of electricity as it came, bit by bit. It was like the waves of the sea, coming in slowly from far away then rising up in white foam as it hit the shoreline before receding and coming in again. Each new electricity pole that was erected spoke of certainty. They were made of good wood and stood tall over the bare landscape. Long strong wires connected them all together, like an army. This was the future, now visible to everyone. It was no longer unknown, but a wire that physically connected today with tomorrow. All the teenagers threw chuckie-stones at the ceramic holders on the poles, which made a singing sound with every hit. Cuagach certainly knew that it was important to claim the future, because today depended on it. For if you didn't know tomorrow's weather, how would you know whether to sow the grain or prepare the boat today, for an unexpected storm or downpour could destroy it all tomorrow? So you needed to constantly fathom the future. Whenever it rained he always went out immediately afterwards to judge what good or harm it had done to the earth. There was nothing like the smell of hay after the summer rain. If steam was rising from the thatch on the byre that meant endless days of good dry weather.

Unlike the changeable sky, where the new poles were, the earth remembered everything. It always paid you back, one way or the other. It was good when everything was washed clean. The land always looked best under a rising sun or a full moon, when the sea and the grass and the rocks and the sky were new-born and clear. Everything needed to have meaning in some kind of cosmic order. You couldn't just do a thing impulsively, or just for the fun of it. It would imbalance everything and have all kind of dangerous consequences. Cuagach once walked a different way home because he was in such a hurry and couldn't get out of his bed the next day. It was as if some kind of tremendous weight was holding him down every time he tried to rise, he said.

What he lacked was human company. Or more precisely, anyone who understood him. When he spoke, people looked at him with incomprehension. As if he was stupid or daft and ignorant. It's that look that says,

'Really? You expect me to believe that?'

And they had reason. For what he said and did often had no explanation. He baffled neighbours who were always looking for a reason for a thing, as if there had to be a reason for everything.

He was incomprehensible even to himself. For how can you explain that which you don't understand, how can you put into words that which you see in pictures and symbols and visions? How was he to know what a sudden flash of light in the sky was, unless he had already seen lightning? Only he knew the signs and omens, and he lacked words and ways and means of transferring that vision to anyone else in a language they could appreciate. Which is why he blessed them with two words and cursed them with another two and maimed them with needles and altered their minds with charms and threads and amulets and healed them with running water. These were the only means he had. For you need to have some way of influencing things. Of altering the inevitable. Of changing someone's mind. If a storm is coming, the least you can do is to tie threads of twine round your fingers to tame it. The house itself was as secure as it ever would be with stones and ropes holding it down. There was enough natural light around, from the sun and moon and stars, to do all that was necessary. You didn't need to add to the danger.

Niall Cuagach was afraid of not seeing his shadow, for to walk in the casting omnipotent sun without throwing a shadow was a sure premonition of death. He saw things that others didn't. A falling leaf was an illness, depending on the kind of tree. Pity there were so few trees around, limiting his language. Birch falling was a migraine; willow a stomach-ache.

The shape and colour of a thing was also important. A five-leaved clover might heal a hand or foot. A spider's web fixed any septic wound. A yellow rose meant that the woman who grew it would have a child. A red rose that she would have three, but probably more, depending on the number of petals. When a bee hovered over a window-pane it meant a letter was coming. If the window was open and the bee entered, the letter would bring good news. It's not that you believe everything you see and hear but that it becomes part of you, like dust on a shelf or like a will-o'-the-wisp in the darkness. Cuagach himself always carried a wisp of straw sticking out of his pocket as if he was still at the Martinmas market, and refused to turn any wheel on Martinmas day, as that was most unlucky. I don't think they call it that now. It's been overtaken by Armistice.

As a child, Cuagach's clothes were always held together by safety pins.

'That was just so he could use the pins to hook worms on for fishing on his way back home from school,' Dad said. For Cuagach, being at school was like walking with someone bigger and taller who took longer steps all the time so that he had to hurry to keep up with him. He never slowed down or took your hand or said or did anything kind except shout at you to hurry up. And what was the point of school anyway? All it did was take you away from home and the land. And the other thing was that teachers always made you speak. Even if you didn't know the answer and had no idea what they were talking about, you couldn't just stay nice and quiet, but always had to give some kind of rubbishy answer, even though you knew fine it was completely wrong, so that you then looked daft and ashamed and everyone laughed at you. And even if you were right, you became as much afraid of being right as being wrong. They would just call you Smartypants.

He was born with a limp. Hence the name – Cuagach means lame. He dealt with it by being the most stubborn and single-minded person in the place. In olden days he might have been left out on the moor as a changeling or drowned as a fairy-child, but all that vanity vanished years ago. Education dispelled these myths and replaced them with certificates of progress. All those poor children crying out on the moor until they were silenced by time. The Schoolmaster used to tell us that plain ability was no better than plain stupidity. That stupidity was doing one thing when you could just as well be doing something else if you bothered to think about it.

'You're best to excel in one or the other,' he said when you solved a puzzle or failed to write straight.

'Be either completely smart, or completely stupid. Either stay at peace in your islands of ignorance or venture out to the continents of thought. Don't be shipwrecked in between.'

It sounded very much like something he'd learned, or like something his own teacher had drummed into him. And isn't it terrible, despite all our best efforts, how much that rubbish keeps coming back to us? If only I could forgive the whole world for the way it is. If only I could change it. The way Mam did the washing every Monday, all the sheets and blankets and towels and shirts swaying clean and fresh in the wind.

Growing up, it felt as if success or failure was a destiny beyond anyone's individual effort or ability. And you had to go to the mainland to succeed, because land there was endless, Duncan said. Unlike this tiny rock we were born on, where you had no room to grow or expand or conquer. Who was there to conquer anyway? That old wifie MacInnes who lived in her tumble-down thatched cottage up the hill, or crooked MacAskill who thought he was the Lord Lovat just because he had acquired three crofts for himself? If you wanted to get anywhere you ought to emigrate. There was no end of land and cattle and jobs in America, where everything was new. Though Cuagach could never say the word properly. Always 'merica, which Dad said was no country, but that didn't bother him. Must have heard it somewhere said that way.

When he was seven, Niall Cuagach was given an extra high left shoe so that he could walk straight, but he had become so used to waltzing over the moors that he felt strange walking evenly. It wasn't him. The things others do to try and change us! To help us. So he walked as he had learnt to walk, like a sailor on the deck of a swaying ship. We could see him from miles away, up and down through the bogs like a yellow yo-yo from Donnie's shop.

It was always fun to go shopping at Donnie's with a list from Mam.

'Half a pound o' tea,' and off Donnie went hopping to the shelf to weigh it into the brown paper bag.

'And half a pound o' butter,' and off to the other side to wrap that. Goodness, looking back on it, how environmentally friendly it all was, with not a plastic wrapper in sight! And best was at the end, ordering the sweeties and watching him climb the rickety ladder to get a quarter of cinnamon balls. We always hoped he'd fall and clatter all the jars of sweeties down onto the floor so that we could scoop them up, but he never did! Poor man.

And boy, could Niall Cuagach run! Despite appearances. Dad said that no one ever beat him in the school races when he was younger. They'd start quicker, but five or ten yards into the race Niall appeared at their shoulders like a phantom, hardly breathing. They heard his feet clomping up behind them with a pony-like trotting, up-and-down and clip-clopping, and next thing he was racing on ahead like that amazing horse they all watched one day much later in Farquhar MacDonald's house. Red Rum he was called. They all remembered that because Farquhar gave them all a swig of rum from a dark bottle he snatched out from beneath the sofa.

Farquhar was the first to have a telly in the district. His first cousin Murdo was Inspector of Police in Hong Kong and brought it back with him the last, and only, time he visited. The Inspector wore leather patches on the elbows of his tweed jacket. I remember that, because everyone asked why someone with such a good job and salary still wore patches as if he was poor. Even if they were leather.

'No way. I'm not turning into a pillar of salt,' he said when asked if he was staying home for good to look after the old place. The stones have been removed from the ruins of that old house now, so that you would never know anyone ever lived there unless you had seen them with your own eyes. I once heard a horse neighing from the ruin as I walked by in the dark. These places are always full of faraway noises.

Niall Cuagach's parents died when he was twelve. Some fever they caught while visiting relatives in Skye. They never returned and were buried where they died, at a place called Tiumpan, for fear their corpses would carry the fever back to Niall. After that, he never took anything for granted. Not even the sea. He'd miss it so much if it wasn't there. The salt in his nostrils. He fended for himself from then on in a long wooden shack on the edge of the moor. The shack got bigger and wider and higher as the years went on, as if success always lay in the next bit added, which would be drier and better. He was like someone trying to distract the future by living in the most primitive conditions. As if the future would then leave him alone to get on with it. Which it did.

It's a lonely place, out beyond the loch, beneath the copse of trees that Captain MacKenzie planted in the 19th century. That's Murdoch MacKenzie, the legendary skipper of the clipper ship 'Dundonald' who won the Great Tea Race from China in 1865 and planted trees because he believed in the future. Even God had planted a garden, Captain MacKenzie said, because He believed in the future. Niall Cuagach had an old painting of the ship with Captain MacKenzie at the helm, sporting the longest beard in the world, running down past his knees, though others said it was just a reproduction of that man who used to advertise Player's Navy Cut cigarettes once upon a time. Though it couldn't have been, because his beard was much shorter. A rowan tree still grows by the door of Niall Cuagach's hut and a yew tree which rustles in the wind on quiet nights and shrieks all night long through the winter. He could see the stars from his bed, which meant he was part of infinity. Sometimes the moon shone in through the window and lay beside him in bed. Eventually she would move silently across his body and vanish out the wall on the other side.

He kept horses. A dozen Eriskay ponies that smelt of myrtle and roamed wild across the moors. He only had to whistle and one of them appeared at his side, ready to take him to the shop. He knew that once you teach a horse a way he will remember it forever. The village watched him from behind their curtains as he bobbed up and down across bog and hill. He carried a tiny bell which he tinkled in the horse's right ear to turn right and his left to turn left. He also heard things. While I heard the birds singing he heard them talking.

'This way, this way, this way,' advised the little sparrow.

'Beware, beware, beware,' warned the crow.

He was also the only person in the place to give his horses a holiday. Every first Saturday of the month he led them down to the shore and gave them all afternoon and evening to paddle and trot and bathe in the salt water. They'd run around, their halters hanging free swishing in the sea foam. We all ran down after him of course and begged rides, which is the reason some of us eventually learnt how to stand on one leg on the back of a pony while singing 'Heigh Ho, Heigh Ho' at the top of our voices, without falling off! I wonder if I could still do it?

He had his own names for things and places that no one else knew or understood. The river that we called 'An Abhainn Dhearg' (The Red River) he called 'Abhainn Dhùghaill' (Dugald's River). Dugald lived there in the early eighteenth century, and often met with Niall by the bend of the river underneath the hawthorn tree. He'd fought in both Jacobite campaigns and was killed in an instant by musket-shot at Culloden.

'I had no time to die, so here I am forever, now taking my time,' he said to Niall. 'It stands still, which is why it is forever.'

The campaign had been both exhilarating and terrible.

'No one else joined the first time, except myself,' Dugald said. 'They didn't believe in the cause first time 'round, but when the Prince himself came in '45, we all went. And why wouldn't we? We were young and foolish. You should have seen him, Niall. The bravest and bonniest looking man you ever saw. Handsome. A proper Clan Chief. And he proved it all in battle, unlike those MacDonald bastards who didn't turn up, and the spineless Munros who killed me from afar. They didn't even have the courage to come near. A musket shot rather than a sword. What kind of fighting is that, Niall? That of a coward. Shooting from afar. I was glad to die for the Prince, even though I wasn't able to thank him as I fell. I've thanked him ever since. Sometimes I see him here and we sit together and have a wee dram. I sit on the lower chair of course to give him his due and allow him to talk. He's good at that, with a beautiful accent and a love of Scotland that has never ever diminished. He wishes he could start it all over again and do it differently this time around. Wishes he hadn't listened to those others at Carlisle. All of them feart. Cowards. It's easy enough to tell the truth when it doesn't matter, same as it's easy to believe when things are looking good. But what about believing when you fear? Ought to have gone on, of course, all the way to London. Trusted his own judgement. I tell him that, even though it was not and is not my job to tell him that. I don't have the authority, Niall. But nevertheless he listens to me and respects my opinion. And despite his sadness we then have a dram together. "Slàinte," he says, in that beautiful way of his.' And then Niall would always pause, watching the Prince sailing eastwards across Loch na Cloiche.

There were three paths to Niall Cuagach's shack. The high road, the middle road and the low road, folk called them. The high road followed the deer tracks across the steep part of the moor. The middle road led from the main artery through the island, while the low road took you down to the loch and round by the old sheep-fank, past the trees. They gave him choices. The last thing he wanted was a proper road. That's how the Romans had conquered people like him in other parts of Britain. There was no track to the north where the cliff-face holds the ocean at bay. Invasions came from the north. The wild Vikings came from there. Driven mad by the snow and the cold and needing to do something to keep themselves warm, flashing their swords and raping and pillaging and setting fire to everything they saw. Never from the south. Soft Romans who turned back at Mons Graupius as soon as they were attacked by the rain and the midges. Too used to lying in the sun and eating olives and drinking wine. They ran when they saw the wild men and women with the tattoos.

The sea road: now that was a proper highway. Took you places while you caught shoals of herring on the way. On winter days

Niall would stand on the cliff edge in the snow flashing his torches to warn all shipping. For not everyone was as aware of changes in the atmosphere as he was. Mist makes everything look the same. But once it evaporates, everything becomes blue. If only there was something mysterious hidden in the mist, except what he knew was there: all those old cleared villages.

The torch in his right hand was covered with red coloured paper, the one in his left with green. Fearchar and I used to do it with Dad's torch, sending signals across the fields to Dolina and to Fearchar's best pal, Iain. It matters as much when you do a thing as how you do it. Always best to signal in the mirk or in the dark.

'Red to port, green to starboard,' Cuagach bellowed out in the mist, for there is nothing more frightening than being lost silently in the fog. The further out he could see to sea the more he wanted to stay on dry land. Snow, rain, hail and winter were not punishments but only part of nature, just like the sun and summer.

Cuagach knew the boundaries of the place like no one else. Whenever there was a dispute over the rights to grazing or to croft land, he was informally consulted. Someone found an excuse to walk along one of the three roads, where Niall met them, as if accidentally. His word carried the weight of ancient unwritten law.

'No,' he'd say. 'MacAulay's croft ends exactly there. See. Where the oblong stone stands at the edge of the ditch. West of that belongs to young MacDonald. His grandfather won it in a wager over horses. The horse was called Adag. The contest was about which horse could jump furthest over Brian's stone wall. Adag won. Jumped eighteen feet.'

Boundary lines that were invisible to everyone else were clear and distinct to Cuagach because nothing was incidental. Ditches and culverts and tracks were where they were for a reason. That half-finished trench because MacFarlane got fed up digging it and headed off to the war and never came back. The underground stream marked the exact division between Slagan and Druim Sgairbh, and the iron pin long wedged into the crevice of the rock was where Diarmaid MacGregor was tied captive after the Battle of Inverlochy.

When he stood on the cliff edge, Niall Cuagach could see forever, even through the fog. Bright cities shone far to the north, illuminated by gaslight. The mainland, however, seemed much further away than the stars and planets he saw swirling above him every night.

'That's the German Ocean to the east,' he said to Duncan and Fearchar and I. 'And the Pictland Firth separates it from us. There's no snow over there for the sea air dissolves it.'

He looked out towards Skye in the distance and called it the East Hebrides. Bad winters came from there. From the east. That's where all the plagues came from. He grazed his cattle near the cleared village of Hangabhat, which had been dis-peopled in his grandfather's time.

He knew everything about nature and the tides, which was some help to Duncan and Fearchar and me in our geography lessons, though the phrases we learned from him confused the teacher because a lot of the places he talked about didn't exist any longer. The Island of Thule, for example, which the teacher said never existed. But we knew it did – Innis Tìle, which the teacher and all her books called Iceland!

Cuagach called the tides impetuous and named things after the colour of the sky or the shape of the clouds. It was important to name a thing, he said, otherwise how would you know what it was? If you didn't have a name for it, then how would you know if Dugald the Auctioneer was talking about a cow or a sheep or a horse since they all had four legs? How would I know I was Annie unless people called me that, he said. We laughed at him, of course. Called him daft behind his back. Probably believed that a plane was just a tractor ploughing the sky.

He had a beautiful sleek pony called Mackerel, after the speckled clouds that predict a fine day to come, and another one called Dawk, whose back was marked like the drizzling rain. He spent a good deal of time sitting on top of the hill, believing that the mountain breezes purify the air, and drank from a spring whose waters are lighter by one-half than any other water in the island. He measured it, putting the water in a dish on one side of a balanced bar of wood, with white stones on the other side as counterweights. The water from the well balanced at two small stones, while every other water required at least four. He always kept a scallop-shell filled with sea-water by his bed because he could then smell the ocean in his sleep and know that he was still alive. Stones had virtues, after all. They could even surprise you. Look heavy but be as light as feather, and vice versa. You never knew until you tried lifting them. White ones gave you strength and courage, dark ones wisdom. They worked negatively too, and if you placed or removed stones from near certain places or people their strength and courage was diminished. He was forever on the lookout for broad flat stones to place things on.

He had so much to remember that he once told me he sometimes wondered whether he had made it all up. Otherwise, how would he have remembered it? Better to wonder than doubt. He had a faraway memory of his father and mother bartering for everything, giving a day cutting hay in exchange for a return day at the peats, and as a child going with his grandfather to the cobbler, who made a pair of shoes for him in exchange for a basket of herring. Could it be that the swaps we made, or saw, as children shape the adults we've become?

Cuagach especially believed that things need to be a certain shape. They had been made like that, by time or place or fortune or design. That things have a right and a wrong size, and when they're the wrong size they're stretched, and tear like an ill-fitting pair of trousers, as if perfection excludes all imperfection. Christ was the only man who was six feet tall, neither an inch more nor an inch less, he argued. Hills that were once high melted and became valleys, rivers that were once long and broad were made small and narrow by dams. A field ought to be no bigger than can graze seven cows. A house ought to be no bigger than the needs of the people in it. Some folk now live so extravagantly, having three rooms when one could do them. And houses ought to be built with curved corners to soften the wind, rather than the sharp hard corners that had become the fashion. The sitting room always ought to be on the right after you entered the front door. That was how things ought to be, he argued. Things were out of balance. Out of proportion for him.

He loved the moon especially. It explained everything to him, as if all life depended on it. Which it does. He hunted rabbits in the moonlight. By the light of the moon, when it was waxing, never by the dark of the moon, when it was waning. He always sowed his crops when the moon was waxing so that they would grow well as the moon became full. A south-east and north-west moon caused high water, which gave him plenty of oysters, mussels and cockles.

Thing is, the moon never grew old. He'd watched and counted, and it only ever reached twenty-eight or twenty-nine days of age, then it was born again. He told me that once, as a child, he accidentally cut his toe at the change of the moon and it bled a fresh drop of blood at every change of the moon ever since. And besides, he found the moon simply beautiful to look at in all its ever-changing shapes and forms. 'I think it feels everything we do,' he said. 'That's why it goes red when my toe bleeds.'

When he was a child, his old neighbour Eòghainn Steele told him he'd been to the moon.

'It was just like Uist,' he said, 'except it didn't have a machair, so I came back home because I don't think I could bear to stay somewhere I couldn't get machair potatoes.'

Just like Dad. He always felt he hadn't eaten if he hadn't had potatoes for his dinner!

For Duncan and Fearchar and all the boys the moon was a ball, because they played football. I always saw a rabbit there, with its dark ears twitching beneath the passing clouds. None of us wanted distant stars and a dark sky that were remote and shapeless. The heavens were filled with ploughs and anchors and wheels and bears and the seven sisters of Deirdre who always came out to dance in a glittering circle on frosty nights. The moon never stopped looking for lochs and puddles to see itself in. The best way to see yourself is to look into the water and watch how you ripple and change shape or disappear when a stone falls in or a fish jumps to disturb the surface.

When Cuagach wanted to harness his pony at night, the moon shone down like a soft torch so that the pony was at ease. Moonlight was a special kind of night light, which his mother must have loved. She must have. When it shone, it was all that mattered. We all knew that without its silent brightness all life would cease. It would be like turning the electricity off now. A good night is a gift of God, and on still nights we could hear Cuagach singing up in his shack,

> *On Saturday night I lost my Mum*
> *Guess you where I found her,*
> *Up in the moon, singing a tune*
> *And all the stars around her.*

He was so lonely he must have wondered if he was still alive, because that's what happens to me. Wonder if a thing has happened at all if I'm not able to tell anyone about it. Say when his cow was ill and he healed her with the plant of the tansy, or when one of his sheep had a lump in her throat and Niall took a turf from the roof of his house and set it alight, putting the nose of the sheep over it to inhale the smoke until the nose and mouth watered plentifully. You needed to know lots of odds and ends to survive. The fat of a heron slain at full moon cures rheumatism. The cuckoo always leaves on St Peter's Day. A spoon made from the horn lost by a living cow heals all kinds of diseases.

But what was the use if no one saw it or if he wasn't able to tell anyone about it? It was as if the miracle hadn't happened. Say if he thought of something and wanted to say it and no one was there to listen or hear it, had he thought it at all, and if he had, did it matter? It's so difficult to know what a thought is anyway because it is one thing one moment and another thing the next.

6

James Campbell

JAMES CAMPBELL HAD other means. He was the big shot in the place, imagining he was smarter than everyone else because he was a businessman and had a big house and a big car and money. How could anyone have these things and be honest? Though now that I think of it, it was all probably borrowed from the bank. An invented world just like Cuagach's. That magic trick of making something out of nothing. He had the power of speech, though he sometimes mistook words for ideas. Which no one was much interested in – they preferred to hear practical things about sheds and windows and sheep and cows and fences, not fancy things about co-operation and diversification and progress and development and planning. He spoke the language of the future, making him a traitor to everyone who didn't see happiness this side of heaven.

Ideas were dangerous things which you needed to get rid of as soon as you could before they caused any lasting damage. It was really quite remarkable that looking after cows and sheep and pigs and hens and drains and byres was like a new thing to them every day which they tackled with endless enthusiasm. Where the future was nothing more than the easy repetition of the past. You could see them all puffed up and proud because they could hammer a fence post into the ground or judge a beast by its appearance.

'If it's fat in the head it will be fat on the rump,' as if that was some kind of eternal truth. Big things were always admired. They'd walk backwards and stand and look at a big horse for ages.

Private school and university-educated, Campbell knew how to use words so that they sounded as if they meant one thing while they meant another. He polished his words until they glowed and he believed in them, as if they were inspired and had come to him rather than from him. Except the more you listened to him the less you trusted him. Even though he always did what he said. Or maybe because of that. There was no room for mistakes with him.

He hadn't planned on being a businessman. It's just the way things worked out. The way things do. You need to be in the right place at the right time and have the right attitude. You made your own future. So it was important to know your market. If you offer people what they like, then they will believe in it instinctively because they trust their intuition more than their knowledge. Same as with songs and stories. People don't want long complicated obscure things. Just songs that they can hum along to. Speed bonny boat like a bird on the wing, over the sea to Skye.

Campbell's argument was that too many folk in our community were relaxed, come day go day, not bothering about wealth when, at the end of the day, it was all that mattered. Without it, life was miserable. Scraping seaweed from the shore and keeping their scrawny hens and dung-covered cattle in their broken down byres when they could be done up and rented out to visitors. He wanted to persuade them that tourism was better than the traditional poverty they were accustomed to. I heard him say that prisoners become so accustomed to their chains that they feel lost without them.

He was the only son of Richard (Dickie) Campbell who was the estate ghillie for over thirty years and was a neighbour of ours. Dickie Campbell originally came to the island from the mainland as an RAF technician, but spent most of his time fishing the river and lochs which he came to know like the back of his hand. Loch na h-Eala was best for trout, while Loch na Caiplich on the east side of the mountain was best for salmon. He had an option to leave the services after five years, which he did, immediately getting a job as ghillie on the local estate. He married a local girl, Janet MacGregor (she was distantly related to Mam), and James was their only child.

Although Dickie Campbell didn't have any Gaelic, Janet did, so James was brought up fluent in both English and Gaelic. He could switch from one language to the other without any difficulty or hesitation, and unlike most native Gaelic speakers I knew, he tried to avoid all traces of anglicisation in his speech. So that instead of using the word 'heilicoiptear', for example, James would say 'inneal-sgiathan' (a wing-machine). Sometimes he pretended he could only hear in Gaelic so that we'd be forced to speak it to him, which we hated. So we always just answered him in English. He tried to make us feel guilty about it, saying we had a responsibility for the future when all we wanted to do was play however we wanted and speak whatever we wanted and be normal. The local lads thought he was being pretentious, and told him so, but he had more than enough confidence to sweep that aside, stating that all languages need both integrity and constant renewal.

'Survival of the fittest, lads. Adapt and survive. The problem with you guys is that you're so conservative you'll all end up in a museum.'

For a while, he shaped things almost as much as the sea and the mountains did. He went to the local primary school, but when he reached secondary school age he won a scholarship to a mainland boarding school that specialised in outdoor pursuits and country matters. It was an all-boys school. The school desks leant forward so that he was forever sliding and having to pull himself straight. That's why he had such a straight strong back, he told us.

'You're not here to enjoy yourselves,' the teacher said, 'but to learn. And that's never painless.'

Over and above the normal school timetable, Campbell and the others spent most weekends out on the hills, learning the trade. During the grouse season they acted as beat-keepers on the moors, with the deer-stalking season then carrying them through to the middle of February for the red hinds and on to the very end of April for the fallow bucks. In between, there was the extra fun of game shooting, helping the guests shoot everything from ducks to partridges. He was a quick learner, and realised quickly that he learned faster than he could be taught, whereas others in his class could be taught forever and not learn a thing. It was better to be smart than diligent.

He liked the house system. The whole school was divided into four tribes, each named after a saint. There was the House of Columba, of Ninian, Mungo and Andrew, and they competed all the time for points and favours. The boys got points for washing dishes and cleaning floors and spelling correctly and not fidgeting in class and not eating too fast and shining their shoes and all kinds of things which made some better than others, for it was always good to be better than someone else and best of all to be better than everyone else.

He loved gaining points for his team – the famous House of Columba, which won every year he was there, celebrating every triumph collectively by running across the lawn, arms raised with their hand-made wooden swords and all shouting 'Death or Victory!'

A school friend got him interested in flying. The Piper Cherokee Club met most evenings at the local disused Second World War airstrip and anyone who was keen on flying got free lessons. James loved it. He was a quick learner, and was airborne within six weeks in the small Piper Cruiser. It was a heady mixture of danger and control for a sixteen-year-old, and a sensation that continued to drive him in business as well as in his personal life. He could soar or crash at any moment. Though he himself put his interest down to Aladdin, whose magic carpet fascinated him as a child. The carpet in *The Arabian Nights* was red with blue swirls and curved at the end when Aladdin flew through the air. Nothing flat ever flew properly. It had to have curves and wings, like a bird.

He thought of entering the RAF, but instead studied Architecture at university because of his fascination with the way things worked. The Piper Cruiser itself was wonderfully designed. A bird could have made it. A swallow, perhaps. He liked to say that it was born, not manufactured. Elegant and balanced, looking right both on the ground and in the air. James wanted to study not so much how things were built or made, but the designs that gave them life. And he discovered, to his delight, that house construction worked on the same principles: the hand was only as good as the eye. Or, as he preferred to put it, the house was as good, or as bad, as the imagination.

Appearance was half the battle. Secrets could be hidden as long as the surface looked fine. Though Mam knew better. Scones had to taste good as well as look good. You should never cheat, which is what the shops do, tarting up their scones with sugar and chocolate drizzle. When you eat them it's literally like eating nothing. Especially the ones without any raisins or sultanas. Campbell used to do the same with his flocks. They said that just before the cattle sale he used to feed salt to his cows so they'd drink endless amounts of water and look fatter until they emptied their bladders. But by then the cash was in his bank.

Campbell was lucky. It was the time when mainland house-buyers began to look for houses that 'articulated the vernacular' as they put it in their brochures, and what better than stone and thatch in the Gàidhealtachd, and wood and red-roofed zinc elsewhere? It paid to give people an image of the past as a vision of the future.

Everyone wanted a touch of the countryside with a sea view, but within twenty minutes of the shops, so James Campbell stepped into that open market. All those tiny, draughty windows behind which folk had tried to shelter from the storms were replaced by large panes of pure double-glazed glass, the sin of poverty replaced by shining displays of progress.

Campbell was conscious all along that development and the environment need to be as balanced as a bird on the wing. He called his housing developments after them. Seagull Crescent. Eagle Avenue. Owl Terrace. Corncrake Cottages. He was environmentally friendly. The housing developments he built on the mainland were small-scale, but profitable. Folk wanted privacy as well as community, so shared parking spaces and play areas dominated the central areas with the houses themselves hidden behind hedges and trees. Everything was country within reach of town.

A thing needed to be possible before it became probable, and the challenge locally was that people hadn't even got to that first basic stage. You'd go into folks' houses and nothing ever changed: that old grandfather clock still ticking away in the corner as if it had nothing else to do, the same old tea pot, the same flowery wallpaper they'd plastered on fifty years ago. Some people had been old forever and would still be in hovels if the sanitary inspector hadn't forced them to move. Mrs MacDonald papered her kitchen with the *Oban Times* and you could sit there forever reading news that never changed. Miss Catherine Beaton was forever the Argyleshire Gathering Gala Queen.

Strangers were welcome as long as they conformed. It was like at school. We didn't have gangs as such, but everyone knew who was friends with whom, and if you wanted to be in with a particular group then it was fair enough that you played by their rules. Dolina and Morag and Katie and I, for example, always wore a yellow ribbon in our hair, and our socks folded down at the ankles as a sign that we were pals, and if anyone ever wanted to join any of our special games they had to come to school dressed like that too, then go with us behind the wall at playtime, huddle, cross their hearts and hope to die if they didn't promise to stick by us no matter what happened.

A committee, with a paid project officer, led the development. The chair was Mr Marlboro himself, James Campbell, who also owned the local construction company. Dad said he had the ability to sell you something and make you feel grateful for it, as if he'd paid you to buy it from him. He was a very fine piper and singer and also conducted the local Gaelic choir.

People said he was handsome, with his ruddy features and thick black hair, but I knew his hair was dyed with boot-polish because

I could see the flecks of grey hidden beneath the dye every time I served him tea when he visited our house. And his eyes were weak, like the white of an egg. His voice was lovely, however. Folk muttered that he walked about with an air of entitlement but all I could smell from him was uncertainty and anxiety, as if he was not quite what he wished to be.

The development of the local airstrip was almost, but not quite, a hobby for Campbell. There was his love of flying, of course, but equally important for him was 'the development as a symbol of the future built on the relics of the past,' as he pompously put it in one of his leaflets. And it wouldn't make a financial loss either. Anything to rescue the villagers from their twin addictions to the past and the future. Forever going on about history or heaven as if the present didn't exist. Preferring to remember rather than live.

'Nothing stands still,' he said to anyone who complained about destroying the old ways.

'It's called progress. Like penicillin.'

He knew fine that there were still folk about who could remember their parents and grandparents talking about the bad old days when children died from coughs and consumption because they couldn't afford to go to the doctor. Campbell recognised that important decisions are made from memory or desire, not reason. Progress had to bypass that, since memory is fallible. It needs to trample over the past if necessary, in the same way that gravediggers have to walk over the grass and flowers and other mounds on their way to a new burial plot.

Old people can be as mistaken and foolish as the young. Campbell believed that nothing exists for its own sake, without some utilitarian purpose. I suppose even daisies are there for a reason, if only to beautify the grass. Bets some bugs need them to survive.

Campbell was only like the clan chief of old, knowing better than the common people themselves what was good for them in the great arc of civilisation. Compared to Niall Cuagach's old strange knowledge, Campbell's language was clear and distinct. He knew that the future, just like the past, was economic, not social. Stories and songs were fine for the hearth or for passing a long cold winter's evening, but long-term survival depended on jobs and incomes. Without the puritan energy of business and enterprise, as he put it, nothing would happen. The soil itself was filled with treasures if only the people weren't wilfully blind to it and too lazy to dig it. Idleness, next to drunkenness, had always been the chief sin of the Gael. The problem was that a lot of the young people had already left to get better educated on the mainland or simply to get jobs, and only the old were left, for whom time and progress no longer had any monetary value, with their accounts elsewhere. And, good Lord, what infinite credit they had.

'That man would sell the wind if he could,' Mam said. And eventually he did, with his windfarms. He argued that tourism was the way forward, and that we were in an ideal situation to benefit from it. Preferably older environmentally-conscious high-spending visitors who wouldn't trash the place with wild parties and overcrowding. Just good folk who would fly in for a week or so and stay in the local hotel (owned by his cousin) and enjoy fresh local produce, go bird-watching and sight-seeing and get a taste of the local culture.

'Not just good for the local economy, but for the overall well-being of the place,' he said at the first meeting. 'We're losing young people all the time, and the more activities we have on here the better. Cèilidhs don't take place in a morgue. And they don't just fill the silence.'

He was right. Cèilidhs owed their existence to a crowd. This was before there were any visitor-centres or cafes in the place, because every home was one. The public spaces then were the machair and the moor, though they too were mostly apportioned to families who had crofts, so that you were always treading on the borders of someone's inheritance. I always felt that fences and walls were barriers to sharing things, designed to keep people out rather than to keep sheep and cattle in, as the crofters argued. 'An offence to both taste and liberty,' Mùgan claimed in one of his half-drunk speeches.

I particularly hated barbed wire, which tore my boots and clothes every time I crossed a field. In the old days it was never like that, according to the songs and stories, with shepherd girls and boys roaming the moors, before we all accepted the enclosures as the natural and profitable order of things. Fences and walls protecting us from strangers and enemies. The next thing we all had private gardens with flowers as extra rooms for display and admiration rather than for growing more potatoes! Mùgan asked 'What's the point of growing something you can't eat?' Even worse was the sin of mashing the potatoes. They had to be eaten full, in all their goodness in their skins, without being crushed like sand.

I think the grown-ups feared Campbell because he just got on with things without getting their approval. Duncan and Fearchar and I admired him for that, because that's what we liked to do ourselves when we could get away with it. Which was difficult, because we always needed some adult's approval for whatever we were doing, whether playing skipping-jumps on the rickety old bridge or doing a drawing in the jotter at school.

'Lining his own pockets, while pretending it's all for our benefit,' said Cuagach. 'That's the problem. Just because he's been to Oban, thinks he's Alexander the Great.'

Campbell had a beautiful singing voice. Baritone. We liked him when he was singing. Perhaps it was more grudging admiration. Unlike my mother, though, he never sang any of the grace-notes, because he said they slowed down the song. But you had to admire his sweet tone. The priest used to say that a holy mystery was seeing one thing – bread and wine for instance – and believing another – these ordinary elements transubstantiated into the body and blood of Christ. So that when Campbell sang it also seemed like a mystery – this selfish man bringing forth all the glories in a love song and all the tragedies in a lament.

It was as if you didn't need to hear any of the words he sang.

They reached you without listening. At times he reminded me of Frank Sinatra, on other occasions of Johnny Cash. He could also sing bass baritone, and if you closed your eyes while he was singing 'The Eriskay Love Lilt', you'd think Paul Robeson himself was on stage. Especially when the local music teacher, Mrs MacDonald, accompanied him at the official concerts on piano. Sadly, he never sang any pop songs, though sometimes he deigned to sing country and western, his favourite being 'Lipstick on My Collar'. It was as if he were two different men: the businessman in his flashy car and the beautiful singer at the cèilidh. I suppose one relied on the other.

7

Lisa

THE PROJECT OFFICER for the development was Lisa. Lisa Cornhill, who previously worked in the hotel. Dear, gentle Lisa. She lived in a renovated thatched house in the northern village of Dùn Chamuis, where she also ran a small tourist enterprise renting out bicycles. She was nervous and pretty. Her cup and saucer shook slightly as she held them, and I was always tempted to ask her to leave the cèilidh with me and to go and play outside with my shells, but I didn't, because she was a grown-up and I didn't want to take her away from the songs and stories, and besides folk would disapprove and look down on her as if she were a child and not acting her age. Later, she told me she wished I had.

I never knew Lisa's age. She would have been in her mid-20s I suppose, though to me she was like a big sister. Or cousin, though we were not related. She was from the other end of the island and worked down about our area as a development officer, though I wasn't sure what that meant at the time and when I asked her she said she helped people to do things.

She taught me how to cycle. Properly, I mean. I'd learned before, when I was really wee on a three-wheeled little wooden scooter-like thing Dad made me. Two small wheels at the back and a slightly larger one at the front, with a wooden batten connecting the two on which I stood. I could only stand and go fast on it downhill though, even if that was a bit dangerous. But I knew which small grassy hills I could go on. Otherwise I stood on it with one leg and pushed myself along with the other. Duncan and Fearchar said it was a girly kind of thing, and wouldn't allow me on their slightly more fancy bikes, though even those were just rubbish contraptions which didn't work properly unless you were freewheeling down the big hills with the wind at your back.

But Lisa had a proper bike: a dark blue one with gears and everything, and even more impressively it was a 'man's bike' with a crossbar, which had only ever been seen used by men before. No one disapproved however, because she was an expert cyclist who could outspeed anyone on the flat machair and climb the mountain peat-tracks as if the bike was a goat. And she had a red saddle and matching helmet that I thought were the coolest things on earth. Especially because no one else in the area had a bicycle helmet at the time. It was a Raleigh bike with six gears and front and back lights and a proper pump and bells, and flashes on the spokes and mudguards and pedals and everything.

I was playing on my tricycle (I disliked the word at the time, but that's what it really was) one day as she cycled by and stopped.

'What a lovely bike,' she said to me, 'and you can go so fast on it!'

I couldn't really, but I believed her wee fib. For some things are more believable than others. Who didn't want to travel fast like the birds of the air, which one moment would be sitting on our chimney pot and the next be miles away over in MacPhee's field because they'd seen a snail or something interesting over there? You could go from here to there in a jiffy if you wanted.

'Do you think I could go on a big bike?' I asked her, the same way as I'd asked Duncan and Fearchar, who said 'No'. They said I needed to be at least as tall as them before I could do that, because I wouldn't reach the pedals, or if I just stood on the pedals then I wouldn't be able to reach the handle-bars and even if I did I then couldn't steer properly and would just fall off and injure myself.

'Probably even kill yourself,' added Fearchar.

'Of course you could go on a big bike,' Lisa said. 'Except not this one, for this one really is too big. But next time I'm down I'll bring one for you.'

And she did – the following day. It was a proper bike my size. Lisa sat me on the saddle and told me that the secret was to steer with my whole body, not just my hands and feet. We practised on the grass for a while. Lisa pushed me on the bike at first, asking me to steer by moving my body first to the right and then to the left so that the wheels and handlebars turned according to where I leant. After a while I steered the bicycle both sides without using my hands. It was easy-peasy after that, putting my hands on the handle-bars and going round in larger and larger circles. The other secret she gave me was that I ought to turn the pedals with the soles of my feet or heels rather than with my toes or the front part of my foot: the bike then moves with little physical effort. Try it!

Once I learned to cycle properly, Dolina and I liked to ride the bikes on the wrong side of the road. We formed a secret club called The Wrong Side of the Road Club. It was nonsense really, because there was hardly any traffic except for the occasional tractor and horse and cart, but then the local council came and put white lines along the road with a sign telling us to keep left, so we deliberately kept right because it was more fun to break rules. The roads were so quiet that they were half grass and you were more likely to meet a cow grazing in the middle of it than any vehicle. The real danger was the regular flicking of a cow's tail covered in dung as she tried to swat off the flies as you passed. We became experts at swerving round them.

The freedom our bikes gave us! One minute I'd be at home, the next I was over at Dolina's in the next village, and moments after that both of us were free-wheeling down the big brae to where Katie and Morag lived, which before we got bikes seemed so so far away. When we pedalled fast enough we were blurs. Invisible actually. Then we both bought bells from the catalogue through the post. Dolina's was green and went ding-dong like a door bell (which no one had then!) while mine was blue and went tring-tring-tring like a phone (which only the Schoolmaster and Effie the Postmistress had in their houses, though there was a lovely red phone box outside the Post Office), and when we rode side-by-side down through the villages we hit both bells simultaneously and all the cows galloped off across the field in fear of their lives. After a while they got so used to it that they just continued grazing without even looking up as we ding-donged and tring-tring-tringed past them with all our might! We deliberately cycled through all the puddles so that we could hear the tyres singing.

Sometimes we stopped at the phone kiosk and pretended to phone someone. We didn't have any money anyway and even if we did, who would we phone, for all our friends lived just a cycle-ride along the road? Except for those who had moved to Glasgow, and we didn't have numbers for them, even if they had phones, and Great-Aunt Isabel who lived in Canada and sent air-mail letters to us from Vancouver and a beautifully wrapped parcel every Christmas with gifts in it for all of us. Once, Duncan got a train set and Fearchar got an aeroplane he could wind up and fly, though the wind was so strong that it blew away and smashed into the byre and broke. My favourite present was a *Rupert Annual* she sent me for my ninth birthday. Great-Aunt Isabel also had beautiful handwriting and wrote in calligraphy, 'For my dearest Annie, 9 today! With all my love forever. G-A Isabel xxx'. I liked Bingo the brainy Pup best because he invented amazing things like a mini submarine so he could go to the bottom of the ponds to see all the toads and frogs at work and play.

One Christmas, Dolina's Auntie Marion sent her a tennis racquet and ball, but since that was the only racquet on the island we couldn't play tennis with it, so we just played plainy-clappy, hitting the ball with the racquet against the barn wall at different speeds and angles and then catching it after clapping your hands quickly behind your back or touching your heels or toes or turning round. Every child in the world must have played it one time or other! I was best at it, and once I caught it fifty times in a row. The secret was to know that the ball was always trying to get back to the place it had left. So you could always predict where it was coming to, unless it hit a dip or a curve or a bump in the wall that destroyed its gravity. Someone once told me that's what speed is about – an attempt to stay where you are.

I've always liked the rhyme and still chant it every time I play the game!

> *Plainy, Clappy,*
> *Roll the reel to backy,*
> *Touch your heel,*
> *Touch your toe,*
> *Touch the ground,*
> *And all around.*

And if you don't touch a thing it doesn't count.

Once inside the phone-box we could talk to anyone we liked. Dolina pretended to phone Cliff and ask him how he was, and then sang 'Summer Holiday' along with him, while I then crooned 'Are You Lonesome Tonight' down the line to Elvis. We then jumped on our bikes and both sang 'She loves you yea, yea, yea' at the tops of our voices as we free-wheeled down the bumpy machair track swerving round the cow-pats.

The machair track always tried to tell us where to go, but we did our best to avoid the existing ruts and forge a new path every time, even if it took us across the uneven fields. As long as Grumpy MacGregor wasn't watching, 'cos he'd just bawl at us for destroying his precious turnips. What did his stupid neeps matter to us! He'd sold his cows and sheep and planted turnips everywhere saying that he was now specialising because that would make him more money. Though he still went round in rags because he was so mean.

On the shore, we wrote our names in the sand and then drew two long lines side by side with our sticks. The lines went every which way round and backwards and forwards and in circles and our challenge was to ride between the lines without touching them or crossing them and by the time we'd done that half a dozen times the tide was coming in so we cycled home while our marks and names were still clear in the sand.

Once, a girl from the mainland came to stay with her granny for a while and was in our class and because she was new we found her fascinating and tried to make pals with her. But she wasn't very interesting, and left after a month or so. I think her name was Jean. It was also strange how we disliked some children not because of anything they did or said, but because of things they didn't do or say. Becky, for instance, who never said anything, and Ranald who never joined in any of the games. And besides, they both wore specs which made them too careful and afraid to play proper games like wheelbarrow races or walking the high wall because the only time they tried, their glasses fell off and they'd be sprachling about on their knees for ages looking for them and that spoilt the game.

Still, I liked Dolina best because we could sit on the grass together for ages and ages saying and doing nothing and be perfectly happy and content. It was enough to be together, the same way it's enough to sit with a cup of coffee in a café not because you really want coffee but because it's so good to be in some warm place even if you're on your own and no one is talking to you. Still, you hear the buzz of conversation and the clanking of cups and machines and the glow and noise of human beings all around you, which is something.

Then, after sitting on the grass together for a while, one of us would say or do something and off we went. It was good being best pals with Dolina because if I was feeling sad about anything she wouldn't just tell me to forget it or that things would be better tomorrow. She listened, and would then slip her arm through mine in that special way and we'd go off for a walk together down by the sheep-paths not saying anything and by the time we were halfway along we'd be running and skipping without a care in the world.

I could also tell her anything. Even things I was ashamed of, like the time that I was in a bad mood and just for spite, I chose Katie for my playing team instead of her, and when I told her she said that it didn't matter. And I knew that it didn't because of how she said it. She also had a curl in her hair which looped over her left ear all the time no matter how hard we tried to pin it down, once even using glue which just made a mess, though the curl still bounced free after a while.

Lisa was so good. It was as if she became my age, though wiser, when with me. Her mind must have been on her work, though we didn't talk about it often. It probably helped her as much as me. All I knew was that Lisa preferred to cycle rather than drive, even though she sometimes had to drive for her work because of the long distances involved in rough and windy weather. She told me she disliked it. Thing is, she didn't want to be an accomplice, which she feared she was by default. I told her not to worry. That Miss Marple was the same. Sometimes she also *pretended* to be an accomplice so as to find out what was really happening. I was reading too many Agatha Christie books at the time I think! Lisa liked that.

'Okay, then,' she said. 'I'll be Miss Marple. As long as I don't have to be an old maid like her!'

I was just a child and didn't need to justify anything, but looking back I now understand the mental hoops she must have gone through. The place needed jobs and progress to replace the dead weight of the past. If folk had their way, they would do nothing. Lie in bed all day, for to preserve what you have is safe, while it's dangerous to move out of the cave until you have to. There might be bears and dragons and monsters out there.

'You need God most when you're in least peril,' Mam used to tell us.

'Danger past, God forgotten,' Dad always added.

Lisa and I cycled a lot together so I got to know her well. Though I was years younger than her, she never treated me like a child; perhaps because in so many ways she was a child herself. Or at least wanted to be one now and again. She could relax and be daft with me. My best trick was to cycle with my feet steering the handle-bars, so she also learned to do that, silly and dangerous though it was. It took her mind off the stress of work. Off doing unlikeable things when all she really wanted to do was to cycle the machair paths all day long.

Initially, she was glad James Campbell was the Chair of the Development Board, for he was smart at manoeuvring his way round difficult issues. Days after she started her job, a multi-national company approached them with plans to site a fish-farm and feed-plant on Loch na Cloiche. Loch na Cloiche was just over the hill from us. They were seeking planning permission from the council, and support from the local community was critical. She was at the initial meeting as secretary. The presentation was slick and professional, with the company confident about their proposal, though she had her personal reservations. Her dad used to fish there and it had lovely wild trout. She loved how they always lit a wee fire on the shore afterwards and cooked the fish in foil. The councillors asked questions.

'What about the environmental damage?'

'We're not here to save the world,' Campbell said. 'All due diligence has been exercised on that front.'

Statistics and graphs and figures were produced to show that all the legal and ecological requirements were met. The drawings were all coloured, she said, as in a child's universe. She showed me the way she used to draw the sea a perfect blue, and the houses all neat and rectangular as if there was never any wind or damage.

'And jobs?'

'Seventy during the construction period, then fifty after.'

'Full time?'

'Thirty full-time. Fifteen part-time. All high-value jobs.'

It was like a road which narrowed as hazards approached. She feared betraying the community. Herself. Taking the tarmacked main road instead of the sand-filled machair track which bumped you all the way from Àrdglas to Linsiadair.

She said it was all dry and factual until Campbell intervened.

'Statistics don't move people. Emotions do. They want to feel it belongs to them, that they have a real stake in it. Individually, I mean. Not as a community. Remember, it's the individual who's sovereign here, not the state. They still imagine themselves as hunter-gatherers, not consumers and customers like all the rest of us.'

So the company compromised, offering every individual within a five mile radius of the development a percentage share in the company, up to an overall limit of 15 per cent.

'What about those six miles away?' Lisa asked.

'Tough luck,' replied Campbell. 'There are enough within the five mile radius to carry it.'

And they did. Every home benefited individually – some bought new double-glazed windows. Everyone's ambition was to see the sea and not feel or hear the wind.

'To see everything and hear nothing,' as Dad put it.

Others got tarmac to their houses, extensions to their dwellings, new fencing for their crofts and bursaries for the children who were going on to further education. Everyone gained, except for the poor trout which were destroyed as soon as the cages were set in the loch. But who cared about them anyway, because the farmed trout tasted just as good. Duncan always covered his with tomato sauce, Fearchar with brown sauce, and I preferred salad cream, which wasn't as sweet or gooey.

8

Electricity

THE EVENING SOUND of my childhood is the hiss of the paraffin tilley-lamp hanging from a nail on the ceiling. We could measure time by the sound, for the lamp went quieter as the fuel burnt through. And the smell is the sweet odour of the paraffin when it took that first flicker of flame and slowly lit up the globe. It lit purple first then white before settling down to a warmish orange glow. The mantle hissed.

There was a lamp in each room, and when dusk fell Dad went round the house checking there was enough fuel in them and that the wicks were dry, before pumping the paraffin by hand through the wick to light it. From as soon as we could walk, Duncan, then Fearchar, then I dreamt of the day we would be allowed to pump the tilley to life. We watched them glow ever brighter and brighter and then there was always that moment the light began to fade and we all ran to be first to the pump to renew the brightness.

It looked easier than it was. You needed both strength and delicacy: enough strength to pump the oil through, but if you did it too vigorously or too lightly the wick went up in flames or didn't light at all. Like everything else, it was balance: slow and steady rather than fast and strong. Truth was, the tilley-lamps didn't provide that much light – just enough to make sure you could see things, and then after a while the light began to fade and dim, but could be given extra life for a while by pumping more paraffin through. The oily smell lingered on Dad's clothes until the day he died.

The worst thing was to let the tilley fuel exhaust itself. For then Dad had to start the whole palaver of filling it all over again, moaning at us for not keeping an eye on it. As if we had nothing better to do! I remember the hiss of the soft light and the security we all felt as we sat under its unsteady glow. I had no notion at the time that my Mam and Dad would have had to buy the lamps and paraffin somewhere, and repair or replace the mantles and wicks and globes and pumps and the lamp itself when it broke down. To me the tilley-lamps were as guaranteed a part of my childhood as the sun rising in the morning and setting at night.

We discovered light and shade. My room had both an east-facing and a west-facing window – tiny skylight windows – so that when the morning sun shone early and I was still in bed I could watch the light gradually moving across the wall, and then in the evenings reverse its path, throwing the places it had left behind into the shade. One moment the wildflowers in the small vase on top of my table were bathed in light; the next they were resting in the cool of the evening. It was as if the walls shifted according to the light. At certain times, I could lie in bed and make shapes with my hands which became rabbits and elephants and Reynard the Fox on the wall. Flap your thumbs and that's him on full alert.

The best was waking early during the school holidays with the window open and smelling the summer outside while the flies and the bees buzzed everywhere. Everything was new. I could imagine no better world than the one that existed. It was where I most wanted to be. Katie was afraid of the bees and ran away when they came near, until Dolina and I told her that they were not the least bit interested in stinging us, and were our friends. They were just singing their own song. We told her to buzz like a bee and then they would think we were one of them.

'All they want to do is dance from clover to clover and gather nectar to make honey,' Dolina said. 'So the only way they will ever sting you is if you frighten them.'

And Katie was forever fine after that.

It's only now that I fully realise what a terrible struggle it must all have been. The constant effort Mam and Dad must have made to make sure we were warm and fed and educated. There was shame, of course: I remember having to go to the shop on a Tuesday, just before the Family Allowance arrived on Wednesday, for groceries with a note asking the shopkeeper to 'Please Oblige'. As if lending was an obligation rather than a choice. He did, except for one Tuesday when Fearchar and I handed over our Mam's note and he looked at it, shook his head, and said, 'I'm sorry, the sum is too high already.'

Sometimes Dolina chummed me to the shop and if she had any money we bought jelly squares and chewed them as slowly as we could all the way home. But no matter how slowly we chewed and promised not to swallow, by the time we got half-way home the jelly squares were all finished.

The problem with the shop was that it offered us things we couldn't buy. When Christmas came the shopkeeper had spinning tops and coloured beads and rattles and sweet cigarettes and everything on his shelf. We bought them when we were a bit older and used to sit on the gate leading up to the fank. I was Greta Garbo and Dolina was Marilyn Monroe.

'Let's go to the shop,' I suggested to Dolina, the day we became film stars.

'Aye, let's,' she agreed.

Duncan and Fearchar and I had secret electricity, however. Even though we were off-grid, we could access the whole world once we left the house. A few neighbours had television, though they never put anything on except for the boring news and weather, as if we needed to know that: you just had to look outside and up to know that it was raining, but with that small patch of blue high to the north-west, it would be dry and fine for playing in half-an-hour or so. My recollection is that in our village Alasdair Mòr and Jessie Sinclair had small televisions with two channels in black and white, but that the pictures were always full of falling snow so that you couldn't see anything anyway. Then we could make up the things hidden by the snow, like Duncan claiming that the policeman had killed the woman, even though I knew it was the thief. Nevertheless, the snow melted and *Dixon of Dock Green* soon became a hero like Fionn to them.

Radio was better. Duncan loved football and listened to all the commentaries sitting behind a haystack on the machair with a little transistor his friend Norman gave him. I listened with him and liked the way the roar of the crowd rose then died away in disappointment. It was like listening to the surf on a winter's night. Norman got the set in Glasgow and Duncan paid him £5 for it. He got the £5 by rearing and selling two lambs the previous spring. Unfortunately the battery expired and he couldn't replace it. The local shop only sold things like sausages and paraffin and sweets, which old MacLean carefully weighed out on his brass scales as if each sweetie was made of gold. While the battery lasted, folk walking past the haystack on the other side of the river heard music and later said that it was coming from the fairies who had made the good crop. Though some of them were surprised at the sort of music the fairies were making nowadays.

The electric came to the island when I was eleven. Poles with wires began appearing from the north, mile after mile. They changed the sound of the wind, which now whined through the cables. Duncan told me they were called 'telegraph poles'. If you got the bus up to that end of the island you could see workers hanging from the skies tying wires and clay pots to the poles, and the best thing of all was watching the men harness themselves before climbing the iron-stakes like monkeys right up to the top.

Duncan's friend Alex said that he saw one of the linesmen touch the sky with his extended hand, and a flash of lightning followed that lit up the whole island. He said that for a moment he was able to see through the walls of all the houses as if they weren't there and that he could see people in their beds and cooking and even sitting naked on the toilet and everything.

'Did you see their... their things?' Duncan asked, as if I didn't know what the things were called.

'Of course,' said Alex. 'They're just the same as footballs.'

At school everyone who lived at the north end of the island talked of the marvel. You just entered the house and pressed a switch down and you could instantly see everything. It was amazing how many things could happen all at the same time in so many places. It was as if everything was happening at once. And there was no smell of paraffin or oil or peat or wood or dust or anything from it. There was no smoke either from the bulbs or the new electric fires to make your eyes sting or cloud over the room so that you could barely see in front of you. And you had no need now to go tramping up the hill in the rain to cut peats and then have to spend the whole summer drying them and stacking them while fighting off the midges and clegs and then having to haul them home on your back because all you needed to do was press a wee switch and the electric fire would glow for you all day and all night if you wanted without any need to clear out all these dirty ashes.

But who could believe those north end people? They lived so far away. Twenty miles at least, so we didn't really know them. They'd all gone to a different primary school and church and had different pals and everything. We couldn't trust them, for they could just be making things up to make us look daft at the other end of the island.

'But everything is so clean and safe and quick,' Patricia said. 'We can wash any time, day or night, and we don't have to make the fire or clean the ashes or handle dirty peat any more. My school shoes aren't covered in dust anymore – look!'

And they weren't, for they shone black and bright and clean.

Some folk had already bought radios to replace their old wind-up gramophones and it was said that young Alex, the schoolmaster's son, had also ordered a colour television. You could see the whole world on the television, Alex said. Boxing and football and people kissing and everything. Duncan knew that, for he'd seen that already at the Film Guild pictures. All that girly stuff, Duncan complained, that spoilt every cowboy film, because he always turned away until he heard the sound of gunfire when it was safe to look again.

All the big Primary Seven boys from the north end began to play a new game called Z Cars, arresting criminals all over the school playground for robberies and murders. Strange that no one was robbed or murdered for real where we were, though they seemed to be getting killed all the time on the radio. Though Niall Cuagach once told Duncan that the last person to be killed on the island was a travelling packman called George Wilson who was waylaid and bludgeoned to death out on the moor on New Year's Day in 1864. His sack contained Spanish doubloons and twenty golden guineas. Niall Cuagach said some of them were still buried in a pit, and he knew where they were, but he wouldn't tell where because they were cursed.

The strangest thing was that the birds sat on the wires and weren't killed. For everyone was warned that electricity was dangerous, and that if you touched the wires, or even looked at them, you would be killed instantly. Mùgan said the real danger was that if you were holding a dog and leant against a telegraph pole the electrons would travel back and forth through you, and next thing you might start barking and chasing sheep. There were even big clear notices stuck on the poles saying 'DANGER OF DEATH'.

'That's because birds have special feet,' Niall Cuagach said. 'They only feel living things like air and water and sand. Man-made things can't touch them.' Though we all knew that couldn't be right because he himself hunted with a bow and arrow and feasted regularly on pheasants and cormorants, so they obviously felt things all right. It wasn't like in the comics where if a cat or dog or a boy or girl was run over by a road-roller they then sprung up again like elastic. It was the one magic gift Dolina and I wished we had. Not because we feared getting run over by anything, but because it would have been so much fun being able to make ourselves so thin that we could slip away out under the school door without being seen whenever Mr Morrison started the dreadful times tables that we already knew off by heart.

Speaking of elastic, I always made the best catapults in the place. Duncan and Fearchar always wanted them, but couldn't make them to save themselves, but because I'd learned how to sew with Mam I knew how elastic worked, so whenever they wanted a catapult they always pleaded with me to help. I made all kinds of special ones, because it all depends on how you set the elastic into the wood. Of course Duncan wanted a catapult that would fire things miles and miles, but I taught him that was stupid and that it was better to have one that was really tight and strong and accurate rather than merely relying on length. So I made one for him that could not just ping a tin off the top of a post every time from a distance of ten yards, but would also send it flying another thirty yards onwards from the impact. Of course he didn't want a catapult just for knocking tins off a wall. His favourite escapade was lurking behind rocks or sheds by the roadside and firing off pellets towards anyone who was walking or cycling past. It didn't take long for Dad to confiscate all the catapults.

Mam had an elastic body. She was by far the fittest of us all. Or at least the most supple. She was the only one in the house who could put the palms of her hands flat on the floor without bending her knees (she used to scrub the floor like that), and she could do it in reverse if we asked her, bending her body backwards and touching the floor with the tips of her fingers. Her never ending house and croft work was the yoga and gym of the time.

I was lucky because I spent most time with Mam, who was patient. If I couldn't do something she explained it to me and if that didn't work she took my hand and guided me through it again and again. Hold the needle this way, lick the end of the thread, then twirl it tight and it will go through easily enough, see? Or we would knead the dough, her hand over mine as we rolled the flour slowly in small circles. First clockwise, then the other way. See, there it is, as thin as a winter's cloud. Duncan and Fearchar suffered because they spent more time with Dad who gave them terrible rows if they made a mistake. It made Fearchar frightened to try anything new and Duncan reacted the other way, as if he knew everything in the whole world without anyone having to tell him.

Summer was best, when the tar melted on the roads and the creosote dripped down the telegraph poles. Duncan and Fearchar and I gathered empty jam jars and filled them with tar and creosote which we then sailed down the stream towards the ocean. We liked the bits where the water ran fast and straight because the boats then raced quickly along, but we liked it better where the river curved and looped, because then we could follow our jars bobbing and weaving and tumbling and crashing this way and that all the way down to the wee waterfall. I liked going down there on my own sometimes just to listen to the water tumbling over the stones in the quiet.

The hardened creosote and tar weighed the ships down with ballast, making them sail straighter and faster. We had proof it worked best, for other things didn't work half as well. Sailing empty jars down the river was useless, for they just floated aimlessly about like corks, moving this way and that, while filling them with stones made them too heavy and filling them with grass too unstable. The jars then overflowed with water and sank. Tar and creosote were perfect. One of my boats once sailed across the wee loch to the Spanish Sahara, which doesn't exist anymore. I always wanted Dad to make me a proper play-boat of wood with bright red sails and a mast and a name and everything, but he always said he was too busy, and never did. The boat would have been called the Santa Maria. Instead, Dolina and I made endless iris-boats which we sailed across the loch. They were green with yellow daffodil and lily petals for sails.

Making something was the best thing in the world. And the best thing we ever made was a wooden spinning-top which we then painted in different colour circles so that they all blended into one multi-coloured whirl when it spun. Dolina had a multi-coloured pom-pom skirt and she could also do that trick where she spun round and round, though when I put it on and tried it I got dizzy and just fell over. She could spin for hours and hours and see things like the school that were normally fixed in one position moving to different places as she whirled round. I wonder who the first person was in the whole world to make a circle and spin round and round taking the world spinning with them? I suppose it was the first thing anyone ever did. Hazel was doing it all the time. She wasn't even doing it for show. It was just her.

Our ship's voyage began on the east side of the wooden bridge near the main road. Duncan said all voyages should begin from the east and head west, for that's where America was. A flat stone was the pier, and once we launched the jars the journey to America was long and hazardous. The first challenge was under the bridge itself, where nine times out of ten our boats got stuck in the rushes. But that was part of the adventure. It happened to all the great sailing ships and armadas and liners, some of which had been shipwrecked and others captured by pirates in the Spanish Main. We then crawled under the bridge with the water knee-high and released the liners to sail down the rapids on the other side. Sometimes I was the pirate and captured Fearchar and Duncan's boats and demanded the usual ransom of a double caramel or a Spanish doubloon, which were Mam's old coat buttons.

There was one rule – none of us were allowed to touch our boat by hand. They had to be steered by sticks collected on the sailing day. The sticks weren't allowed to be gathered or prepared beforehand. Just the best one we found on our way from the house to the river. It was the longest and widest and deepest and biggest stream in the world because it was also the Nile and the Amazon and the Mississippi where our pals Tom and Huck and Becky were at the same time sending a boat towards us from the other end of the river. One day the two boats would meet half-way and we'd exchange flags and greetings and we'd all sing 'John Brown's body lies a-mouldering in the grave' together.

Truth was, our boats never reached America. They sank in the mid-Atlantic storms which had also taken the Titanic and other great ships. The jars always got stuck in the boggy part down by Ronnie's byre, and we all knew it was too dangerous to wade in there, for it was soft and deep and deadly. Old MacArthur drowned there some years ago on his way back home from the pub. If you went down there on your own on a dark winter's night you could still hear him singing as he walked and then hear the huge splash and the fearful cry as he disappeared and was sucked into the mud. The dead were always wailing and crying in those dangerous places where they'd drowned. I think they found comfort in us hearing them. All the rivers on our side of the island ran west, and our elders always told us that if we ever got lost in the dark up in the hills all we had to do was follow the river down to the villages by the sea. Murdo MacInnes once told me that if I ever found myself in trouble he would sail his trawler from Rockall, laden with prawns and lobsters, and come to my rescue. No wonder the seas would all gang dry if we ceased to love. I think of him every time I see these poor asylum-seekers in their flimsy boats in the English Channel and how Murdo would lift up them on board and give them a hot mug of tea and a plate of soup and a warm place by the stove.

Duncan never took the transistor home. Not because he feared Mam and Dad, but because he didn't want to disappoint them. He listened to them the day the man came to offer a connection to the grid. The man, Mr Johnston, was smartly dressed in a blue suit with a red tie. He had a beautiful car. A slim silver thing with two separate exhaust pipes, so you could hear him miles before you saw him.

'Japanese,' he said to Duncan as soon as he saw him admiring the car.

He did a strange thing. He knocked at the door, which no one had ever done before, for the door was always open and never locked. Why would it be when it was protected by common poverty? Hens and dogs and folk came and went as they pleased, except at Hogmanay when the guisers couldn't get in until they recited a poem. It was as if, once a year, entering someone's house was a privilege rather than a right, and as a child I wondered why it couldn't be like that all the time, so that folk could only come in if they sang a song or chanted some magic first. And besides, that Hogmanay business was so unfair for only Duncan and Fearchar and the other boys were allowed to go round while us girls were stuck at home. It's all changed now, and girls go too!

Once inside the house, Mam made Mr Johnston a cup of tea, for there was a law that no one could enter any house without being given a cup of tea. He sat at one side of the table, with Dad at the other. Dad always wore a cap, even when he was inside, because at any moment he might go outside to work. Except he took it off when eating dinner. Duncan and Fearchar and I sat huddled together on the bench that lay between the stove and the door. No visitor should ever cross between the householder and the fire. My job was to shove away any hens that tried to venture inside. They liked coming into the warmth, and when Dad wasn't there Mam allowed them in to peck the crumbs on the floor. The world was theirs as much as ours. They were even known to slip in and lay their eggs under our beds, so we always made sure we looked in every nook and cranny of the house in the morning in case some lovely fresh brown eggs were there for breakfast! The old hen, Murdina, was my favourite, for when she was allowed to come in she would jump up onto my lap and coorie in like a baby doll. She'd lie there with her eyes closed and I'd stroke her feathers while she made soft cooing noises just like a baby. She even snored when she fell asleep.

At least we had rugs to impress him, for the two sisters down the road, Miss Agnes and Miss Peggy, still had sand on their bare floor. They swept it all out of the house on the last Friday of every month. Then got Dad to bring them a cart-load of fresh sand up from the shore to carpet it afresh. Mam always swept our house morning and night, as if dust was something unnatural to be swept away rather than normal and left alone, as in their house, where it floated in the air like a million angels. Their stone floor was uneven. The first time they called me in I stumbled in the big hollow between the front door and the kitchen corner, but once I got used to it I was fine. The rest of the floor went up and down in various places, just like being on Dad's boat. They put milk out for the cat in one of the wee hollows by the fire.

They must have been quite lonely, for whenever I walked past their thatched house they'd call me in to talk. It looked a bit like the gingerbread house Hansel and Gretel lived in, and at first I used to carry wee white shells with me in my pocket, just in case. Even though Miss Peggy was deaf she could always sense me going by, even if I was creeping ever so quietly, and suddenly appear at the door shouting my name.

Every time I entered they fetched an old white lace tablecloth from a drawer and spread it on the small table because I was a stranger and they had invited me in, and the special cups and saucers came out because they needed to show them to someone as part of a gracious ceremony. I am grateful that their old strange ways prepared me for the ways of the world. Dad called them the Alpha and the Omega, though I didn't understand what he meant at the time. I now know they were the widow's mite.

The first time I went in they gave me tea and a scone, but the tea was boiled like tar so I only ate the scone and every other time they called me in I said I wasn't thirsty. Their kettle was always on the boil. It made a different music from ours: hummed endlessly, and then when they wanted to make tea Miss Agnes moved it a fraction and it began to sing. Ours whistled. The two of them sat opposite each other at the small table, both of them dipping their big digestive biscuits into the tea until bits of them floated to the surface. There seemed to be a clear division of labour in the house, for Miss Agnes did all the cooking and housework, while Miss Peggy would always be seen outside feeding the hens and goats they kept at the back of the house.

The scones were lovely though, always freshly made by Miss Agnes on the griddle over the open fire. Sometimes she put a newspaper in front of the fire to draw the air and brighten the flames. I always hoped the paper would catch on fire to see what would happen, but it never did. They had cows and hens and ducks and did everything themselves, because if they didn't, who else would do it? Miss Agnes said the ducks were blessed creatures because they once hid Jesus under straw when he was being pursued by his enemies. After milking the cow Miss Agnes always made the sign of the cross on the cow's back with the cream from the bucket. Dad said Miss Peggy could read my fortune in the tea leaves and Miss Agnes in the white of an egg, though I never saw them to do it. Later on, he said they would have read them anyway and would have known my future but would not have told me unless I asked, because they had such good manners.

It was so dark inside their little house. Cosy, as if the three of us were tucked up in bed together, along with a several hens and cats. Any chink of light from outside was instantly swallowed. The two tiny windows so hidden that you had to put your face right up to them to see out, though Miss Agnes and Miss Peggy moved effortlessly about the place like bats in a cave. I don't think a different nest would have occurred to them. It always took me ages to get used to the darkness inside, but after a while I got familiar with it too and could make things out, starting with the loud ticking of the grandfather clock which was the only noise in the room. I always hoped to be there when it rang the hour slowly and solemnly. If Miss Agnes and Miss Peggy were doing something when the clock started beating, they stopped and listened intently as if it was sounding for the first, or maybe the last, time. Sometimes it struck the hour the same time as the kettle hissed and it was as if the clock and the kettle were talking to each other. The clock with its deep old voice and the kettle with its impatient cry. 'Let me off this stove, it's far too hot, I'm boiling,' the kettle hissed while the sleepy old clock beat on, as if it had all the time in the world.

If you just sat there and waited long enough you got your bearings. They knew everything that was going on outside by the tiny noises things made. Someone moving a cart far off, doing something useful. A hen scratching in the next field. After tea, Miss Agnes always sat by the tiny window looking out in case anything moved to break the silence. She could see the whole world from there.

'There's Archie's cow grazing by the river again,' she said.

They still used the old way of telling the months. Never January, February and so on. Always 'Ciad mìos an Earraich' ('The first month of Spring' – which was February). The thatch kept the house cool in the summer and warm in the winter so that it always felt like being inside a nest. They had no pictures on their walls. Just pots and pans and ladles and brushes hanging on nails made out of heather roots. If you couldn't use a thing, what was the point of having it? Though they had two matching red and white china dogs, one on Miss Peggy's side of the fire the other on Miss Agnes's. But the sisters were just like me, because they too liked shells and had stuck them in cement on the floor in front of the fire.

'As a decoration,' Miss Peggy said.

'It's so that we don't slip,' said Miss Agnes. 'They give me a good grip.'

It was too late before I realised how much they knew. At the time I was more fascinated by how they behaved rather than what they said. Each of them had a snuff-box they treasured. Miss Agnes's was black with a silver colour she imagined was pearl on top, while Miss Peggy's was brown with a picture of a castle on it. It was fascinating watching them at differing intervals – they never did it together – open their box ever so carefully, then pinch the snuff delicately between their coarse fingers, place it on the back of their hand and sniff. Sometimes they sneezed, more often they didn't.

'It clears my head,' Miss Agnes always said afterwards. While Miss Peggy, sitting in the other corner, crooned a tune she said she once heard out at the pier:

> *Julius Caesar made a law,*
> *Augustus Caesar signed it,*
> *That everyone who made a sneeze*
> *Should run away and find it.*

And they'd both chuckle.

The sisters spoke an older form of Gaelic which I only half-understood, using many archaic words and phrases, and also sort of chanted rather than spoke, one finishing the sentence for the other so that the first could think about the beginning of the next. I liked the way Miss Peggy said my name ever so slowly – she called me Annag – as if it was a precious object that would fall apart if she handled it too quickly.

When talking, their hands moved all the time as if they were acting out everything they were saying in case it didn't exist if it wasn't made visible as well. They bore the last remnants of the native sing-song voice which has since evened out and disappeared altogether in most places, though there must be a corner of heaven where saints like Miss Agnes and Miss Peggy make scones forever as they chant and lilt away, waiting for all their friends and descendants to arrive as the grandfather clock beats on, even though time will be no more. That won't be its job any longer. Only to be itself, tick-tocking eternally for the pure joy of it.

We will know our friends there as we do here because they will rise and put the kettle on when they see us. I look forward to seeing them again, though it will be strange for us all to be covered in dazzling light! Surely there will be a candle-lit cottage sanctified by a peat-fire especially for them so that they will know that they are happy? I'm sure they will be allowed to let it die down and be lit afresh every new Mayday.

The man was always called by his full name, Mr Johnston. Strange how people from the mainland, and teachers, didn't have first names. Duncan was taught by Mr Ferguson. Fearchar by

Mrs Ferguson, and I was taught by Miss MacNeil and then by Mr Morrison. Though it wasn't completely true, for when the travelling packman arrived they called him by his first name. Ali. But he only had a bicycle. Maybe that was the difference. Maybe strangers had first names too, until they got cars. Ali used to walk his bike along the road. I suppose because his case took up all the space between the saddle and the handle-bars, though people used to say it was because his Dad before him travelled the same way with a horse, creels filled with clothes and knick-knacks hanging from each side, and a bit of string for a halter. It was how it was done.

And the other mystery about teachers is what they did on Saturdays. Maybe they talked to their own children then, for they never talked to us during the week. Not properly anyway, for when they spoke they didn't speak as normal people did, back and forwards in sort of half-sentences, but just sat or stood there giving us information. That five times three made fifteen or that one line down and then one line meeting it straight across was a 90-degree angle, whatever that meant, and if we asked why, they would just say that's the way it is or it's the 'rule of mathematics' or something, as if that explained anything.

They were always 'explaining' things to us, however, as if a thing had only one meaning and accuracy was all that mattered. It was shameful not to have an explanation for something, so of course we invented answers just to please them. But it had to be a made-up answer that they liked. If they didn't like it, they punished you. Mr Morrison asked Duncan why sea water was salty and since he didn't know he said it was because of all the shipwrecks where everything, including all the bags of salt in the galleys, spilt into the sea. He got six of the belt for that.

There was only room for certainty, as if a thing had to be what it was called and nothing else, when any idiot knew that a stone could just as easily be a goalpost and a heap of grass a bed for a cow. Strange how exact and certain things were in school and in church and how uncertain and conditional they were everywhere else, where things always depended on the weather or how much money you had in your pocket or whether the paraffin had run out or on what mood Mam or Dad or your best pal was in.

And besides, the teachers were always correcting us – even our opinions.

'You're learning an important skill that will be useful to you later on,' Mr Morrison said to me the day I told him it was unfair that us girls always had to tidy the dining tables up while the boys went out to play. Though he moaned about that as well, as if playing was a waste of time. I often wish I'd wasted my whole life playing. And any time I did a drawing, a teacher would appear at my shoulder and sniff and then add a line where there should be no line, or tell me to paint something in, or change the colour, or add something, as if I hadn't made a choice to leave it blank in the first place. It was as if anything we did or thought or said was never good enough. As if it was always insufficient. It was unfair, and unfairness is always remembered. Try not to be unkind to anyone, for despite all our bravado, we're all as fragile as a reed.

Mam poured the tea into the best china cups.

'Sugar?' she asked Mr Johnston, and he said, 'Yes. Please. Two.' Which was quite an extravagance. He had very clean hands as if he'd never changed a bicycle-wheel or anything.

Mam put two spoonfuls into his cup. He stirred it round quickly, looking as if he regretted something. Maybe he normally stirred the sugar in slowly, the way Dad did. Or in a different direction, because if he was anything like me, he might have just gotten flustered for a moment and stirred the sugar clockwise when he normally did it anti-clockwise.

These things matter, for they can really throw you for the rest of the day if you forget to bring the right kind of pencil to school for example, because the ones in school don't draw the line as clearly as the one you left at home. They smudge, and all you then get is a row from the teacher and when you explain that's because you left your proper pencil at home you just get another head-nip. 'Serves you right for forgetting, then. That'll hopefully remind you to bring everything you need to school from now on.' And then the teacher would give you a rubbishy pencil as a punishment or as if it didn't matter, when it actually makes all the difference in the world what kind of pencil or spade or knitting-needle you use.

Mr Johnston sat on the edge of the chair as if he could leave at any moment. At the cèilidh, folk always sat back as if they were never going to leave once they got settled and had their dram or tea and scone. He was nervous, for he was tapping his knee with his fingers and speaking in short clipped sentences. I think it was the first time I realised the difference between speaking and singing. He wore a lovely black watch with big white dials and a silver strap, which he tightened round his wrist now and again. He relaxed as he sipped his tea, explaining the advantages of electricity, as if we didn't know. To Dad, who had transported electricity poles through the Panama Canal decades before, and to Mam who'd danced in the glistening ballroom of the Adelphi the night before she left Liverpool. Glass chandeliers shone like a thousand stars.

He talked as if the old world was useless. Darkness was to be extinguished. No more cutting peats and lighting dirty fires and slaving over a hot stove and pouring dangerous smelly paraffin into lamps and looking for matches and stumbling and falling over one another in the dark. Although we all quite liked the fun we had the days we spent cutting and gathering and stacking the peats, even when it was misty and wet and dawky and we had to stand in the bogs wet up to our knees and covered in clegs and flies and midges, and we liked the smell of the paraffin lamps and whispering things that magnified to each other in the dark. Best was taking a corner of a newspaper and lighting it in the fire and then running across with it to light a candle. You never knew when you'd set the whole house on fire!

Instead, all would be clean and quick and easy. And much safer – no danger of a candle spilling over in the night or of a spark from the stove starting off a blaze. That was how Iain Gobha, the first ever blacksmith, set the volcano on fire. He forgot to close the forge door.

All that would be gone. One flick of a switch and a kettle would boil. Cookers with four hobs and two ovens. An electric fire. A washing machine to keep everything clean. An iron for our Sunday clothes. An electric alarm clock if we wanted, instead of those daft cockerels crowing whenever the fancy took them. It just meant that a new day was dawning anyway, not that we were all heading off to betray one another, as Cuagach claimed. Lights in every room. No danger of flames and death. A television if we wished.

'It's just like a new crop for you to harvest,' Mr Johnston said. 'Look on it as a new type of potato that will nourish you day and night through the whole year, summer and winter. As a greater man than me said, it will abolish day and night. You'll be able to shear your sheep and milk your cows any time. For where there is darkness there will be light, as the good book says.'

Duncan and Fearchar and I loved it. We wanted the man to talk forever. About light and speed and sparks and sound and how you could see the lights of Glasgow from a hundred miles away and how the world was like a lit ball from outer space, with only Africa and where we stayed as dark spots. He sounded like Dad when he told one of his great stories. Like that one about Conall Gulban who had the magic sword on which there were carvings of lion and leopard, of griffin and striking serpent, fiery and scaly, with an edge which could cut an apple on water and a single shaggy hair from the head of a wild bear. Television would have stories like that, except better, for there would be real pictures rather than pretend ones.

We would miss toasting bread on the open fire, however. Those late winter nights, with the wind howling outside, when Dad gave us the special long fork and we took it in turns to toast the loaf through the grill of the stove. None of us could manage it in one go. It got too hot, our hands burning until it became unbearable. So we took turns, squabbling over who would get the last shot, when the bread turned crispy and golden brown. The best thing was then putting the butter on, watching it melting and swimming like honey all through the slice. The challenge was always to try and keep the butter on the bread, balancing it well so that it would not pour off down the edges. We all liked the brand new sliced white Milanda loaf we bought from the travelling van and which was rapidly replacing homemade bread in most houses. It was a sign that we were better off. That, and Ambrosia custard. We all fought for the thick back-slice, but Mam made sure we each took a turn. She kept a note of it in her pocket. Best of all, Duncan quickly discovered that the new white bread made a great eraser to correct our spelling mistakes in the school jotters. Thing is, though, we were always hungry very quickly after eating it.

'That's because there's no life in it,' Mam said.

'All very impressive,' Dad said to Mr Johnston. 'Except we don't want electricity. Don't need it. We're perfectly happy as we are.'

Which we weren't. As if you could keep the ghost away by hiding under the blankets. He'd be there with you in the darkness. I saw Duncan's lips move and he almost said something, but didn't. He would very much like it. As would Fearchar. And I. We wanted whatever old people didn't want. Things for us, not for them. They would all die soon. We were longing for the future with all its promises. It would thrill us to bits. We'd be the first to hear things. Dolina didn't have a radio yet. She could come over to mine and we'd listen and sing together. And dance. Not these old fashioned dances we had here to long slow Gaelic music, but fast dances. Up and down and back and forwards and from side to side. Dances we could do on our own without anybody asking us. I'd seen the pictures. It was something to look forward to.

It would make a change from watching the clouds to see if one would turn into a dog or an elephant. But of course they didn't, they were just the same old boring clouds that went from white to grey to black and then became rain. Though Katie said to us that she'd once seen a cloud which had grown from a kitten to a dog to an ostrich to a crocodile and then became one of those huge -sauros things, but we didn't believe a word of it. At least watching the clouds was more interesting than the past-time of some adults who spent their days looking out the window to see if big Effie was at the washing-line hanging out her long drawers or the shorter ones, which were much bigger and longer than anyone else's in the first place.

I looked at Mam who sat knitting by the fire. She was making a cardigan, stitching in that slow, precise way of hers. In and out, with the wool threaded over one finger as the ball grew gradually smaller and the sleeve longer and larger, for she always made the sleeves wider at the bottom than at the top. Nothing was ever hurried, the needles perfectly synchronised as the sleeve extended. It was the same as when she handled the scythe, as if everything was useless unless it was used well. It was sacred, like the way the priest consecrated the host.

Someone would be kept warm as a consequence of her labour, for Mam never told who any work in progress was for until it was complete. Then it was given as a gift, for if something isn't given as a gift it's worthless. Maybe she only decided who it was for at the last minute or once it was done, but I suppose not, for she would have had to work out measurements and dimensions beforehand. She knew people's sizes just by looking at them. Watching Mam, I realised that nothing could ever be made without two things working together. Needle and thread, kettle and water, flour and butter. I only ever understood myself through her.

Mr Johnston looked over towards her, but she said nothing, continuing to knit. I loved the click-clack sound the needles made as she wove the stitches together. I never loved her more than at that moment. Mam knew everything. Because she made and darned all our clothes she could work out at a glance what people were hiding under their garments, from Fozy's large bodice to Mr Blair's invisible corset-belt which kept his floppy belly under control.

That's probably how I learned to examine people too. Mam said poor Mr Blair spent all his strength on keeping up appearances.

What Dad feared most was that the fire would be extinguished. Ever since humans had discovered it, it was the centre of life. I wonder how they found out? I'm not sure about that old story about some caveman sitting there rubbing two flints together and then seeing sparks flying. Why would he have rubbed two flints together in the first place? A sense of wonder I suppose, to see if anything might happen. That's how we discovered things too.

The fire provided warmth, cooked the food and gave light. It was amazing really how much light it gave. I could read by it, even when I was furthest away from it by the door when Mam and Dad and Duncan and Fearchar claimed the best places nearest the fire. Words always looked better by firelight, and when the flames flared up or settled down the pages sometimes shimmered as if they too were on fire or were dying. As if the words themselves were in flames.

It was never allowed to go out but was always kept smouldering overnight, so that all that was needed in the morning was to stir the ashes and add a few dry sticks and another day began. Seeing smoke rising from a chimney was a signal that someone was alive. Mam worried when someone's chimney was silent. And smoke falling instead of rising was a sure sign of coming rain, she said. Lots of folk who had gotten lost out in the dark had been guided home by the light of a distant fire. In the olden days it was lit anew once a year, at Beltane, but that practice had long gone: everyone now kept it going all the time, smooring it down overnight. To extinguish it meant certain death. How could anyone think of replacing an eternal thing with a switch you could turn on and off at will, Dad asked? And what if the switch broke? What then?

Johnston spoke of the day he'd spent with Murdo Clark, the man who'd wired MacLachlan's house. MacLachlan had offered them both a dram, then sat stoking the fire with peats, watching with wonder as Clark laid wires throughout the house. MacLachan's chimney went on fire every few years because he never cleaned it, believing that the sparks from his fire cleansed the outside air from devils and evil spirits. At last when the miracle of the lights was switched on, MacLachlan, who was the best piper in the place, asked the electrician, 'Do you play the pipes?'

'No,' said Clark. 'I don't.'

'Impossible,' said MacLachlan. 'How can you do the magic you're doing with those wires without also being able to play the pipes?'

Electricity was a just a new tune he needed to learn. Poor MacLachlan hadn't realised he wanted light until he saw it. Unlike others, he'd never been away from home. He'd seen men go sailing and off to the wars and come home changed. He wouldn't need to do that now, for he could be changed sitting where he was, whether he liked it or not. If television had been there at the time all these young boys needn't have gone off to the Somme, he said. It was like MacCrimmon's piping, which altered everyone who heard it. Folk who never cried before burst into tears and the biggest cowards in the place lifted up their swords and headed off to war as soon as they heard him playing. They say old Bellag stood on a chair just before she went to bed the night she had the electric installed and spent hours trying to blow the bulb out like a candle.

'Aye, she's not as thrifty as she used to be,' her neighbours all said, watching her lights glowing all night long. After that, she couldn't bear the dark.

'Well,' Johnston said after a while. 'We'll just leave you then. We'll bring the poles down as far as your road-end anyway, so that if you ever change your minds you can just let us know and one of our engineers can call by to connect you to the outside world. You'll be the last in the village. On the whole island.'

The whole world, he meant. You're forgetting Niall Cuagach, we all thought. Johnston knew of him all right, but hadn't bothered to climb the hill to his solitary, remote shack. Some failures aren't even worth the effort.

As he left, Duncan dared.

'Would you…'

'Of course,' the man said. 'Just to the main road.'

The inside of the car was as shiny as the outside. Fearchar and I sat in the back. Duncan could see his reflection in the gear knob that was so unlike his father's tractor. Dozens of coloured dials and little clocks glittered and flashed on the dashboard.

'Revs,' the man said. 'And that one's the speedometer.'

It was pulsing at 60, moving towards 70.

'Temperature. 20 degrees in. 14 degrees outside.'

'What's that one?' Duncan asked.

Mr Johnston pressed a button and it crackled, displaying a moving red line.

'Music. What kind do you like?'

Duncan didn't know.

'All kinds,' he said.

'This?' Johnston asked, and a woman was singing. He flicked another switch. 'Or this?'

A man sang.

'Or this?'

Some fiddles played. Johnston changed gears, touching Duncan's knee as he did so.

'Sorry,' he said.

'This is the road end,' Duncan said. 'We need to get out here.'

The car stopped. The man was about to say something, but ceased. We ran all the way home.

9

Mrs MacPherson

MRS MACPHERSON WAS small and round and fat as butter and the most loved person in the village. Not because she could sing or tell stories, but because everyone felt better if they saw her, as if they'd seen a saint. She was Dr MacPherson's widow, and as a midwife and nurse oversaw every birth in the place over the previous fifty years. She told me that when babies didn't want to come into the world she just opened the doors and windows and out they popped. That's why everyone should have windows that open wide and aren't all stuck with paint, like John and Margaret MacLean's house, though I don't suppose it mattered to them that much because they were very old.

Mrs MacPherson had a marvellous memory despite her great age and still saw everyone as the infant they had been. She liked colour and attached ribbons instead of names to babies' wrists when they were born. MacDonalds were green, Campbells blue, MacInneses yellow and Nicolsons red. She saw them in colour all the way through their lives until they themselves became grandmothers and grandfathers. If there were different MacDonald or Campbell or MacInnes or Nicolson families she shaded the greens and blues and yellows and reds to distinguish them from one another.

She had easels and paints and brushes and all kinds of marvels in the extra scullery she had at the side of the house where she sat and painted in the evenings in the soft warmth of the late sun. She said that made the paints themselves kinder. She taught me how to hold the brush properly, not like a pen sideways as we did at school, but more like a feather, which she held lightly with the thumb and fore- and middle-fingers, painting from the top down as it were.

'Hold it like this,' she told me, 'as if you're looking down from heaven to earth, because colours contain the whole of heaven and earth. And remember the grass doesn't have to be green and the sea blue! It doesn't have to be grass and sea at all. As long as every brush stroke means something. A snail, a horse, your Mam or whatever. It doesn't matter what, as long as it's something real. Which gives you heaven and earth to paint.'

Best thing she had was a cardboard box filled with birds' feathers she used for brush strokes, including an eagle's feather Dr MacPherson had found when climbing Ben Mòr. So ever after that, whenever I found a bird's feather, from a wren to a seagull, I picked it up and took it to her. Eventually poor Mrs MacPherson had to tell me that she had enough gull's feathers for a whole lifetime, thank you very much Annie! And anyway I was supposed to leave seagulls alone, for they were dead fishermen returning to their grounds and how could they ever get back home without all their feathers, even the ones that fell off, for they'd notice they were flying slower and would turn back to get them and what if they weren't there?

When I tried to paint I wasn't very good because what I liked doing was putting dabs and blobs of paint of differing shapes in different places, rather than drawing anything recognisable, because I saw no point in that. I could see sheep and cows and dogs and people and fields and lochs and walls and mountains any time outside and all I wanted to see on the paper were the colours that all these things were, or could be. I later read that was called Impressionism, so maybe I wasn't useless! But Mrs MacPherson, like my school teachers, just wanted me to draw gates and houses and horses and things they could 'see' all the time, and since I didn't want to do that, I gave up. I tried painting flowers for her, but because I always found the gaps between the petals more interesting than the petals themselves they never looked like 'flowers'. Nobody liked my drawings because they were full of what looked like blank spaces.

'Which is nothing,' Duncan said.

I learned from her that there are warm colours and cold colours. And that there is a difference between light and colour. Light shines, colour dances. The warm colours approach you, the cold ones retreat from you. Like the sun and the moon. There is a time to draw near and a time to draw back. Yellow is warm. Blue is cold. But then you can mix them, and that becomes green, which is the colour of summer. In fact, if you mix the colours ever so slightly, one thing slowly – or sometimes quickly – becomes another. Just as in baking.

Her own favourite colour was vermillion, which she made by mixing red with water and then quenching it with blue. Next to purple, it's my favourite colour, though it's hard to find with the same thick glow that Mrs MacPherson made it with. She later told me her secret was using the white from inside a plover's egg to give the paint its sheen. And these are ever so hard to find, and it's now illegal to pick them.

She was painting a river one evening when I called in to see her, and she asked me what I thought was a strange question.

'Annie – when I say a word like "bee" to you, do you see the bee or hear it?'

'See it,' I said, but then when I really thought about it I thought I didn't – I could hear it buzzing away as it picked the nectar on the machair flowers. Same as when I now think of Mam, I hear her singing and scraping some dirt off the stove, and when I think of Duncan I hear him whistling as he cycled along the road and when I think of Dolina I hear her chanting

> *In and out the dusty bluebells,*
> *In and out the dusty bluebells,*
> *In and out the dusty bluebells,*
> *Who shall be my partner?*
> *Tappity tappity on your shoulder,*

Tappity tappity on your shoulder,
Tappity tappity on your shoulder,
You shall be my partner.

I can hardly remember what they looked like, only what they sounded like. Much later, when I worked as a nurse with children who had learning difficulties, I studied the difference between what medics call verbal and non-verbal learning, which is basically the difference between learning words by hearing the sound they make and learning them by making a mental picture of them. It's like the difference between east and west: if you go west, there's the sea all the way to America, and east, the hills where the heather grows and the sheep and cows graze all summer long. I worked with many patients who were dyslexic, for example, and it was always helpful for them to get a picture of a word.

Which is not half as easy as it appears! It's easy enough to make a mental picture of words like 'dog' or 'house' or 'river' for example, but what about words like 'it' and 'where' and 'why'? If, as a child, you don't know how to pronounce them, how on earth do you make a mental picture of them? I always encouraged children to remember words by rhyming and repetition, for to repeat is to remember!

In a dark, dark wood, there was a dark, dark house,
And in that dark, dark house, there was a dark, dark room,
And in that dark, dark room, there was a dark, dark cupboard,
And in that dark, dark cupboard, there was a dark, dark shelf,
And in that dark, dark shelf, there was a dark, dark box,
And in that dark, dark box, there was a pale, pale GHOST!

It helps to speak out your fear. You can then call to him and tell him to go away. And if he doesn't, after a while, you realise he's even more scared than you are, so you can just wave to him, like an old sad friend. He likes that, especially if you smile. That really scares him!

*

I always went out of my way to call in and see Mrs MacPherson. On my way back from school, or if I was sent on an errand to the shop, I made sure I climbed over the stile that separated our crofts so that I'd have to cut through Mrs MacPherson's garden. It was the only garden in the place which was kept. I mean she was the only person who grew flowers rather than vegetables, saying she preferred carnations to carrots! Everyone else had cabbages and leeks and onions and turnips and potatoes growing, and considered flowers an unnecessary luxury – something that merely used up space. And if you needed them for any special occasion you could order them from the mainland, where they grew bigger and better and brighter. It may have been a folk memory of the famine, but if you couldn't eat what you grew, folk saw no point in it. Beauty and colour and scent for their own sakes were superfluous. Though her flowers were freely used by everyone, with lilies or primroses or roses from her garden decorating the church altar every Sunday and adorning every bride to her wedding. In those days, no flowers were ever seen at funerals.

She liked her flowers best in the garden and not in vases inside. I always wanted to pick and cut flowers and put them in my hair or in the jam jar in the window. Sometimes Mrs MacPherson allowed me to pick and cut some, but only if I did it properly. Cutting with her secateur just above the stem, and always keeping more of the green leaves than the coloured petals. She couldn't bear people who plucked flowers and then sheared off all the greenery just to show off all the bright colours in their windows. It was selfish and crude, she said.

The other thing is that we were allowed into Mrs MacPherson's house, unlike some of the other older people who kept everything hidden. They'd call us over as far as their door and ask how Mam and Dad were, and sometimes give us a bit of cake with a thumb-hole in the middle, but we were never allowed in over their thresholds into the darkness beyond. I now realise that they would have been simply hiding their poverty because they were ashamed of it. The little wealth we had (I had ankle socks with flowered patterns on them!) was a reminder of what they never had and a sign of change. At least they had their poverty and their silence for their possession. My memory is that poverty and goodness went together. As if poverty itself made folk kinder, aware of how fragile everything was.

Mrs MacPherson's garden was a riot of colour in the summer and autumn. It was very much like the English Country Garden we sang about at school. Mrs Wilson was the visiting music teacher and we saw her once a month, when we all assembled in the big room. An old piano stood in the corner, which was never used except when she visited, and she'd sit there for half an hour trying to teach us a song. She played the tune on the piano, then stood and conducted us, mouthing the words as we sang:

> *How many kinds of sweet flowers grow*
> *In an English country garden...*

And then those marvellous names which sounded so much more beautiful than any of our native thistles and irises and dockens and daisies – meadowsweet and lady smocks, gentian, lupine and tall hollyhocks, roses, foxgloves, snowdrops and forget-me-nots, until Mrs MacPherson told me that of course we had all these except we called them different names – Crios-Chuchulainn, lus a' chrùbain, gall pheasair and so on. She reminded me that we even had songs about them and then she and I would spend time singing Duncan Ban's song to Ben Dòbhrain with its primroses and St John's wort and orchids. It was only much later that I realised we sang about wild things rather than cultivated ones. After the music class we all of course sang our own words to the song out in the playground:

> *What can you do if you can't find the loo*
> *In an English country garden,*

Pull down your pants and piddle on the plants
In an English country garden...

Despite the permanent salt air and the constant wind, Mrs MacPherson managed to cultivate miracles in her garden. Hidden behind her old stone wall by the roadside were her little friends, as she called them – daisies and clover and nasturtiums and bluebells and primroses; then she had a little rockery, where heathers and round coloured shrubs with Latin names grew, before she led me into the sheltered south-facing section where all the roses and geraniums and lupins and a fragrant climbing honeysuckle were on display. I just knew that if flowers could be that sweet-smelling and beautiful then anything in the world was possible.

She had a small glasshouse at the gable-end where she nurtured seedlings and grew tomatoes and which was regarded as the ultimate in extravagance by some of the older crofters. A special corner of her garden was given over to herbs – mint and tarragon and lavender and balm o' Gilead and Lus nan Laogh which you dried and boiled, and if you drank the juice it cleared headaches as well as all kinds of infections, and Lus nan Gadmann which, if you mix it with fresh butter, cures baldness. She also always warned me to carry a bite to eat in my pocket in case I ever stood on Lus an Acrais (the hunger plant), because if you tread on it you lose your strength and if you haven't anything to eat you will lose the ability to move. It's good advice. Always carry a bite to eat, even if it's only half a biscuit, for you never know what straits you might find yourself in with no one to help you, or which poor child you might come across whose life will be saved by the giving of your biscuit.

She got me to water the garden from an old tin can, which I thought at first was unnecessary given the amounts of daily rain we got.

'But that's completely different,' she said. 'That rain comes pelting down. What these plants need are little sprays of mist, so that they know they are individually loved rather than part of a deluge.'

Everything in the garden had its say. Even what others called weeds. She cultivated and nurtured them, telling me that everything in the world has its place and that nothing is useless or ugly or superfluous. My own favourite flower was the fragrant white jasmine which fought the wind and rain to bloom again every June and July. The simplest thing I learned from Mrs MacPherson was that things always grow upwards, towards the sun. If they're blocked from the sunlight she showed me how the little stems wind their way round things to emerge again up into the light. Even if they have to circumnavigate the globe to get there. Nothing can stop us moving towards the sun. I was about to pick some flowers one day when she stopped me and said this strange thing to me.

'No. Leave them please, Annie. They haven't grown up yet. That's what I'm interested in – what they will become. Even though I know already. Though you never really know.'

She looked at me steadily.

'You might not appreciate this just now, Annie, but value yourself like a flower. Be generous to yourself so that you'll bloom. People say they only last a season, but they last forever. The fragrance and the colour and the memory.'

And they have, as I still see her in her light blue dungarees bending over to weed in the peaty soil between the long rows.

After we admired the flowers and praised the garden I'd go into Mrs MacPherson's kitchen where the range was always on, summer and winter. She was the only woman who made double pastries, sometimes covered with almond or coconut flakes, rather than the common cheese or fruit scones which everyone else made. The kettle was boiling and I tried not to look up at the top cupboard where she kept the tin of chocolate. Once the kettle boiled she said,

'I don't suppose you'd like a hot drink, Annie?' and I'd nod and run across to the table, take the chair over to the cupboard, stand on it and take down the chocolate. Unlike Mam, she didn't give me a row for standing on a wobbly chair. We made it in a pan. A drop of milk first, then the chocolate and then the boiling water, stirring ever so slowly as it heated up until the first froth appeared. 'Beannaich a' bhò,' she always said as she poured the milk in.

Mrs MacPherson herself drank coffee, which no one ever drank back then. She kept the beans in a glass jar and then poured a large spoonful on to the chopping board and hammered them down to powder. She gave me a small wooden mallet to help her and I loved bashing away at the beans, even though I made such a noise and mess. Or maybe because I made such a noise and mess! The first time I helped her I asked her if I could taste the coffee and I did, and it was awful. I preferred the smell to the taste!

As we sipped the chocolate and coffee, Mrs MacPherson fetched out the registration book where she kept the colour chart for all the children born in the area. It was fascinating to follow all the family lines: the green MacDonalds, the blue Campbells, the purple Galbraiths and so on. Later, when I travelled in London on the tube, I sat there looking at the green District line and the blue Piccadilly line and the purple Metropolitan one and the extended family that was London. Everywhere connected one way or the other. If you get the underground from Green Park to Holborn, for example, you can then jump off and without going up for air catch another to Marble Arch or Lancaster Gate or wherever. As the train rushed through the tunnels I thought of how much Mrs MacPherson and Mùgan would have liked being called connecting stations.

Before she married, Mrs MacPherson was Fiona Smith. The Smiths had built and repaired everything in the place over the previous two hundred years. Carts and axles and ploughs and anvils and hoes and spades and wheels which then lay rusting and resting in fields and ditches and dumps and byres. Strange how things retain their shape without being themselves. Carts without wheels, ploughs without shares, spades without blades. They grew old and outdated so fast. The first Smith was Tormod, who walked down from the north centuries ago bearing a forge on his shoulders, with his wife and seven children marching behind him carrying all the tools of the trade. He set up business behind the mill at Lòn an Inbhir, where Niall Cuagach claimed that sparks could still be seen flying out of the rocks on clear winter nights.

'For a master craftsman's work outlasts him,' Niall Cuagach said.

Mrs MacPherson's two brothers, Norman and Sandy, continued to run the mill just across the road from us and every so often we'd collect a firlot of meal from there. Dad always gave me a hurl in the empty barrow on the way across, and then replaced me with the bag of meal for the return journey, running precariously on the way over, trundling carefully on the way back. Sometimes Mam did the journey instead, and then I always got her to sit in the barrow on the way over as I ran with her as best I could while she bounced up and down in the barrow shrieking and hollering.

Mrs MacPherson's gift was to encourage everyone. When she looked at you it was a sign of friendship, but if she went as far as holding your hand you knew she loved you. She sang the cèilidh choruses with joy, listened to every conversation with complete focus. She shivered when Old Murdo told his ghost stories. Held her hands tight when Niall Cuagach gave his prophecies. She hoped Hazel would forget them. The veins on the back of her hand were clear as rivers.

'You need to learn from what never happened,' she whispered as Old Murdo and Niall Cuagach spoke.

I sometimes sat on her knee, the way Hazel used to. When the cèilidh room was crowded, with pipe-smoke stinging our eyes and the smell of whisky in the air, Mrs MacPherson opened up her hands, a signal to me to come across and be rescued. To sit safely on her thighs for a while. I'd rest back against her ample breasts. When she turned on her side I could hear her heart beating steadily. It was slow and deep like the old clock she had in her sitting room ticking solemnly towards bedtime.

Whenever James Campbell spoke, Mrs MacPherson hugged me that bit tighter. She told me later that as part of her nursing studies forty years before, she'd done a short course in Clinical Psychology and all she remembered from it was the thing the Swiss doctor Jung said about a thing called shadows. She remembered it because it was so common in her own childhood. Folk who had the second sight and would stand still watching phantom funerals passing by, or seeing shrouds draped over the living. They were so reluctant to tell what they saw, but others knew by their posture that something serious was afoot, because at the sight of a vision the eye-lids of the seer rose up and the eyes continued staring until the object vanished. If they blinked, the vision was gone. She didn't have that full gift, though she had enough of it to see through people. She said it was like seeing the sun through the rain.

Strange how some folk can't see what's in front of their very eyes while others see what isn't. Maybe we just see what we want to see, and others see what could be there?

'Folk now see less because they see more,' Mùgan said. 'We don't have time any more to see the things we're not looking for. We just find what suits us.'

'The thing is,' Mrs MacPherson said, 'it was a gift, and often an unwanted one. Those who saw realised the danger of wanting to peer into the future. It made it inevitable rather than changeable, which is surely what we all want? The chance to change things? If it's already there, it can't be not there.'

I suppose those who had the gift of second-sight could see things because they were hesitating between two worlds – the one that was vanishing before their eyes and the one that was hurtling towards them at electric speed. They could simultaneously see the past and the future because they were living in both and didn't blink. Campbell scoffed at all the prophetic palaver since it was perfectly obvious to him that you could forecast the future from past behaviour. He imagined he knew more about what folk believed than they knew themselves. How wrong he was, for no one knew.

Mrs MacPherson felt there was something false about his language, though he talked so directly and eloquently and told no lies. She told me he was a fraud. Strange that most things that Old Murdo said were complete fictions, yet we believed every word, while Campbell was always factually correct yet everything he said was questionable.

'What a beautiful afternoon,' he'd say, and immediately everyone questioned his motive. Who was he trying to please? And why? Thing is, we knew that lying was really bad if you were just trying to benefit yourself. It wasn't so bad if you were lying to protect someone else, like trying to keep your pal out of trouble at school. That was just a white lie. Silence was just as bad. At school we always knew who was clyping because they'd sit there quietly saying nothing when the teacher questioned us all. They'd pay for it later.

When I sat on her knees, Mrs MacPherson acted as a kind of medium. She knew the world is made up of competing visions and voices. That everyone has their own ghost. It was obvious that the people who lived by the sea, such as Janet MacPhail, talked about seeing selkies and mermaids, while those who lived up the glen saw horned men and singing maids and lost souls. If some of the words in Old Murdo's story were fearful, she interpreted them for me. So when Murdo said, 'The ghost walked through the wall,' Mrs MacPherson whispered into my ear, 'That means he's going away.' And the candle flickered as he swept past.

She'd learnt that everything everyone said could just as easily mean the very opposite. Folk said all kinds of things that could mean anything, and once you defined it for them, they disagreed. Unless it didn't really bother them and then they agreed. And there were some people who never agreed with anything, even when they privately did. They used to come to Dr MacPherson's surgery all the time with ailments that didn't exist or disguising ones that did. For anything that existed once existed always.

'What's the matter?'

'I'm not feeling well.'

'Anything sore?'

'No. Not really. Except I get a headache now and again.'

'What kind of headache?'

'Just a headache. Like a throbbing. Here.' And the patient would point to their forehead. Nurse MacPherson would stand and feel their forehead, which was slightly hot. But that could be the heat from the room, or the long walk the patient took to the surgery.

'Did you walk here?'

'No. I cycled.'

And so, by a long sequence of exclusions she'd reach some sort of diagnosis and judgement. It was difficult for people to admit things. Just as at the cèilidh, where what folk didn't say mattered as much as what they said, their body language telling more than their words or songs or stories. What they liked or disliked was what they believed or disbelieved. Hazel always sat crouched on the floor, nervously smoking. She studied everyone and knew where all their pimples and scars were.

Everyone sat down where they could at the cèilidh. Some on the floor and on whatever stool or chair they could find, except for Campbell who stood singing his pompous songs while I rested on Mrs MacPherson's knees, leaning back on her soft chest. Everyone talked about the weather first, and when asked how they were, everyone was fine, except for Mùgan who always had some new ailment every time. Unlike us children, all the grown-ups spoke in half sentences as if full ones couldn't be trusted except when telling a story. It was a language of hints and movements, shrugs and glances, which only made sense if you trusted the person who was telling the story or singing the song. It was obvious that the virtue of the words depended solely on the teller. You didn't have to believe everything you heard or saw.

The house cèilidh was much less formal than the occasional concerts which were held in the school or church hall. The highlight of these official concerts was Mùgan's impersonations. He would spend five minutes slowly and carefully preparing for his act, then suddenly head off and do something completely unrelated. As if a sensational new idea had come to him which superseded everything else. So that, for instance, he would bring a pole and put flour on his hands and march up and down for a while as if he was preparing to pole-vault, then at the last minute before he made the final run towards the high-bar would lie down instead, tuck a blanket over himself, and go to sleep, snoring. We laughed because we realised how daft we were, spending so much time preparing for things that never happened or didn't matter, including watching Mùgan on the stage. Mùgan himself claimed he was trying to teach us that what we chose not to do was more important than what we did.

The Cèilidh

I USED TO watch and listen to them all at the cèilidh because it was like watching a play before we had television or anything like that. At least now with television I can always switch it off or choose what to watch. Then I had no choice. Niall Cuagach used to sit on the three-legged stool by the window while James Campbell always stood nonchalantly by the fire, leaning against the whitewashed wall.

Mam always washed the wall after he left, because he tended to leave his mark. He even wore galluses as an affectation. They were the preserve of old men, simply to keep their trousers up when their bodies began to sag, but of course Campbell had to show off, pretending didn't care whether he was young or old. Nevertheless he must have cared, for we all did. We had endless arguments over whether we were ten or ten-and-a-half. It made all the difference in the world because the half made you so much nearer being eleven, which was so much better than being just a baby of ten, and we also knew fine that everyone over thirty stopped remembering their birthdays because they didn't want to get any older.

Naturally, Campbell's braces were bright and narrow, because he had to shine – his were blue with yellow stripes, while the older men wore the standard thick grey ones from the local shop. The same with waistcoats. His were always quality tweed, always with yellow buttons made of brass. Now and again when everyone was silent he would sit down for a moment on the edge of a chair, merely so that he could stand up again. If you watched and listened you learned everything. He even started growing his hair long and talking about the Rolling Stones when it was obvious we all preferred The Beatles.

Parties are the same everywhere, I suppose. Fit in or leave. We were moulded by the opinion of others then as we are now. Everyone liked the good singer and the good story-teller and the good maker of bread and cheese and soup and cakes and tea and scones. You could be excluded or excommunicated from the cèilidh as much as from anywhere else. Those who were just blatherers, or were deemed unsuitable. Those who had no long old stories to tell and no old songs to sing or who were, simply, undesirable or awkward company. Who smelt or were drunkards or used filthy language.

Telling a story or singing a song badly was as shameful as telling a lie. You knew whether a story was true or false from the eyes of the story-teller, not from the words. If it was true, their eyes were calm and still except for illuminating the action. Though I could also tell that by the voice. I always knew when Katie was telling fibs just by the way she spoke. Her voice was then lower than normal, and a bit sweeter. You always know when something is wrong because you've once seen or heard it right. Nothing is a mistake.

Sometimes Campbell sang one of Mam's old songs and everyone then looked at the wall or at their feet while he sang, because stealing someone else's special song was as despicable as stealing their food. And making words up was just as bad, because everyone knew that's not how the story or the song was in the first place. That was like going into someone's house and taking things and moving all their furniture about.

The coming of radio and TV was a huge blessing to those who couldn't sing or were useless at telling stories, and to many lonely and isolated people who, at long last, found the terrible evening silences replaced by the sounds of human voices in their room. It was an extra blessing to recovering alcoholics who couldn't go to the pub anymore, because all those fascinating regulars in

Ambridge and at the Rovers Return came to visit them. Became their companions and friends. Someone to listen to. And besides, a lot of people never came to any cèilidh because they didn't believe in it. Idle folk sitting around talking and making things up when they should be out milking a cow or thatching the barn or clearing drains or doing something useful. And the time for it was nearly over, a flickering candle replaced by a bright, solid switch. Goodness, the washing and scrubbing that took place when the electricity came and everyone saw the dust and dirt under the new proper lights.

The way people sat or stood or dressed said as much about them as the way they talked. We were all taught one thing about dressing – that going out forced you to wear your best, or at least decent, clothes. Otherwise folk would wander about in pinnies and boiler-suits and Wellingtons all day and night. They said that old Smith slept in his. And he certainly smelt like it. Funny how we dressed up. When there was a concert in the village hall, a proper thing, we dressed up in nice bright colours, whereas for a cèilidh at a house, that was considered pompous. It was drawing attention to yourself rather than to the songs and stories.

Mr Blair the merchant always wore a white suit, which fitted him well, though we all wondered how he kept it so spotlessly clean, and everyone knew that when Mùgan put on his Breton beret it meant he was heading off to the pub on one of his big sprees. So they all kept an eye out for his headwear and gave him food and lifts home for the next seven days while he went his merry way. Dad said he was searching for something he was afraid to find. When Dad asked him why he went drinking he just said that he didn't have everything he needed at home.

'If I did, I'd never need to go to the shop or anything. It would just be me here and the world there.'

Mr Blair claimed to come from a distinguished Perthshire family that had fallen on hard times because of his father's gambling addiction, so he was reduced to earning a living. His shop was out next to the pier where you could buy what Mam called 'useful things' like ropes and tins of paraffin and nails and lamps and Wellington boots. His white suit was a flashy signal of better times, and sometimes he carried a silver-topped cane and a black hat. And an umbrella. He always sat neatly, as if he could rise and leave at any moment. The only thing that let him down was his voice, which was high and squeaky.

When he spoke to us out at the shop we never really understood anything he was saying because the way he spoke was so strange, as if he was making up sounds as he went along. So that 'because', for example, sounded like 'bee-caws' and 'tomorrow' like 'two marrows'. It was only after you left him you realised you had understood him perfectly though at the time it was like watching a fish talk. They said he beat his wife and children till they were black and blue, and sure enough his wife wore a lot of make-up any time she appeared in public and his two daughters were off school every other Monday. He also had a doorbell on his house, which no one else had. Later on, Mr Blair was taken away to Craig Dunain Mental Hospital in Inverness in a white van. We didn't want him to leave. We watched as it drove over the brae and we never saw him again.

'Poor man, hiding everything away,' Mam said.

We lived at the furthest end of the village – myself and Fearchar and Duncan and Mam and Dad. At the flat end, near the machair, where we could hear the corncrakes on quiet evenings. Just like Niall Cuagach out on the moor, we lived off-grid, so nothing much disturbed the silence except for our own voices, the sigh of the wind and the hiss of the tilley-lamp in the dark.

Dad loved the silence and Mam tolerated it. Duncan and Fearchar and I just wished we had television like the rest of the world. Sometimes I woke up just before dawn and it was so still that I could hear the grass and wind wondering what they would do that day. I suppose it depended on the sun, which hadn't risen yet. He would tell them what to do when he woke up. If the sun was strong the grass would grow and the wind would go away and play somewhere else.

We were lucky that ours was the cèilidh house, because so many other houses never had any visitors at all, just old men and women sitting in silence on their own all year long. Sometimes Mam asked us to take milk or bread along to these houses and when you entered the darkness all you could ever hear was the slow tick-tocking of their clocks beating out time over the fire. It was like waiting to die.

What a gulf there was between children and grown-ups in those days. Be seen and not heard and all that. When folk came to the cèilidh at ours they often whispered at the start to each other and passed some gossip along as if they were sharing a cake, leaving us children out. As if we didn't know that big people also had their pals and favourites as well as their spites and jealousies. If a place was empty, it was filled with gossip about the person who was absent, since nature abhors a vacuum! I learned that you didn't have to say much, for others then quietly fill and expand the gaps, the way you fill a balloon, slowly and steadily.

'Did you hear about George?'

'No? Really?!'

'Goodness, the smell off him tonight.'

'Did you see that belly? All that beer I suppose.'

'Poor woman.'

The men always held pipes in their hands and the women handkerchiefs whenever they spoke, as if these things were part of what they were saying and they wouldn't be able to say or do the things they did without them. Mrs MacPherson had a beautiful blue silk handkerchief which always smelt of lavender. I'd pretend to have a tickly nose and she pretended it was true so that I could sniff it. She was one of those women who always knew what needed to be done or said, whatever the occasion.

Mam and Dad said more folk used to come, but some died – it's what happened to old people – and others now had better things to do.

'Whatever things those are,' Mam said, rolling her eyes. They used to meet most winter Fridays, but by the time I was a child it was about once a month. Although our house was small, it seemed to expand so that everyone fitted into the same space that felt tight when the five of us were on our own.

When everyone gathered and had a dram they spoke loudly all the time, except for Mrs MacPherson who whispered, so that you were forced to listen to what she had to say. Most of the others spent their days outside calling to dogs in the constant wind and had long forgotten that they could quieten their voices when inside. They missed the fields. I've often wondered if the land and weather shapes our voices, so that people who live by the sea raise and lower their voices like the tide and those who live in cities speak fast and in stops and starts to keep up with the traffic and the changing lights.

Softness was a rare woman's gift, apparently. Us girls also had a 'whispering space' at school, just next to the stone wall where Dolina and Katie and Morag and Peggy and I would crouch to tell things to each other. It was as if a place didn't exist until we played in it and told secrets in it. It was the best and safest place in the whole world. The boys never went there. Not because we stopped them, but because they didn't want to.

Sometimes the five of us lay there, side by side, looking up at the sky and watching the white smoke of a jet curving high. We all guessed, because guessing was as good as anything and great fun and better than all these boring calculations we had to do in class. As if there was a correct answer to everything.

'London!'

'America!'

'Japan!'

'Australia!'

'Stornoway!' from Peggy, the daftie, just because she had a cousin who stayed there, as the jet-stream faded into the high clouds, becoming part of them. It all meant something, though we weren't sure what. Dolina once said to me that she was glad the two of us were alive at the same time in the same place so we could play together, which was such a strange and beautiful thing to say. One night we were allowed to camp out by ourselves in the garden. We watched the shooting stars.

'It would be no fun watching them without you seeing them too,' she said before we went to sleep.

Old Murdo specialised in ghost stories that left Duncan and Fearchar and I in fear of our lives. You could see and hear the ghosts when he spoke, for though we all made our own ghosts, his were especially terrifying because they were people who had recently been alive and had not yet forgotten the geography of the place and knew all the houses inside out and where we kept things and where we slept and where we hid when we were frightened, so there was no use in hiding from them because they would always find us, and any gust of wind during the night after the cèilidh became the host of the dead and whenever Fearchar turned in bed Duncan's heart almost stopped beating.

Every creak and squeak and croak was The White Ghost slowly climbing the stairs with terrible certainty, for he knew where every step was and where every one of us lay. He even knew where the squeaks were, so he'd step over the fifth and ninth floorboards silently. We hid under the blankets even though we knew that would only hold him off for an extra few seconds. Closing our eyes was the last defence. It was now or never. And by the time we opened them he'd gone and you could see the wall closing where he'd gone through.

But the ghosts were bound to come round some time or other, because the world itself was round and it was therefore obvious they'd have nowhere else to go to except round and round in an everlasting circle and back to where they were at the beginning, like Dolina and I did if we cycled down to the machair and then turned right so we passed all the same places on the old circular road until we got back home. We always took ages to do things together because then they lasted longer. Although the faster we did things the more they stayed the same because if we ran really quickly along the shore the incoming tide could never catch us.

The other thing is, the ghosts Old Murdo spoke of were always local, haunting the fields just down behind our house where there were no high walls or fences or deep ditches to stop them coming. And even if there were, it would make no difference, because these ghosts could walk through walls and peat-stacks and houses as if they were not there. The only reason they did that, Murdo said, was because these walls and peat-stacks and houses hadn't been there when they were alive, so obviously they didn't see them now because they were travelling from memory. We asked Murdo once if he'd ever seen a ghost laugh, and he said he hadn't, but maybe they did elsewhere, maybe on the mainland, though he didn't think so because they were quite lonely and lost and sad. They wanted to be remembered. To have friends. People to see and play up to and scare, the same way children put a scarf on and shout Boo! They were scared of the dark and of being alone too, he said.

He wasn't sure if they had bodies, though they could probably conjure up bodies if they wanted to. He doubted it though, because he'd never seen them eating or drinking or digging a ditch or playing football or going to the toilet or anything normal like that, and of course they walked through solid walls as if they weren't there. They must have missed the old places and people they'd known. Their stories had never been properly listened to, so they were still travelling about in the hope that someone would ask them in and listen to them and maybe understand them. Or give them a hug.

Sometimes windows opened on their own in the howling storms, letting them in. Maybe he was a ghost himself, Old Murdo said once. When folk finally stopped telling ghost stories the ghosts themselves disappeared because they became homeless. Once people stopped talking about them, they died again. When people scoffed at him, Murdo said that if ghosts didn't exist, then nothing existed. Nobody had ever seen the soaking ghost down by the well until Cuagach saw it. Then everyone did.

Mam had hundreds of songs. She remembered them because she'd always listened carefully. She said she never learned them, just listened to them. When she sang, it was as if no one had ever heard the song before, though they'd already heard it a thousand times. They received the songs as if they were accepting a newborn baby into their arms to cradle for a short while. They all liked babies because there used to be far more of them in the village when everyone had big families, and they could remember them crying and playing about the place, but they had all grown up and gone away. The songs she liked best were 'Maol Donn' and 'A' Bhradag Dhubh', which gave equal praise and condemnation to the MacNeils and the MacDonalds.

Mam herself was a MacNeil before she married Dad, who was the great storyteller. His favourite story was Conall Gulban, Son of the King of Ireland, whose sword could cut nine men down as it went from him, and nine nines as he drew it back. Whatever that meant. I suppose it sounded better and less brutal if it rhymed. Every time he told a story he finished by removing himself from the drama, sitting back and saying,

'And I left them there and they gave me butter on a burning coal and shoes of paper and they sent me off with a shot from a big gun on a great road of glass, and they left me sitting here at home.' And you could hear them outside leaving on their horses in the rain.

No one ever clapped after someone told a story or sang a song – that was kept for the formal concerts in the church hall. To applaud after Mam sang or after Dad or anyone else told a story would have been as stupid as applauding the priest once he'd given his homily or clapping the teacher when he told us that five plus four made nine! I suppose it was also strange we never danced at our cèilidhs, though that's not the sort of occasion it was. Dancing would have been considered very showy. And, besides, there was very little room for it. You'd be forever bumping into the stove or the bucket or the cats and dogs and hens and the table. Dancing was kept for the hall, where things were much more formal with all the proper steps done by the grown-ups. At least by those who were sober. The ones who were drunk or half-drunk just swayed or fell about the place.

We dressed up for the dances, because that was going out. The cèilidhs were just in people's houses, so that was staying in. You didn't want to embarrass the household by flouncing in wearing something fancy. What if they only had their old breeks or the floury pinny they had on? At the dance, Dolina and Katie and I always preferred the fast dances where we'd be flung about by the older lads. We liked the boys who swirled us round fast but held on to us strongly so that there was no danger of being sent flying across the room and showing your knickers to everyone. We knew who cared by the way they held us.

The house cèilidh was the place where boundaries and taboos were settled. What was not permitted in real life was glorified in a story or song, where you could do anything and anything could happen. Where every wish was obeyed and decorum was set aside. The songs and the stories gave you permission to do anything and go anywhere for a while. You could go to Greece and marry the King's son or daughter or kill thirty of your enemies with one swift cut of the sword or sail across the skies on a wisp of straw or become a mermaid, whereas here in real life your boyfriend would just be wearing sweaty Wellingtons and carting the dirty muck in the byre, and if you fought and injured anyone you were clapped into Constable Murdo's locked back room for the night before being sent off the island next day to Inverness Sherriff Court and fined and jailed for thirty days as happened to poor George Smith when he hit Mr MacIntosh the bailiff at the last annual cattle show. I don't remember any of the women ever telling long traditional stories, though they had them, of course. Miss Agnes and Miss Peggy had them, as did Mam, though she left the public telling of them to Dad.

After a story there would be silence for a while, until someone suggested a cup of tea. That was my special job. The best china cups taken out earlier from behind the patterned curved glass, and the bannocks and scones and crowdie and cheese and jam already in their blue ceramic dishes beneath the white cloth. There was just one kind of tea. Sun-Ray Tips from the van. Mam said to me,

'If anyone comes into the house when I'm not here, never ask them if they would like a cup of tea. Just make it and set it down to them. And always with a scone.'

Except for Niall Cuagach who always brought his own cow-horn and drank out of it, slurping like a pig.

Dad knew the stars and the constellations in the sky by name. He learned them when doing his navigation course at sea. They weren't just bright sparkly lights shining namelessly out there somewhere, or omens as Niall Cuagach believed. Sirius and Castor and Pollux and the Pleiades were as clearly defined as Hector's Field, which was next door to our house and Mairead's Stack which was half-way up the hill. That was a huge rock cloven in half, in which young Mairead Steele had sheltered for five days and five nights at the time of the great snowstorm of a century ago, staying alive by melting the snow in her mouth. She went on to live until she was one hundred.

Some of the younger ones sat at the table while the older ones were served where they were. Mrs MacPherson poured her tea into the saucer and drank from it like Bessie the old mare at the stone trough. Niall Cuagach was given a tin of treacle and melted three spoonfuls of it into his cow-horn. Effie the Postmistress asked shyly for a sherry, saying she had a sore head. She liked to drink her tea black from the blue Japanese cup Dad brought back from Tokyo. She was always clutching a beaded purse in which she kept Pan Drops. Some people called her Fozy, but she didn't like it, so we tried not to.

Pipes were stuffed with tobacco while Fearchar moved 'round the room with a lighted wick to get them all going. He could smell whisky from John the Shoemaker, sometimes known as Peter the Proverb, who sat nearest the door on an upturned wooden bucket, passing wind silently as he moved secretly from side to side, as if no one noticed. Though we all did and pretended not to. Peter always wore dungarees with a one-fold two-foot slide-rule in his thigh pocket. When he wanted to demonstrate something he'd take it out and measure things in the air, as if that proved everything. Hazel lit a cigarette. It was just a thing that was done. Life was meant to be enjoyed, not endured.

Where people sat was important. It signified degrees of friendship and enmity. If you paid someone a compliment it was made to sound accidental. It was always best to sit in a familiar position, where you sat last week, in order not to disturb anyone's order. As in church. Stay to the right of Mùgan and to the left of John. Otherwise someone might be offended. Little consolations took the place of affection. You never told someone you loved them: you just gave them extra potatoes, or an extra strong cup of tea. Machair potatoes in their floury coats with a heap of fresh butter if you were really fond of them.

The room was filled with smoke and smelt of sweat and peat and tea and whisky and perfume. I could close my eyes and move about in the darkness, knowing by the scent and smell where I was and who was near. The rancid smell from Old Murdo's boots. He had a strange moustache, though it was quite interesting watching him waxing it as he sat there, twirling the ends as if they were odd pieces of string. It was a grim yellow colour from nicotine. He claimed that when he was at sea he could smell icebergs miles and miles away because they smelt of the land and vegetation. 'I could smell the sheep grazing on St Kilda from here,' he said. 'Depending on the wind.'

Mrs MacPherson smelt fresh, like the shore after the early spring storms. Niall Cuagach of treacle. Mùgan, who spent decades at sea, of salt. Effie the Postmistress of talcum powder. Flecks of white dust lay on her hair and shawl. When she slapped her thighs a cloud rose into the air like that picture of the hydrogen bomb we'd seen in the paper. She was a good listener and heard everything; even those things that people just thought. Hazel smelt of cigarette smoke. I wore perfume. Eau de cologne it was called then, which my aunt Katherine gave me for my tenth birthday.

Once the tea things were put away, the cèilidh continued. Even though the tea and scones and cakes were part of the cèilidh, we all understood that it was also an interval, and less significant. Bits of gossip were then told and folk went outside 'to smell the air'. The men always made sure they stayed inside until the women who had gone out returned, and then headed out with their pipes. It was a bit like school itself where we could play and do secret things outside and only do permitted things inside. Even the windows were built high up so that looking out and seeing cows and flowers and things wouldn't distract us from doing Sums. The teacher was always keeping an eye on us and ringing that awful bell as if the open air was an enemy because he knew we could be better controlled inside. I suppose that's why meetings are always held indoors.

Mam then sang. Words that only the oldest fully understood. It was about a man who went to Ireland and met another girl, leaving his sweetheart behind, heartbroken. The abandoned girl is like a galley without oars, like a tree without roots or branches, like a day robbed of its sun. If you love the tree, you love the branches. But she wishes him well. Wishes him long life, love and happiness and many children. As Mam sang, Campbell smoked in the corner. He was the only man who smoked cigarettes and not a pipe. A lovely white packet with a flash of red at the top. Marlboro written on it. When he took one from the pack he tapped it three times on his right knee and then once on his left before lighting it with a silver lighter. The magic of ritual. He made smoke circles too. Seven normally, though once I counted twenty before they all faded into nothing. You could see he was afraid of himself. He wore a tin badge of Tintin on his lapel which all the grown-ups thought was unseemly for a man of his age and position.

Lisa sat in the small window chair which I used when reading. The light came from the south and shone directly onto the book when I sat there. Sometimes I had to squint my eyes because the light dazzled the page and the words became blurred and invisible, so I'd just make them up. I'd hear snatches of conversation and remnants of stories and bits of song, because when someone spoke, what they said suggested or reminded someone else of something else, so that talk of weather led to discussion about crops and on to food and prices, or the mention of the new baby boy born to Kirsty in Linsiadair meant that he would have the same name as his maternal grandfather who had composed the song about the rabbit and cormorant pie in the year of the long snow storm which lasted from Halloween to Easter.

There's a myth that in those old days of my childhood the seer saw a vision which he then told, as if he were Moses coming down from the mountain. Except it didn't work like that. What was unspoken was as significant as what was said. What really happened is that someone – Niall Cuagach, for example – would come to the cèilidh and, after someone had told an old, familiar story and someone had sung a song, would say,

'Chunna mi dreag an-raoir' ('I saw a shooting star last night').

'Càite?' ('Where?') Mùgan would ask.

'From above Linsiadair and falling over Àrdglas.'

Which meant a death in Àrdglas. Everyone thought of who they knew in Àrdglas. Though no one would say anything, and tea might be served or someone else would tell part of the story about Fionn and the Giants.

Then later, Dad would say to Niall Cuagach,

'Are you sure it fell over Àrdglas?'

And Niall Cuagach would hesitate and say,

'Well maybe it was more towards Kilaird. Sort of half-way between the two.'

Others would say this and that about it, and by the end of the night the company reached a kind of collective decision about what Cuagach had seen, and what it meant. And that was the vision. It was clear to me that nobody knew anything.

Nothing was as it seemed. Because everyone listened silently, without nodding or anything, you never knew what they were listening to or hearing or agreeing to or thinking. It was dangerous to let people know what you really thought. As wrong to say anything new as to put your feet up on the table. Though everyone knew that some dafties would walk through these villages the following morning to see if any algae was lying around. A sure sign of the remains of a falling star.

Sometimes folk would also gather in our house to play cards. I suppose it offered them a calculated risk rather than the daily run of fate. Something unexpected might happen after all, instead of the usual rain and wind. Whist and Catch the Ten, mostly, and what always surprised me was how keen the players were to win! They were all old respectable people, and there was no gambling and no prizes to be won, yet they played as if all their wellbeing and fortune depended on having the right card. And maybe it did.

'It's all about choice, not chance,' old Seònaid always said after she'd won another hand. The cards themselves were so lovely and full of colour, the Kings in red and the Queens in beautiful long blue robes. I once saw Seònaid and Marie almost come to blows, playing as a team, because Seònaid played a Jack when she should have played a much lower card as a decoy. And the language! It would make a maiden blush, as my Mam used to say.

Mind you, we weren't much better, for sometimes Duncan and Fearchar and I played Snap and it always ended up like World War Three. And I'll tell you why – because I was always quicker to see the snap-cards and would move my hand down to snap the one on the table, but they were stronger and always grabbed my wrist and pushed my hand aside so that they could win. As if the game was about strength rather than speed.

The other end of the village was 'ripe for development' as the local paper put it. The old disused airstrip lay there, with some ancient hangars the RAF used during the last war. A mile beyond, over the hill, lay the harbour where the ferry berthed three times a week. It was the big wide seaway to the world. If we climbed the hill we could watch the ferry until it became a tiny dot on the horizon before disappearing out of sight beyond the skerries to the invisible mainland. When we saw ships from a distance we couldn't tell whether they were coming or going. Next day we could be in London and might see the Queen, or even New York and see the statue. We used to go out and see what was happening some evenings. Old people always seemed to be crying when arriving and young people laughing when leaving. The elderly carried heavy suitcases and young people small rucksacks. We couldn't wait for the day when we would also leave. I would take the blue shell and that would be it.

Campbell even offered to build the new aircraft buildings from his own pocket as an incentive to boost the local economy. Making a profit was the least of his worries. That would happen anyway. The challenge was to do something worthwhile, for we all like to be remembered for the good we do.

'It's a certain winner,' he declared at the public meeting. 'A little airstrip that will bring high-quality, high-value and high-spending visitors to the area. Good people who will appreciate the good things we have to offer – peace and quiet; fresh air, excellent walks, local food and a taste of the local culture. We shouldn't deny the future, but invite it in.'

I was looking forward to seeing all these people, for who doesn't get tired of the same boring old faces all the time? Duncan, Fearchar and I couldn't wait to see planes flying in and out. The bigger and faster the better. We wondered whether they'd have parachutes. Twenty wheels and six engines and a hundred windows.

'Just think,' said Duncan. 'I could fly out of here in the morning. See Celtic play in Glasgow in the afternoon, and be back to milk Rosie before supper!'

'You'd need a rocket to do that,' Fearchar said.

'If I had a rocket I would go to Canada right now,' I said.

My overseas friend was a pen-pal from Canada – Naomi Lanier – who used to send me beautiful pictures of British Columbia. It was full of green and red trees and amazing paddle-boats and I promised her I would write to her forever, but then I sent three letters in a row and never got any reply, except for the third time when a note arrived from a Mr Latimer who said that the Laniers had sold their house to him a year previously and moved elsewhere and that he was sorry he had no forwarding address. I never heard from Naomi again, and though I vowed to trace her when I grew up I never did, for then it felt like a thing from the past and I didn't want to intrude on her new life. I've never forgotten her, and still have a wee picture she sent me of herself ice-skating on Lake Windermere in my best album.

Even though I was a child, I always found meetings interesting. Not because of anything that was said, but for the way people behaved, and the strange ways they prepared themselves to speak, and the actual way they spoke. They were like our own playground games, with an 'It' at the head, and everyone running and hiding while someone counted before she tried to catch us. We took it in turns to be 'It', though Katie always tried to hog it, the daftie that she was, not realising that it was far more fun running around and hiding rather than standing there with her hands over her eyes counting ever so slowly to ten or twenty or sometimes even to one hundred while we found the best hiding places in the world. Even though we all knew the hiding places, still they were new every time. It was frightening though, because sometimes as I crouched behind the Bran Stone I thought – what if they don't even bother looking for me? What if Dolina and Katie are now the best of pals and skipping across the grass together hand in hand and dislike me so much that they won't even come looking for me? Or worse. What if they don't care? And then one of them would suddenly appear, shouting 'See you! You're

IT.' And so I was. And when I was 'It' I would count fast but then they'd all complain so I'd have to slow down and count normal, except I then went extra slow just to show them, so that they'd get bored and peek out to see what was going on and then I'd catch them and be back running and hiding, which was best.

I watched the grown-ups carefully, because like when you are playing 'It' you need to hide ever so quietly when you're hiding and look everywhere when you're looking, and I could see ten minutes beforehand when someone was preparing to speak. Mùgan would straighten his back, as if he was preparing to go off on a long walk, and James Campbell would slick his hand though his hair several times, while Lisa tucked her knees in and brought the sharp points of her shoes together as if she was gathering all force to make a particular point. Everyone spoke with their bodies before they actually said anything. It's a bit like these pole-vaulters you see on television, rocking backwards and forwards for ages before they launch themselves off to hurtle over the bar, which they then clatter into in failure most of the time.

Meetings were new things to most folk. Up until then people were just told what to do, so it was quite difficult for them to believe that anything they said would make any difference. Choice was a terrible burden, Fr John always said. Dad said that if everything grew naturally like the grass we wouldn't need meetings. They were only a sign that people didn't speak properly to one another when they met at the sheep-fank and at the shop. It was like the songs of the birds in the air. Why would they reduce their thousand individual songs to one note, croaked by some buzzard high up on a branch? That's what meetings did to you.

And then when they spoke, everyone stood in a different way: some standing rock still, others swaying backwards and forwards or from side to side. No one ever spoke sitting down, but stood up as if they were back in front of the teacher. In school, we always had to stand up if we were asked a question. Most had nervous ticks, as if they were unsure of what they were saying, and not certain that they could find the words to say what they wanted to say. Maybe it was like a sum, and they didn't know the answer, for I never knew the answer to any of these multiplication things the teacher asked me either.

With some people, I always wondered why they were saying the words they were saying when they could just as easily have been saying different ones, for that's what I'd heard them say privately. It was mostly the men who spoke, who seemed well pleased with themselves once they sat down again, as if they'd opened a window and breathed fresh air and then snapped the window shut, pleased with what they'd seen, while any woman who spoke then looked anxiously at her immediate neighbour to see if she'd done okay.

The best meeting I was ever at was when Cailleach nan Cearc (the Poultry Woman) came to the school to advertise the best-laying ducks and hens for the crofts. She was a small, solid, well-built woman and wore a red coat and orange bonnet which she removed for her talk, though she put it on immediately afterwards to answer questions. Her hair was parted in the middle which made her look like that fat man we used to see in the film reels who made us all laugh. The best thing was that she had a slide machine on which she showed us pictures of different kinds of hens. I was given the honour of closing the curtains so that it was dark enough to see the slides, and though I've seen hundreds of films since, in large and small cinemas, none of them have ever beaten the thrill of that first night I saw images projected onto the wall. The curtains were brown velvet and once closed they shut out all the light, and all that you could hear was the loud hum of the slide projector as people settled into their seats to watch the show. I can't remember how many duck and drake and hen and goose pictures she showed, but I wanted them to stay up there on the white wall forever, for it seemed that my whole world was suddenly magnified and made multi-coloured and significant. There were red hens and brown ones and white ones and speckled ones, and then beautiful close-ups of all the different kinds of feathers, and I just knew that my Mam would love them to decorate her Sunday hat. The only breed name I remember is Rhode Island Red which sounded like poetry to my ears, and ever since, if anyone mentions hens to me I always ask them whether they are Rhode Island Reds, and try and hide my disappointment if they're not. The hen woman seemed old to me then, but now I know she would only have been middle-aged, which these days is no age at all. As with Naomi, I always wonder who she was and where she stayed and if she was married and had children and what happened to her, though I realise that, like the magic of the slides themselves, the picture is as it was forever that night, with those beautiful hens pecking at the golden corn.

Mam knew, because love can never be hidden. So when I became a teenager I was given the responsibility of looking after our ducks and hens. I made sure they were fed and watered and safe from any predators and in their well-wired-in coops at night, and of course had the pleasure of collecting the eggs every afternoon. Those nice big round brown ones were best, and I put aside the biggest and the best for Easter time for painting, because Dolina and Morag and Katie and I then had a wee competition to see who best painted the eggs. I always remember that at Calvary, Our Lady gave a basket of eggs to the soldiers in the hope that they might treat her  Son more kindly, but of course they didn't and his drops of blood fell onto the eggs turning them red, so I always made sure I put streaks of red across the middle.

But I'll give you a wee tip about the ducks and hens – if you want plenty of eggs from them you should keep them in their coops till mid-day. Otherwise, if you let them out in the morning they will lay their eggs all over the place and the crows will come and eat them. And another thing – when you set eggs out for hatching you should always put out an odd number, or all the eggs will be addled.

One Easter, Mam knitted little yellow woollen chick-jackets

for Duncan and Fearchar and I, and put an egg inside each of them, and though the eggs have long gone, I still have the tiny jacket in my box of special things beside my bed. The others lost theirs.

The usual suspects led the opposition to the airport development – folk who were against all developments because it would change things. It was impossible for them to believe in something that had not previously happened. Why fry an egg when it had always been boiled? And they didn't want anything new because they knew it would cost. And, besides, what was the point of improving anything – digging a ditch, for example, so that the fields wouldn't be flooded, when it didn't legally belong to you, and your improvement would just be used by the landlord as another excuse for increasing the rent? Who could believe fat Soutar anyway, that crooked Factor, who always hinted that you could grow two blades of grass where only one grew now, as if money could magnify the earth itself? And besides, you were going to die one day and inherit the new heavens and the new earth instead of these barren wastes. So why bother?

'I wonder,' I asked Mam after the cèilidh, 'if Catrìona ever married?'
    'Catrìona?'
    'Yes. Catrìona. In the song. The one you always sing'
    'Oh, her. She did. Yes, she did. Married Martin, the Laird's son. They had seven children. One of them was called Annie.'
    'The one in the other song?'
    'Yes, the one in the other song.'
    'Will you sing it?'
    'No. You sing it. You know it as well as I do now. You know them all.'
    'Only some of them.'
    'Some is enough.'
    And so I sang.

A Mhaighread òg, 's tu rinn mo leòn
Gur cailean bhòidheach lurach thu
Gur guirme do shùil sa mhadainn chiùin
Nan dearc air chùl nan duilleagan.

'You'll be fine,' my Mam said that night. 'You'll be fine.'

I wish I could translate it for you, but I can't because though I know what the words mean in English I just want to sing them to you as they are. It's like Burns said: 'you seize the flow'r, its bloom is shed.'

11

Fair Saturday

THE BEST THING about Saturday was that there was no school or church. The cèilidh was usually held on a Friday, so for those who worked elsewhere during the week, Saturday was a chance to do some of the croft work while trying to laugh about that ghost story from Murdo or the vision shared by Niall Cuagach. Depending on the kind of day it was – bright with sunshine or dark with rain – the ghosts magnified or vanished and the vision was fulfilled or forgiven. It was never as simple as just believing or not believing in ghosts. They were in the air too, and if you couldn't trust the air you breathed, what could you trust?

It's not that the stories made much sense anyway. The ones we read at school always had a beginning and a middle and an end, and whenever Mr Morrison asked us to write a story he'd put 'B-M-E' up in big chalk on the blackboard so that we'd remember to do it properly.

'You need to give a reward to your reader at the end,' he always said, except we'd remember Dad or Mùgan's stories, which strayed all over the place and where the best things were always the wee laughs and songs they stuck in along the way so that sometimes there was no end to them because of all the distractions on the way, from Mrs MacPherson's sighs to Fozy's secret biscuit-crunching in the corner. It took me ages to realise that was the story, not the 'proper' story that was being told!

Saturday always brought its own free story. No school, woo hoo! It's hard to imagine things differently when the sun's shining and you have work to do and the ghosts have vanished. For the grown-ups, if there weren't cows to be milked or fed or sheep to be sheared or moved, there were ditches to be cleaned or walls repaired or a byre cleaned out or that old tractor started up again. Jobs like that helped you not to think. No difficult decisions had to be made, except whether to use a spade or a shovel and when and where to stop to have your tea and piece. Work cleansed the mind. When he was full of drink Mùgan said that everything had gone to the dogs the day people started using spades to till the earth.

'We were meant to be hunters and warriors,' he cried, 'not crofters and farmers.' Which was a bit rich coming from a man who lived mostly out of tins and bottles.

Grocery vans came round the villages twice a week. It saved walking miles to the shop. 'And saves me buying rubbish I don't need when I go there,' Mam said. Though some of the women had catalogues and somehow found time and money to order new shoes or a vest or a nightgown for the winter. All the women wore cotton stockings, but Dolina once ordered two pairs of silk stockings from the catalogue and gave me a pair, so when we wore them to church the following Sunday we were the bees' knees, and all the other girls our age were in their usual ankle socks, as if they were little children beside us. Ali the packman was ill that year and we missed him. No one knew how he managed to contain the whole world in his expanding suitcase. I know now: it was simply that our world was smaller. Dolina and I sometimes spent a whole winter's evening looking through the catalogues, circling the flowered dresses and pointed shoes we'd buy when we grew up. We thought we could do that always and forever together.

The Saturday after that particular cèilidh was special. It was the day of the Annual Fair, when marvels arrived from the mainland. Coloured tents and cranky machines that went round and round and up and down, and a man with a hurdy-gurdy and another with a drum on his back and cymbals between his knees and a penny-whistle in his mouth, and endless drinks and cakes and sweet things. One year there were coconut shies and a man came selling canaries in cages, but he never returned. The other stall-holders said he'd sailed off on a big ship to South America to bring back some exotic parrots, but they hadn't seen him since.

I woke very early, then Fearchar woke early. He knew that if he tapped the wall I would hear him. Tap. Tap. Tap. I ignored it. Make him wait, as in a proper game. He tapped louder. Tap. Tap. Tap. I tapped back twice. Tap Tap. Good Morning.

'Tap tap tap?' asked Fearchar. 'How are you?'

Tap. 'Fine.'

Then I tapped four times.

'Is Duncan awake yet?'

He tapped back once.

'No.'

'What time is it?'

'I don't know.'

'Has the cock crowed yet?'

'Don't think so. I didn't hear it.'

'Must be the middle of the night then?'

'Suppose so.'

'Good night.'

'Night.'

Hours later, the cock crew, as if he had just discovered the morning and wanted the whole world to know about it. We had three cockerels, but Red always had to crow first. Otherwise the others were beaten to near death. He left them alive but wounded, so they would remember. But as soon as he finished crowing his heart out, then the others were allowed to caw. Though at a lower level, and not for so long. I timed them. I could count to sixty before Red stopped. Topper could get to forty-five, but the youngest one, Ginger, was never allowed beyond thirty. A flap of Red's feathers was enough to silence him.

I woke with a headache, which was the first time I ever had one.

Mam put her hand on my forehead and said I was fine because I had no temperature. She gave me an aspirin and told me it would go away. And it did. We were allowed to go to the Fair by ourselves. After all it wasn't that far away – ten miles to the north by road, though if we took the machair track and then cut across by the ford it cut the distance by half. Duncan wanted to take his bike, but Dad told him not to be selfish and to walk his younger brother and sister. Unlike Duncan, Fearchar and I had not yet reached the age where we wanted to be older. Especially not on the day of the Fair.

'Keep an eye on them,' Dad said.

Duncan knew that was to keep him within bounds as much as to keep the younger ones safe. What could happen to us anyway?

'We could be kidnapped by gypsies,' I claimed.

'Or fall into a bog and drown,' added Fearchar, 'while you're having a good time to yourself on that magic horse.'

'What magic horse is that?' asked Duncan. 'That old nag MacFarlane brings with him every year? The rogue charging a shilling a time to sit on that scraggy beast. You'd be better off sitting on a stone and believe you're flying to the moon.'

'Waw!' I said. 'What a fantastic idea! Where's that stone?'

He looked at me with what I now know to have been love and pity.

'I'll tell you one day,' he said. 'Let's just get there.'

Dolina and I said 'Let's' a lot. When we wanted to jink school, I'd suggest it and she'd say, 'Let's.' Or when it was rainy and windy but she suggested we go cycling, despite the weather I'd say, 'Let's.'

Duncan led the way. Down by the old mill, then left over the stone bridge and along the old cart-track to the shore until we reached the skeleton of the beached whale. We always stopped there.

'Will it eventually disappear altogether?' I asked.

'No,' said Fearchar. 'Remember those other bones at the old shieling? They've been there thousands and thousands of years. Millions in fact. So will this.'

We heard the Fair before we saw it. A kind of glassy sound

at first, as if someone was smashing bottles. Which no one did, because you got pennies for them when you took them back to the shop or out to the hotel. But we could see the whole thing once we reached the top of the small hill. It was all colour, like a cloud of mixed butterflies, while everything else was brown moor and grey stone. As though the thing we'd dreamt of had been whooshed into being. There were lots of people there already, for we could see them moving like Fearchar's puppet-shadows in the lamplight. These were the drovers, for the cattle sales started first thing in the morning, and we knew that if we ran down the hill we'd still have time to listen to the drovers' special fast language as they sold one cow after the other.

The three of us stood leaning against the stone wall as the auctioneer fired out words the way we threw stones at empty bottles placed on a fence post. One was bound to hit sooner or later. The men were all standing, looking important. Except for Flora who had brought her single cow for sale and was holding her with a halter to the side. We couldn't make out any individual words, yet all the drovers understood him, one nodding his head, another raising an index finger, another his stick.

'Twoamabidforabidamabidandthreeamabidamabidamabid amabidanditsfouramabidamabid' until the auctioneer smacked his hand down on to his thigh and the cow was taken away and another led in by rope on the west side and it all began again and again and again. It was like when we threw stone after stone into the loch. We never did it just for the sake of it or out of boredom. We did it to hear the splash and watch the ripples getting bigger and bigger and bigger. I once threw in a big stone that made fifty circles until I lost count.

The rides were short and simple, but miraculous. One gypsy had a small brass horse on a stand and I sat on it as the man turned a handle to make the horse jump up and down. Faster and faster and higher and higher until I felt dizzy and faint and the man slowed down and lifted me back down to earth, reeling and disorientated. The best thing was standing in line waiting for another turn. Duncan and Fearchar then carried me across to a tent where a woman was selling sweets and lemonade and gingerbread and sat me on the grass as they bought a paper bag of toffees and a large glass bottle between them. It was fizzy, and that too make my head spin.

'Don't drink it all in one go,' Duncan said. 'Just one gulp each, okay?'

The boys went off to play football with some other lads who were there for the day. Dolina came up and sat beside me.

'Are you going?' Dolina asked.

'No. And besides I don't have any money.'

'But I do,' Dolina said. 'I can pay for both of us.'

'Don't want to.'

'Chicken.'

'She's just a liar anyway.'

'No she's not. Everything she said last year was true.'

'Like what?'

'About the shoes. That I'd get new shoes. Black ones.'

'Pah! Even I could tell you that. You always get new shoes when school starts.'

'Aye, but. She said the size and everything.'

I just shook my head.

'You're daft.'

Dolina ran over to the caravan on which there was a red and

yellow sign saying 'Madame Petrovna, Fortune Teller.'

She was smiling when she came out of the caravan.

'So?' I asked her.

'So what?'

'So what did she tell you?'

Dolina leant in near.

'Can't tell. It's a secret.'

'It's not a proper secret if I don't know.'

Dolina looked at me, wondering if that was true.

'It's just a secret secret if only you know,' I said. 'It's a proper secret if the two of us know, and then keep it secret from everyone else. That's a proper secret.'

Dolina was almost convinced.

'It makes it really special then,' I added. 'Just something that only the two of us know.'

Dolina sat down beside me.

'Promise?' she asked.

'Promise,' I said. 'Cross my heart and hope to die.'

'Promise promise? By the stream then.'

We ran over to the stream and held hands over the running water, which made the promise binding and eternal because the river was running from east to west which it has to if something is to last forever. The sun and moon and stars do it all the time. We would always do the best by each other. She whispered something indistinguishable into my ear.

'Show me your hands,' I said.

I stood up, in shock, still holding her hands but looking at her face where, as every fortune-teller knows, every future is foretold. The hands are only a ruse.

'Really?'

'Really!' shouted Dolina, 'And anyway, she said she could only tell my fortune, not change it. That's up to me. Let's play.'

'Let's.'

And both of us ran over to the tent-stall where Dolina bought a skipping-rope. It had blue and red and green strands entwined together and when we skipped it was like jumping through a rainbow. I was dizzy. Everything was a circle as we skipped. Strange how a rainbow was never a circle, just half of one. Probably the other half was under the earth where we couldn't see. And the two of us had the best rhymes in the whole world.

'Gooseberry, raspberry, strawberry jam,

Tell me the name of your young man,' chanted Dolina, and as soon as I took the rope I chanted,

'Mary Ann, Mary Ann, make good porridge in a pan,

Make it thick, make it thin, make it any way you can.'

Then we played that game where one holds the rope as both skip together, chanting in unison,

> *March, march, two by two,*
> *My little sister lost her shoe,*
> *I love coffee, I love tea,*
> *I love the boys*
> *And the boys love me.*

Our rhymes were always in English because that had more magic. The more marvellous a thing is, the more power it has.

Dolina had enough money to buy a bubble-jar. We took it in turns to blow the bubbles up into the air, trying to make bigger and bigger ones so that they would float slowly and land on people's heads. Maybe one of them would totally cover the auctioneer and he would be forever caught inside a soapy bubble and have to float like that back home to the mainland blabbering away in his fast language with no one paying any attention to him. His wife and children would be astonished and he might never get out of the bubble again, though she would probably just prick it with a safety-pin and he'd pop out all wet and soaking. Still, bets that wouldn't stop him speaking fast again as soon as he got out of the bubble.

The bubbles we blew made colours in the air, some were green and some were blue, and the best were multi-coloured, and I finally blew twenty in a row which we chased over past the sheep-fank but couldn't catch because they rose higher and higher into the air and disappeared out of sight high up into the clouds.

We then spotted a butterfly and ran after it, trying to catch it, flinging our cardigans into the air as if that would trap it, but it always floated away and finally we lost sight of it down by the edge of the loch. We always played that game at school when spring came, with the bleating of lambs over the wall and the primroses shining yellow in their nooks and crannies and the muir-fires burning on the horizon. It was the time of the singing of the birds. That's always when the butterflies appeared and we'd chase the glimpses of colour across the school playground and through the gate and over the moor as far as we could. On the rare occasions we caught one we'd hold her cupped in our hands and admire her beauty – how thin and frail and simply beautiful she was – and then release her back into the air. But you wouldn't tell a butterfly anything for they were terrible gossips, flying away immediately with the news and spreading it all over the place. Though you could tell a bee anything, for he would just sit droning and then disappear into the heart of the flower. Dolina and I are forever chasing that butterfly.

When we returned from the chase we sat on the gate for ages, swinging our legs in unison. As long as whoever owned the gate didn't catch us and chase us away with curses, saying we were damaging their property. As if two wee lassies weighing next to nothing could buckle a solid six-foot wide gate hinged with iron. We liked playing on the wooden gates because we could move at different speeds. 'Will it always be like this?' Dolina asked. If she stood at one end and I pushed, the gate would spin fast all the way across, but if she stood in the middle it would move really slowly like a snail, and if the two of us stood on it together it wouldn't move at all unless we each lifted our legs and helped it along with

our arms. Though the best was when we'd just sit side by side on
it, chanting and swinging our legs backwards and forwards as if we
were little children with nothing better to do than enjoy how things
were. We were going to do that forever.

I saw Duncan. He was smoking over by the beer tent. He coughed
at first, almost doubling over, but the other boys laughed and he
didn't cough again. Some of the other lads had gathered round the
Army tent where a young soldier in khaki spoke to them. I saw
Duncan wandering over.

'The thing is,' the soldier was saying, 'you get paid for it as well.
This year I've been everywhere already. Mexico. India. Africa. And
skiing. We were skiing for a whole month in Norway. Can any of
you ski?'

They all shook their heads.

'Do you know what skiing is?'

They all nodded.

'Any of you pipers?'

Archie and Allan put their hands up.

'Just the chanter,' Archie said. 'But still, I'll be on to the big pipes
next year.'

'I'm already on the pipes,' Allan said. 'And in the T.A.'

'Good lad,' the soldier said. 'Go into the tent. See Major
MacLellan. Anyone else?'

Duncan and the other boys looked at one another and drifted
away. They didn't want to repeat their grandfathers' lives. Older men
were standing around the beer tent talking about dead people and
relatives who emigrated to Canada and never came back. Not even
once to visit. It was dark inside the tent. Mysteries happened in there.

Two local young men, Ronald MacInnes and Joseph MacIsaac,
were wrestling in the centre of a makeshift ring. As if life was that
simple. Ronald suddenly overturned Joe and sat on his chest in
triumph. We all knew they weren't brave. Just strong and half-
drunk and showing off. Those watching applauded. Ronald and

Joseph shook hands. There's always someone stronger and quicker and smarter and uglier than yourself.

Someone was singing inside the tent. A sad song about a sailor leaving Glasgow and heading for Montreal. He wasn't so much singing as undertaking the voyage once again. Bidding farewell to his beloved and making for the open seas. Duncan and the other young lads listened to snatches of conversation from inside the tent. Drunken men reminiscing once again about the good old days. Plenty of filthy words to store away for future use and wild stories about prostitutes and prisons in London and Buenos Aires. Someone talked about cracking nuts and everyone laughed, though none of us understood why.

'You were smoking,' Fearchar said to Duncan when we met up later.

'So?' said Duncan. 'So?'

'So nothing. Just that you were. That's all.'

'Cry baby,' said Duncan. 'So you going to tell, blabbermouth? As if I care.'

Which meant he did, we knew.

'No. I won't tell,' said Fearchar. 'Doesn't mean anything to me anyway. You can do whatever you want.'

Sometimes it was hard to know whether to like Duncan or not. The thing is, he was always a bit mean. And a bit of a cheat and a bully. And a bit lazy. Whenever housework was to be done he always managed to disappear. And he also always wanted to be the first at things. So if snow was forecast or a storm was brewing, he'd sit in the window with his face up to the pane of glass so that if anything happened he could crow for days, 'I was the first to see the snow and hear the thunder and see the lightning!'

He was the last to see Alasdair Mòr walking out on the road that time he headed onto the moor and was never seen again.

'You made him disappear,' Fearchar said, and I think Duncan wondered if that was true.

If someone gave him a bag of sweets he'd never really share them willingly unless you caught him scoffing them, and then he might reluctantly give you one as long as you promised not to tell anyone else he had them. So it was really bribery along with meanness, which was almost the worst thing of all. Though not as bad as stealing – that was the worst sin, taking from those who were as poor as yourself. They said James MacIntosh once stole a loaf from a widow's house and he was found dead the following day having fallen into his own well, though some said that was not just because he stole the loaf but because he lied and said he hadn't when asked about it. If he hadn't lied about it he might still have fallen into the well but would probably have been rescued or managed to climb out himself. It was as if every little thing mattered and had a consequence and then more consequences if you kept on adding to the thing you'd done in the first place.

We walked home at the end of the day, tired and a bit dispirited though we tried to re-live all the good things. What a day we had of it! That first lollipop seemed to last forever. The outside was red when I licked it first, then after a while it turned yellow, then green, then blue and white. The final wee round bit lasted all the way home and even overnight, because I kept it wrapped in paper by my bed all through the night and didn't finish it off until I woke in the morning. Even though it was sticky by then and I had to eat a bit of the paper!

Fearchar won the unofficial hill race. Down past the fank then across the river and half-way up the hill to the old shieling and back down through the heather on the other side. Best was going through the river: all the other lads took ages crossing it, stepping from one stone to the next, but he just plunged straight through it. The worst that could happen is that you'd get wet. Which was fun in itself. Dolina and I cheered him on.

Duncan remembered the first deep breath of nicotine he managed to hold. It swirled round his stomach and then all the way through his body in a surge of pleasure. That's what flying must be like, he said. It would be good to travel like the people at the Fair, we all thought. Moving with all these bright loud things by horse and cart and wagon and tent from one place to the next, owing no special allegiance to anything except what you liked. It must have been such a pleasure for the stall-holders to see children everywhere enjoying themselves. What if we all ran away and joined them and Duncan looked after the horses and Dolina and I painted the caravans and Fearchar sold all the sweets and lollipops? What if?

James Campbell had an open-backed Land Rover and beeped the horn three times as he drove up behind us while we were walking home. Once for Duncan. Once for Fearchar. And once for me. As if we needed to hear as well as see his vehicle – show-off! He stopped and waved for us to come into the vehicle. Fearchar and I sat in the front beside Campbell. Duncan had pride of place in the open truck at the back, feeling the wind racing through him as we drove uphill. We loved the view from up high in the front, with everything looking so small down by the road.

I secretly feared we were squashing all the caterpillars on the tarmac as we raced along, but I didn't say anything. Maybe they were lucky and lay unmoved and stayed safe and cosy between the wheels. They probably weren't like us and wouldn't be frightened by the noise. And maybe they were deaf. Maybe they didn't have ears anyway.

'Are caterpillars deaf?' I asked Fearchar. 'Do they have ears?' But I don't think he heard because of the noise of the Land Rover. He just shook his head, which might have meant that they didn't or that he couldn't hear what I was saying because of the noise.

Instead, I studied all the dials that clicked and whirred and moved alongside the noise of the engine as I sucked my lollipop. Campbell was singing. 'By yon bonny banks, and by yon bonny braes, where the sun shines bright on Loch Lomond.' The song was loud and brash, like his Land Rover. He sang lots of grace notes, which he never did when he sang at the concerts, pompously exaggerating all the vowels. But then he stopped, and all we could hear was the sound of the wind above the engine because we were travelling so fast. The sun was shining on us too, lighting up the heather on the moor which was just beginning to turn purple. I had the sudden thought that the future could never match this moment. It might be like the day the byre roof came off and we all sat in the window watching it swirling in the air before it disappeared towards the Sound of Barra.

'Have you been to the airport?' Campbell shouted above the noise of the wind and the engine. We shook our heads.

'Shall we have a look then?'

We nodded. He drove south, towards the disused site. Of course we'd been there, but not officially. Illegally, as it were, because there were big signs that said 'No Entry' and 'Forbidden' and 'Danger'. Which is why we went in there in the first place. But it was no more dangerous than our own bedrooms. Just some old dilapidated wooden buildings and two locked corrugated Nissan huts.

'But it says "No Entry",' Fearchar said.

'Only for ordinary mortals, not for us,' Campbell said. 'Just a precaution, in case a sheet of zinc falls on you. Anyway, that's not what I want to show you. All that old broken stuff. I'll show you what it could be like. What's to come. I know this place like the back of my hand. Chained like a dog by conventions. Whatever you do, don't do anything differently is the mantra. Don't stand out, or everyone will talk about you, and what they don't know about you they will invent. Even your secrets. Don't you guys ever be like that. You're young. Show them. Just look around you,' he said.

We all looked around at the dilapidated buildings and the corrugated huts.

'No,' he said. 'At the whole place. North, east, south and west. Look up at the wide blue skies.'

We did.

'Mark my words,' he said. 'One day this will not just be an airport but a spaceport. Because it has everything. Big wide spaces, no people and those deep blue empty skies. Nothing, my friends, between us and Mars.'

He parked the van by the locked gate and we all climbed over, walking towards the Nissan huts. Campbell probably had a key for the gate as well but decided to make it a bit of an adventure for us. Though once inside the perimeter fence he then took a large key from his back pocket, put it into the rusty padlock and unlocked the shed. It was a complete surprise, because though we'd tried to peek inside the shed it had always been boarded-up and dark and we could never see a thing.

A beautiful aeroplane sat there, gleaming in the sun which was now shining in through the wide-open door. The plane was painted blue and white with the letters G-SUJC written in silver on the side. We ran over to try and touch it, though it was too high for Fearchar and I. To touch it was to fly it. Same as when Dolina and I wanted to go on an adventure, we just had to rub the blue slate pebble clockwise with our right thumb three times and we were wherever we named. Campbell and Duncan stood there with their hands on the aircraft as if they were already in the air.

'You're the first people to see it,' Campbell said. 'I flew it in one night a few years ago under cover of darkness when everyone was asleep. I asked everyone afterwards if they'd heard or seen a plane during the night. No one had, though some mentioned they'd dreamt of a plane passing overhead. Did any of you hear it?'

We all shook our heads.

'Of course I've worked on it since then. It was in a sorry state when I flew it in – something of a miracle I actually managed it. Or maybe skill? But I've replaced bits and pieces here and there.'

He looked at us, one by one.

'And painted it of course. Blue for the sky and white for the clouds so that it will blend into the heavens when it flies.'

We all gazed at the plane.

'Would you like to sit in it?'

We all nodded. Duncan was first to the door, Fearchar behind him and then I.

'Okay guys,' Campbell said, 'ladies first,' and he lifted me up into the cockpit. There were ten little round clocks on the left-hand side and a steering wheel a bit like the one on Dad's tractor on the right-hand side. Except that it wasn't fully round – just two bits to the side with a sort of handle on the middle, like on the milk-churn.

'How do you start it?' I asked.

He laughed.

'That's a trade secret, Annie. But once everything is working properly then you can learn that as well. Do you think you'd like to be a pilot when you grow up?'

'No. I want to be a nurse.'

I surprised myself, for I had never spoken that dream out.

'They used to have flying nurses round here you know. So that's nothing new. Come on Annie, jump down and give the boys a chance.'

We all loved it. It was like you could press any button and anything could happen. Like when you throw a stone into a loch and it splashes and frightens the birds, and the bigger the stone you throw the bigger the splash and the more birds that take off into the skies. Because you don't just throw a stone into the water for the sake of it but so that you can hear the splash and watch the ripples growing bigger and bigger and see the ducks paddling away for dear life. And the same with skimming – the point is to see how many skips the stone makes. I once made twenty-eight, which was better than Duncan or Fearchar ever managed. They just said I cheated and had counted wrong, which of course I hadn't. But though we pressed all the buttons and flicked all the switches, nothing happened.

'That's because the engine is turned off,' Campbell said. 'Nothing happens until the engine starts up. I'll need to fix it properly, one day.'

He led us over to the other Nissan hut which he unlocked and opened up. This one was laid out with tables covered in all kinds of papers.

'These are all the plans for the airport,' he said to us. 'See here

– this will be the main runway, south to north. It's always best to take-off into the prevailing wind. It will be five thousand feet long. That's almost a mile. There will be two smaller runs as well, for training. The cafe will be here. Parking there. And here's where the hotel will be.'

The main runway was drawn in red, the two smaller strips in blue, the cafe in green, the parking area in grey and the hotel in purple. Maybe rain had fallen on the papers, for they were smudged. The lines and colours were not as clear and pretty as those of Mrs MacPherson. She used thick crayons which left a texture when you drew a line. Maybe his coloured pencils weren't as good.

'Where did you get the pencils?' I asked.

He smiled.

'Oh, I don't know. I didn't draw them. An architect did that. In Glasgow. I'll ask him for you if you'd like.'

I nodded.

Campbell drove us back to the road end. From there we could take the hill track down by the loch and be home in ten minutes. As we descended the track, we saw him weaving up and down the brae next to us. Niall Cuagach. He soon caught up with us because he could move by magic. He knew every short-cut in the world. A narrow pass through the gorge takes him to the other side of the hill through a tunnel. That's where he lived.

'Were you at the Fair today?' he asked us.

'Aye.'

'What prices did the stirks fetch?'

'Ten pounds,' said Duncan.

He grunted approval.

'Did I see you down at the airstrip?'

'Aye,' we all said, protecting one another.

'See the plane?'

How did he know?

'Yes,' said Duncan. 'How do you know it's there? Have you seen it?'

'I know things. I heard it coming. Saw it coming. Saw him wheeling it into that Nissan hut. There are no secrets around here, Duncan. Things start small then grow bigger. You know that. Anyway, you'd best be away home. You'll need proper food after eating all that rubbish at the Fair.'

He took three newly killed rabbits out of his bag. Trickles of blood were still seeping out of the corners of their mouths. Mam would skin and stew them.

'Give these to your mother and father. They'll make a good stew.'

And off he went up the hill.

While we were at the Fair, Mam and Dad had the day to themselves. It was and wasn't a day of leisure. Mam was always up first and made breakfast for us before we headed off, and then also prepared pieces for us to take with us in a haversack for lunch. Bread with mutton and cheese.

'Take this bottle with you and fill it up at the well on the way,' she added. Water from the well was a sacred thing. Folk had not forgotten that pure clean water had kept them alive in times of disease and plague. The well was in a dark crevice beneath a big rock so the water was always cold and fresh. It made us all shiver when we drank it. Cuagach said there were two special wells over the hills, but it was a risk to drink from them. 'One gives you the gift of wisdom the other the gift of foolishness, but no one knows which is which, so no one but me as had ever taken the risk.'

As we were getting ready to leave, the two of them sat down to have breakfast. On Saturday mornings it was always ham and eggs. Ham from the shop and eggs from our own hens. Big round brown speckled eggs.

'We should get some pigs,' Dad said, because he always said that.

'Och, you say that every Saturday morning! And who would look after them? Me?'

'They look after themselves.'

'A Sheumais, nothing looks after itself. Not even you. Or I.'

He began to sing.

'Takes two to tango, two to tango... we used to sing that on the ship. Louis Armstrong I think it was...'

'Are you going to finish the barn roof today?' Mam asked.

'No. I'd rather finish the hay in the top field.'

'Then I'll come with you. After all, it takes two to scythe. One to cut and one to gather...'

'And one to bind. And one to stook.'

'So there's no end to it.'

'The less the hay is turned the better.'

We could see them from the ridge of the hill as we walked to the Fair. Mam took first go at the scythe, with Dad shaking-out after her, because that's what they did every year. They switched over after a while. Dad spat on his hands before handling the scythe. I'd always seen him do that whenever he lifted an instrument. If he didn't they might chaff. I liked their hands. The way Mam held hers when singing, the thumb and forefinger of her right hand gently caressing the pinkie of her left, and the way Dad's hand rested ever so easily on the tiller of the boat when we went out fishing, easing it this way and that with an invisible touch. A silver flash in the water was the promise of herring.

By lunch-time half the field would be done. There was always a right way to do things and a wrong way. The right way is to hold the scythe like a feather, so that it does all the work and you merely guide it as you walk along behind it. Even though the blade is curved, you cut in a straight line, otherwise you lose the harvest at the edge. Strange how simple things always worked. Mam's dad used to say that the best way to scythe was to cut eleven rows of hay with one sweep of the blade. Though no one bothered with being that precise these days, for the blades were better and longer.

The best thing about our scythe was that it had an adjustable handle so that it fitted both their different swings. For Mam was taller than Dad. And there was a proper way to bind and stack, so that the wind ran through the hay to dry. You worked out from the centre, layering gently. Then it was time to pause and have the tea and sandwiches. In the old days, you were entitled to as much hay from the laird's field for your horse as you could scythe between the sun moving from the peak of Horabhal to the peak of Heabhal. That was 42 minutes on a good autumn day. You never shaved close but always left a good measure of stubble for the creatures and the mist and rain.

We saw them as we descended the hill on the way back home from the Fair, after seeing the plane. Mam picked up the scythe and cut ever so smoothly from right to left with Dad half-crouched behind her picking up the hay and binding it with small swift movements. Apart from them, the machair was empty. It was as if they were the only man and woman in the whole world. I still see them there, Mam binding the last stook tight and Dad putting the scythe on her shoulder as they prepare to walk back home.

12

Frog Sunday

OUR SUNDAYS WERE quieter than other days. I loved them. In the morning we all went to church, and in the afternoon we played football or went for a walk or to visit relatives. Everything seemed silent, because we were all allowed to do a thing without being hurried or corrected by a teacher. Dolina and I used to lie in the grass and count the blades we could feel with our outstretched fingers.

Mass was a thing we all did together. It was as if, for one day, everyone was equal. For an hour or so no one had a bigger peat-stack or better potatoes or whiter house than anyone else. The shopkeeper was on his knees same as everyone else. You had to get there at the right time. Neither too early nor too late. Maybe about ten minutes before the service was perfect, for it gave you time to cross yourself properly and genuflect and get a seat and bow your head and do your prayer and see who else was there and maybe watch the latecomers. Hazel sometimes walked with us, and on the way she'd pick up some wild mint from the roadside and crush it behind her ears and under her chin and on the front of her neck to smell nice.

It was always the same people who were there and always the same people who were early and late. Most people had perfected the time and walked there steadily, though you could always see some grown-up dawdling along by the roadside to lose some time or – worse – almost running along the road like a horse to make up time. Some people never learned. Or just couldn't get out of old habits, same as Seonaidh MacIntosh's ducks which kept waddling along to his kitchen door for scraps even though it had been boarded up months before.

Everyone was clean and smelling nice and the sun was shining through the big long windows. We were happy gathered together. Like the hens laying those beautiful round brown eggs every morning, pleased with the way that the straw they lay in has been freshly made.

We enjoyed the liturgy and chanting prayers with one voice, though you could always clearly hear Mrs MacPherson a word or two ahead of everyone else and Mùgan with his deep nasal mutter trailing behind, as if he lived in a slightly different time, and the incense and the candles and the singing and the closeness to each other. I always tried to sit next to Dolina and Hazel, though our parents always ushered us away towards their friends.

It was as if the church building itself – its shape and where people sat – was part of the worship. Though it may have been the other way round. That the way the congregation breathed in and out at different parts of the Mass shaped the building itself. The roof sloped where the choir was. We were here in the pews, and the priest and the altar-servers were there in the sanctuary, so I suppose we all learned that there are spaces and places which are special and which you can't enter whenever you want just because you fancy it.

'Just because you can shear a sheep doesn't mean you're King David,' Fr John said to Dad the day he helped him at the fank.

The homily was in Gaelic though the whole of the liturgy itself was in Latin. It made us Romans and citizens of the big wide world. For though we didn't understand the meaning of most of the individual words themselves we didn't need to, because we knew what they meant since we spoke them every week. *In nomine Patris et Filii et Spiritus Sancti* meant 'In the name of the Father, the Son and the Holy Ghost' and other parts like *Dominus vobiscum* meant 'The Lord be with you' and *Kyrie eleison* meant 'Lord have mercy'. I just knew that some other girl like me would be saying the same words, even in Rome, which also meant that maybe somewhere in Mexico two girls like Dolina and I would also have bikes and go for rides along their paths, bumping over the mounds and swerving round all the potholes, just like we did here.

I enjoyed the round direct sound of Latin, because we didn't hear it anywhere else. And the words could be said just the way there were written, unlike English, where if you saw a word like 'through' we didn't know whether to say it as 'thru' or 'troch' or 'trowch' or whatever. *Dominus* was Dominus and *vobiscum* was vobiscum. It was a holy and exalted medium, and felt like a better language for public worship and veneration than our native Gaelic, which was good for talking about fishing and sheep and cattle and songs and the places around us and local things like that. Though Dad said Latin was only used to keep us ignorant. While the priest chanted his Latin I could hear all the women beside me caressing their rosaries and praying in Gaelic.

We didn't need to make a new prayer or song because the ones we had were fine. The *Salve Regina* and the *Te Deum* were as familiar to us as Fionn's escape from Ireland. And the glorious names that exalted the special days – Shrove Tuesday and Ash Wednesday and Maundy Thursday and Good Friday and Holy Saturday, all leading to the sun dancing on Easter morning, when I could discard my winter boots and wear my flowered frock and white hat with the long yellow ribbon.

We had a family picnic once a year. Every Easter Sunday afternoon. On Saturday morning, Mam produced the old wicker basket from some hidden recess in her bedroom, which signalled that the fabulous day was happening again. Gathering the stuff for it was a half-mysterious, half-miraculous affair, for we were supposed to do it secretly, though it always turned out the same every year, which is how the best miracles are.

I gathered and painted the eggs (though Mam helped me to blow them out), Duncan always somehow managed to make five kites for us, Fearchar saved five shillings which he hid at the picnic place for us to find, Dad secretly collected five different bottles of lemonade to share, and Mam made five individual cakes so that there would be no squabbling over who got which piece. Those magic numbers! Seven and five and three. There were seven stars in The Plough, five in our family and three in the Blessed Trinity.

We always rolled the eggs down the same bit of the hill, because the marvel would be broken if we ever rolled them down anywhere else. Spells always work best when they know they rhyme.

> *Lady Queen Ann,*
> *she sits in the sun,*
> *as fair as a lily,*
> *as white as a swan,*
> *we bring you three letters,*
> *and pray you read one... Abracadabra,*
> *catch me if you can!*

Mam always made fancy sandwiches for that day, cutting them into neat little triangles with some cress in them and making sure that the crust was cut off, which Dad complained was a terrible waste. He collected all the crusts and then used them later to fry herring. The other thing was that every year the fairies left five chocolate sweeties under a stone at our picnic spot, as if they knew we would be there. Thing is, Duncan and Fearchar and I always ran up there the day before to check and the sweets were never there then, but they always were when we arrived the next day with Mam and Dad!

I loved the smell of church. The men reeked of smoke, but they mostly sat on the far pews to the right together and I kept clear of them. The women all smelt of very sweet perfume, struggling through the holy fragrance of candles and incense. Unlike the other scents, you could see incense: when the altar boy gave the censer to the priest, the incense smoke rose high into the air in thick sweet clouds. The sound of the altar bell forgave everything. I always vowed to be a better friend to Katie every time I heard it. I would have loved to have lit the candles and swung the censer and rung the bells, but girls weren't allowed to do it in those days, and we thought that was unfair, but that's the way things were, and when I finally got the chance to do it at St Gabriel's the childish wonder and simplicity of it was gone.

I especially loved the permanent little grotto at the back of the painted church and all the medallions and colourful saints' cards and beads and the mementoes from Lourdes and Fatima you could buy to adorn it. Some of the cards glittered, and when you turned them a certain way you could see angels that you couldn't see there at first. Above the grotto was the beautiful statue of the Virgin Mary. She had a long white dress with a bright blue cloak and always blessed us with her welcome, hands outstretched. She proved that anything was possible. We weren't supposed to touch her, but none of us could resist placing our fingertips on her feet, knowing she loved us. She brought heaven nearer – within touching distance – and why would anyone object to that? Besides, we could tell her things and she always listened and helped. We knew that it wasn't who we saw that mattered but who cared for us. We prayed with our eyes as well as with our lips. It's good to have your own guardian angel. Mine always took my hand when I ran across the moor quicker than anyone else and when I crossed the fast-flowing river and whenever I walked home in the dark.

I've always loved votive candles because I know they belong to the Catholic poor. We had something which was ours. All the men wore their best suits and the boys their best trousers and jumpers and shoes and the girls their best dresses to Mass. Maybe that was the glory of God the priest always talked about. Nowadays everyone scoffs at all that Mariology, dismissing it as the superstition of the simple. If that is so, I'm glad I'm simple. Sometimes we went to Benediction as well, which was at 5pm, but mostly it was just either Mam or Dad who went to that on their own. When I went, the early evening light softened everything. It was a more subdued gathering of older people who had come a long way on an arduous, patient journey. Some Friday evenings I went to the Stations of the Cross service, the images all beautifully carved in slate on the walls of the church. I especially liked the 6th Station, Veronica wiping the face of Jesus. It's what Mam did when we cried.

I spent half my time at Mass admiring the squares and headscarves the women wore. Some of them were plain, but most were beautifully decorated with little flowers and emblems which you could trace all across the lace, for you could worship God as much by dressing up and looking lovely as by prayer. After all, we had to wear ordinary work or school clothes every other day of the week. Surely God wanted us to look as smart and as beautiful as we could? We all knew that Jesus loved beggars and tramps and the lost and the forsaken, but also knew that after Legion was saved he was then found dressed and in his right mind!

A few of the much older women wore black mantillas, though it was going out of fashion, probably due to Vatican II, and of course the highlight for us was when we had our First Communion and Confirmation when we were allowed to dress up for the day in pure white. Even white shoes! Which were so difficult to keep shining clean all the way there and back through the mud and puddles and rain. Mam put wild flowers in my hair. Daisies and marigolds and butterworts and clover. I remember some of the petals falling off and drifting down my face all soft and smelling of the summer machair. It was the happiest of days.

And the way the older women breathed when they prayed always surprised me, with their heads bent as they said the Hail Mary, as if every breath was life or death. They always managed it in one breath down to the name of Jesus, and then paused and inhaled before continuing. 'Hail Mary full of grace the Lord is with thee blessed are thou amongst women and blessed is the fruit of the womb Jesus' – and then they would breathe in and continue – 'Holy Mary Mother of God pray for us sinners now and at the hour of our death Amen.' Though all of us young people could do it from start to finish without pausing or breathing in or out at all. Dolina and I practiced doing it fast and slow and we could easily do both without drawing breath! The worshippers were such good, innocent people.

I can't remember a time when I didn't know when to stand and when to sit and when to kneel and when to close my eyes and when to pray. It has been like walking and eating and breathing. I continue to go to weekly confession and communion, even though that seems such a strange thing to do these days. As I take the wafer, I sometimes kneel as the girl I was and sometimes stand as the woman I am. My patron saint was (is!) St Anne. We even have the same birthday (26 July), though that's not why I was named Anne – that was after my Dad's Mam who died the year before I was born. 'Sweet Star of the Sea' has always been my favourite hymn.

After Mass, everyone stood outside talking. It's like when you come out of a clean river after swimming, which Eric and I did a few times in Perthshire. You breathe and take in the air, renewed by the water and glad to be alive at that moment with that person in that place. No one was in a hurry to get away. It was still the place where news was shared. Many hadn't seen each other since the previous Sunday. Morag was feeling better. John was due home on Wednesday. It was going to rain until Tuesday, but it would be dry after that, for the wind was turning to the south, though you could never be one hundred per cent sure. Behind every fact lay a possibility. Dolina had a new dress. Arrived in the post the night before. It had a fringe and everything.

Some men cycled away, others walked, in twos or threes, except for Niall Cuagach who limped off over the hill on his own. A few women walked arm in arm down the road. As Mrs MacPherson and Miss Agnes and Miss Peggy walked along, I saw shafts of gold fall on them. Others climbed into the new bus. No one talked about the homily or anything like that. Just about the weather and pipe tobacco and how good the new potatoes were and how their relatives were getting on in Glasgow and things like that. We went on the bus sometimes when it was raining heavily. Sitting up at the back, well clear of the old men who sat there shredding and cutting their plugs of tobacco, arguing with one another about the better merits of Condor and Black Twist.

We usually walked home, however. Mam and Dad together, side by side, but not holding hands. No one did then. Fearchar paced some yards behind them, followed by me and then Duncan. He was dawdling, trying to put as much distance as possible between himself and all of us. I kept glancing back at him. He wasn't a child anymore, even though we knew he kept seeing snails and worms and caterpillars and small things that only children noticed. He saw a frog in the ditch and bent down to examine it before remembering he'd put such things behind him. But it was too late. I'd seen him. Goodness, the world that is in a ditch!

If he couldn't be a child now, he never would be again. So he called out, 'Annie! Look! Look!'

I ran back to see what he'd found, though Fearchar walked on.

'Waw!' I called. 'Let's take it home. Go on. Let's.'

'Ok,' he said. 'Let's.'

'Can I carry him?'

'Of course. But be careful. Frogs can leap for miles. You need to cup your hand. Like this.'

He showed me how to cup my hand so that it was like a bowl, even though I knew how to do that already. I liked to let him think he was teaching me. He then placed the little frog in the hollow of my hand.

'Careful now. No shivering. And walk slowly. Very slowly.'

The distance between us and Mam and Dad grew bigger. Mam glanced back now and again to see us in the distance playing together. Fearchar was some thirty yards ahead, kicking a small stone as a football. Sometimes he had to climb down into the ditch to retrieve it, and every time he did so the score increased. By the time we got home he'd beaten England 50-0.

The frog sat still in the hollow of my hand. Its shell was grass

green and its eyes were grey. It had amazing feet. Five long thin toes
but only four stubby fingers. Its little chest was rising and falling as
if she'd been running for miles.

'It's a girl frog, isn't it?' I said to Duncan. As if he'd know, or care.

'Suppose so. I don't know. Can be if you want.'

'Flora. That's what I'll call her. She can live in the pond.'

'She'll swim away.'

'No she won't. It's not a river. Only a pond. She can't get out.'

'Might hop out though.'

I hadn't thought of that.

'You think so? Then I'll build a wall round it. A big wall of stones.'

'Can hop over that too. And climb. They're good climbers. See –
if you placed her at the bottom of that wall, next thing she'd scarper
up the stones and disappear over the top. Bets.'

I was tempted, but didn't want to risk it.

'No. I'll take her home and put her in our own pond. Her own
pond, I mean. I'll call it Flora's Pond.'

'Suit yourself.'

I headed for the pond as soon as I got home.

'There you are,' I said to Flora, releasing her slowly into the
water. 'Off you go and swim. There's plenty worms and things there
for you to eat. If not, let me know and I'll get stuff for you. We've
got some nuts in the house. Think you'd like that?'

I looked down at her little legs paddling in the pond. I was
always either looking down at things, like the wee frog in the pond,
or up at things, like the teacher at school. It was only when all us
girls sat together outside playing, with our knees bent under our
bodies that we were all the same size and we could see one another
properly side by side without being a dwarf or a giant. The boys
never sat together like that. It was as if one of them always had to
stand up and be the captain of the team or the skipper of the ship or
the master of the spaceship.

The same with grown-ups. Sometimes they'd see all us girls sitting
round in a circle not moving. And because we weren't talking or

singing or shouting or running around or anything, they presumed we were just being lazy and sitting there doing nothing, when actually it was an important part of the game. We might have been counting silently or remembering or thinking, or maybe the whole game was that we had to sit stock still up to the count of a thousand and if anyone moved or made any sound they were out of the game. But some grown-up would come along and tell us to move because his cows or his dogs were coming that way. As if it would bother the cows or the dogs!

Then Mam called. Dinner was ready. We never called it lunch. It was breakfast and dinner and then tea. Sometimes supper too – toast or Indian bread. Breacag Innsinneach we called it – an Indian Bannock. That was always my favourite – cooking it with Mam on the griddle. Beremeal, plain flour, baking soda, cream of tartar, buttermilk and a sprinkling of salt. Nowadays it's made in an oven, but then we used the open griddle on top of the stove, which needed to be almost white-hot. Fearchar used to complain that Mam always called out 'Time for dinner' just as he was in the middle of a game when he wasn't even hungry.

'We should just eat when we're hungry,' he cried, 'not when it's "time".'

We sat where we could, not in any pre-defined place at the table, though Dad always sat at the end, where the salt was, which we had to ask for. He said that a meal without salt was like a day without light. Everything rotted and decayed without it. We needed to protect everything from destruction, because it was so difficult to replace things. There was always a barrel of salt herring at the back of the house which was horrible to eat though Mam and Dad thought it was wonderful. Duncan and Fearchar and I always just complained about the bones which always got stuck in between our teeth or in our gums. Dad always wiped his hands against his shirt when he finished dinner.

The clock was ticking good and strong as it always did on

Sunday, because we wound it up every Saturday night, and as the week progressed the ticking got softer and softer until you could hardly hear it the following Saturday when it was time to wind it up again. Dad brought the clock home from Marseille from one of his voyages and it had a beautiful picture of a harbour with yellow yachts behind the clock-face and ding-donged once on the hour, up until midnight when it stopped until six o'clock. We took it in turns to wind it up because it was such fun climbing in behind it and turning the big key as if you were a magician. So each one of us – Dad, Mam, Duncan, Fearchar and I – got that treat in turns on a Saturday night (along with toast on a fork!) every five weeks.

On that Frog Sunday, as I've called it since, we had mutton pieces with gingerbread and jelly and cream for pudding. I scoffed it all down in a hurry and headed back out to the pond.

'Flora,' I called. 'Flora.'

Nothing. Not even a splash. I went down on my hands and knees and searched the edge of the pond. Mud and little stones and more mud and worms and shells. I crawled slowly round the whole edge of the pond, but couldn't see her, so took my shoes and socks off and waded out into the middle. It felt deep then, but in reality would only have been a foot or so. I crouched down and searched the bottom of the pond with my hands. It was too muddy and stirred-up to see anything. I didn't find her. But it didn't worry me, for I knew Flora must have made a little house for herself in the mud. That's what I would have done. And frogs need a wee place for themselves too. She could dig with those little claws, and would have hollowed out a house for herself and lined it with shells. The shells were so pretty. I had dozens in my bedroom, decorating the table and the window-sills and the walls and the floors. Sometimes in the summer when the light was not so scarce Mam allowed me to melt some candle-wax into one of my shells and then put the stub of a candle in and burn it. It never provided much light but that wasn't the point. It was very pretty and flickered and made a sweet smell.

I always loved shells. Knew – and still know! – the names for all of them. There were cockle shells and mussel shells and clam shells and crab shells and scallop shells and snail shells and conch shells and razor-fish shells and the big round sea-urchin shells and lots and lots of others I won't list just now because the shapes and the colours were always far more important than the names.

I kept hundreds of them in a box outside the byre and would take them out now and then and lay them in long rows on the broken big wooden bench. I always laid them out in order. I used to do it by size at first, the little ones at the front and the big ones at the back, but that was too much like school where Primary One sat in the front and Primary Seven at the back, except in Miss Gillies's class where all the 'dafties' as we called them sat at the front and all us smart ones, who were never ever given the dunce's cap, sat in neat perfect rows at the back. Of course it didn't work out properly, because friends always wanted to sit together and my best friend Dolina was told to sit in the front row while I had to sit next to Arthur MacT. who, though he might have been as smart as Einstein and could do the multiplication tables backwards, smelt like sewage. And he was always chewing the end of his pencil, so that when I was trying to work out my sums all I could hear was him gnawing away like a rat.

Miss Gillies said she didn't choose whether we were clever or stupid. It was just our fate. And neither was it up to us to choose our future. There was nothing much to learn anyway. As long as you paid attention sometimes, you picked everything up fine. Whenever Sgliugan did something wrong – he was terrible for picking his nose then throwing the snot at someone – he was given a book to read as a punishment. I suppose someone has to be the village idiot.

She was also always picking on poor Gordy MacPherson who could never remember whether Catherine of Aragon's head rolled down the hill before Anne Boleyn's or vice-versa, because he came from a starving home and spent all his time thinking of what he might get to eat from someone at playtime instead of the order of the beheaded queens. And besides, as Miss Gillies said, none of them would ever have lost their heads in the first place if Henry VIII had been a good Catholic and kept to just one wife as was right and proper. Miss Gillies's lower lip always quivered just before she spoke, as if that's where all her thoughts lived instead of in her brain.

The best thing about Gordy MacPherson was that though he was daft as a brush he had the best jammy pieces in school. I sometimes let him copy my sums in exchange for his pieces. Mam always insisted on giving us home-made bread and cheese for our playtime piece because it was 'healthier', but that didn't count for much in a swap. I quickly discovered that doing daft Gordy's sums for him offered a far better exchange rate. And the other thing was that he even had different jams on his bread every day. I can still remember the order – strawberry on Monday, raspberry on Tuesday, marmalade on Wednesday, plum on Thursday and damson on Friday. That was my favourite day.

I don't suppose I was any fairer than poor Miss Gillies, for I too laid out my shells according to whim. For once they were out of the salt water they were just ornaments. I basically ranked them in order of prettiness. My favourites were the long blue razor-fish shells. They were streaked with different shades of blue through the thin white shell – shells that were so fragile and brittle that you could see right through them, especially if you lifted them up to the light. I often think that was the real reason I became a nurse – admiring the beauty of the shell, which could break so easily. They were like natural, organic x-rays, without my realising at the time. Fragile objects which somehow survived all these fierce Atlantic storms.

My other favourites were the small green round ones that I found in the shingle. I'd lay out the blue and the green side-by-side at the front, until I realised how unfair that was on the ones that were not so colourful. Just like at the school dance when all the pretty older girls were chosen first, and Angela Smith and Hazel were always left sitting on the side with us younger ones. So every year I'd sit with them and if anyone asked me to dance I'd tell them they had to dance with Angela first, because it's her turn, and then Hazel's. And the girls didn't mind because they knew I was doing it to annoy the boys, not because I pitied them. Then during the last two years at school I didn't even bother waiting for all that palaver. The three of us just danced together in the centre of the room and who cares what anyone thought, we had such a great time. And you know what? Once we did it, everyone did it. So, that's how things change.

After all that, I began selecting the shells more or less by instinct. This one because it was broken. That one because it was smaller than all the others. This one because it was the most beautiful in the whole world, and that one because it wasn't. I gathered that particular one after the big winter storm, which seemed to have thrown half the ocean's contents onto the shore. A wrinkled lump of a thing with crusts of hardened black sand all over it. Once upon a time I would have thrown it away, or at least scraped the sand off, but I left it just as it was because it had managed to travel all the way across the Atlantic from somewhere like Jamaica just to land on my doorstep, and all that stuff on it had kept it warm and safe though all the dangers and storms. The crusts of sands were its clothes, for I knew that everyone needs a jumper and jacket and coat when it is cold and windy and wet. I spent the whole afternoon of that Frog Sunday playing with my shells. I made a shop out of them and a doll's house and a village with a road and cars and houses, because everything had to be made before you knew what it was. I sang to them too. If I sang a song into the shell and then put it to my ear the shell sang the song back to me the same way a baby gurgles and sings back when her Mam sings to her.

Meantime, Duncan and Fearchar walked down to the machair to play football.

'I'm not playing in goals again,' Fearchar said to me before he left. 'I'm tired of it.'

He said that to Duncan too as they walked down the machair road.

'I always have to be in goals. Why don't you go today?'

Duncan had the ball, bouncing it as he went along.

'We'll take it in turns then,' he conceded. 'But you first. And when I score twenty, then I'll go into goals.'

'Ten.'

'Split in the middle. Fifteen.'

'No. It's too high. That'll take forever. Twelve?'

'All right. Twelve it is.'

Our football area was next to the fairy knoll because it was nice and soft and green. Hazel and Dolina and I often played there. The fairy rings were perfectly round, and Hazel said that was because the fairies danced properly, in order, round and round, again and again, not like the wild and uneven reels our grown-ups did in the hall. That was because they all drank too much, Hazel said, whereas the fairies only ever drank milk and one thimble-full of mead, whatever that was. Hazel thought it was honey straight from the bees.

There was no proper pitch or goalposts or markers or anything, which was part of the joy of the game. Making it every time we went there. Sometimes I went down with them to play. Though they were reluctant to let me in at first – simply because I was a girl – the truth was that I was quite skilful, so they accepted me readily enough. I could 'read' a game well, as the modern commentators put it, though it was really just common sense – anyone with an ounce of wisdom could see where all the players were standing and could work out quickly enough where to pass the ball.

The problem mostly was that none of the boys could ever properly anticipate things, so that whenever I passed the ball into a space, no one would have moved there and then they would all shout at me and criticise me for not passing the ball directly to them, where they stood. As if I'd passed the ball nowhere. Idiots! As if the game wasn't about moving into the empty spaces which lay all over the machair like oases. I very quickly understood that the main thing was to get the ball, no matter what position you were in, no matter what complicated grown-up tactics Duncan would spout at us before we started, which everyone then instantly forgot as they started chasing the ball whichever way it went.

We made goalposts with our jackets and jerseys, but whether the ball had gone in this side of the post or missed outside was a matter of eternal argument.

'Did.'

'Did not.'

'Did so. In off the post.'

'Liar! What post?'

'Cheat!'

'It went over the bar.'

'Did not. It hit the bar then bounced down and went in.'

'Aye, but not over the line.'

'Alright then, we'll call it a draw.'

'No. We'll decide by penalty shoot-out.'

And then the penalty itself would go over the jacket rather than inside or out and the argument began all over again. Because a goal was never a goal until it was agreed that it had crossed the invisible line under the non-existent bar between the jackets. So anything was possible and nothing was ever conclusive.

'Alright then. We'll need to start the game again. Right from the start. Who's got the whistle?'

Really, the game could last forever.

Others always joined in, walking through fields and over gates and walls and fences from all directions. The twins, Donald and Iain Morrison, then Norman MacPhail and his pals Finlay and Ruairidh and poor Sgliugan (Snotter) who couldn't tell his right foot from his left, so he was always stuck in goals saving nothing and letting everything fly past him. He could never be blamed, only constantly told that it didn't matter. He stood open mouthed at every goal scored as if it was a miracle, cheering and clapping even when it was scored against him and it was clearly his fault and everybody on his own team was shouting and blaming him. He was so happy to be playing that even losing was a joy for him, since the point of playing was not winning or losing anyway. As long as he touched the ball now and again by hand or foot or by any part of his body he was happy.

Whenever the ball was lost or blew away in the wind far across the sand-dunes, Sgliugan was always sent to fetch it and came back with it as if it was a newly discovered ball found for a new game. Nobody called him Sgliugan when he was within earshot, though he knew fine that's what he was called. He frothed at the mouth if he heard anyone, either by mistake or through malice, call him Sgliugan. Even though it was such an accurate name, with his nose constantly streaming big wet blobs. His real name was John. He was always looking up into the air as if he expected lightning to strike any moment.

It was four-a-side most days I went and Duncan and Norman got to pick the teams, because they were the biggest. If someone had a coin to toss, Duncan always said, 'Heads I win, tails you lose,' as the coin was flicked so that he would always win. If no one had a coin, we picked up a stone from the machair and whoever flung it furthest had first choice. It was always best of three, however, for if it was just once the loser would complain for the rest of the day. Whoever won the toss always picked Fearchar first for their team, for he was easily the best player on the island. Not strong, but really skilful with his left foot. Duncan then always picked Donald Morrison first because he was fat and made an excellent defender. It was almost impossible to get anything past him. Norman picked Iain, Duncan selected Finlay, Norman picked Ruairidh and Duncan was left with poor Sgliugan, who jumped up and down as if he'd been chosen to play in the World Cup Finals. It's as well Sgliugan was there because it saved the second last from feeling useless.

Sometimes I would be referee and would give the poorer side free-kicks and penalty-kicks and goals that were marginal to say the least even though they all complained! And they had every reason to complain because it was clear to all of us that not everyone was equal and that some were better than others.

We'd be careful not to tell Sgliugan to play in goals, but to ask.

'Right, John. You want to go in goals?'

Duncan always carried gloves in his pockets for the match. He'd throw them to John, who was always delighted to put them on, as if they were a present he'd never seen before. Duncan knew he'd have few saves to make anyway, since hardly anything would get past fat Donald.

The final score of the first match I refereed was 36–34 with a long-lasting dispute over the result because Duncan claimed that the last two goals they scored were offside.

'No they weren't,' said Norman. 'Sgliugan was playing everyone on-side. He was standing like a dummy there on the goal-line all the time as the last defender.'

Thing is, Sgliugan would have been nowhere near the goal-line had Donald not been injured early on. He caught his foot in a rabbit-hole and had to go and lie down beside the pitch for most of the game.

'Otherwise,' said Duncan, 'we'd have won 34–0. And we scored the best goals. Did you see that free-kick I scored direct from my own half?'

The worst thing was when the ball burst and the game had to be abandoned, even though Fatty Morrison always seemed to have a bicycle-repair kit in one of his pockets and would try to repair the ball for a while with a patch until it fell apart completely and we'd all drift home moaning about whoever had last kicked the ball when it burst ,as if it was that player's fault. For the best thing about all our games was the bit after, when we talked about everything we'd done. The game was never finished. The goals and the saves and the misses and all the unfair decisions replayed forever. Big Donald tripped me. So he did. Aye, but it wasn't deliberate, it's just how he is and he couldn't move fast enough to get out of the way. Eh? Of course he could, if he wanted.

There was another world. While the boys played football and I

played or refereed or played with the shells, our parents went to bed. Sunday afternoon was the only regular time they had the house to themselves with nothing else to do. Or the only time they chose not to do anything else. There were always hundreds of things to do, from darning socks to repairing fences, but these things could sometimes wait.

Dad made the bed from oak beams found on the shore. He always said it could bear the weight of a horse, and I always had a picture of what it would be like to see a horse putting his pyjamas on and lying down and tucking himself in for the night. And speaking of darning, I once caught Dad trying to fix a hole in his socks with Copydex! I never told Mam.

Mam always lay on the inside against the wall and Dad on the outside towards the door.

'It's a cave instinct,' the skipper on his ship had told him once. 'The warrior always lies at the door protecting the tribe from lions and other predators. That's why I always sleep facing the door. Old habits die hard.'

It was colder that side. Any draught came in through the door, while Mam lay nice and cosy in the warmth at the back. He felt good about that. Protective. Maybe, after all, there are better ways to love than words. The best is always lying there in the stillness embracing each other. Strange how we coorie-in knees-to-back-of-knees at other times, but love makes us face each other, since we're scared of being alone. I've always been wary of people who don't look at you as you speak to them. There is nothing good about solitude. Lying there breathing together must have been their tenderest hour.

Mam always got up first. Washed her face in the blue porcelain bowl and tidied her hair. Made the tea, which she brought him in bed. If I was outside playing with my shells and the wind was quiet, I could hear the movements and then the kettle boiling on the stove and the tinkle of the china cups being fetched out of the cupboards and all the tea-making and pouring noises that followed.

By the time I came from the shells and Duncan and Fearchar returned from the machair they'd be sitting quietly by the fire. Mam knitting a bonnet and Dad reading through his favourite book once again. It was the only book he ever read. *Shane* by Jack Schaefer. He would always hum a tune (which I later learned was 'Shenandoah') as he read it. The book had an orange cover with a picture of a cowboy on the front. I read it as well, even though Duncan scoffed, saying it was a boys' book. As if there was such a thing! Pages were missing here and there including the last two pages, but it didn't really matter because Dad had read it so many times he'd memorised the pages when they'd been there, so when I got to these empty places he told me what was on the page. Word for word, he said. And he was right.

Funny too how we all read differently. Dad only ever read sitting down in the armchair by the fire. Mam at the table. Duncan always read lying on his back, one hand behind his head, the other holding the book, or more often than not, the comic. Fearchar always crouched over, on his knees, reading on the floor, while I always preferred to lie flat on my tummy with the book on the floor and my chin resting on my two fists. I turned the pages with my tongue and teeth! I wonder whether it gave us different experiences? Much as I would like to try and experiment, I'm afraid if I tried that position now I might never get up again! Maybe I've just turned into Dad, for there is nothing better now than sitting in the comfy chair by the fire reading, with the light shining from over my shoulder. Even though it's decades since I last read *Shane*!

We were lucky because we had good peats. Hard black ones from the hill which burned red and strong, as opposed to the soft mushy ones from the lower bogs that provided lots of smoke, but little heat. It was a matter of history: those who had been given crofts in the nineteenth century or after the break-up of land after World War One had the best peat-banks high up in the hills, while those who came later were given the inferior, boggier banks down below. Sort of like first-come, first-served, so that the first at the table get the biggest slice of the sausage! Sometimes Dad carried me on his shoulders out to the peats and I remember his big hands holding my ankles as we bobbed up and down through the bogs, jumping across the ditches as I held on with my hands around his eyes and him letting on like he couldn't see. I could see forever because I was up so high on his shoulders. All the houses and villages were just little specks in the distance.

13

Old Murdo and Mùgan
and John the Shoemaker and Hazel
and Effie the Postmistress

I DREAMT OF Reginald Maudling last night. He was Chancellor of the Exchequer once upon a time, and I used to see him often on television. He had thick-set glasses and reminded me of Mr Gardner, the Chemistry teacher I had at high school, who needed a magnifying glass to check our experiments. So many strangers lurking around. Jeremy Paxton, Martina Navratilova, Gladys Knight and the Pips and so many others who seemed so significant at the time compared to all those Murdos I grew up with.

There were countless Murdos, so they had to be distinguished by place or age or job or some other trait. So we had Fair-haired Murdo and Dark-haired Murdo and Young Murdo and Murdo the Tailor and Murdo Claw-hammer and Murdo Club-foot and Murdo of the Moor and Murdo Mainland and Murdo the Minister and Murdo the Mariner and Wee Murdo and Big Murdo and Old Murdo. Though Old Murdo was always called Old Murdo ever since he was nine months old because then his younger brother was born whom his parents also called Murdo. So he became Young Murdo. Old Murdo was named after his father's father, while Young Murdo was named after his mother's father. And Old Murdo the father's father was named after his Uncle Murdo – Murdo the Shepherd – who died in the Opium War, while Young Murdo the mother's father was named after his uncle – Murdo the Sailor – who was drowned off Cape

Horn. And that's before I start on all those poor girls called Murdina.

The original Murdo, they said, was an Irish seaman called Seumaidh Muireadhach who sailed in a coracle alongside St Brendan, but became separated during a storm in the Minch and ended up in Iceland as a Viking mercenary. The natives there couldn't quite pronounce his original Irish name and said it as Murchadh, and when the Norse invasions of Scotland happened centuries later it was again changed to Murdo, with the variant of Murphy once the warriors reached their ancestral land of Ireland. The best warrior name to have during these long centuries was Muireadhach Muireadhach or Murchadh Murchadh which translates as Murdo Murdo. The last Murdo Murdo, known colloquially as Murdo the Soldier, perished at the Battle of Balaclava in Crimea in 1854.

Probably because he was called Old Murdo from the cradle, our village Murdo always behaved as if he was old. His father claimed he was a changeling and wanted to abandon him on the moor, but his mother held tight to him and refused to let him go. He'd frown when other children smiled and took to smoking the pipe from age seven. No one challenged him as he sat there on a stone at the school gate puffing away in a cloud before the bell rang. When the teacher told him he couldn't smoke he just said,

'But you do it yourself.'

The only rule was that he would not smoke in the actual classroom. So Murdo and the teacher sat back to back on the stone, puffing away. He left school aged fourteen and joined the merchant navy where he served for the next sixty-five years. That's where he learned how to smoke and hold a clay-pipe properly, and he was so proud of the fact that he'd never given way to fashion and didn't use the new briar-pipes like the others, including old Flora who smoked like a chimney day and night, the pipe hardly ever coming out of her spitting mouth, whether she was making food or planting potatoes. You could see a couple of unlit stuffed pipes sticking out of her pockets in church. Old Murdo was much more delicate and took great care to let us know how to hold the pipe properly when smoking – by the stem with two fingers on top and the thumb underneath. We all tried to smoke, but most of us coughed and hated it and didn't persevere long enough to become addicted.

He lived down the road from us, and Mam and Dad said he seemed a hundred years of age even when they were children and somehow was now still the same age. His face was etched and brown, like my Mam's crumpled oven paper, because he spent most of his time outside in the sun and wind and rain. He looked like a lobster. He had one tooth in the bottom part of his mouth, and told us that his wrinkles were a personal gift from Neptune for having sailed the seven seas.

And he would then name them – the Adriatic, Mediterranean, the Black Sea, the Caspian Sea, the Persian Gulf and the Arabian Sea, and ramble on about the five oceans, none of which were as astonishing, he claimed, as the silver Minch which surrounded us, daily giving us herring and mackerel and lobsters and tangle and seaweed and salty lips and faces and fresh healthy complexions.

He'd spent thirty years as a seaman on the Great Lakes and now spent most of his days sitting by the window playing Cribbage using matchsticks for counters. He was expert at it because long practice had made all the moves automatic for him. He still counted on his fingers. Not because he couldn't do it mentally, he said to us when we smirked, but because it slowed him down and gave him time to think of his next move. He liked it best when he lost against himself.

If anything happened, he always imagined he was the first person to know it.

'Did you see that sunset last night?' he'd ask, wanting us to say no so that he could tell us all about it. Nothing seemed to be as good as it used to be for Murdo. Not even the sunset, so that you always felt it was a bit of a mistake to be alive now rather than then. The dead and the long gone had better stories and songs and solutions, no matter how smart and creative anyone was now. And besides, in the good old days if you made a song you were paid properly, given a cow in exchange for it. Or sixteen geese.

'If only you'd been here fifty years ago, my dear, then you'd have heard the proper version. Or five thousand and four hundred years ago, when Adam himself spoke the best Gaelic.' He said he'd worked it out.

He smoked like a chimney, as if he was a house. He saw ghosts, though they were not really ghosts but the broken memories of his long life. The phantoms of things he once glimpsed somewhere. Turbaned sailors he met in Cairo, and ringleted women he danced with in Cadiz who wore red and white ribbons on their shoes, and a memory of his mother leaning over the cradle singing to him. They got jumbled up like cards and appeared to him as he walked down by the fank or when he had his Saturday night bath in the tub by the fire. There were a thousand times more spirits in the world than there were villagers around him. Same as Gladys Knight and the Pips! They kept him company and populated all the empty spaces around him. They were like electricity, lighting up the darkness. None of the ghosts frightened him. They were friendly and told him of the past, which is only the present of another time, though when he told others what he saw they'd shiver and shrivel as if shifting time was strange.

'Nothing – not even what you call time or anything that has happened since – changes the past,' the ghosts told him. They broke all the rules of space, for there were no fences or walls or locks and keys where they travelled, despite the claim that the church and the cemetery were the only places where the living were expected to meet the dead. They must have been lost, for they were not supposed to wander about all over the place, moving between heaven and earth. Though Dad said it was Murdo himself who was lost.

He had the tidiest house because he kept everything which he wasn't using at that moment in a trunk – cutlery and pots and pans and his shirts and trousers and shoes and hammers and all kinds of odds and ends. He hoarded everything. Never threw anything away, and still wore the same Sunday suit he was given when he was eighteen, and always used the same plate and cup and saucer, as if nothing new had been invented or discovered in the sixty and more years since.

When he needed something he just rummaged about in the box for a while and fetched out a cup or a vest or whatever else he needed at that moment and when he was finished with it he washed it and dried and put it back in the box, so that the small space in his house always seemed as huge and empty as the hall in between the weekly dances. He kept to the old way of only bathing and shaving every Saturday night, so that as the week wore on he smelt more and more and his grey stubble grew and grew, but at Mass on Sunday his face looked as smooth as my Mam's best silk nightshirt and if you passed him he smelt of the carbolic soap my Dad sometimes used after he'd been cutting the peats.

He used to live next door to Arthur Smith the ghillie, who died, and because he was unmarried and had no relatives the ghillie's house was sold and bought by Miss Cranshaw, who used to come on holiday to the place every summer and stay in the hotel. But once she bought the house she did this strange thing – she gave it a name, as if it belonged to her and not to the Smiths who had lived there for centuries. Everyone else just had croft numbers.

'Goodness,' Mam said, 'you only give names to babies.'

'And dogs and cows and horses,' added Dad.

But Miss Cranshaw had a sign made with 'Seaview' written on it and of course everyone laughed behind her back, saying,

'Well, what else do we all see every time we look out the window or the door but the sea? So why call it that? Daft. It's like calling your dog "Dog".'

Thing is, we had the best view of the sea in the whole place. Especially from our outside toilet, which Dad built for us at the end of the garden. A little stone hut with an upturned old boat for a roof and when you sat there on a clear night you could see all the stars and watch the Atlantic surging white foam onto the long stretch of sand. It was as if it was singing in Gaelic.

I think Old Murdo used the old pastoral calendar, so only four dates really mattered to him, the quarter-times of the year. Thing is, he was always late. Maybe because time was measured long. Rushing into church after the priest had already blessed the people, arriving at the travelling van as it left, missing the ferry by hours. He blamed it on the weather, for he'd always used two broken bottles sealed together and filled with sand for telling the time. On good dry summer days the sand would take an hour to run through the glass, at which point he would turn it upside down to mark the next hour, but when it rained and the weather got damp the sand of course ran more slowly so that the hour extended and because of that he also claimed he was only half the age he really was.

As children we'd call in to see him so that we'd get the chance to turn his sand-glass on the hour and tried to tell him that it was running more slowly when the weather was damp, but he refused to listen, saying, 'No, no. It's not that at all. It's just that time varies constantly and is different from day to day. It's not me or the sand-glass that's wrong but everyone else who holds to their artificial clocks as if everything is fixed. Don't they know that when it's eleven in the morning here, it's four in the afternoon in Egypt? Nothing is fixed.'

And on the way home we knew he was right, for we found dandelions by the roadside and each of us blew a different time even though the dandelions were similar and we all breathed the same length of time with the same strength.

Nevertheless, every home had a clock tick-tocking away proudly on the wall or over the fire. They were there as much for decoration as for use, since most of them either ran fast or slow. Since we could tell the time by the sun anyway, what folk actually admired were the different sounds that all the different clocks made. Some loud and deep and sonorous, like a Gaelic song, others small and light and tinkling like the ones on the radio. Mrs MacPherson even bought a cuckoo-clock from the catalogue and everyone called by to watch the beautiful little yellow bird with its red beak popping out to say hello every quarter hour. I had the treat of winding him up every afternoon on my way back from school.

'No more than eight winds or the spring will break,' she told me.

Mùgan had been an officer at sea. So he said. He was a smart-looking gentleman. Every day for him was a clean-shirt-day, which Dad thought odd. Twice a week was good enough for everyone else. Mùgan had a little white well-trimmed beard, with his shoes always shining. He had a variety of them. Black, brown and even white which he wore to go dancing. He was easily the best dancer on the island, so light on his feet that sometimes he looked like a feather floating gaily in the breeze. He never married, and some people said he was strange, being so neat and tidy and doing his own washing and drying and everything. He had the loveliest clothes-line in the place and was as vain as anything. While others just stuck ropes into rocks or even dried their clothes on the rocks themselves, he had two individually-designed clothes-lines. One on the west side of his house for the blankets and heavy materials, so that they caught the prevailing wind, and one on the south side for his shirts and socks and underwear to catch the warmth. He was always the first to hang out his washing, as if it was some kind of competition that mattered to him. And not only that – the lines were made of silk to protect his garments, and even the clothes-pegs he used were multi-coloured. A scarlet cord always hung from his gable-end window. He knew people looked and wondered and it made him important.

He painted the east side of his house (the side facing the road) yellow, which was unheard of, so that when you passed his house on a breezy day it was like walking through the pages of a comic, with colours fluttering in unexpected corners as a prize. He even had a large white towel which he claimed the company sent him as a gift. It flapped like a ship's sail in the wind, with 'Rinso Sunshine' written on one side and 'Out of the blue comes the whitest white' on the other. Perhaps he was still sailing the Pacific. After a while the words faded on the towel, though none of us have ever forgotten the message. I suppose he thought that if he tidied his house and displayed colours it made the world neater and brighter.

He was also what they called a 'fresh-air fiend'. Summer and winter, Mùgan's windows were always wide open during the day, for he remembered how his parents had died of tuberculosis and his grandparents of consumption. As an extra precaution, he never drank milk. He was also the village barber, though we were saved from his terrible bowl-cuts because Mam cut ours. With scissors too, not with the open razor he used.

Mam held our hair in tiny folds in her left hand, ran her fingers through it, and then clipped it ever so softly and gently so that you wouldn't know she was cutting it. The boys always wanted the same haircut, but I was quite happy to have mine different every time, so sometimes she cut it short and wavy, other times she left it long. Once she put her curlers in mine because I wanted to look like Dusty Springfield, but I only looked like a daft old woman, so we washed it out immediately and straightened it with a wet comb and brush.

Mùgan dressed well because he despised how casual the world had become. He told us he hated people not living up to their station. They were like ships without sails or engines, he said. The schoolmaster, for example, whom he'd seen going tie-less to work, and the day before, the priest walking along the road wearing brown cords and a red polo jumper as if there was no such things as social distinction or as if that distinction could be disguised by dressing up like a commoner or for fun. His job was to be a shepherd, not one of the sheep. The least he could do was wear a woollen coat or hat if he was to be one of them. And what was he doing walking? With his hands in his pockets too, claiming that made the birds of the air feel less threatened. Only people who had nothing better to do, such as tourists, walked for its own sake. It was simply indecent. They ought to live up to their uniformed vocations, for order was the first principle and a man is exactly how he looks.

'Clothes matter because they distinguish people,' he said to us. 'When I was young you'd know an artisan from a labourer because the artisan had a long tail to his coat. It distinguishes class from carelessness. If you're penniless but dress well, people will respect you,' he preached. Mùgan liked order, and dressing well was part of that discipline – highly-polished shoes, an ironed shirt and a good jumper – cashmere was best.

He had a portrait of Bonnie Prince Charlie striding across the heather at his front door and if anyone asked about it he'd say,

'That's where the Prince got out of his carriage and walked. But even though he walked he was still well turned-out, because he was a gentleman. The thing is, if you don't respect a thing, you despise it.'

So whenever we called in to see him Mam always asked so that he could hear himself.

Because Mùgan was a relatively short man he tended to stand on his tiptoes, like a ballerina, when he spoke to people. Effie said it was because he thought that brought him nearer to heaven, whereas he'd be better off on his knees if that was his hope.

When things disintegrated, he went on the drink and by the end of his alcoholic bout was more ashamed by the state of his clothing than anything he may or may not have done while completely drunk. Everyone knew when a spree was coming up because days in advance he'd carry chairs and place them strategically at various points along the roadside to rest on when the time came. When he went to the mainland on a binge he regularly sold his dog for drink, knowing full well she'd make her own way back home in a couple of weeks. All the ferry workers knew the dog. He didn't need a ticket. Every time he came back he looked like Rumpelstiltskin.

'That dog's not only my best friend, but my best bank,' he'd say then. 'Though I always make the same mistake – of foolishly believing that the mainland is just a different version of the island. But of course it's completely different. It's over the water, which is everything. I so miss Tangier and the smell of the sea, and feel trapped inland like I'm in an oven.'

He'd then blubber how the mainland police, whether in Leith or Liberia in the old days, would slam him into jail overnight for being drunk, whereas here someone would always carry him home and make sure he was tucked up safe in his bed. He was like the old Irishman Eric and I once met in a pub in Grafton Street who kept saying to us, 'I wish I was on the Old Kent Road wishing I was here.'

Maybe that's why he always carried a pocketbook and pencil with him, and whenever he headed off to the pub we'd watch him stop at various places, such as the old Pictish standing stone, take out his notebook and jot down his bearings with little crosses, as if to reassure himself that some things remained steady and solid. It was a pagan stone, but had been converted by John the Shoemaker who had once incised a cross on it.

When he was at sea he was also the unqualified ship's doctor.

'They gave me a book called *The Sailor's Medical Manual* and whenever anyone was ill they came to me for a consultation. The previous skipper had left five cloudy bottles in the medicine cupboard but I had no idea what was in them. They were just marked one two three four five and if anyone was ill I'd give them a spoonful from one of them and if they were really ill I made a cocktail of all of them and gave that to them. If they survived, they survived, and if they didn't they didn't. Most of them were glad to be pitched over the side into the waters we loved with a Gaelic prayer and a benediction.'

As he weaved his way home from the pub he never went in a straight line. Not because he was drunk but because never sailing in a straight line was an article of faith with him. He knew the difference between seamanship and navigation, and regarded the land simply as an interruption of the sea, causing a man like him to lose his bearing.

'The best instruments are your eyes, your ears and your experience. It may appear on first sight that the quickest way is always to go straight from A to B, but if you know the sea like I do you'll know that the Roaring Forties and the Trade Winds get in the way, so you have to take what is known as the Great Circle, which is the shortest distance between two points even if it doesn't look like it. Only fools travel in a rum line. Speed is always the enemy of safety. It's like telling a story. Always go round with the elements rather than against them. Get to know them rather than fight them. Always be a friend, not an enemy.'

And he'd weave his great circle using the cardinal points of his unique compass through the different villages, south to Eairdsidh's cottage where he knew he'd get a tot of rum, then nor-by-nor-east to Murdina's where a plate of soup and a heap of home-made bread would be waiting for him. On dark clear nights he navigated his way to port via the Pole Star. He always made it home eventually via Balik Papan and Cape Horn. Dad had an old compass which was broken and Duncan and Fearchar and I sometimes took it and sailed round the world on our bikes with it.

John the Shoemaker was named Peter the Proverb because of his love of rhyming proverbs. The Schoolmaster sometimes invited him into school to spout proverbs at us which we then wrote down in a book that he was supposed to publish some day but never did. He spoke in quotes, hardly having any vocabulary of his own. It made things easier for him not sharing any original or dangerous thoughts, because proverbs never questioned anything.

If Mam or Dad or anyone asked him, 'How are you?' he'd say, 'Like my old shoes, ever getting worse.'

'What's the right time, John?'

'Time and tide wait for no man.'

'Are you busy just now, Peter?'

'Better sit still than rise and fall.'

He came from a long line of shoemakers, though he wasn't one himself. No need for it, he said.

'Everything comes in a parcel now. Even fiddlers can buy their own shoes nowadays.'

He played the fiddle badly and drank too much. When he drank he couldn't fiddle, and instead went round folk's houses diddling, becoming the fiddle himself.

'Dal da di di cher da dael di dal i da da dam pa di...'

until they sobered him up with soup and cheese and he returned to his silence and his proverbs.

'The tune that will make one fiddler happy will make another unhappy,' he'd announce as he left the house sobered up, already thinking about his next drinking bout.

'Ah! The dust of the world still clings to me. It does. It does,' he'd chant when in his cups.

I sometimes wonder whether I made them all up. Except they're all too innocent to have been invented, for years later I saw them again in Sardinia and Greece and in rural France.

Hazel was a special child and became a special grown-up. I loved her because she was the least like myself and was happier than any of the rest of us could ever be. She had the gift of silence. Dr and Mrs MacPherson adopted her as a baby, and though they knew her birth-mother, Hazel didn't want to know.

'I just love you,' she said when asked if she wanted to know about her real mother, so they left off asking.

She saw things in pictures, and read through colour rather than words. Happiness was yellow, and sadness was blue, and anger was red. The gold colour of the corn on the machair in autumn was Eden, where she sat for hours leaning against a haystack, moving with the sun until it sank into the sea. It was as if the hayfield itself, and the sea, rather than the sun, was shining. It could rain some other time, and that too was perfect.

She always walked slowly, as if moving fast was inappropriate, and whenever she saw a white pebble she picked it up and took it home because it was sacred. I think she was the only person in the place who could have been transported anywhere in the world and still remain unchanged.

When we played races she didn't refuse to play, just danced along while we ran, so that she was always last. Not that it mattered in the least, for when we raced it wasn't about who was first or second or third or last anyway! That wasn't the point of racing. The fun was in the things we did as we ran along. Sometimes we hopped or swerved or ran with our knees bent or jumped backwards all the way, or did it blindfold, which meant that anyone could win accidentally, and the fun was in seeing Dolina or Morag or Katie or myself falling over or going in the wrong direction. My favourite one was called Giant Steps, when one of us stood at the front and then gave instructions to each of us in turn either to hop or jump or stretch. Sometimes we'd have to scissor-jump, or if the leader shouted 'Crocodile', we'd have to crawl along on the ground like a crocodile, and if she shouted 'Crocodile Roll' we turned on our sides and then rolled along all dizzy to the finishing line.

The boys always played it by spitting, which I hated – they'd start the game over by the fank and then sit and run to where their spit landed and then spit again and run again until the first one reached the school wall. Dirty beasts. Think of the germs.

The Schoolmaster then almost spoiled everything by introducing what he called Athletics and making us do competitive races against each other when all we wanted was just to run for fun, not to win and lose by crossing a line first, for there were other and better ways to do that. The funniest, or the daftest, for example, would normally win or lose when we made our own rules. I once won a race even though I was last because I ran all the way round carrying big fat Marie on my back the day after she broke her ankle. But that wasn't good enough for the Headie who made it all rules and flags and whistles and timings and winners and losers, which always meant one winner and the rest of us a whole bunch of losers, having to suffer Katie and sleekit Dan Thomson smirking away for the rest of the day, flashing their daft cheap paper badges as if they meant something.

While I'm remembering school, the best thing I learned there was from the new nurse who came in one day and taught us all how to clean our teeth properly.

'You're supposed to brush them, not scrub them,' she said, and fetched a set of plastic dentures out of her bag and demonstrated how to do it, working slowly from the back of the bottom tooth at the left. She then gave each of us a toothbrush. A soft brush.

'It must be a soft brush,' she said, 'for you need to be gentle in all things.'

We could choose the colours. I chose purple, of course! It was only much later that I heard the word Zen, and the most Zen-like experience I've had every day since (and three times a day too!) is brushing my teeth. Take time. That's the most important thing. No rushing! Put a tiny drop of toothpaste on the brush, find a comfortable seat and brush each tooth gently and slowly in circles, as if you were painting an eternal O. Oh, and if you ever get toothache, go find a caterpiller, gently wrap it in a rag and place it next to the tooth, and the pain will disappear!

Hazel became anxious and depressed in the winter when the days were long and dark as her hair. She visited us often and Mam would ask to make scones with her, and while Hazel mixed the flour and butter and raisins Mam sang. Mam always wore an apron in which she gathered herbs and small potatoes and clothes-pegs and eggs and things when outside, until it contained the whole world. Once she put a bleating lamb in it and carried it home and we fed it with bottled milk until he was strong enough to go and graze on his own. As Mam sang, Hazel saw birds flying in the sky and when Dad told a story Hazel saw the story like a film on the wall because the story never happened then but now.

'There he is, running,' she'd say, when the hero was chasing the deer, or she'd look at the blank space on the white-painted stone wall and see the man bending down and rubbing his hand across his face when he goes blind and begins searching for the healing spring. The healing spring was in the alcove by the fire. She was especially fond of dancing and asked me to chum her to the weekly dances in the church hall. For luck, we always wore something new to the dance, even if it was only a shoelace. If she wanted a boy to ask her to dance she wore a yellow flower with the stalk upwards in her hair, and if she wanted a girl to dance with her she wore the stalk downwards. The boys all danced fast and rough, and the girls swayed like corn in the wind.

The other thing was that we danced so differently from the adults. We moved up and down rather than sideways, and snapped our fingers and clicked our heels and touched the floor with our fingers while the grown-ups clapped and stepped as if they were following pre-set diagrams and patterns on the floor and in the air. We so admired the older girls who all wore flowery dresses and wore their hair curling down at the side and climbing up to heaven on the top. There was no toilet inside the hall so when we went outside to pee the girls would all go to the left side of the building and as we crouched there we could hear the older boys talking and clinking whisky bottles together on the other side.

Hazel was daring because she was innocent, and she was innocent because she had no ambition, so that she would do things and go places the rest of us were afraid to go to. Like the steep gully by the eastern rock which she could climb easily like a goat, and all these forbidden paths where ghosts and bogles and the spirits of the dead would jump on you. She went there and came back and told us about it so that we didn't have to go ourselves because we didn't want to and were afraid, even when she said that all she saw was the bog-cotton dancing in the breeze and the wild white horses grazing over at the back of Stùlabhal. After all, she might have been making it up, and we didn't really want to risk it. You could never be sure.

'She's just like Christopher Columbus,' Fearchar said. 'He was the first to prove that the earth wasn't flat and that you wouldn't fall off it when you travelled so far, right to the edge. But still there are folk around here who refuse to believe him.'

As if any of that scared us. No – it was just that we wanted to leave all those infinite spaces for Hazel to explore. We had enough going on where we were, around the house itself and down by the shore. I realise now that she was dyslexic, which gave her the gift of orientation so that she saw all things three-dimensionally, as if she was constantly looking down on the world from the sky.

There was more sky than earth where we were. Everything happened for her now, in the present tense. It was as if she was always seeing things for the first time, without remembering them from before like we did, who got bored of things so quickly. That's just the bus we'd say, whereas for her it was like a bright travelling thing she'd never seen before. She could do the same thing again and again and again as if every time was the first time ever. Even jumping on a bike and shouting at the top of her lungs at the wonder of moving once more.

Effie the Postmistress was round and fat. She also believed in Niall Cuagach's string theory – that if she got stressed she'd lose weight and become as thin as a piece of string and grow weak instead of being a strong rope which could anchor down a boat and thatch on a wild and windy day. So she ate a lot because she didn't want to disappear, and preferred to give information rather than an opinion so that if anyone said to her, 'What a beautiful day,' she replied, 'Some days the sun shines. Other days it rains.'

She lived as if everything had already happened and nothing more could ever be imagined.

'There's always been electricity,' she said when folk talked about this new thing that was coming our way. 'From the day God said "Let there be light". What else are the sun and moon and stars but electricity?'

Her hobby was collecting weather data. She had a wooden barrel at the end of the house where she measured the daily rainfall. Folk thought she was daft because it was clear to them – of course it was – when it rained and when it was dry. But that was different from measuring it and recording it. She calculated from the barrel, morning and night, with a ruler, and logged the rainfall in a little book she always carried in her bag, a little canvas satchel she called her dream-bag. Sometimes I helped her and the best bit was when I was allowed to dip the ruler into the barrel and then write down where the wet line lay. Everyone considered her habit both unnecessary and eccentric, though her wee pile of books can now be studied in the local museum and are of considerable interest to climate scientists.

She was also the only person in the village who had a decorated gate. Everyone else (including us) had old wooden things here and there which were regularly falling apart, though some had the new tubular steel gates bought from the Department of Agriculture and Fisheries store, but Effie had proper ornate cast-iron gates hand-made by a blacksmith called Smith from the Borders. She said that ugly things never worked properly. Her gate was beautiful, and adorned with roses throughout and with a little latch that clicked when you opened it and clacked when you closed it, and everyone knew that Effie just loved the sounds whenever anyone came to or left from the Post Office, so we would often go down there for a stamp or an envelope when there was no need for either or when we could just as easily buy a whole pack of them if we wanted, just so that we could give poor Effie the pleasure of hearing her click and clack.

One day I went to the Post Office to get stamps for Dad and I found Effie sitting alone crying behind the counter. I must have been seven or eight, and it was the first time I'd ever seen a grown-up crying, so I was a bit confused. When I cried, my Mam always gave me a cuddle and when Dolina or Morag or any of the other girls cried we'd also cuddle each another, so I climbed over the counter and cuddled Effie as best I could, which was difficult because she was so big and stout. But I held her tight around her neck because she was sitting down and she cried and cried for what seemed like hours. At first I had my eyes closed when I cuddled her, because that's what you do when you cuddle properly, but then I opened them and watched her big round tears flowing down her cheeks. They were like the raindrops on the window in the winter, except they made no sound. When they finally stopped flowing I dried her cheeks and face with my hankie and she smiled and became a child and said to me, 'I steam open people's letters and read them, Annie. I just can't help myself – they always look so personal and interesting, with stamps from faraway places and the next thing I find myself boiling the kettle for a cup of tea and putting the envelopes under the steam and reading them as I have my tea.'

She started crying again. It was like when I opened my pillowcase and all the hen feathers flew out.

'And the worst of it is that none of them are worth reading anyway – just scraps of shabby gossip and useless information and things about weather and dogs, and I feel so dirty and soiled once I've read them, as if – no not as if – but because I've broken trust and secrecy.'

I sat beside her stroking her long white hair as if she was a dolly, or a dog, until she calmed down and breathed nice and steady. Her hair was still strong and thick and curly despite her age. She fetched out her own lace handkerchief and dabbed some drops of perfume on it from a small glass bottle she had on the shelf and patted her brow with it. It smelt a bit like Dettol, except sweeter. I once made a corn dolly out of three stalks of wheat, and called her Goldielocks.

'The thing is, Annie, everyone wants to help, but no one understands. The things I could tell, though,' she blubbered. 'Though I won't.'

I didn't understand either, but that didn't matter, because I listened. She was only as daft as everyone else.

She looked just like wee Fiona Thomson did at school when she was punished for always getting her sums wrong. How can anyone be expected to do everything right all the time? Even if multiplication is explained to you, that doesn't mean you understand it. For some reason, at that moment, I thought Effie should have a canary as a pet to keep her company, but she didn't. I'd probably read of old women who had kept canaries and sang with them when they sang, and stroked their feathers when they were sad.

Then she stood up and asked, as if nothing had happened,

'Did you come for stamps, Annie?'

I nodded and she gave me a book of stamps with a picture of five silver bicycles embossed with the words Commonwealth Games on each one. They were special stamps which she kept in a sealed box beneath the counter along with other beautiful ones which had pictures of flamingos and penguins and animals and birds I'd never seen before and didn't know the names of. But we had broken some kind of secret barrier, and whenever I called in to post a letter or get a stamp or envelopes after that, we'd talk if no one else was there. It was as if she allowed herself to be my age from then on rather than be a Postmistress. We played Eye-Spy and Put the Tail on the Donkey and – her favourite – Pitching Pennies into the Jar! I was happy that she showed me her stamp collections. The ones from others islands like the Fair Isles and Fiji and the Isle of Man were her favourites.

The Post Office was a counter and some shelves and drawing and weighing-measures in her porch. You then went through the curtains to Effie's warm kitchen. I remember she got a new carpet and it changed everything, for any visitors then had to take off their shoes before entering through the kitchen to her sitting room, where she kept back copies of newspapers, so most folk stopped coming. They would probably have been embarrassed by their darned or smelly stockings. But I was happy enough to take off my shoes and walk across her soft carpet and admire her treasures – a silver brooch that had belonged to her granny and the framed letter from the Postmaster General himself congratulating her when she sent the hundredth telegram from her small Post Office.

She had the sweetest Sacred Heart Lamp which smelt so nice because she always added linseed oil to the paraffin. Yet the thing I noticed most in her sitting room and kitchen was that both of her clocks were out of time, the kitchen an hour early, the sitting room an hour late. When I asked her about them she simply explained that one was set for summer time and one for winter time to save her opening them up at the back and changing them every Spring and Autumn.

Her shelves were newly lined each week with freshly folded

newspaper. She kept her special things in a curved glass display cabinet – plates with pictures of Queen Victoria and Prince Albert, and dainty little cups with rabbits on them, and silver cutlery which reflected everything around. And her dresser was gorgeous, painted bright yellow with the edges of the shelves a dark blue.

'Would you like some tea?' she asked and though I didn't like tea I always said 'Yes' because I knew she wanted to take her special pot and cups and saucers out and show them off as objects of use rather than of mere display. The decorative plates were never used for eating. Isn't it lovely that children and old people like special things which we don't use for common purposes? I still take your Mam's dolls out now and again just to freshen them up, and I dare anyone to touch the silver teapot my pal Audrey gave me for my sixtieth!

In public and at the cèilidh, as she scoffed some more cake, Effie took extra care not to confuse any emotion with fact. Another sticky bun seemed the answer to most problems. When she wasn't eating a bun or biscuit she always sat with her hands clasped together, constantly circulating one thumb round the other. A dozen times clockwise, then a dozen times anti-clockwise, and on and on forever until she was offered a cup of tea. Then her thumbs rested, one on the cup and one on the cake.

When folk suggested that electricity would change the place she reminded them that they also said that about the wheel and the clock and the bicycle and the telephone and the telegraph and the chairs they sat on and the newspapers they'd all been using for more than a century.

'Probably even said it about the sun when they first saw it shining up there in the sky,' she said.

14

The Meeting

THE BIG MEETING took place on Monday night. Everyone was there. The Monday night after Frog Sunday, though I never took to calling it Frog Monday. I often think of that meeting as if I'm watching an old black and white film.

My favourite is *Murder on the Orient Express*. The original one with Ingrid Bergman, not that rubbishy version they made more recently. Though I know every conversation and movement in the film, it still thrills me – the steam from the train as it leaves Istanbul on the great adventure, and the puzzle of always working out who did what, even if I know, for you never know. They might do something different. They might. There's nothing to stop them, after all, beyond the decisions Agatha made all those years ago. Every time I watch the film though I realise how daft that is. Like trying to change the outcome of the Boer War or something.

I like imagining their reasons and motives for myself. For I'm sure my guesses are as good as theirs! And how beautiful everyone looks, in those divine suits and dresses. I don't want to sound like an old fogey, but I do think we dressed better in those days. Dressed with style. My Mam had that – whether she was wearing a kitchen apron or a Sunday dress, shoes or wellingtons, she always looked elegant. Even her hard-worn hands, which she never hid with gloves.

The meeting was scheduled to be held in the church hall, but slates had fallen off the roof during the last gale, so it was moved to the school instead. Peter the Proverb blamed his neighbour Gormul MacLean who was a witch with the power to raise air: the power to raise a storm by incantations. Miss MacLean lived on her own and had no one to talk to, and yet he'd heard her blabbering and murmuring on dark evenings before great storms, and the quieter her voice became, the greater the storm.

I suppose she needed to make her voice heard one way or the other. They all avoided her, though some of them visited her secretly in the dark when they were in desperate need and everything else had failed. They said she could turn into a hare or a coil of rope or a hawk or anything, so you had to be careful what you said when you were out and about in case a snail or a swallow or a wasp or even a stick was listening, which was really her in disguise. Sometimes indoors as a moth fluttering round the candle flame as you spoke.

We only had three public buildings – the church with its hall, the school and the pub. The first was for everyone, the second for us children and the third for men. All three, however, were the first places to have electricity, and when you went outside in the dark you could see them shining on the horizon beneath the stars.

Most people hadn't been at the school building for a long time. Not since they were children, with all their hopes and fears, and you could see these memories and scars fluttering like little coloured flags as folk walked to the school. Old men and women who could hardly move in normal times hurried, as if they were heading with their satchels filled with pieces for their first day in class and didn't want to get into trouble for being late when they got there. Others dawdled, as if by delaying their arrival the lesson they feared most (Arithmetic!) would have passed.

The answer was always wrong, no matter how hard you tried. You just knew how many sheep could fit into a fank, and how many stitches you needed for each finger of the mittens, so why would you need something like long division and factors and things like that? What we all remembered was not so much anything we learned at school, but who our real chums were, and whether the teacher liked us or not. You sensed from the first day in Primary

One if the teacher approved of you or not. That's what lasts – the knowledge of being loved or not.

Sometimes we were allowed to make things up in a test called composition, though Mam told me that was basically just a spelling test. What you wrote about didn't matter. You only got marks, and sometimes a prize, for spelling the words right. And the teacher was forever telling us to pay attention, as if there was something to pay attention to in the first place.

Everyone remembered that the best time in their lives was the walk to and from school when you were in limbo, neither under the control of your parents nor the power of the school. You created this makeshift world between two orders, where everything was possible, from making a shirt out of moss-cotton to discovering a half-crown in the ditch. It was the place where freedom was permitted and you didn't have to please anyone or be useful. Where you could play instead of carting cow dung. Best of all was chumming up with someone on the way to school so that you could be doubly protected from what was to come. Fun protected you for a while.

We played at being grown-ups, which was a thousand times better than being a grown-up, because you knew it was only a game. Most of the things big people said never happened anyway. They were just hopes and threats and promises. Being a grown-up isn't really any more important than being a child. You say lots of things and hardly any of them happen for real. Though it was good to pretend for a while. The person you could be if it wasn't for your Mam and Dad and brothers and sisters and teachers and Katie. Or the teacher or the spot on my nose or the way my hair always went curly when I wanted it to be nice and straight like Audrey Hepburn. And the ball always bursting and the bicycle always having a flat tyre and the paraffin always running out and all these other people and the government and the lack of money and opportunities and where you stayed which was so far away from everywhere with the ferry always breaking down or storm-bound in Oban.

If we fell out with our pals on the way to school it would be all made up by the time we walked home together, whereas some grown-ups hadn't spoken to their neighbours for nearly forty years because of something, now completely forgotten, their fathers or mothers or grandparents had once argued about. So many things have unknown causes.

On the way to the meeting I saw some of the old people touch the standing stone by the road three times, once with the right forefinger, then once with the left and then once with both hands, just as I did every morning on my way to school and every afternoon on my way back, because that brought good luck. The stone smiled when you touched it and frowned when you didn't. And worse if you started and didn't finish. It had seen so much. Some of them even remembered the special way to walk to school, and I could see a few of them making sure that they didn't step on the lines on the road in case they fell into the dragon's lair which lay beneath. For once you do a thing you do it forever. I still ride a bicycle, even though it's now an electric one!

At the school itself, some entered fearfully, remembering thrashings they received in the building decades before. A wooden ruler across the knuckles for writing unevenly. A hard slap across the ears for listening to their friend. And the tawse itself for speaking worthless Gaelic. That filthy tongue of the byre and the old-fashioned and useless language of the fireside, not of books and learning and education. Good enough for singing and telling stories, and carting manure and digging ditches, but if you want to get on in the world, boys and girls, speak English. They exchanged their native ignorance for superior wisdom and quickly acquired this beautiful language of improvement and progress that has opened the world for all of us. It was like a constant lesson we all heard echoing on and on inside our heads.

Christopher Columbus discovered America which didn't exist until he found it, the same way that Thomas MacDonald found the unknown hidden loch over the big hill which was teeming with wild salmon and trout and which ever afterwards was named MacDonald's Loch after him. He caught a salmon and brought it home alive in a basin and kept it in a small pond at the back of his house which had the surface of a mirror. When he needed to know anything he went out there and looked at his own reflection in the water and stroked the salmon until the fish told him everything until they both passed away at exactly the same time on the same day.

Our own history was inadequate because it was unwritten and therefore remembered wrong and our geography irrelevant because nothing important ever happened here. Neither Christopher Columbus nor Florence Nightingale had been born around here. And even if they had, they wouldn't have amounted to much. Chris would have been out there on the skerries in his dripping oilskins lobster-fishing, and Flo probably making the mince and tatties in the school canteen.

Though Mrs MacPherson told me how surprised she was when she went to school that everyone in the class was given the same book to read, as if there was just one book in the whole world. And they all had to read at the same slow pace, even though she could skim through the whole book in minutes while daft Flora who sat beside her took a whole morning to read a single sentence. The cat sat on the mat forever and ever. Her own parents never learned how to write.

'Why write when you can remember and tell?' her father had said. 'The only thing they ever taught me at school was that there were lots of pirates in the Horn of Africa. Not that I've ever been there. The thing is, you can't remember more important things if they fill your head with all that stuff at school. Other people's words and thoughts.'

Some had happier memories. Anna Bheag still remembered the way she learned the English alphabet, attaching a name to each letter, though she didn't know then what many of the names meant. A is for Apple, B is for Bear, C is for Custard, D is for Donkey, E is for Everest, F is for Finlay, G is for God, H is for Hector, I is for India, J is for John, K is for Kilmarnock, L is for London, M is for Mother, N is for Nurse, O is for October, P is for Peter, Q is for Queen, R is for Russia, S is for Sugar, T is for Tea, U is for Up, V is for Victory,

W is for War, X is for what hens lay, Y is for Young, Z is for Zebra.

And besides, English had more letters in the alphabet than Gaelic, which obviously made it much better than a language that didn't even have X, which in English also meant that you loved someone, Alexina said. She was so lucky, having an x in her name!

Some of their names are still scratched on the old desks from decades ago, when the pen began to replace the plough. Everyone heard Mùgan calling, 'Here, Sandy,' and Alexander walked over to admire his initials from all those years ago. 'A.M.I.', Alexander MacInnes.

'I got six of the belt for carving that,' Sandy said. 'But it's lasted. I did a fine job of it. It was a good knife, though. A black Commando one my father brought back from the war.'

And others too spent time examining old scrawls and scratches, working out who made them and how many of them were still living and who was long dead though their names lived on. There had been so many wars.

The meeting was chaired by Sir Bert Morrison, who was Chairman of FlyAir. We knew him well because he sometimes stayed with us. It made him feel better. He could take his tie off and play with us and have a dram by the fire and feel normal. He arrived one evening at our door with MacPhee the councillor, who said that Sir Bert was looking for someone to take him out sea-fishing and that he couldn't think of anyone better able to do that than Dad. So he did, and while they were out fishing they got talking and Sir Bert told Dad how tired he was of travelling and staying in hotels and this turned to that, and when Dad mentioned that we had a wee closet room beneath the stairs Sir Bert said,

'Perfect. A cabin-bed. Just like my grampa had.'

So he stayed with us when he came on his airport visits. I thought he looked a wee bit like Bill the Badger, Rupert's friend from the Annuals, with his two bits of hair parted in the middle. Sir Bert smelt of strong after-shave as if he was trying to cover up his sweat, which we could always see on his forehead, though he never dabbed himself with a handkerchief as he ought. He just swept it away with the back of his hand. He always ate two boiled eggs for his breakfast, though he ate them a bit like a baby, taking them out of their shells and then mashing them along with butter on a fork and putting them on his toast and cut as soldiers.

He always washed his hands after eating, never before. Maybe it was his way of pretending he hadn't eaten so much. And he slurped his tea, like a wee boy. Dad always had bacon, sausages and fried eggs, Mam toast and porridge, while Duncan and Fearchar and I had cornflakes, which was the only cereal available at the time. Sir Bert always disapproved, saying we should be eating something healthy. As if he had any right to give advice, given his fat belly! And he always crossed his knife and fork when he was finished eating, which we all knew was bad luck.

But he seemed very important. Whenever he spoke to Mam or Dad he would lower his voice as if he was going to tell a secret or give some great revelation, which only turned out to be the most banal of things. That rain was forecast, or that he wouldn't be back that day till very late. Despite being jolly all the time, he always looked as if he dreaded something.

He had a badge on the night of the meeting in case anyone was in doubt that he was in charge. It said 'Sir Bert Morrison: Chairman FlyAir.'

'Which means it's an important meeting,' Mrs MacPherson whispered to me. 'If it was less important, James Campbell himself, or the local councillor, Michael MacPhee, would chair it.'

'Everything depends on how far up the monkey tree you go,' I heard him say to Lisa as they made preparations for the meeting. I looked around for the monkeys and unfortunately couldn't see any.

Sir Bert lived in Aberdeen, though his own people were originally from Skye, where he still had a holiday home. A little white cottage by the shore which would never lose value because of the splendid sea view and the developing market for rural hideaways. Though you needed money to live off the scenery. He'd learned that. He wished he could live there all the time, watching the tide rising and falling. But he had duties. Responsibilities. You can't be a child forever. Truth is, he didn't really want to stay there full time. It was fine for a holiday – as an aisling – but when winter came it would be all rain and wind and isolation, which was not good for a man of his age.

A lawyer by profession, Sir Bert had retired five years previously, and devoted his time since to good works, chairing a number of charitable companies, though his real passion was yachting. He had two boats. One at Findhorn for sailing round the Moray Firth and another on the Clyde for summer cruising over to Ireland and up the west coast.

When he stayed with us he often sat up late by the fire, sharing a dram with Dad and telling us things. He was a member of the local choral society and especially loved their annual rendition of *The Pirates of Penzance*. The highlight, he said, was always his one-verse comic solo of 'I Am the Very Model of a Modern Major-General', which he sang to us at the end of the barn the night before he left. He was also fond of poetry. Not the modern stuff. His favourite was Wordsworth. Truth is, he told us late one night when he was drunk, his knighthood only magnified his sense of failure. He'd thought about it. Maybe it went back to when he failed the Bursary Examination, which disappointed his father so much. 'You'll never succeed, because you don't know what you want,' his father had told him.

Every night when he went to bed he bent on his knees and we could hear him praying out loud like a child, 'Now I lay me down to sleep, I pray the Lord my soul to keep; Guide me safely through the night, And wake me with the morning light.' And we all whispered, 'Amen.' It's still my favourite prayer and I whisper it every night just before I go to sleep, trusting I will wake up in the morning.

Sir Bert was Chair because of his charm. He had learned to stoop slightly forwards all the time so that it looked as if he was always gracefully bowing to you and paying attention. Fearchar said he looked like Big Uggy in 'The Topper'. His job with FlyAir was more or less a decoration, just like his gold pocket-watch. Though every time he looked at it, it had none of the glory of the little toy wristwatch his girlfriend Jean gave him for his seventh birthday all those years ago.

'A picture of a plane on the green flower-covered machair is worth more than any accountant can price,' he said one night as he took his bedtime toddy.

He arrived at the school early and shook hands with everyone at the door. He also had enough Gaelic, which he'd practiced in our house, to welcome everyone with 'Feasgar math' (Good evening), which they all recognised as a gesture, but a nice one nevertheless. He had not forgotten what he had been as a child, once upon a time. He wanted to make a good speech, for he feared mediocrity – maybe feared the thing he had become. Maybe I was lucky in that I always knew I wanted to be a nurse. Like having the second sight, nothing then disappointed me.

He told Dad that as a young man he had noble ambitions – he laughed at that strange, old-fashioned word – to be a Parliamentarian, but life had got in the way and by the time he was ready to throw his hat into the ring he was too well known as a businessman to attach himself to any other party than the Conservatives who already had a life-long Parliamentarian in his constituency, and his family commitments prevented him from bidding for a safe seat elsewhere. He could as easily have stood for the Liberal Party, except that they too had a local farmer in the seat for life, and he wasn't interested in carpet-bagging somewhere else. Sir Bert lacked the courage. He liked his whisky and talked a lot as he sat by the fire. Talked about himself as if he was telling an old, familiar story, like Dad.

The community meeting was held in the big room, where primaries five, six and seven met during the day. World maps and charts adorned the walls. In 55 BC Julius Caesar invaded Britain and in 1934 *The Flying Scotsman* became the first steam locomotive to reach 100 miles per hour! I saw Old Murdo and Niall Cuagach looking up at the maps and charts, like little children back in school. The maps were bright and beautiful, with every country marked a different shade of colour in perfect order. Canada was big and yellow. Africa was all kinds of colours, as if they were allowed to use every crayon and pencil in the cupboard while the Arctic and the Antarctic were glittering white with dazzling flags on both poles.

'That orange bit used to be British Somaliland,' said Niall. 'And the inkwells have all gone.'

'I always wanted to go there when I was at school, but by the time I got there it was Somalia,' said Murdo, puffing his clay-pipe. 'Many's the time I sailed into Berbera. Trucks and cigarettes in, goats and spices out.'

'And that bit there was Tanganyika.'

'Tanzania.'

'The colours are different too.'

'They're not like that in real life, though. The grass in New Zealand is green like here. And in Africa. A sort of light green, like boat paint when it dries. I could have stayed on in New Zealand. Maybe should have. And did I tell you of that time just off the east coast of Africa when…'

Sir Bert called the meeting to order. He looked at that moment like a man who came from the mainland to tell us something important – had a brown folder in one hand and a lovely gold pen in the other, and was wearing fine brown brogues and a tweed jacket and a lovely blue tie. We were out of the house playing so hadn't seen him leaving the house all dressed up. He had a good corporation, as Mam called a big fat tummy. He was well looked after. He'd be too old to have a Mammy, I thought, so it must be his wife. Bets he was clever, though, and knew more about everything than anyone else in the room. He must, because after all he wouldn't be a Sir for nothing. I'd read all about Sir Walter Raleigh and Sir Walter Scott and Sir Galahad in the schoolbook and they were knighted because they were clever and brave and daring and had conquered things. Sir Bert stood up and shook the Schoolmaster's bell, which brought a quick silence as if everyone was back in Primary One. If things had turned out differently he would have been conducting an orchestra in Berlin.

Duncan and Fearchar and I sat on stools with all the other children to the side. Dolina wasn't there. She had the mumps. Mrs MacPherson perched herself on a small chair amongst us. Niall Cuagach and Old Murdo sat at the back near the door. Mam and Dad sat in the middle beside our immediate neighbours. When I see Ingrid Bergman and Lauren Bacall and all the others settling into their carriage seats on the Orient Express, I always think it's the same thing! Something good about to start. Lisa had a wee table at the side near the front where she sat by herself, writing. Because she was the official secretary and had to note down everything that was said. She told me it was called minutes, though it had nothing to do with clocks or time. Though there was a big clock up on the wall that ticked so loudly we could still hear it above all the speeches.

We just knew who everyone was, because they were someone's Mam or Dad or Grampa or Granny or neighbour, though we didn't really know them to speak to. Sometimes that was just as well, because it was better not to know what some people said and thought. The MacGregors, for example, who didn't speak to our family for some unknown reason. I think it had to do with a cow or a bull a long time ago.

The local councillor, Michael MacPhee, was at the front beside Sir Bert, with James Campbell on the other side. Campbell was tapping his pencil impatiently, as if he hated the lack of urgency in everything and things taking so long, which must have meant he wanted the thing over and done with as quickly as possible because when Dolina and Hazel and Katie and I played our games we wanted what we were doing to go on and on and last forever. Councillor MacPhee was wearing his smart woollen blazer with the perfect triangle of a white embroidered handkerchief in his top pocket like a flag. He must never have used it to wipe his nose for it was always clean and never moved from its position. All the boys in my class just wiped their noses with the sleeves of their jackets. You could see the wet sticky patches all the way up to their elbows when the sun shone.

I saw the schoolmaster's son, Alex, sitting in the corner at the registration desk. He had a small square machine in front of him which he told us later was a cassette recorder his Dad had been given by the education authority. He was that kind of boy: recorded everything he could, from the sound of the boat arriving at the pier to boring old meetings and concerts, simply because he wanted to know how the machine worked and what it was capable of. Just as well he did. They're now online and such a precious resource. Rubbish as the recordings are, with lots of noises and hisses and breaks, it's amazing to hear Mùgan's sing-song voice emerging out of time. He speaks ever so slowly, and sometimes still when I can't get to sleep I play the archive on my phone and within minutes I'm asleep, his long slumbrous speech like the last wave settling onto the distant shore as night falls.

Listening back to these old recordings always reminds me how things that seemed so important at the time now seem negligible. Like when the wind rose on a winter's night and we feared the roof would come off the house, but in the morning all was quiet and as before except for the old gate which was off its hinge and repaired before dinner time. Perhaps, after all, Niall Cuagach was right and it's a holy thing to choose to stay silent. Then when you raise your voice it's a surprise, like hearing the fairies sing.

I noticed Sir Bert spoke differently in public than he did in private in our house, as if speaking publicly was more important. He would have been taught that at school just like we were. Or maybe he was a coward, just like Arthur MacT, who always lisped when he spoke with the teacher, because he was afraid of him. He never lisped when he was outside, playing. Sir Bert's accent was like an ocean wave, with every sentence starting softly then finishing with a flourish. What he said didn't matter as much as how he said it.

'Good evening and welcome, ladies and gentlemen,' with the emphasis ever so slightly on the last word so that the men felt better already.

Old Murdo put his shoulders back, for it was lovely to be called a gentleman. And then Sir Bert paused, looking towards us children and said,

'And boys and girls.'

Like Old Murdo, we also were delighted to be publicly acknowledged. Though Katie stuck her tongue at me, meaning at him. Mrs MacPherson wrote down two words,

'Good manners.'

We were taught never to ask for things, because giving something without being asked for it was the highest grace. Things were always spoilt if they had to be asked for. For instance, it would have been so wrong to go into someone's house and ask for a cup of tea or scone. Mam would have been mortified if anyone had to ask for anything. Sir Bert also seemed to know that, for he didn't ask for anything, just explained how good things would be once we had an airport and we could come and go when we pleased. We could fly out to Glasgow in the morning and go shopping or visit friends and relatives for the day and be back home by the fire for the evening. And the daily papers, with all the news, would arrive first thing every morning without having to wait for some storm-bound ferry.

It's fascinating listening to Sir Bert now, across the crackly decades. He spoke as if everyone believed the same thing, which would become self-evident as he spoke. All he could do was to re-assure the ones who would vote for the development anyway that they were in the right all along; the trick was not to pointlessly upset the others, who would vote against it no matter what he said. No one should be made to feel that they had lost. We sometimes did that when playing games at school and needed full teams but didn't want to upset those who didn't want to play, so we'd change the rules a wee bit to include them, knowing we'd still win, and then everyone was happy. It was like a wee game of hopscotch, jumping over the lines, for none of it mattered much in the end except the fun you had hopping from here to there as if your life depended on it. It's best done on one leg, the fun being in trying not to touch the chalk with the other.

Even I could work out on the evening itself that what he was saying and what folk were hearing were two different things. Like when Dolina or Katie said the same thing to me it always had one meaning coming from Dolina and another from Katie. When Dolly said 'Let's play' it meant have fun together whereas when Katie said it, it meant 'Let's see who's best.'

Duncan listened to the early speeches, and Fearchar and I and Katie and Morag and the other children didn't. They were a background noise while we played, for Mrs MacPherson gave us crayons and pencils and plain paper and colouring and puzzle books, so we drew and fathomed our own world. I was inside a maze for ages where I had to lead a kitten back to her mother. The kitten was called Kitty. My first efforts all ended in a cul-de-sac at the back of a tall hedge, and I had to cheat to get Kitty out of the maze. Mrs MacPherson was also wise enough to have given everyone rubbers so we could play and then replay the game until we finally got it right. After I got the kitten safely through the maze I also sat back and listened. Sir Bert had finished his long introduction. Soutar the Factor then told everyone that this was the opportunity of a lifetime. As if anyone would pay attention to him anyway. Always speaking for himself.

I suddenly realised that everything was unique and inevitable. This meeting at this school with these people and these men speechifying and objecting and rambling and us children colouring-in in the corner and the women adjusting their hats and bras and corsets and the vote and the way the plan would go ahead and not matter that much in the end because what really counted was that everyone would then go home and stoke up their fires and have tea and toast together. And for me what really counted was being best pals with Dolina and making the longest daisy-chain in the whole world with her and playing football now and then with Duncan and Fearchar and eating toast and pilchards with Mam and Dad and I think that's when I truly decided to be a nurse and help people through it all despite, or maybe even because of, all the speeches. Fozy was the only women that spoke, nervously twining her fingers as she did so. That's how you always know if someone is telling the truth. They're not too sure of themselves.

We could see that MacPhee feared the way the wind was blowing, so he proposed a show of hands. You couldn't be in two minds.

'All those in favour of developing the airport?'

'It should be a secret ballot,' Niall Cuagach called out. 'Like going to Confession. It needs to be a private thing.'

Everyone looked at him with surprise and disdain. How dare he mix up this stuff with the sacred? They were two completely different things. Sir Bert was quick to see the possible danger.

'The gentleman is correct,' he said. 'It ought to be a secret vote, as when we're electing members of Parliament. It's of the same stature and requires the same dignity. We'll therefore hand out sheets of paper and if you'd like this development to happen simply write Yes on the paper, and if you're against it simply write No. And because the future belongs to them, I propose we give all the young people who are here tonight, whatever their age, a vote as well. After all, they've bothered to come out to listen to us.'

He knew that the young would all vote for an airport because the future belonged to them. He smiled, looking at Old Murdo. 'There's no upper age limit either, for we all know, don't we, that with great age comes great wisdom.'

'Doesn't matter anyway,' Old Murdo said. 'Whichever way you vote, you'll regret it.'

Duncan wrote Yes, so because Fearchar saw that he wrote No. I wrote No because I knew Mam and Dad would write No, but mostly because Mrs MacPherson, who was sitting right next to me, wrote No with a silver fountain-pen. Mrs MacPherson had beautiful handwriting, starting the N down at the bottom left, then an elegant thin line upwards, a short line at the top, a lovely diagonal line across the paper, up once more and another across. And the 'O' Mrs MacPherson drew was the most beautiful thing in the whole world, drawn in one perfect loop anti-clockwise with the left curve of the letter marginally fatter than the other side. If I could learn to write like that anything could happen.

'Will you teach me to write good too?' I whispered to her as I wrote my own squiggly No. Later in school I was taught how to write 'properly', though none of it was as lovely and elegant as Mrs MacPherson's. I thought letters should be any shape they wanted to be but Mr Matheson insisted that they had to be the way he said. A needed to be just like that, even though I thought it was much more interesting and much more fun to put it on its side ▷ or upside down ∀ or even like the way other languages I'd seen in the *National Geographic* had it with double dots and lines over it, but he got very cross and told me just to behave myself and write as I was told.

'There are two spoiled votes,' James Campbell announced once he and Councillor MacPhee had counted the papers. Someone had written Chan eil, which was outwith the clear instructions, though no one confessed or argued, and Old Murdo's vote was also discounted because he just put an X where Yes or No should have been.

'That was me,' he announced when the mistake was pointed out. 'And it wasn't a mistake but a choice. For why write when you can remember? Make of that what you will.'

Not that it made any difference, for the majority voted Yes.

'Fifty-one for, twenty-nine against, and two uncounted spoiled votes. So that's 63 per cent "Yes" and 37 per cent "No" of all the votes cast. Thank you everyone for coming out and making your views and your voices heard. Oidhche mhath,' announced Sir Bert, to polite applause. There's nothing more dispiriting than polite applause. Roddy MacTavish, who'd spent his life as a butcher in Oban, passed us on the way out, muttering, 'If God had meant us to fly surely he'd have given us wings?'

Daft so-and-so!

15

After

DAD HAD BINOCULARS and through them we could see forever. Or at least as far north as Àrdglas. He'd bought them from the chief engineer on the fisheries vessel, and once we fine-focused the lens we could see things in wonderful detail. Dots far out at sea became sailors scrubbing decks on finely-decked ships, and a hint of silver in the air was a beautifully feathered eagle hovering over Loch nan Dubhaich. On clear starry nights we could see lights blinking far out west, which Duncan said were big lorries in New York.

Niall Cuagach stood in the doorway of his shack halfway up the hill. A button had just come loose from the top notch of his trousers. When he stood, he held them up with one hand. He ate breakfast with the other. He fixed the button before he ventured out. He yanked the top button from his shirt and tied it with a safety pin to his trousers. It would do. Outside he stood urinating, his back to us and to the wind. Tied the safety pin back on again. Strange how buttons were always perfectly round and never here and there like the stones and rocks and fields. What if his thoughts were more real than all these solid things?

On quiet nights, such as the night before, he could hear the fishermen talk down at the slipway miles away. Herring and ring-nets. The fishing banks were called Cuile-Mhoire (Mary's Treasure) because they were filled with the fruits of prayer. For no mother will ever refuse the good pleas of her children. He missed his mother. She used to tie his bootlaces with a double-knot in the shape of a flower when he was small. The Seven Sisters had not yet appeared. When they did he could go out fishing in deeper waters. The seas knew everything. They knew the future, just like the stars. He thought of how James and John had left their father's boat to follow Him. Maybe he had done the same, turning his back on the world. Even if he didn't have much choice.

The island was spread out before him. Sometimes he felt the place wouldn't survive if he wasn't there. No one was up and about yet. Just fields and tracks and lochs. Houses and the school and the church. More water than land really. Bits of white and red on the machair. The fields beginning to turn green. It was like looking at the old world map on the Primary One side of the room. An old, brave landscape, empty of trees and shelter. The sea grey to the west. The world must have been created on a morning like this.

Nobody had yet spoiled the day. The houses scattered into villages from south to north. He always scanned them that way, clockwise. Otherwise everything would be arse-to-elbow and nothing worked out because of the disorder. You have to name things, otherwise they don't exist. There's The Loch of the White Swan. And the Red River. And The Hill of Plenty. And there's Janet's old house. And the sheep-fank where Angus MacIntosh broke his leg. Unless you named a thing it could become anything. Donald MacLean had a dog he didn't name and it behaved like a duck, forever wandering about with the ducks in dirty puddles and quacking instead of barking because he hadn't been called anything from the moment he was born.

All the old houses faced east towards the rising sun, though all the new ones had discarded that old convention and faced every which way. No wonder folk were drinking too much. People had improved themselves. The original blackhouses in ruins, and the newer white houses a few yards from them now inhabited by hens and machinery, and the brand-new Department of Agriculture bungalows where the people were still sleeping shining in the morning sun. As if the cockerels hadn't woken the whole world hours ago. Folk are stupid. Replacing those round walls which ease the wind round them with square ones which face it full on. No surprise that everything is going to ruin.

There were 140 houses in five villages. Linsiadair, Slagan, Druim Sgairbh, Kilaird and Àrdglas, where the world began. 450 people altogether. Though some are away working and at college. Cuagach knows where they all are. There's the school in Linsiadair, and the church in Slagan, and the shop in Druim Sgairbh. It's simple. The place created the people, and the people created the place. It's good to have the world in order, neat and tidy, like things on a bench, so that when you stretch out your hand you'll find the object you're looking for. A Bible here and a clay-pipe there and the small hammer and a packet of nails and some tobacco and buttons in the silver-plated tin box beside it. Whenever we visited Niall, Mam told us not to touch anything in case it meant having to re-assemble the whole house. Because that's what happened when Dad once moved Cuagach's herring-pail from one side of the door to the other.

He stands there. The old airstrip lies between Kilaird and Àrdglas. Àrdglas has the fishing pier and the ferry pier, where emigrants departed and drovers arrived. His people were from there as far back as memory and records go. Some families are good at fishing, others at farming. That's just how it is, learned over the generations, and you crossed from one to the other at your peril. It took time. Boundaries were there for a reason. How else would you account for anything?

If you were a fisherman you fished, and if you were a teacher you taught. That large stone that divides Linsiadair from Slagan. They say Coinneach Mòr put it there in the first decade of the twelfth century and it hasn't moved an inch since then. He is glad he was born at the end of the earth. It's not a wild frontier any more though. The crofts are now carefully marked out, as if God's earth could be parcelled and divided up that easily and belong to individual people. There was no knowing where things began or ended, unless you'd listened and watched and learned over the years. Even then you couldn't be sure. Without God, the borders would vanish, the same way his crops rotted when left unharvested.

The day was moist and warm. Cuagach watched Ruairidh and

the sons of Coinneach getting their boats ready for the lobsters. Not even a wisp of tea-smoke rising from Seonaidh MacIntosh's chimney. The lazy bastard, still lying in bed. There's nothing more selfish than sleeping on after the sun has risen. What if the sun did that? If it couldn't be arsed getting up, leaving us in a perpetual winter? No wonder MacIntosh's fields are full of thorns and thistles. He gets the same sun and rain and wind as everyone else, yet he produces bugger all. Scratches at the earth rather than digging it. Unlike everyone else who's under an obligation to do their best. One of those fools who expect things to be better tomorrow than they are today for no other reason than that time has passed. When all that's required is just to get on with things. However dreich things might look, mushrooms still grow out of cowpats. You find treasures in the most unexpected places. Cuagach thought it would have been good to be a Viking. To be rude and wild and fearless. To be a conqueror. Kill people if they were in your way. And admired for it, because that was the way of it.

There's nothing like cultivated soil to show the quality of a people, Cuagach always said. The shoreline to the south and west has eroded forty yards since he was a child. He remembers marram grass where there is now only sand. He's glad he lives up on the hill, though he knows fine that one stormy day the tides will also reach where he stands. Maybe when he's gone, because things take a while, then they happen all of a sudden. The seven geese that have spent the past two months on Loch Fada are heading north to Iceland. As they should. By rights they should probably have gone last week. Cattle are beginning to munch their way east towards the moor. Specks of dust float in the air. It couldn't be otherwise. Donald John is on his boat on the sea, so he can't be elsewhere. It's impossible to be in two places at once, even though you can imagine it.

There's nothing like a beginning, Niall thinks. It's the purest thing in the world. The land is being worked, which is good. To work the land is to praise God. A few folk are now down on the machair, inspecting the fields and ditches. Though they are miles away, and mere specks on the horizon, he recognises each one of them by their little movements. They do the same things day after day. That fat round blob is Effie off to collect the public mail from the box at the road-end. She'll then put the kettle on, of course. The thin line down by the river is Dickie Campbell, checking his net. It's land that always needs to be worked to prevent it from reverting to nothing, but if you do it slowly and steadily you finally get there. You can't do it quickly, overnight, or even over a lifetime. It takes generations to form those ridges and ditches and fields. To shape the land. Landlords used to rule. Now everyone does. And things are so strange. Tourists are now coming round with cameras taking pictures of the land, as if it's something to admire rather than something to grow potatoes on.

He could have stood there forever, making the world. Putting bits together. Seonaidh's stone wall could be extended north and connected to the fank-end so that the whole thing would run together properly as one. Everything seems bigger than itself. Heaven and earth are his witness. Each year, in February, he works out what the land can bear. If the primroses are out by the stream by St Bride's Day all will be well.

Cuagach grows his own stuff. While others go to the shops and buy tins and tasteless bread in coloured paper, he makes everything himself. The cows give him milk and he makes crowdie and cheese and cream. And when it's time he butchers them himself and has his fill of beef. As a child, he noticed that all the animals always drift to the left when you leave them on their own to cross a field, so he has placed his gates to the right. One at the top of the field and one at the bottom. It's theirs to choose, for not everything is fate. There's freedom too. He also knows that they always graze and rest facing the same way, south to north and north to south, never east and west. He likes how their coats shine and glisten when they wade through the river on the way home every evening after grazing high up on the heather.

He kills sheep in the winter to keep him going, salting the meat in barrels. Good mutton, which makes the best of soups when salted. He'd bring us cuts now and again. In springtime into summer it's lamb, and in between, venison from the deer he hunts on the far side of the hill. He has a gun and shoots cormorants and shags and geese and wild ducks. Sea-birds are most easily caught when the weather is tempestuous and rough. He grows potatoes and onions and turnips and cabbages. He has a small rowing boat over at Bàgh a' Bhile where he catches mackerel and plaice and herring and haddock in a net. He does it quietly, because noise kills fish and he wants them fresh and new. He makes small crosses out of the fish bones to bless his daily bread.

He built his own shack, crafted from wood from the shore and odds and ends gathered here and there. It has a tin roof and when he lies in bed at night he sings at the top of his voice, the rattle of the rain on the roof giving him the rhythm. Everyone hears him though no one joins in, except sometimes I hum along. He's never alone because he can hear the sea in the distance, forever coming and going. In the mornings, he smells the cattle manure steaming fresh at the end of the stone byre while listening to the sweet song of the skylark's ascension. If he hears the cuckoo calling once in May he is content, for he knows then he will live another year. Though he never counts the number of calls it makes, for that predicts the exact number of years he has left to live. It's better not to know. That's why Adam and Eve should never have eaten that red apple. Little wonder they turned into eagles, living down Galway way.

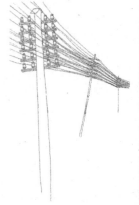

He has eyes like a hawk, not needing any binoculars. Mùgan is already hanging out the washing. Mrs MacPherson is waiting by the old byre for the daily bus which will arrive in ten minutes. The careless MacFarlanes are letting the liquid manure go to waste when it should be enriching the soil. That's what all these people do. Always. Every day. The telegraph poles are arriving from the north where the power station has been built. They stretch all the way south, connecting every house except his and ours to the outside world. Everything leans towards the south, away from the harsh light of the north. Though he doesn't really have a house as such. Just a place of abode. A hut, some call it. A bothy. A shack. His refuge. Home.

He had a variety of saws and wanted to cut the poles down, but they looked tough and creosoted. The best saw he had was the large one which needed two people to work it, one at either end. Maybe Dad would do it with him, though he doubted it. He'd be afraid. Wouldn't want to go to prison and shame himself and the family. Would say it was pointless. A fruitless gesture. And dangerous. Though the poles were only wood and as long as he kept clear of the wires he'd be fine.

Niall Cuagach was the man who wrote Chan eil on the paper. It meant No. Though it's not exactly the word for no – it's more the rejection of what is being proposed. As when someone asked him, 'Are you cold, Niall?' he replied, 'I am not.'

So it was really quite a positive no. A statement that he was what he was not, or that he was not what he was. He told me that, and so much more, when I nursed him years later.

He taught himself to read and write, so no one instructed him how to read things, or what they meant. When he read a sentence such as 'I am going to the zoo' in a book, what he understood from it was that he, Niall Cuagach, was going to the zoo. And he argued with the text, saying that he was not. He learned to read first in Gaelic, from an old Bible he found in a trunk, and discovered that as soon as he could read in Gaelic, he could also read in English. So he thought that reading had nothing to do with language but with the ability to see letters together. He knew they weren't letters, just symbols – things that stand for other things, like when he wanted to go to sleep he thought of a bed and off he went into it. He had to see things before he could name them, for if he couldn't name them how could he then find them?

The trick was to see that everything was connected and that a word like 'zoo' had no meaning until he gave it meaning by putting animals inside it. It was just like looking out to sea where he could see everything all at once – the water as well as the waves, the flying gulls as well as the boats. None would exist without the other. Which is why he was not alone. His favourite book was *The Rights of Man*, which he found at a jumble sale at church. He liked the swing of the words in the tattered copy he had, because they connected meaning to facts. Though the previous owner had put lines through the word Rights and replaced it with Responsibilities. Just because he was on his own didn't mean he didn't have anyone to talk to. We could hear him on quiet nights reading out loud.

The morning after the meeting, Niall Cuagach stood looking down towards the small clump of trees where the airport would be. Old pines which had somehow miraculously survived the Vikings, the weather and the sheep. It would be a pity to use them as logs, though sometimes needs must. No. He'd use them to replace the roof beams on his shack and add another shed. A shed is always useful, for there's no end to the things one collects. Ropes and carts and ploughs and saws and buoys and shears and all kinds of useful and strange objects that the tide brought in daily. You never knew when another glass bottle or a wine cork would come in handy. There were so many things to put in bottles, from sheep-dip to iodine. And they were really handy for peeing into on wild winter nights when it was dangerous to go outside. The wine corks were just perfect for filling in those little crevices which always appeared between the stones as perfect avenues for the wind. Only thing was that once he filled one hole another appeared elsewhere, as if the wind was playing Tig with the stones as willing accomplices. He used to play that at school.

He spent half his life protecting himself from the elements. Enduring another winter was always an achievement, as good as escaping from an enemy. He could endure anything as long as folk didn't call round to give him advice. You needed to eat a lot of fish and mutton and potatoes and cabbages to survive. Some folk were always deceived, believing that winter was worn out when the first sign of spring came, forgetting that it hung in there even when the sun was shining and the buds were beginning to flower. You had to test promises. You couldn't just trust them. The light never failed him though. There was morning and afternoon and evening and night with their separate jobs and duties. Feeding things in the morning, moving them in the afternoon, settling them in the evening, resting them during the night. Success is always quiet. And steady.

In many ways Niall Cuagach had the least, and most, to lose. The least because he lived furthest from the airstrip, but most because it would be something else to take into account in his pre-ordained world. A familiar thing would be suddenly changed. Fields and ditches and culverts and land which had taken centuries to shape and mould would be altered overnight. It was unseemly. It's not that he was afraid of new sights and sounds: every day and night he saw and heard new things. But these were things of nature, beyond his control. He congratulated the sun for rising differently every morning. In summer, exactly over the highest ridge of the mountain, then an inch further to the south every day until midwinter found it rising over the bay, before it worked its way back to the beginning again. The sun knew what it had to do. Which bits of the land to warm up and which bits to shade. When to glow gently and when to burn. When to hide behind the clouds or to cheer the whole world up by shining clear and bright. Then the crops grew well under the steady breeze while the cattle lay down in the shade of the few trees.

Sometimes it was white, sometimes red, sometimes invisible. Cirrus clouds to the north-west were always a favourable omen. And sounds also changed by the moment, every day. The night before, it was a soft thing flapping in the wind. He went out and searched and found an empty carton of paper caught in a wedge in a rock, blowing in the gale. It was when he lay in bed in a gale that he missed his mother most. This morning it was the cry of an infant in Linsiadair. Effie MacDougall had been expecting.

He liked going to church because the same words and prayers were repeated every week without error. And yet they were always new, because the priest's voice varied from Sunday to Sunday. Sometimes you knew he had spent time with God because his steady voice breathed peace and calm; sometimes it rasped with concern; sometimes it choked up and was nasal, simply because the priest had a cold. That didn't matter. He was only a servant too, ploughing as best he could.

Niall Cuagach also went out of his way to sit in a different place every Sunday. He considered it strange that others sat in the same place week in week out. Some even climbed over people to get to their historic spot, or shoved the person who was sitting in their usual place along the pew. Everything has its time and place and shape. In church he sat behind Bald Donald whose shining head would now be spoilt if a wisp of hair suddenly appeared. That was not the kind of miracle that was useful. A shepherd and a lamb shone in the stained-glass window above the altar, and that too would be spoilt if the artist had drawn a rabbit instead of a lamb.

For things have a specific form, and if that alters they go out of shape and become something else and the world goes all wrong. Niall Cuagach knew that when he gets to heaven everything will be as it ought to be, for to have a heavenly body is to have a heavenly mind. Who then will remember that Niall Cuagach lived here as an isolated cripple, scoffed at, in this remote shack, once upon a time which will be no more? Until then, he would measure things right, for to measure them wrong is to endanger heaven itself.

The thing was, Niall Cuagach knew his ancient rights. The field where the airport was to be built encroached his ancient grazing rights. As he knelt in church he made his decision. He would put seven cows there, because that's the right number for that size of field. More and they wouldn't get proper grazing, less would be to overfeed the blessèd beasts.

16

The Den

WE ALL HAD a den we shared. Some, like Katie, and Alex the schoolmaster's son, were lucky enough to have their own, in corners of disused byres or in rickety self-made constructions behind stone walls, but the one we all shared was a new development. It was situated in the ruined castle that was abandoned after a fire centuries ago. We played in what had once been Magnus Barefoot's lair, making it our own. Folk said it was haunted, but Duncan and Fearchar and I and most of the other children knew that was just said to frighten us and keep us away from harm. Still, we realised it was dangerous, with crumbling walls and tumbling staircases and falling masonry, which made it all the more exciting. Especially because we could see each other getting scared and frightened. Having your own den is fine, but what's the point unless the fun and danger is shared?

The main den was down the stairs in the old cellar. It must have been the laird's wine cellar, for a few empty bottles still lay about the place, though Duncan heard that's just where Hector MacRae used to drink before he sobered up and became a minister. They say he used to heal the sick after that by kneeling at their bedsides praying and fanning their faces with the leaves of the Gaelic Bible until they rose healed and praising God.

Duncan discovered the den. Or at least he was the first to go in there, haunted and abandoned as it was. He skived off school one Friday afternoon and headed down towards the ruin. There were no other places to hide. Everywhere was so open and flat, and unless you wore an invisible cloak or until you were inside the old castle ramparts you could be seen by every old nosy biddy peeping from behind their lace curtains in the surrounding villages. That was the whole purpose of the place as an ancient fortress: a stronghold from which you could see everywhere all around, knowing friend from foe on the horizon. Once inside, you were as invisible and as powerful as any ghost. You could only be imagined and feared then.

The castle lies across a marsh, but Duncan had seen MacRae weaving his way unsteadily over there, down by the loch across the warning stones which were half-hidden under the water. They seemed solid enough, but every step was shoogly, the stones constantly moving beneath him. The nearer he came to the ruins the more frightened he became. No wonder MacRae needed drink to strengthen him. Duncan tried not to listen, but he heard noises and voices, some low and soft, some loud and hissing, and was about to turn back when the owls and pigeons and bats all fled from their haven, terrified by his arrival.

The place was covered in bird-droppings, which didn't bother him much. Like humans, they have to live. Two broken stairways led to the upper floor where there was nothing now but empty air. Downstairs was bigger and darker, with three rectangular openings on each wall. He could see all around him through the openings. North, east, south and west. Perfect for seeing enemies approaching. Firing at them with stones and arrows and bombs and guns and cannons and mud and insults. And it had a roof, so we'd be dry when it rained.

Odd that no one had dared before. As far as he knew. But here he was, king of the castle. No – much, much more than that: King of The Castle. He will clean it up. His slaves and servants will do that for him. Fearchar and I, for example. Upstairs will be his look-out point where he'll put his soldiers on guard. The bravest will manage up the rickety steps or they won't qualify to be in his army. His friend John, now Major Sgliugan, will lead the troops. Or maybe he will keep the castle and all its powers to himself. For the best way for his peasants to respect power is for them to have none. No. It will be much better for them all to share it, under his command. It will be more fun. For rulers need subjects. We were still to learn that our weaknesses and our stupidity were greater than our powers and our wisdom, and made us better people.

It took a while for him to mention it to us. We were all playing outside one night when he said,

'Know what, Fearchar?'

'What?'

'Know what, Annie?'

'What?'

'I went.'

'Where?' Fearchar said.

'Promise to keep a secret. Or else.'

'Or else what?'

'Or else this.'

He slammed a fist into the palm of his hand.

'Promise.'

'To the castle.'

'That ruin?'

'It's haunted.'

'See any ghosts then?'

'No. I scared them away.'

Silence.

'What's it like?'

'Amazing,' Duncan said. 'Will make a great den.'

'Who for?'

'Me. You and me. You and me and others.'

'Others?'

'Aye, others.'

'Such as.'

'Such as... well, we can work that out. You can be in charge of that, Fearchar.'

'Really?'

'Really.'

'I'll need to see it first, to see how many folk can live in the castle.'

'All right. We'll do that tomorrow. After school.'

And we did.

'It's dirty,' Fearchar said.

'Well, that's why we need servants. They can do that work. It will be a condition of membership of the clan. Of membership of the den.'

Brushes and spades were gathered and servants signed up. Within weeks it was clean enough for a king, even though some of the evicted owls and bats and birds still hung about unwilling to leave their homes, for they too have a long memory. Some found new, quieter nests elsewhere, and the ones who stayed seemed to realise that they had new tenants and tolerated us. The owls sat in the eaves where no one could touch them and the sparrows in the high ivy crevices beyond human habitation. Some things are outwith even the reaches of kings.

Duncan made a throne of stones which he placed in the centre of the room, and anyone who entered had to bow when they came in. Fearchar and John got hold of two long sticks and stood at the entrance guarding the king's castle.

'Treat every stranger with suspicion,' Duncan told them. 'Everyone is a potential enemy.'

Dolina was the chief cook, making splendid stews out of marram grass and cowslips and seaweed and worms, while I negotiated myself into the position of Queen, reigning in Duncan's absence when he went off to war.

'Every castle needs a Queen,' I argued.

The battles were ferocious and always triumphant, though with some casualties. We spoke in bubbles, for all you would hear was 'Injuns! 'Aaaargh!' 'Eeeek!' 'Achtung!' and 'Gott in Himmel!' as we screeched and fell. I don't suppose these words ever appear now, do they? When we were (supposedly) hit, some always fell long and slow in agony, and others dropped quickly like stones. I always fell quickly, to get it over with! And I don't know if you ever use bows and arrows nowadays, but the right way to use a bow and arrow was always to put the arrow next to your ear so that it would fly straight. You knew from the ping in your ear whether it was any good. If it was all soft and gooey it was a useless shot and wouldn't kill anyone. We knew the sound of these things from hunting rabbits and cormorants with Dad, so it was easy to pretend. You did it quietly so that the rabbit and bird wouldn't hear, and the next thing they fell where they were. We made a stretcher out of old blankets and spent hours carrying the battle-scarred back from the muddy field.

Duncan himself invariably led the charge, always routing the enemy, only to be wounded by a stray arrow or by a fragment of shell or bullet at the last moment. He'd lie there writhing and moaning and dying while his devoted soldiers pleaded with him to live, for they couldn't survive without him. They then carried him on the stretcher back to the castle where they washed his wounds with water and dabbed him with comfrey root and gave him juice to drink and soon he was restored back to his rightful place on the throne. He thanked them all for their courage and service, and made a big speech.

'If the soldiers are cowards, it does not matter how big or small the army is. Same when it comes to courage,' he proclaimed from the window of the castle. 'The brave will always triumph, even though they die.'

'All for one and one for all,' we all shouted together, and one of the soldiers – usually Fatty Morrison because he acted as a sort of king's guard – then called,

'Three Hurrahs for the King! Hip-hip!'
'Hurrah!'
'Hip-hip!'
'Hurrah!'
'Hip-hip!'
'Hurrah!'

'We need better communications,' Duncan announced one day. 'Though this is an old castle, we must deal with modern times. With modern warfare and methods. So to defeat the enemy we need up-to-date communications. Not just spies and guards and look-outs on the ramparts and swords and shields and bows and guns on the field but agents out there in the bogs and swamps and trenches who can tell us what people are planning. We need to infiltrate their homes and steadings and towns and cities. Who's with me?'

All hands went up.

This was not a sudden idea. Duncan had been planning it for some time. He knew that an enemy doesn't just attack on the spur of the moment. Ideas were just the same as his bootlaces, a matter of tying things together. An enemy thinks about it. Plans. Has a strategy. The secret is to know what they're thinking so that you can imagine against it. It's a two-way process. You need to be both here and there: making your own plans, but also aware of what the other side is doing. We weren't imagining anything. Only re-enacting what we'd seen in the comics. It's what Braddock did. Going round in circles, pretending.

Duncan was actually thinking about electricity, and that man Johnston. The swish car he had, and all the fancy shining dials inside it. It was fast, like electricity itself, where everything happens at once. Because I was Queen he talked to me about the long line of telegraph poles and the power they carried. It obviously worked like everything else – there was a source of power somewhere, which was then transmitted along the wires to those who used it. Except it didn't take any time at all to get from A to Z. Electricity didn't flow like a river, it moved instantly and was everywhere at once. Just as he could be, as king. When he sat on the throne he had power and the orders he gave were executed. Instantly. Or else.

Though he also knew it wasn't as simple as that, for sometimes we refused to do what he told us, because it was too dangerous or we didn't like it. Even though he made up all the rules, they still had to be obeyed or they'd be useless. He had to judge what we'd enjoy doing, or it wouldn't happen. It must have been quite a burden, working out our limits. Maybe even worse than being a servant. He tried to bully, but it didn't work. We just said we'd all go home and not play anymore. To be fair to him, he asked my advice.

'You can't be a king without any people,' I told him.

Someone needs to say the difficult thing.

What he really feared was being replaced. That one of us would usurp him and become king of the castle instead. So he made sure there were rewards, and that everyone felt part of the uneven game. For he knew it was uneven. Tyrants always do. Fearchar complained one day.

'So how come you're always king of the castle?'

''Cos I found it. And I'm oldest.'

'No, you didn't find it. It was always here. Been here for hundreds and thousands of years.'

'So? What difference does that make, idiot? No one was using it, were they? I was first to come here and make it a castle for us. I discovered it, didn't I? Finders keepers. I was the one who wasn't feart like you all were. That gives me first call on things. Being the bravest and all that.'

'Still, you should give everyone a chance,' I said. 'Otherwise it's unfair.'

'Well, you're Queen aren't you? Isn't that good enough? Or do you just want to be a girly princess or something, sitting in front of a pretend mirror all day putting curls into your hair?'

I leapt at him, shouting, 'I'm as brave and as wise as you are,' but he held both my hands by the wrists.

'But not as strong,' he said. 'And the strongest has to be king.'

We let it go at that, though we remembered it, and he was conscious of the wider discontent among the gang. That evening, on the way home, he said to us, 'Maybe I will give them all a shot at being king, after all. One day.'

We all knew fine that one day was no day. Meantime, he made efforts to include all his subjects in his new Communications Plan. He called a General Council, because that's what Oliver Cromwell had done, according to the history book we read at school.

'What I want to do,' he explained, 'is to have a Central Control Panel here in the King's Room. I will send messages from here, and some of you will have receivers out in the field of battle. Once you receive a message from me, each receiver will respond with these words "Message Received. Loud and Clear". Is that all understood?'

Fearchar put his hand up.

'Will the message be written as in Morse Code, or just said?'

'That will depend,' said King Duncan. 'Sometimes it will be in Morse Code. Or in some other kind of code, for complete secrecy. And sometimes it will be spoken. You need to keep the enemy confused.'

'Aye aye, Sir,' said Sgliugan, slapping his wellingtons together as if he was in some kind of different play. Sgliugan always carried a shiny shilling around with him and whenever anyone died on the field of battle he'd put the shilling in the corpse's hand to pay the underworld ferryman. He'd then hoist the dead boy on his shoulders, cross the stream in a slow march, claim the shilling on the other side, and run back through the water with the revived corpse chasing him. If caught, he made duck noises, and if you didn't know it was Sgliugan you'd think you were strangling a duck!

King Duncan's central control panel was an empty fish box with the fading words 'Peterhead Fish Merchants' written across it. The telegraph operator had two large nails which he tapped at different intervals and with different strengths to send the signal. The receiving units were large shells which I provided and which our friends placed over their ears. Some placed them over one ear, some over the two.

'Received. Loud and clear,' was heard from various locations, despite the cows lowing and the honking of the greylag geese and the shrill calls of the corncrakes.

Duncan worried about his troops' abilities. For it was no use them pretending: they had to learn to work the equipment properly, or it would be pointless. They'd have to spend time training on the different ways to tap the nails on the fish box so that they made distinctive sounds. One tap 'A', two taps 'B' and so on, though it was much too complicated, for if you got a message like 'Enemy Manoeuvring to the North' it took forever to tap out, and by the time you had tapped the fish-box they'd be upon you and you'd be dead.

So we simplified it. One tap was 'No Enemy Here'; two taps meant 'Enemy Located'; three nail taps, 'Enemy to the North'; four, 'Enemy to the South'; five, 'Enemy to the West'; six, 'Enemy to the East'; seven taps meant 'Enemy Approaching'; eight signalled 'Attack Enemy'; nine, 'Enemy Engaged'; and ten, 'Enemy Conquered! Victory for King Duncan and his valiant troops.' Perfect – ten taps, ten words, for the final triumph. It took a good while, but even Sgliugan worked out the code in the end and wandered about the village with a nail and an old tobacco tin he tapped every time he met anyone, as if action was possible at any moment. Maybe he was the only one to realise that for a thing to become something else it needs to be what it was as well as what it will become.

That was only the technical side of the operation, of course. Duncan's real challenge was to maintain discipline, but above all courage and enthusiasm. It always is. I don't know if you've ever seen those old pictures of Blondin walking the tightrope above the Niagara Falls. He never looked down. That was his secret. Only doing what was essential.

'There will be greater things,' Duncan promised us. 'For technology doesn't stand still. I'm working on a new system that will be even more thrilling.'

He showed us the book – one he'd borrowed from the school library and read through several times. It was called *The Radio Experimenter's Handbook*. None of us could make heads or tails of it, but Duncan memorised some of the words to impress everyone. Duncan's ace card was this sentence, which amazed us all for a while:

'Wavelength in yards is equal to 59·6 multiplied by the square root of the product of the inductance in inches by the capacity in microfarads.'

'Waw!' exclaimed Sgliugan every time he uttered the sentence, though the rest of us soon understood that it was just mumbo-jumbo which he knew nothing about. Still, I loved the book too, for the best thing about it were the drawings which he sometimes shared with his inner circle – Fearchar, Sgliugan and I. This was always the one we liked best and afterwards when Dolina and I were down on the shore with our bikes we used to try and mark out the shapes with our wheels in the sand, the best fun doing the grid coil circles without stopping once.

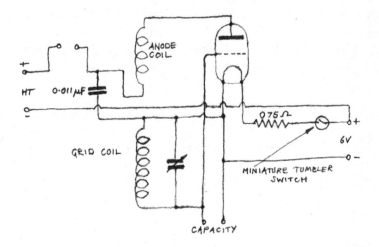

What we all realised after a while was that the game was better than the reality. Our game was unhampered by broken machinery and bad transmission lines. Everything was possible and fixed quickly either by a piece of string or a magic word, and though the troops wounded and killed one another and lay dead in ditches and upon the ramparts of the castle, they always rose to fight again, time after time. Even Duncan's permanent and unfair kingship was tolerated because the rest of it was so much endless fun, and because we also sensed that none of it would last.

The accident was inevitable, for every time any of us climbed the ramparts or the stairs we were dicing with injury and death.

None of us really knew yet that it's smarter to avoid danger than overcome it. Young Rory MacKechnie was in many ways the most daring and also the most foolhardy, and it was also probably quite inevitable that he was the one who fell while traversing across the old window on the second storey.

He was crossing from Mars to Saturn by rope at the time, even though that had nothing to do with the battle going on around him. Maybe that's why he fell. He broke his spine and had to be helicoptered to hospital in Glasgow. He couldn't walk after that, though every time I saw him he still said that he would not have exchanged the fun of those days for the ability to walk.

'Danger and risk and adventure are part of life,' he always said, wheeling himself at speed down through the machair villages.

17

The Cows

NIALL CUAGACH MOVED his seven cows into the field the night before the JCBs arrived at the airstrip. They were fine looking beasts. Four dun and three black short-legged Dexters which ambled about the village as calm as a summer's morning. Nothing bothered them. Niall could fire a rifle over their heads and they would still just keep on slowly munching the grass. When the JCBs arrived at the gate they looked over as if a few crows had landed on the fence, and continued grazing, for there is nothing as good as eating fresh green grass. We all wandered down to see what was going on.

It was a problem for the drivers, who had no instructions as to what to do in such circumstances. Their orders were merely to go in and flatten the site, starting from the direction of the old hangars up to the river on the south side. The Dexters were grazing between the river and the hangars. They were spread out as if each of them had been told to patrol a specific area, covering the whole field between them. The south side was particularly rich in clover, where the largest of the fine-looking beasts was feeding. There is something sacred about a cow eating clover.

One of the drivers suggested moving the cows.

'Where to?' the others asked.

'Anywhere will do. Just out of here.'

They opened the gate and approached the cows, who continued to graze.

'Shoo,' one of the workers called, as if he was dealing with flies. The cows didn't budge.

'Maybe we should get a stick?' another said. 'Or a dog?'

'Don't be daft. That's for sheep.'

We were standing with Niall Cuagach, who walked over towards the drivers.

'Morning, gentlemen.'

'Morning.'

'You bothering the cattle?'

'No. Just trying to get them to move out of here. Into the next field. We've work to do here.'

Cuagach took a folded parchment out of his pocket.

'This field belongs to them. Grazing rights established by Dr Alexander MacAskill – An Dotair Bàn – and signed here in 1830. It has never been legally revoked.'

The JCB drivers glanced at the ancient document.

'Latin?' one of them asked.

'No. Irish. Legal Irish.'

The workmen didn't want to cause trouble, so retreated into their machines. It wasn't really their responsibility. They were there just to do a job which they were being prevented from doing. One of them was sent to find James Campbell, who would surely sort something out. He was gone for hours. The other drivers sat in their vehicles, yawning and sleeping. Niall Cuagach sat on a stone watching the cows grazing. Things keep moving unless they're stopped.

At mid-day Campbell drove up, followed by the JCB driver.

'What's this document?' he asked Niall Cuagach. Cuagach showed it to him. He studied it.

'Out of date,' Campbell said.

'Really?' said Niall Cuagach.

'Really,' said Campbell.

'How?'

'It's obvious,' said Campbell. 'How old is this? Two hundred years old? This place has been bought and sold plenty times since. Clanranald to Cluny to Lord This-That-And-The-Other, then to the government and on to me. This parchment means nothing. Except maybe to a museum.'

'Prove it,' said Niall Cuagach.

Campbell sighed. That old delaying tactic. Lawyers. And paying them. He'd have to. He'd learned that much. Never to proceed without solid legal grounding. Not necessarily for his own sake, because he knew where the rights lay, but for the other person's. Despite their fixation on the invisible, these awkward locals never believed anything until it was presented to them in black and white from a court lawyer. For all their talk of faith, when it came to land and money these peasants would only believe a thing when they could touch and feel it.

And even then they would snort as if they knew better, muttering that common usage mattered more than paper law. People who sought security in their poverty and backwardness, like an old blanket to keep them warm. Living in the haze of an imaginary past because the present was so miserable for them. Folk who carried their grievances in the same way he carried his ambitions.

And there was no point in giving in to their grievances because, like his own ambitions, he knew they could never be satisfied. It's like a packet of sweeties. As soon as you open it, you finish it. Once one particular summit was climbed, another mountain always appeared on the horizon. Once one ambition was fulfilled, another took its place. Once one grievance was settled, a fresh one replaced it. As in the old story where the giant, Sannt, could never be satisfied with enough and at last ate himself, starting with his big toe. As if Cuagach's endlessly methane-farting cows were any better for the environment than Campbell's occasional plane.

'Okay,' Campbell said. 'I'll get the evidence for you. In black and white. Because law always trumps custom, Niall.'

'They're the same thing,' Cuagach said.

Campbell told the JCB drivers to leave, telling them, 'I'm sure it will be all sorted to start tomorrow.'

Except that nothing is easy, for the law is as rigid and flexible as custom itself. Back at the office, his secretary apparently couldn't find the actual land-deeds document. All the other documents were there, from planning permission to scale drawings, but not the land transaction certificate. Phone calls were made, but still nothing was found. Campbell phoned the JCB guys to instruct them to cancel the job in the meantime. He knew how long these things take.

Niall Cuagach was right. Through a long series of legal omissions, the bottom field which the airport development needed to extend to regulation length had slipped through the net. The old parchment was never revoked when one landowner sold it to another over the generations, because they never used that bit of land anyway. Dr MacAskill wrote an amendment into the original legal document which gave the use of the land for grazing rights in perpetuity to the Nicolsons, the latest descendent being Niall Cuagach.

The amendment stated that even if the land itself was sold, this particular field was to remain as grazing ground 'in perpetuity in lieu of the service provided to this community by Alexander Nicolson at the time of the famine.' Because the document itself was in Irish, the lawyers argued over the exact meaning of the words 'gu maireann' (in perpetuity), but the High Court finally agreed that it meant what it said, and was legally binding, no matter the language it was written in. As if any law could be above the language it was formed in. Though there are always courts of appeal which can find an obscure clause which can change everything.

Campbell had a dilemma. To cancel the whole project or proceed with the development on a smaller scale, or move it elsewhere. He marched off to see Sir Bert. We followed him like all those children in the story about the Pied Piper of Hamelin. He even whistled a pipe tune as he marched along, and we beat our feet against the ground in time. Have you ever played a game where you tried to change the rules just a wee bit to give you a better chance of winning? We used to do it all the time, say when playing rounders and you just knew that you'd never get round the sticks in time, so we'd ask if the sticks could be just that wee bit closer together when we were batting! And depending if the other team were daft, sometimes we got away with it!'

'Can we buy him out?' asked Sir Bert. 'Or rent the field from him?'

Campbell laughed.

'More chance of buying or renting the moon,' he said. 'It's holy ground to him. Or at least to the beasts he's put in there. You can't talk to him. If he didn't have cows to talk about I don't think he'd ever speak at all.'

'Can we develop in the other direction then? To the north?'

'Impossible. The river runs through it. Would cost too much to divert that. And the conservation people would raise hell. You know how powerful they are, ears and voices in high places.'

'Elsewhere?'

'The original strip was here for a reason. It's the best bit of flat land available.'

'Can we proceed on a smaller scale then, without Cuagach's field?'

'Could do. But would have financial implications. Smaller aircraft, less profit. And besides, there's the plan for the hotel…'

'Hmm. Bloody cows. You're sure he can't be bought?'

'Positive. Money means nothing to him.'

'What does?'

Campbell knew.

'Ratio, I think. I think ratio matters to him.'

'Ratio?'

'Aye. As in proportions. As in open fields. Seeing things from afar and not being enclosed and hemmed-in. Space is semi-divine to him. Says it's only space that prevents flies and clegs and cows and people being all glued together in one big sticky mess. Doesn't see it as an empty thing to be filled by houses or anything. It's as if they have a life of their own. Rivers. Tracks. Moorland. Heather. The moon. The stars. Says there's a rowan tree on the moon. Thinks the stars are hauled across the skies in a cart by a Clydesdale horse. Without these things he's lost.'

'Aren't we all? Except we have to live in the real world. The one where you starve if you don't earn. We can't live off nature and a nice view. We all have to compromise. Build schools and hospitals and churches and roads and bridges and ships and even airports. I presume he uses some of these things?'

'Well he was born in a deer shed, hardly went to school, doesn't drive a car and never been to hospital as far as I know.'

'But others have. That's the key thing. We don't live for ourselves alone. He can't be that selfish, thinking the world belongs to him alone.'

'No, Sir Bert. But then again he wouldn't be alone in thinking that.'

Sir Bert laughed.

'No, James. He wouldn't. But we should try and get him on board, for the sake of this community if not for ourselves.'

Good luck, thought James.

'And what can we offer him?' he asked. 'What can we give a man who doesn't want anything?'

'Nothing, I suppose. Except to remind him that no man is an island entire unto himself. Not even Niall Cuagach. He couldn't survive without his cows. And his cows couldn't survive without him. They depend on one another. So that when it comes to right or wrong it's like him and his cows. Truth lies in the middle.'

How wrong you are, thought Campbell, that's where falsehood lies. Though he didn't say it out loud. For if truth doesn't lie at the extremes neither he nor Niall Cuagach could be right.

18

Cycling

LISA LOVED THE freedom cycling gave her. Feeling the wind and rain while moving through it instead of avoiding it behind glass. She was like me. Never stayed in waiting for it to dry. That evening she went for a long ride along the machair track. I saw her and jumped on my own bike and she slowed down so that I caught up with her. It was drizzling a bit, but that didn't matter. Everything smelt of things growing. Clover and wild garlic. The poppies were waving their little red leaves in the breeze.

We cycled up through Àrdglas. Niall Cuagach and his seven cows were still there. We saw them from afar. The seven cows were perfectly spaced in the field, grazing clockwise. They munched some grass, then moved fractionally forward, almost in unison.

Niall Cuagach was leaning on the gate. He'd made it himself, for that was his speciality. Making – and especially hanging – a gate properly is not easy. The bought ones never last, and when you make it yourself you have to be ever so careful to hang it right, so that it will swing open at a touch and stay shut properly without the latches or the bars or the spars hanging loose. The secret is in having good sturdy hinges and brace posts, with everything correctly aligned. For there's nothing worse than a badly-hanging gate. I used to help Dad doing it and it was ever so difficult. Sometimes Mad Meg chased us with a stick if she saw us swinging on the gates. As if our tiny weight would damage any hinges! Not if they were made properly. We cycled up to him and stopped.

'Evening,' Lisa said.

'Evening.'

Strange how grown-ups always pretended to be formal, when 'Hi' or 'Aye aye' would do.

'So. You sent them away?'

'No. I just showed them the parchment, and then they went away.'

'Can I see it?'

He handed it to her. She read it carefully. I looked at it and couldn't make sense of it.

'I understand some of it,' Lisa said.

'I understand all of it.'

'How come?'

'My father told me. And his father told him. And so back.'

'But you can't read it?'

'No. But that doesn't matter. Being told is the same. And Crichton the lawyer agrees. He's read it.'

'They'll find a way eventually. To disprove it. They always do. You know that.'

'I know. But eventually is not today. Why are you with them anyway?'

'With them? I'm not with them. I'm with the community. With us. We're all in it together, to work for the best for this place.'

Niall Cuagach scoffed.

'Rubbish. It's always them and us. The rich against the poor. It's always the strong against the weak. I know animals. Eagles lift lambs, birds eat worms. Everything to its prey.'

She came down off her bike. Stood by the gate. I cycled round in a big circle trying to make it smaller and smaller to see if I could eventually turn round and round within the space of the bike itself. It took ages, and as soon as I almost got there the bike would cowp over and I'd have to start all over again.

'We're not animals, Niall. Some may be, but we're not. I'm not. You're not. Seumas MacDonald isn't. Nor Curstag. Or Duncan or Fearchar or Annie or Hazel or Mrs MacPherson or any of the others. You'll lose this field in a court of law. And the airstrip will be lengthened and visitors will come, and they'll be entitled to come, for they've as much right to this place as you or I. You can't resist change just for the sake of it.'

'I'm not resisting for the sake of it.'

'Then what for?'

He couldn't say. His childhood, and those memories he had of things, and that other feeling that everything was disappearing. Like trying to put a jigsaw with most of the pieces missing back together again. It seemed impossible, leaving him desperate and angry. Like a loch in a sudden squall. Maybe he was dying.

'It's to do with size and shape,' he finally said. 'A collie is not a pig. When things get too big they go out of focus and lose shape. I can't shear a sheep or move a cow now without filling in a form for someone somewhere to approve and certify that I've done it right, as if I didn't know. Excuse my language, Miss Cornhill, and Annie, if you're listening, but I can't even shit nowadays without flushing it down a pre-assembled plug hole as if it's got nothing to do with me. That it's someone else's product and someone else's responsibility. Same with everything.'

'That was the moment I changed sides,' she told me later. 'Even though I'd just said there were no sides. He was right. There are. Of course there are, because there are always sides. Men and women. Young and old. Believers and unbelievers. Right and wrong. Those who destroy the world and those who care for it. Even if there are so many grey areas between them all. Maybe it's not even that there are sides but that you sometimes just need to choose because not choosing is to side with the strong. That was the reason I returned home in the first place, Annie. That and my homesickness. Like a migratory bird sensing the seasons. I knew I wanted to help people control their own affairs. To own their own stuff, as Niall Cuagach put it. That strange man sitting there on the fence letting his cows stop aeroplanes might be the future. I thought of saying that to him. Had the strength to say it. He liked folk being direct. Instead, you might remember I just said, "The main thing James Campbell and Sir Bert are interested in is money. It's really that simple. But the problem, Niall Cuagach, is that you're too strange to defeat them on your own."'

He let the strange bit go.

'There's nothing wrong with defeat. Or being on my own. Even though I'm not. Things are with me. The grass and the river and the moon and the stars.'

'They don't have a voice. Or a vote.'

'No? Well, without them there's nothing. Then you're truly on your own.'

'You'd be better off with folk alongside you, supporting you, Niall. The young people, for instance. Duncan and Fearchar and Annie admire your ways, but are afraid of you. Alone, up here on the moor. It makes you...' She hesitated. 'Unusual. Strange.'

'But not dangerous?'

'That too,' she said. 'For whatever is odd is dangerous. To many.'

She wanted to ask him to include others in his world. To teach them his peculiar way of seeing things.

'Maybe they are the ones who are strange? Crowding together, as if there aren't miles and miles of empty moorland and mountain and bog and hill and machair.'

'It gives us strength. Being together. Surely you get lonely out here on your own? Is that not why you too came to the meeting, and go down into the village, and to church?'

'No. I went to the meeting to give my view. I go down into the village to move the cattle. And I go to church to worship God.'

'You could do that here, on your own.'

'I do. For there is nothing there which is not here.'

'So what will you do when they win the day in the High Court and the JCBs roll in again, this time with full permission?'

'I will take my cows up to the high pastures,' he said. 'Nearer God.'

'Maybe resistance is better done on lower ground. Down where the people are. Where the kids like Annie are, who own the future.'

'Maybe,' he said. 'Maybe. And I'm sure she can speak for herself. I'd better move the cows now, don't want them getting upset with all this noise.'

He turned.

'And one other thing, Lisa. Never try to influence anyone. It's a mistake. Let them – let me – make my own mistakes.'

19

Flying

IT WAS GREY and raining steadily from the north. The whole world was wet and crumbly, a bit like peat-ash. Water ran down the eaves of the house. The window panes were a blur of mist. The rocks outside glistened. The loch had burst its banks. The stream was overflowing. The hens tried to flap their heavy wings and the horses stood backsides to the rain at the south end of the barn.

I liked it when Dad took the horses along to Old Gillies for

shoeing and we stood by the flames in the forge as he shaped the shoe with the hammer and anvil. It was as if the only purpose of life was to shoe a horse. I was sometimes allowed to plunge the iron with the tongs into the large barrel of cold water and loved how it sizzled and then how the horses were so pleased with their new shoes, setting sparks off the road on the way back home in celebration. The harder the iron was when forged the softer they were on their feet. As if all the hardness has to be burnt out of a thing before it's any use. Old Gillies had special frost nails he used in the winter and my treat for them then when the cold weather came was to press soap into their hooves to prevent the snow and hardened mud from crippling them. Some folk thought he was some kind of wizard, though he was much more prosaic about his abilities.

'I don't just sit on my arse waiting for a spark from heaven. I hit the iron with a hammer, and only then do the sparks fly!'

All the doors were open. Duncan lay stretched out on his bed fully clothed, reading *The Radio Experimenter's Handbook*. Fearchar sat on the edge of his, building a castle out of the remaining bits of Lego. He only had twenty-two bits left. I was to blame. I took them and never returned them. Lost them somewhere on the way over to Dolina's one day when the white bull chased me and I had to jump over the fence through the peat-bog. But the twenty-two survivors performed miracles. Laid circular and flat they were impregnable. Not even Duncan's army could breach the walls. Laid vertical one on top of the other they reached to the sky, which was the pencil mark on the window-wall. Assembled in fours they made a kingdom, with a moat between each castle. Still, if he had more pieces it would be a greater kingdom.

I stood in my room looking out the window. I rubbed it with my sleeve every other minute to clear the mist. If I put my face right up to the glass all I could see at first were the drops of rain like huge bubbles. I could see inside them and everything. They were blue with bits of green. When I closed one eye a single drop of rain slowly streamed down the window until it disappeared. At first I thought all the drops fell at the same speed, but I gradually worked out that each drop rolled down the pane at different speeds. And they also changed shape as they moved – some remained the same, but most got smaller and smaller as they descended, until some of them dissolved completely, never making it to the bottom of the glass.

I liked both the ones that fell so fast that they were almost invisible and the ones that fell so slowly that it was like watching a snail crossing the road. Or a caterpillar, for I liked caterpillars best. We used to lift them off the road in case they got squashed. That summer I had one for a pet and kept her in a glass jar, giving her bits of lettuce and seeds and water, but she died. She was called Alice. I buried her down on the machair next to the old cemetery which the boys said was haunted. They said that about all the places they didn't play in. I knew it wouldn't bother Alice, for I don't think ghosts ever looked down about their feet in case they tripped into or stood on anything. And I don't think they'd care if they did. And besides, by that time they and Alice were eternal.

When I breathed on the window glass it steamed up and I wrote secret messages which dissolved themselves, like the invisible ink they had in the comics. I wrote my name – Annie – and watched as each individual letter slowly melted, until I was just nie and then ie and then just i and then nothing. Sometimes the rain and mist  worked the other way and when I wrote things they stayed there forever. Even when I rubbed the words away, I could still see the faint outline of what was there, days later. So I learned to be careful in case the invisible message was still there centuries on. I love G, I wrote once, and the boys teased me forever afterwards.

'George!' they cried. 'George!' even though it wasn't him and I wouldn't tell them who it really was. Ever. Besides, the rain sometimes changed the letter by itself. And anyway the first letter doesn't have to be right; it can just be a clue within a clue.

I was first to see the car, and I rushed through to the boys' room.

'It's Johnston,' I shouted. 'In that car.'

The silver machine drove through the village in the rain. Past Misses Agnes and Peggy's house and on past Mùgan's and Mrs MacPherson's.

'Maybe it's coming here,' I said.

'Of course it is,' said Duncan. 'Where else would it be going?'

The car slowed down and Johnston came out to open the gate. He drove down the old track towards our house.

'That'll make his car so dirty,' Fearchar said. 'Maybe he'll want me to wash it!'

'He can do it himself,' Duncan said. 'We're not here to serve him.'

'But he'll give me something for it.'

Duncan just looked at him.

Mam went out to meet Johnston.

'Seumas is down at the shore. He'll be back in a moment.'

'Good. I've got an offer for him.'

'Tea?'

'Please. Thanks.'

All was quiet except for Mam putting the leaves in the pot and taking the kettle from the stove. Three spoonfuls. We knew the sounds so well. Clink and swish and pour and stir.

'Kids at home?'

'Yes. Upstairs.'

Silence.

She was pouring the tea. Johnston would be sitting at the table.

'Everyone wired up now?' Mam asked.

'More or less. Except for yourselves of course. Which is a pity.'

'It's what we want. No need for it.'

'Except for how much easier it would make your life. A washing machine, fridge, electric lights, heaters. A proper cooker. All clean and quick instead of smelly paraffin lamps and endless damp clothes.'

Dìleas barked, meaning Dad was returning from the shore. They were both soaking wet. As usual, Dìleas ran up the stairs to say hallo to us. She was not supposed to, but everyone had given up trying to stop her long ago! Dad removed his oilskins and wellingtons at the door, drying himself with a towel. I gave Dìleas a cuddle even though she was all wet. She smelt of seaweed.

'Aye aye,' Dad said to Johnston. 'What brings Marconi here today?'

'Same old, same old,' Johnston said. 'Trying to drag folk into the twentieth century.'

'We are in the twentieth century. Just not the same one as you.'

Johnston smiled.

'So there's no point in me making the offer?'

'Depends what it is. Always open to offers.'

'An apprenticeship. That lad of yours is bright. He'll make a good engineer. We need boys like him. Young, able, intelligent. Bet he has a head for heights too. Would make an excellent poleman, I'm sure.'

Upstairs, Fearchar prodded Duncan hard in the ribs.

'Sshh,' he whispered back.

'Let's ask him,' said Dad.

He called upstairs.

'Duncan.'

Duncan came downstairs, followed by Fearchar, followed by me.

'Did you hear that?' Dad asked.

'Hear what?' Duncan lied.

'Mr Johnston wants to offer you a job.'

'I'm still at school.'

'I know,' Dad said, 'but you'll be sixteen soon.'

'Next week,' I added. 'On the 18th.'

'What kind of job?' Duncan asked.

'An apprenticeship,' Johnston said. 'Electrical engineering. It's the future. A paid apprenticeship, and a full-time job guaranteed at the end. With a good wage. A very good wage.'

Johnston had lovely nails. Long and manicured.

'I already know what I want to do,' Duncan announced.

This was news, even to Fearchar and I. Everyone looked at him.

'I'm going to be a pilot. Fly planes across the world. I wrote to the RAF last month. And I've been speaking to James Campbell. He says he'll help me train here once the airport gets under way.'

Mam and Dad were quiet. Maybe because he'd said so much in front of grown-ups. Four sentences at least. And all together. As if he'd suddenly discovered that speaking was as important as doing wheelies on his bike. I could see they were both resisting the instinct to speak back. Dad to rebuke him. To correct him. To remind Duncan that he was a child and should ask before announcing anything. Mam wanted to praise him. She remembered what it was like to be called a child and blurt things out. To say the unsayable. I could see her thinking. Knowing what you want to be is an astonishing thing. But they didn't say anything.

Once Johnston left, they called us all together. Duncan, Fearchar and I sat in a row on the bench which ran from the door to near the fire. I was nearest the fire, Fearchar in the middle and Duncan nearest the door. Dad sat in the easy chair on the other side of the stove. Mam sat at the table.

'So,' Dad said. 'What's this plan, Duncan?'

'It's not a plan, Dad. It's just what I want to do.'

'You should have asked.'

'You'd have said no.'

'No I wouldn't. I'd just have asked you about it. As I am now.'

'I want to fly.'

'Who put that idea into your head? That rogue Campbell?'

'No. I'm not a cannibal. I don't eat his mince. I have my own ideas. Why does everyone have to sit around here listening to this, as if it's a public meeting needing a vote? It's my decision. My life.'

I'd never heard Duncan put so many words together so well. It was as if they were filled with energy, sparking across the room towards Mam and Dad. Arriving instantly. Like electricity. But they remained calm. You never made decisions on your own. You never replied too quickly. Things took time. Baking a loaf took time. Getting the ingredients. Mixing them together. Adding the yeast.

Waiting for them in the oven. Hauling in lobster creels took time. One by one, taking the individual lobster out and putting it alive in the salt-water box. Throwing the rubbish fish overboard, alive. Dog-fish. It took months for the tatties to grow. Invisibly, under the earth. You just kept an eye on it. Checked them now and again for signs of rot or decay.

'No it's not, Duncan. You're fifteen years of age. A minor.'

'Sixteen next week. Leaving school. Weren't you already at sea at that age, Dad?'

'That's different.'

'How?'

I could see Dad hated not being able to say what he wanted to say. What he felt. For it's so difficult to say what you feel. And even if you find the words, what if? What if they don't come out the way you wanted? What if they don't believe you. Or laugh at you. Mam struck the table with her hand and we all stopped, astonished.

'Don't question your father like that,' Mam said, quietly and firmly. 'He's right. You should talk about these things. Discuss them. After all, when we sit at the table for our dinner, we ask for things, don't we? Pass the salt, please. Can I have some more potatoes, please? Please. Thank you. It's called manners, Duncan. You've been taught that since you were a baby.'

Duncan felt like the child he was. Everyone was quiet. She hadn't nursed us from the cradle without knowing everything about us.

'So, while we're all here,' Dad said after a while, looking at Fearchar, 'what are your plans, lad?'

'Don't know.'

Though everyone knows that we'll all go away anyway. For there's nothing to do here except to plant turnips and look at the sea and count sheep and watch the shape of the clouds.

'Annie?'

I wasn't afraid.

'I'm going to be a nurse. Or maybe a biologist.'

'A what?' Fearchar asked.

'A biologist. That's someone who looks after animals.'

'No, that's a vet,' Duncan said.

'Be quiet,' said Mam in a tone of voice rarely, if ever, heard. Everyone went silent, not daring to move. We looked at Dad who looked at Mam.

'When was the last time any of you bothered asking what I'd like to do?' she said. 'Don't you think that I too would like to have a voice and choose things? I didn't give birth to any of you to watch you head off blindfolded into the dark. To play at being ghosts. Just ask, listen and take advice. And I didn't marry your father to sit here brooding and cooking forever in the half-dark. I too have plans. To live healthily and happily as long as I can. To see you all grow up healthy and happy and secure and prosperous. To love unto death this dear man who's your father. And, for what it's worth, I might even like to have electricity some day. A washing machine, a fridge, running hot water. A bath. A shower. A television. My life doesn't depend on it, but I'd survive it. What difference will an electric kettle make if we can't even talk to one another?'

We all sat still for a while as if dazzled by some kind of light. I thought how little courage we all had, except for Mam. So it was okay to be fiery. And angry. To feel things and say them. I was the only one to move. I ran towards her and clasped her round the waist. I don't know why. I just wanted to cuddle the something big and dangerous she had said which might wither and die if it wasn't welcomed.

Mam kissed and stroked the top of my head. Then Duncan stood up and wanting to say something equally brave, said,

'I will definitely learn how to fly. And when I'm qualified, you can all come on my plane and see everything from high up in the skies.'

He looked at Dad.

'You could even drive it, Dad. I'm sure it's no more difficult than a tractor!'

20

Ploughing

IT TOOK MONTHS of legal wrangling for James Campbell to finally clarify he was the legal owner of the contentious strip of land. The main argument was not so much over the original Irish language document and its precise meaning, but over the legality of which exact pieces of land had been sold and transferred to different tenants over the centuries. The problem was that the boundaries and the common rights enshrined in the Crofters Holding (Scotland) Act of 1886 were perpetually retained by the tenants in most cases, no matter who the landowner was, but these boundaries were difficult to define precisely in the absence of specific maps.

If you conceded an inch to the authorities they'd argue that what had not been seen by their officials did not exist. Land atheists, Cuagach called them.

Niall Cuagach's maps and alignments were different from those offered by the old estate papers and the official Ordnance Survey maps. He had names for places that didn't officially exist as well as a memory of usage which was strictly against the law: his cows should never have been in that field in the first place, but in the field across the wall.

Boundaries were as fixed and fluid as time itself. Campbell's lawyer successfully argued that Niall Cuagach's great-grandfather had mistaken Am Balla Ruadh (The Red Wall) for Am Baile Ruadh (The Red Farm), with the consequence that he had placed his cattle to the south of the red wall instead of south of the red farm, which is where he ought to have grazed his beasts. Crichton, Niall Cuagach's lawyer, argued that nevertheless usage was nine-tenths of the law, but the judge concluded that even though usage might be nine-tenths of the law in popular mythology, possession and usage were legally two different terms, and even though Niall Cuagach and his forebears had used the field that did not amount to the same as legal possession.

The verdict was that the field needed for the airport belonged legally to James Campbell who had bought it off the government a decade previously. A crooked tree will have a crooked shadow, Cuagach said. Niall Cuagach decided not to appeal, because he knew that it was like urinating into the wind. He had quickly learnt as a child to turn his back to the wind when relieving himself outside. The law, like the wind, blows wherever it will.

'Just because he won doesn't prove he was right,' Cuagach said. 'Only that he had a better lawyer.'

As soon as Campbell won his court case he ordered the digging work to resume. The JCBs arrived without any opposition this time. There were only two of them. One started clawing at the north end and one at the south end while Niall Cuagach stood on the hill above looking down on them. He wanted to compare them to dragons eating up the earth, but they were more like snails slowly turning the green field black.

The soil looked rich and promising. He could see the worms enjoying the fresh earth and the birds swooping down on them with equal satisfaction. You've got to imagine a thing first. The new soil would make fine sowing and a good harvest if he took care to weed and harrow and fertilise with cow-pats from the adjacent fields and seaweed from the shore. On the other side of the fence men cut down the old trees and piled them on to the back of a lorry.

Once the JCBs had gone, Niall Cuagach went down to inspect the work more closely. He walked through the mud towards the centre. The field itself was now good black earth. What a marvellous job they'd done, though it still needed some cleaning and harrowing. He went on his knees and worked steadily, picking up the small stones that had been churned up by the machines, and moved them to the side of the field in a cairn. Some day people might imagine it was a cairn to commemorate something. They'd maybe say it was where King Olaf was murdered in defence of his kingdom. Or it would be useful to shelter behind in the wind and rain. Even solid stones had been mud and earth once upon a time. You wouldn't know anything if the stones and sea and grass and fields and sky didn't tell you.

We all watched him for a while, and then became ashamed of ourselves watching a grown man working on his own on his hands and knees, so we slowly joined in. Fearchar moved first, taking up his position to the right of him, then Duncan to the left. Behind them, Dolina and I gathered the small stones they failed to notice, and soon we were joined by Morag and Peggy and Iain and Ruairidh and Norman and by Sgliugan who brought one of his father's creels and put it on his back like a mule so that we could put the pebbles and stones and bits of broken crockery and all the other rubbish we picked up there rather than in our little bags. By the time the sun set and we made our way home, the cairn stood strong and solid like an ancient memorial.

Niall Cuagach then climbed the hill and put the plough on his shoulders. To destroy the developers' work would be a sign of weakness. Far better to plant an alternative. He whistled, and the spotted horses appeared out of the darkness. He whispered to one, Ruadh, and the two of them headed down towards the field. There was a full lantern moon and its bright light illuminated as far as the eye could see. The stars were out too – An Corg to the east and Slighe na Bà Fèinne directly overhead. Where the cows of the Fingalians munched their slow way home every evening across the darkening skies. He harnessed Ruadh and led him down to the field.

He attached the plough and ran the furrows, as was the tradition, from east to west. Long even lines spilling out into the falling moonlight like a child's drawing. He would plant the potatoes on the west side where they would catch the benediction of the evening sun, and the turnips and cabbages on the east side for the angelus of the

morning light. Mice and worms and grubs ran and slithered through the furrows, and an owl hooted somewhere, disturbed by the steady, heavy breathing of the horse.

It was a small, futile gesture. Nothing grows unless a seed is sown. The seed potatoes never went into the ground, the cabbages and turnips were never planted, for when the sun rose in the morning the other workers arrived. The fencers and joiners and builders and bricklayers and line-painters and tarmac-layers with the little neat diggers and rollers. It was like a fair. Duncan and Fearchar and I and all the other young people came to watch, as did many of the grown-ups. The work rate was astonishing. The ploughed field was transformed into a runway by late afternoon, with steam rising from the hot tar, while the shells of new aluminium sheds were swiftly erected on both sides of the Nissan hut which contained Campbell's old plane. Smoke and the smell of sawdust and tar and oil and paint filled the air. It was like when we played with plasticine at school and could make anything we wanted.

Nothing happens instantly. It only seems that way. The control tower was erected and buildings went up. Flags were raised and blew constantly in the wind. They were orange and furled out like small sails. One of them funnelled constantly to indicate the direction of the wind to incoming pilots. Mùgan said it was a complete waste of good canvas which would have made a fine sail for a boat. At least it was some excitement for us, because we could cycle down there and see whether the orange wind-sock was flying east or west. It was something to do and see instead of watching the cows and the clouds. James Campbell had a temporary office next to the terminal. An advert for ground staff appeared in the local paper that week for a receptionist/ticket officer, two baggage handlers, a cook for the cafe and a waitress or waiter.

Duncan went to see Campbell.

'What about a pilot?' he asked.

'You need to be qualified,' Campbell responded.

'And how do I qualify?'

'You train. You've written to the RAF, haven't you? Heard back?'

'Not yet. Couldn't I train here?'

Campbell laughed.

'No, Duncan, my boy. We haven't got the facilities yet. Write to some of the big companies. British Airways would be best.'

Duncan wondered about some of the other jobs.

'What about Flight Controllers and engineers? Won't you need them here as well?'

'We've hired them already. From the mainland. Guys I knew from school. Ex-RAF. They'll start as soon as we get full aviation clearance.'

We always knew when a special letter arrived because Roddy the Postman whistled a particular tune. None of us knew what it was, and when we asked him he said he didn't know the name of it, but that it was an old pipe tune he'd learned from Pipe Major Mathieson during his National Service.

'I only whistle that tune for good news,' he said, and he took special delight in whistling it whenever a rare air-mail letter arrived from Auntie Rachel who had emigrated to New Zealand before the war. She used to send us a box of dried fruits every Christmas. Tamarillos and dates and kiwis and things which we used to cover in custard and eat. We just wanted to eat the custard, but Mam kept on saying that the fruit was good for us.

Duncan's letter from the RAF arrived the week after Johnston's visit. He took it up to his room to read, but of course we were all dying to find out what the letter said. I was sent to find out. I knocked on his bedroom door and when I opened it he was sitting on the window-sill smiling, polishing his Sunday shoes.

'So?'

'So what?'

'The letter. What did it say?'

'Not telling. It's my letter.'

'That shoe-polish is Mam's. She bought it. So don't use it.'

He shrugged, put down the shoe-polish and flung the letter to me.

Dear Mr MacDonald,

Thank you for your application for an apprenticeship with the R.A.F. Can you please attend our depot at Lossiemouth (full address below) on Wednesday 21st at 10:00. You will be shown round the depot by Pilot Officer Philip Coursey before being interviewed and given an Aptitude Test.

We look forward to seeing you on Wednesday.

Signed,
Flt Lt Robert Stevenson.

'What's an Aptitude Test?' I asked him.

'It's a way of finding out how smart I am.'

I was tempted to say that wouldn't take long, but didn't.

Dad tried to keep it secret, but we saw him unlocking the big chest in the hall and giving Duncan a silver coin. It's where Dad kept his few precious things. The thing was, space was so limited in our house that you couldn't ever hide anything. Yet each one of us had a tin sitting on the shelf where we kept our secret things and which no one else ever dared to open. Though none of them were sealed or locked I still don't know what Dad or Mam or Duncan or Fearchar kept in theirs and they never knew what I kept in mine. I still have it, with all its treasures. To have looked in someone else's tin was not forbidden. Just unthinkable. It would have been like searching through their pockets or snooping on them naked. William down the village was a dirty peeping tom and was shunned by everyone until he moved away to Glasgow. He used to steal knickers off the washing-lines but when he also started taking corsets, that was the last straw. They cost the earth and took so long to order through the post. Nothing was forbidden, as it were; it was just that everything had consequences. Still, everybody missed him once he was gone.

The boat took most of the day to take Duncan to Kyle. Then a train to Inverness. He stayed at a guest house near the town centre that had a television in the resident's lounge where he watched a programme called *Tomorrow's World* which said that everyone would have their own personal flying machine by the year 2000. After the programme he walked down through the town. Nobody knew him, so he could do whatever he wanted.

Early in the morning he got the bus to Lossiemouth which dropped him off near the RAF base. Duncan was measured 5ft 7 inches high, 9 stone, 2 pounds. He was then given the Aptitude Test. Most of it had to do with measures. Graphs which showed height and distance, and he had to work out the angle between the two end points. He'd never learned any of that at school, and of course didn't know how to do it. The questions contained words he'd never come across. Parallelogram. Obtuse. Hypotenuse. There was a picture of a man carrying a weight in his right hand marked 182 and another weight in his left hand marked 47 and Duncan was asked to write down the difference. Easy-peasy: 135. He then had to read a short passage and answer questions about it.

It was a passage about a bird with a broken wing that learns how to fly using one wing. The other birds bring food to it so that it can survive. Then he learns he can fly by tucking his broken wing in and raising the good one higher. By the end of the month the one-winged bird is flying higher and longer and better than any other bird. Other birds from all over the world fly in to see him: shoebills from Zambia, lyrebirds from Australia, hoatzins from the Amazon and gugas from Sula Sgeir. They all learn how to fly majestically with one wing and return home to demonstrate the marvel to all their friends. As if any of that could be true. Afterwards, the examiner told Duncan that the principle was about adaptability.

'As a pilot you have to learn to fly no matter the condition of the plane or of the weather. No matter the circumstances, storm or wind or hail or rain or shine or bombs or anti-aircraft missiles. You have to be flexible. Sometimes you have to limp, or soar, home like a bird with a broken wing. That's why birds hardly every sit still. Being earth-bound is alien and temporary to them.'

After the written tests Duncan was taken through to a hangar where a simulation cockpit was set on a platform. The examiner explained the layout to him and then mentioned an individual part by name to see if Duncan could remember where it was. He had a form which he ticked as Duncan answered. Tick, ✓✓✓✓ tick, tick, tick with a flourish of a beautifully sharpened pencil. When he finished ticking he put the pencil crossway in his mouth as he turned the pages of the form to make sure everything had been filled in. It was as if perfection was possible.

Duncan wondered how he managed to get the pencil so sharp and pointed and still work, because he never could. When he sharpened his pencil with a knife it looked beautiful, but as soon as the lead touched the paper it always broke and went back to being a useless stub.

'That's because your hand is too heavy on the pencil. You think it's a spade,' Fearchar always said to him, though Duncan knew it was just the quality of the lead itself, which was cheap and nasty. He once borrowed the schoolmaster's pencil and it was gorgeous, like having a sharp sword in his hand which sliced across the paper as if it was ice. That would be fun. To cut the paper into shreds. That would show them.

Duncan answered every question correctly. Accuracy was all that mattered. The instructor showed him twenty beautiful ticks in twenty little boxes. The simulator engine was turned on and Duncan was asked to steer the plane in a straight line two hundred yards down the runway. White lines ran parallel on both sides and he kept to the centre. He was then asked to repeat the exercise, but at a higher speed. Again he held it perfectly. He was right. It was like driving the tractor, really. You just kept in the middle of the road between the two grassy ditches.

He was always good with his hands, knowing that you ought to be gentle when turning things. Like Mam did with the butter-churn. The thing itself then gives you its secrets. When sawing for instance: the saw does the bulk of the work if you hold it lightly. The worst thing is to grip it like iron. It then snarls the wood rather than running with the grain. Gently does it. Saw to the beat of your heart. It was the same here, except that everything is magnified. He realises that inches are miles in real time. That moving the joystick a fraction means altering course for miles in the air. Like that bird in the story. So he handles the joystick like a new-born lamb. Tenderly, because the lamb feels every movement of your hands as you press him to his mother's udder or caress him for a moment just after he comes into the world. A soft touch makes all the difference between life and death, and the lamb knows it.

His final test was physical. Running on the spot for three minutes. Fifty push-ups. Jumping a few small hurdles. Climbing the wall-bars. Skipping, without touching the rope, fifty times. Dolina had a beautiful skipping-rope and sometimes Duncan and Fearchar joined in with us. Dolina and I would hold the rope and turn it while the boys skipped in the middle. The aim was always to do more than a hundred, so doing fifty skips for the RAF officer was easy-peasy, he said.

'I even chanted your song, quietly to myself,' he told me. 'Helped me focus and kept the jumps nice and steady. I even did it one foot at a time just to show off.'

'What? You chanted that girly thing?'

'Aye,' he said. 'March, march, two by two, my little sister lost her shoe. I love coffee I love tea, I love the girls and the girls love me.'

'It's boys when we sing it, though,' I reminded him.

Duncan then had his eye test, which he failed. Colour-blind. The officer seemed sad to lose him.

'I'm really sorry,' he said. 'For you're such a good candidate too. Passed those physical and aptitude tests with flying colours.'

'Surely it doesn't matter that much,' Duncan said. 'I can still make out the main colours – I know the difference between blue and red and green and yellow and white and orange.'

The officer was hearing, but not listening, for he liked to talk.

'I know, I know,' he said. 'I know you know the difference, lad, but that's a completely different thing from actually distinguishing them in reality. In all their shades. You confused purple with blue and mauve with yellow and violet with green. And that makes all the difference, son, when you're high up there in the skies and sometimes dazzled and confused by the different shades of light. The lights of all the instrument dials, and the lights of the stars and the ever-changing shades of the clouds and the movement of time across the different zones. And that's before I mention anything about actual military activity where it's critical to distinguish things instantly – friend from foe, for instance. It's not mere destiny, boy, it's judgement too.'

He was on his favourite subject, on a roll like one of the Red Arrows looping across the skies. He had no sense of proportion, because he had never failed in anything.

'There have been so many tragedies over the years, mistaking our territory for theirs, our troops for the enemy's. Precision is what matters, and colour precision is at the heart of that. Think of flying over the ocean and looking down at the different shades of blue beneath, and you've got to target an enemy submarine in deep water. Good as radar is, sometimes you have to trust in and believe your eyes. In those circumstances you have to be able to distinguish instantly between the light blue of inner waters and the dark blue of deeper waters and the faint shadow of a whale or a submarine that floats beneath the waves. That's why passing the colour test is so critical.'

Duncan wasn't convinced, but didn't argue with the officer. He thought of suggesting that it had to do with language – that in Gaelic blue was actually green and red was brown, but he knew that was both untrue and pointless. All he would get would be another long lecture from him about precision, whatever the language.

When he got back home we went to see Campbell again.

'I failed the colour eye-test.'

'Ach, that's a pity, Duncan,' Campbell said.

'Can I learn here though? The RAF man was going on about bombing submarines and things, but I wouldn't need to do that here.'

Campbell laughed.

'No. You certainly wouldn't. Maybe an illegal fishing boat or two, though.'

He saw the anxious look on Duncan's face.

'Joking, Duncan. Tell you what,' he then added. 'Though I can't give you a pilot's job, I can offer you a start. We need someone around here to do general work. Bits and pieces, odds and ends.'

'What kind of bits and pieces and odds and ends?'

'Oh, this and that. You know – keeping the place clean and tidy. Running errands. Helping out here and there.'

I could see Duncan thinking. It's not flying. But you have to start somewhere. Like that bird with the broken wing. At least he will be in the daily presence of a plane.

'What about your old plane in the hangar?' he asked.

'What about it?'

'Can I learn to fly it?'

'Of course. One day. It still needs parts. Components which are hard to get because the plane is vintage now.'

He looked at Duncan. Saw himself at that age. 'Tell you what,' he said. 'I'll hire you for that special job. For keeping that plane spick and span, clean and polished. Gleaming. In fact,' he added, 'why don't I hire you to keep all the planes that come and go here clean. After all, it's the most important thing, Duncan. If an aircraft is shining, travellers' trust grows. How about it, son?'

Duncan knew he was being offered a job as a cleaner, but dismissed the word. Polisher might be better. Handyman even, or janitor.

'You can be First Maintenance Officer, Duncan. How about that for a title?'

It could be worse, Duncan thought, so he nodded. Campbell smiled stretched his hand across the table, and they shook on it. He then shook my hand too, for some reason. Maybe just because he wanted me as some kind of witness, or maybe that's what you do when you shake one person's hand – you also have to shake the next person's hand, and on and on and on forever and ever in case anyone feels left out or in case anyone then claims later on that they didn't know anything about anything although they were there all along.

Hydro

'I NEVER HAD anything against it. Ever.'

Sometimes Mam and Dad sat in easy chairs each side of the fire, though usually they sat on the hard chairs each side of the kitchen table. That morning they were sitting side by side on the bench where we usually sat.

'It's just that I dislike things given to us. Sold to us, when we could do it ourselves.'

'We can't do everything ourselves, Seumas. You know that.'

'No? We've managed fine so far. He doesn't own the sea and the skies.'

She turned towards him. This man, still childish in so many ways. In his stubbornness and dream-like world.

'We were young then,' Mam said.

'Still are. Thing is, we don't need Johnston. Or his telegraph poles. His borrowed light. We have a river running by. Used to turn the old mill. Could as easily turn a turbine that will make electricity for us. And there's wind. Plenty of it. We always had sails on our ships to give us extra speed as we crossed the Atlantic. Same thing.'

'I thought you were talking about something else. About Abraham and Sarah. About us.'

He laughed. It was odd. Usually we were excluded from this kind of conversation.

'So why haven't you done it all these years we've been struggling here with peat and candles and oil lamps?'

'No need. And I didn't know. Not until you spoke.'

'Maybe I spoke and you didn't listen?'

'Likely. Probably. I'm sorry.'

'Don't do it if you don't want to.'

'I do. I'm getting older too. It will be easier for all of us. Especially in the winter. It took me a while.'

Mam was quiet.

'A while to realise – well really, to confess – that it's the same thing. Electricity is just the same thing as a plough, or a horse. Something to help us, not to master us.'

'Anything can master us, Seumas. Drink, for instance. Remember?'

'No. I've mastered the art of forgetting.'

'You realise we'll just be like Niall Cuagach. Putting his cows in the field in a foolish attempt to stop the future. Harrowing that field which was tarmacked the day after.'

Dad sat up.

'No. It's a completely different thing, Curstag. That was... that was just resistance. I'm not interested in that... in that kind of gesture. Only in doing it our own way. If only to demonstrate that there are always better alternatives. We don't always have to obey. Be persuaded by men in flash cars.'

It wasn't easy. The old mill hadn't been worked for almost a hundred years.

'Which doesn't mean it's useless,' Dad said. 'Old, decrepit and broken – yes. But not useless, for old and broken things can be repaired and renewed. And anyway, the two essential things are here. A river and a wheel that still turns. Water always moves unless it's enclosed. And if you shut it in on purpose, the secret is then to release it when you want it. Like a tap. All that's needed is a turbine and some other bits and bobs. Electricity is simple enough. It's not magic. Wind or water or sun to generate power, then a way of getting that into the house. It's like opening a window to let the summer breeze in and shutting it tight in the dead of winter. Sun and wind. It's what dries the clothes when you put them on the line.'

He always got excited when talking about practical things, as if everything could be healed by nails or a spot of paint.

The thing is, old broken things were lying all over the place, but no one ever discarded them, for they all said they would come in useful one day. Old carts on their sides at the backs of byres, which made great hiding places, and broken ploughs abandoned on the machair as if the ploughman had just gone off for dinner and forgotten to come back, and abandoned bits of quern-stones lying here and there, and various other iron and wooden odds and ends for God only knows what use which leant against wall-ends and fences and in attics and sheds and ditches.

Nothing was ever relinquished. They still belonged to the people who'd used them once upon a time. They might be repaired some day. Their dead hands were still on them, ready at a moment's notice to push them along. If we tried to move anything someone would shout at us to leave it.

'Someone left that there on purpose. They'll come for it one day.'

They are still there awaiting the resurrection, which will be the day Mam stands by my chair again telling me to put the kettle on.

'More water, Annie,' she'll say. 'Otherwise you'll spoil the kettle.'

As for our own old mill, the first thing was to clear up the debris of a hundred years. Sedge and rushes and thistles and rubbish which were blocking the stream. All the rusted and broken bits that couldn't be rescued or repaired. We cleaned it up until we could see what lay beneath the dirt and grime. Mam and Fearchar and I lent a hand when we could, as did Duncan when he got home from the airport. Dad said the best waterwheel we could have would be the simplest one, but the most difficult thing to make was the simplest one. That's why he believed in God, he added.

The spur wheel itself was in good order, though the pit wheel and the crown wheel needed repaired and a whole number of the wooden cogs had to be made anew. Dad oiled the central axle and it turned creakily and slowly, but the more oil he poured into the joints the smoother it ran.

'The last thing we want is to hear the wheel singing our mistakes every time it turns,' Mam said.

Calum from the local garage helped, bringing various engine parts and bits of turbines from old lorries which we assembled into a working whole. The river had a fall of six feet which was enough to power the turbine and supply us with a form of intermittent electricity. It worked best of course after a storm, when the river was in full flood. Then we had power all day, not just rationed for the evening. The windmill Dad built was much more haphazard and less successful. Later, when I came across the work of Heath Robinson I understood that Dad was just like him. Dad was good at some things (telling stories and cutting hay and stacking corn and butchering lamb into chops), but carpentry really wasn't one of them.

'More nails than wood,' Mùgan said, standing there shaking his head.

Our windmill was basically six old bicycle wheels attached to the roof of the byre, but the angles were impossible to fathom, so it never really worked properly. If we set the wheels too high they were easily blown over by the wind. If too low, they didn't circulate enough. One wheel on its own was insufficient, so Dad and Mam tried to make a connector which tied two of them together, but it was at best wobbly and inefficient. It supplied energy, but only in dribs and drabs, like a dripping tap. The generator sparked up for a moment then fizzled out.

But the improved waterwheel worked a treat. Dad tested it first with one bulb, believing that if it worked with one, it would work with several. He kept the big switch-on moment until dark so that we could all experience the arrival of the electric light in all its glory.

'We should have an official switch-on,' Duncan said. 'Like they do in the pictures.'

He'd once seen a Film Guild picture where the whole town was lit up for Christmas, with the Sheriff's wife switching on the lights.

'We'll ask Annie to do it,' Mam said. 'Seeing she's the youngest.'

*

Mam made a dumpling cake filled with raisins for the occasion and we all waited impatiently until the sun set far to the west, behind the Stac skerries. She would never think of serving herself first. It would have been wrong. We all regretted that it wasn't the depth of winter, for then we wouldn't have to wait so long. By that time it wasn't even getting dark until about nine in the evening.

'It's not dark enough yet,' Dad kept saying. 'I can still see the church.'

Duncan and Fearchar and I crouched in the window trying to measure the dark.

'I can't see Mùgan's house,' I kept saying.

'I can,' said Fearchar. 'See – just there.'

'You're just saying that. We all know it's there – it's another thing seeing it.'

'I am so seeing it.'

'What about Mrs MacPherson's? Can you see her shed?'

'No.'

'Then it's dark enough to put the lights on.'

I called out.

'Mam! Dad! It's dark enough now. We can't see Mrs MacPherson's shed, and that means it's really dark.'

'Okay,' they said, even though they could both see it without even looking.

One time, in the children's ward at the hospital, we brought in a magician to do a few tricks. After the show, he told me the secret: nothing ever appears without being there already. The rabbit was always there, hidden in the bottom half of the hat. The same with Dad's electricity: he'd spent nights preparing the magic.

We all gathered round the switch, which was located above the table beside the door. I stood nearest, on a chair, hand poised over the button.

'Let's do a count down,' Mam said, and we all chanted.

'Ten. Nine. Eight. Seven. Six. Five. Four. Three. Two. One. ZERO!'

I pressed the switch down. Something flickered, and then slowly the bulb lit up just the same way as a candle does until it catches the air and settles. Except that sometimes the wick wouldn't catch and the candle went out and then we'd have to start all over again. Not with the electric: the bulb glowed faintly and then increased in brightness just like the tilley mantle until it was ready to burst. I was disappointed because the bulb only lit up gradually and faintly, and wasn't fast and bright and instant as Mr Johnston and everyone had promised. But that might only be with proper electricity brought in from the mainland, I thought, not our home-made one. The light was yellow and harsh and Mam was mortified seeing the dust and cobwebs she'd never noticed before in the far corners of the ceiling. New things make you see old things better. And even though cobwebs make good bandages she knew fine that wasn't the reason they were hanging there! Dad immediately noticed the crack in the kitchen wall that needed fixed, so the next few days were spent cleaning and dusting and painting until everything that had a light shining on it became light itself.

Everyone wanted a shot at pressing the switch and watching the miracle of the bulb slowly lighting up. I don't think Fearchar, even to this day, understands how it works!

'But the switch is here,' he said. 'So how come the light comes on up there?'

Duncan told him that all the switch did was to connect the wires which then transmitted the electricity itself up to the shining bulb.

'So does it shine all the way through the wire then?' he asked. 'Does that mean it'll shine inside the wall where the wires will be?'

'Course not, daftie,' Duncan said. 'It's just the current that goes through the wire. It only glows when it reaches the bulb.'

Fearchar of course asked him what a 'current' was, but Duncan just scoffed.

'You'll never learn anything. Next thing you'll ask if it's the same thing that Mam puts into the dumplings.'

Once we'd all settled down, I studied the old photograph of

Granny and Grampa above the dresser. They seemed suddenly older, belonging to a previous century, under the new glow of the yellow light. The following day Mam put the grainy photographs away in a drawer. Fearchar and Duncan stood studying the light bulb itself, half-shading their eyes from the glare. The best thing were the wires inside the bulb, which were as flimsy and thin as a spider's legs. It was amazing that something as bright and dangerous as electricity was sparking through these spindly wires. The lightbulbs hung naked until the shop started to sell shades with the flower patterns that softened the colour, pretending it wasn't electricity after all.

It was only the beginning.

'Come with me,' Dad said once our system was more stable, and Duncan and Fearchar and I followed him out. He led us over to the byre where he lifted the old tarpaulin sail which covered the bales of hay in the corner. Hidden within the bales of hay were a variety of objects. A toaster. A kettle. A small fridge.

'Got them from Calum,' Dad said. 'A present for Mam.'

Fearchar carried the toaster in. Duncan the kettle. Dad the fridge. Mam filled the kettle with water and boiled it. Fearchar put two slices of bread in the toaster. Dad wondered what to put in the fridge. Everything keeps as it is – the herring and mackerel and meat in the salted barrels outside, the cheese in the vat in the back room and the milk was always fresh from the cow.

'I'll put what's left of the cake in it after we've celebrated,' Mam said. I put the dumpling on the table and Mam cut half of it into five equal pieces then placed the half that was left in the fridge.

'That'll keep forever now,' I said, though I knew fine it would all be eaten before the night was out.

'It's like manna. You can't hoard it,' Dad said. 'We'll have to eat it all tonight.'

The dumpling was delicious. So delicious that we all took extra time to eat it so that it would last forever. Everyone resisted the temptation to ask for more. When it was finished, I had the nerve to ask the question on all our tongues.

'Will we get a television?'

It was the big moment, and the boys were ashamed they lacked the courage I had.

'I don't think the circuit will carry it,' Dad said. 'Otherwise the lights will go out.'

'That's all right.' I said. 'We can watch the telly in the dark.'

22

Polishing

DUNCAN SPENT HIS time cleaning and polishing things at the airport. Sometimes I helped him. James Campbell had a wood-panelled office which needed lightly oiled and buffed every day to keep it shining bright. Oak wood brought in specially from Sweden, which Duncan soaked with linseed oil first thing in the morning and last thing at night. The trick was to do it in tiny circles, leaving the oil to soak in slowly, without rubbing it. That brought the grain through bit by bit and Duncan and I watched the dark stains getting darker and the lighter areas getting brighter, giving a perfect balance to the wood. A thing should shine dull as if no one had touched it, Duncan told me. He thought it weird that people cut down trees then went to all kinds of trouble to make sure they looked like they did before they were cut down. Though he knew they never would, for once a thing is dead it's dead forever unless it becomes something else. A white butterfly was the soul of someone on the way to paradise. Though they didn't seem to be in much of a hurry, feeding on every flower on the way. Maybe they thought they were already in heaven.

After polishing Campbell's office, Duncan spent time in the cafe. Mostly in the small kitchen area at the back, washing the dishes and pots and pans and cups and saucers, but also occasionally front of house as it was called, serving the soup and sandwiches and tea and cakes. In the afternoon, as the shadows began to extend and point eastwards towards the hills, he cleaned the seating and the walls and the toilets, and sometimes was allowed out with a brush to sweep the dirt away from the tarmac: dust that came from God only knows where, but on wilder windier days also clumps of grass and heather and seaweed which flew down from the moor or up from the shore. He gathered the debris onto a big shovel and then scattered it over the fence in a kind of eternal cycle, like an endless Sunday. Bits of grass and coltsfoot and pink clover were pushing their way up through the cracks in the tarmac, however, so Duncan left those. They added life to the tar. Someday they would cover the whole runway.

James Campbell rewarded him, though. At four o'clock every day he was allowed to go into the old hangar and spend the last hour of his working day polishing the vintage Piper Cruiser. It was a thing of beauty, and often at that time, after school, Sgliugan wandered down to the airstrip and Duncan called him into the hangar to help us. For that holy hour Duncan was pilot and Sgliugan the crew. Duncan sat in the pilot's seat and gave Sgliugan various commands and orders.

'Wash the windows please,' and Duncan sat there making revving noises while Sgliugan dampened the cloth in the bucket and wiped the windows of the aircraft. One bucket had warm water with soap and one had clean cold water. Sgliugan had by now perfected the sequence, dropping the cloth into the soapy water and washing the two front panes carefully, one after the other, in small round circles. It all led up to the highlight of his day when he was allowed to fling the whole contents of the cold water bucket at the glass. Duncan always gave him a countdown,

'Three, Two, One, Fire!'

And Sgliugan watched in daily delight as the flood of water hit the windscreens and poured and dripped down the glass. Duncan always flinched when Sgliugan threw the bucketful of water, convinced that one day he would get carried away and fling the tin bucket along with it. Sgliugan then watched as every last drop of water flowed and seeped down the window, behind which he could see Duncan, wearing his helmet and goggles, navigating the aircraft in to land through the storm and the pouring rain. Duncan waved him away frantically from the runway, afraid that he would run him down as he came in to land.

The best part was then climbing out of the cockpit and removing his helmet with a flourish while Sgliugan asked him where he'd flown to that day.

'O, just a short mission today, John. Over to Copenhagen in the morning, and then down to London in the afternoon. Maybe you can join me in the flight tomorrow? That is, if you're not too scared?'

And Sgliugan would shake his head and say,

'No thanks, Duncan. I'm perfectly happy here making sure things are safe on the ground. Air Traffic Control is even more important than the pilot, Mr Campbell said.'

But Duncan knew. The place was already fixed. At its limits. Like the airstrip itself, for once you reached the end of the runway you had to take off or crash. There was no space for him to grow, and if he stayed he would just become a reflection of everyone else. A shadow of his Dad and his Grandad – always compared unfavourably with them too. Everyone would say they'd been stronger and braver and better. Better suited to the place. Had fitted in better. Ploughed behind horses and fished from open boats and were happy enough as and where they were. Had big strong fishermen's hands.

Two real planes arrived and departed every day. One in the morning came from Glasgow and then returned there, while the one in the afternoon came from and returned to Inverness. The Glasgow flight could carry thirty-two passengers and the Inverness flight eighteen. Council officials and other professionals made up the bulk of the trade, with the rest mostly consisted of people travelling to hospitals for urgent appointments, or family members going to visit a patient already in care. Shoppers and students and general travellers constantly complained that the service was too expensive and so still chose to travel to and from the mainland by ferry.

'It takes ten times as long but is ten times as cheap,' was the common song.

Nevertheless, Sir Bert and James Campbell and the other developers were well pleased. Thanks to Councillor MacPhee, the service was classified as a 'core lifeline service' by the local authority, and hence by the central government, so an annual subsidy to cover all costs and contingencies was guaranteed for the first five years.

'The rest is profit,' said Sir Bert. 'But the most important thing is that it raises the profile of our airline. Makes us a social, not an economic, airline. The blue and white stripes with the eagle's logo will soon be as recognised throughout the area as Nessie herself.'

He knew better than anyone that the real targets were elsewhere. The important connections to mainland Europe and across the Atlantic, and the trade from these places to the oil wells off the coasts. One day oil will be discovered and explored here too, he told us. That would be the day, even if he didn't live to see it. This island enterprise would not make a fortune, but neither would it lose a great deal of money, and he knew that when oil fields were discovered way out west this would be a very useful base for further exploration, to St Kilda and Rockall and beyond, with FlyAir already in pole position with considerable social credit.

He hoped that the airline would be both loved and trusted, for earning the future always depends on investing in the present. I suppose it depends what kind of future you're speculating in.

23

Together

IT SURPRISED SOME people, though it didn't surprise me in the least, for when you are that age everything can be something else. All my fallen shirt-buttons were real money and when Dolina and I cycled across the wee stone bridge we were in Iceland on the far side where everything was made of snow. We'd watched caterpillars turn into butterflies, and lambs into sheep and calves into cows, so when Lisa and Niall Cuagach became a couple, so what? You never knew what a thing could be. Though some said it was witchcraft.

'The evil eye,' Old Murdo said. 'You all know the way he looks at things. She's under his spell.'

She wasn't, for only love creates miracles. I know that sounds trite, but it's really the only truth I know.

Everyone talked about it for a while, until they found something else to talk about. Peter the Proverb put it like this: 'It's like putting half an apple and half an orange together and making a new fruit.'

Mùgan rebuked him. 'Meaning that they were only half-people before? Get a life, man. And anyway, he gave her a trailer-load of seaweed as a gift when she first came back home, so they always had an eye for one another.'

I've thought about it a lot too. They were like two islands which can be forded at low tide. For hours, and sometimes days, an expanse of water separates the islands until the tide goes out and the hardened sand is revealed, which you can cross by foot or cart. And once you reach the other side you look back as the tide slowly fills and covers the strand. The only way back is by boat or waiting for the next ebb tide. It's a bit like being in two places at once. Like when you're in school but your mind is all outside, thinking of better things. And then when playtime comes you say to your best pal, 'Let's play.' And she says, 'Aye, let's.'

For Lisa and Niall Cuagach I think it must have been like discovering things for themselves as when they were children, despite what books and other people had told them. Even if Christopher Columbus himself had been there before them, still no one ever before crossed the ford like they did.

In the same way that no one ever cycled or made daisy-chains like Dolina and I. Same as there never has been another Saturday like this, though there have been so many of them. Wherever Dolina and I went, no one had ever been there before, and no one had ever run or skipped like us before. But we had to play by the rules, otherwise it didn't count. We could only make daisy-chains from daisies, even though Katie, of course, always tried to cheat and used other kinds of flowers if there weren't enough daisies, but we told her that wasn't allowed because if a poppy or a marsh-marigold or daffodil – we called that 'the flower with the bowed head' – was in the chain then it obviously wasn't a daisy-chain any more! It would then be just a flower-chain, we said, which was something completely different, same as Orion was a sword in the sky while the Plough just glittered in the shape of a plough, because obviously there was no earth to till up there, unless Mùgan was right after all and these other stars were the harvest it produced, same as we had corn and hay and potatoes. You have to use the things that are there, otherwise it's cheating. And maybe everything is there anyway.

'It's more like travelling the world,' Mùgan said. 'When I arrived in Java I realised how little I knew. And by the time I'd finished all my voyages, my ignorance was greater than ever, though I realised that wherever I went someone had been there before. But that didn't matter. It was the first time for me. And coming back was also new. For while I was away everything changed, so that by the time I returned I knew nothing and had to learn everything again. I didn't come back to die like a salmon in its birthing pool. Oh no! He who knows nothing loves nothing, as the other man said. Thing is, in every country in the world the sun rises in the morning and sets in the evening. Like putting your clothes on in the morning and taking them off to go to bed at night. And the other thing is that whatever you do with snow, it's only water.'

I think Niall Cuagach's stance against the airport, doomed to failure though it was, emboldened everyone. It was as if folk realised that they could actually do something rather than merely submit to fate. That even if what they tried failed, that was only one way to judge it. It had other value beyond success. Like when you knit a jersey but make it too short. Still, it can be a small cardigan or a shawl, and – if needs be – you can unravel the whole thing and start again from the very beginning. It's only stitches after all.

Peter the Proverb, for example, immediately returned to the original family trade of shoe-making. It was a practical solace – something he could literally put his hands to, and so escape from the endless cycle of words that had entranced him. He carved an iron sign for his gate on which was written 'Peter MacDonald, Master Shoemaker.' He hated the word cobbler, which was an inferior trade, to do with mere repairing. Though any half-decent craft worker knows that repairing a thing is more difficult than doing it new.

He fetched out his father's last from the byre and of course Duncan and Fearchar and I went over to see what all the racket was, and he proudly showed us round his newly-cleaned shed where he had set up all the ancient tools of his trade, each clearly marked with a card in his beautiful copper-plate writing – last, tranchet, horn, bristles, rasps, rings and gudgeons and other stuff I can't remember. We watched him working his old shoes. A twist straightened here and a dent filled in there, forever recasting things and never making anything new.

The so-called Master Shoemaker even showed us how the whole thing worked, taking down an old roll of leather from a shelf and cutting it with scissors before placing it on the last and moving on eventually to stitching and seaming. The best thing was his coil of string which he dipped into a bucket of tar to make the bindings. The only problem is that the materials he used were so old and inflexible that the shoes were no damn use to anyone. So inflexible as to be unwearable, and so they sat there on his desk as strange, unsold works of art. The simplest things are the most difficult to understand.

People mocked him because he also made things that didn't resemble anything else and were of no practical use, and of course if a thing was not of any practical use it was useless. Boots that were shaped more like a kettle than shoes and other bits and blobs and shapes which lay on tables about his yard as if they were some fancy sculptures when they were really only rubbish which had failed to be something else. But maybe everything's a failure, Emily? The problem was that these objects he made didn't have any proper names either. Unlike a spade or a hoe or a plough with which you could dig the earth, these nameless things of his didn't do anything. And if they didn't have a name and if people didn't know what to call them and if they didn't do anything there was absolutely no point to them, was there?

Lisa and I went to see Niall Cuagach the day after he ploughed the field. We all stood on the heath outside his house looking down at the JCBs and steamrollers carving out the new airstrip. They were quite small from a distance. It was like watching a film that you couldn't pause even if you wanted to. It would happen, as things had always happened despite all our fears and hopes and plans and protests. He had a dog once which was easily the best sheepdog in the place, yet he was killed one night by a drunk driver.

'It was pointless,' Lisa said. 'What you did. Just a gesture.'

'Nothing is pointless. Not even gestures. Perhaps, in fact, these are the most significant things of all.'

'I doubt it.'

'I don't.'

He pointed to the newly-laid tarmac stretched out below.

'That's just a gesture too. A grand gesture and expensive gesture, I grant you, but a gesture nevertheless.'

'I doubt it,' Lisa said again. 'It looks very hard and real and solid to me.'

'Though it won't last, Lisa. It will fail, but at least they will have a perfect scapegoat. Someone to blame – me.'

And he was right. It didn't last.

The airport half-operated for a year and then closed down. Six months after it was built, Sir Bert was replaced by Air Marshall Maxwell who ordered an immediate financial audit of all the company's operations. The financial secretary, Cartwright, had long known the true state of things but had massaged the figures in deference to Sir Bert. Freed from that sentiment he laid out the bald statistics, which appalled Maxwell and the rest of the board, who ordered the immediate closure of more than a dozen routes, including the one at Àrdglas. Although they protested, the local council were glad to be rid of the financial burden. It lay derelict and disused for years, weeds growing through the cracked tarmac, the wind whipping round and through the empty buildings, until Sgliugan came to the rescue later on.

Once the airstrip closed, Campbell made various attempts to keep some form of business going there. He even rented a helicopter for a season, attempting to run it as a tourist venture taking visitors on day or night trips over to St Kilda and Rockall, but constant bad weather got in the way and the turnover was not sufficient to maintain it. He then transformed one of the hangars into a traveller's hostel, but that too failed – perhaps he was simply too visionary, attempting something decades before its time.

Duncan worked for him as a kind of glorified caretaker, making sure that the premises remained under lock and key and in a reasonable state of repair, but it was hard to fight against the elements. The hangars were big and cold and exposed, and every gale took its toll: zinc flew off the roof, damp began to moulden the windows, the big steel doors skewed off their hinges, whining every time the wind blew through them. We could all see that it was affecting Duncan who became depressed, wandering about an empty site with ladders and brushes and tins of paint in a futile gesture against the elements. Even the orange wind-sock, which remained bravely flapping for a while, finally tore off, bits of it ending up in the loch and the rest flying west towards the Atlantic.

I reminded him of his other dream. Ever since he was a child, he had also longed for a career at sea, and now and again beautiful booklets would arrive through the post from various Merchant Navy companies promising great things. He was yearning to escape. I can still see the gorgeous ships of The Blue Star Line and The Clan Line and The Pacific Steam Navigation Company adorning the magazines, with the single word, 'Adventure', written across the front.

I didn't want to tell him direct, so one day I asked him if he still had the leaflets.

'Aye,' he said. 'In a box under my bed.'

'Can I see them?'

'Why? You wanna go to sea?'

Again I was courageous enough.

'No. But you might.'

He laughed.

'Think I want to be Long John Silver or something? And anyway I'm colour-blind. They wouldn't take me.'

'That's only for navigation, Duncan. There are other things – you could be an engineer? Or just a deck-hand – that's what Dad did when he was your age. He was a bosun. That means he was in charge of the crew.'

It was a risky thing to say, for he might deliberately then avoid doing anything his father had done. But I knew fine he loved Dad, even though they never showed any signs of affection to one another. It was the way things were in those days. If men showed any physical tenderness – say if they touched hands – they were considered odd. How things have changed – it's now the other way round, and if they don't meet and part with an embrace they are considered equally strange. But Duncan didn't say anything in response, which was a good sign.

He talked to me about it later in the week, however. For things take time. He'd just finished his shift at the empty airport and as I walked home from school he came cycling up beside me.

'Lift?'

I put the satchel on my back and jumped up on to the handlebars, legs splayed out on either side of the wheels. He cycled slowly, as it was difficult to balance everything whilst simultaneously turning the pedals. We'd all tried it loads of time of course, but had never completely mastered it. One way is to sit right back on the handlebars so that your body rests against the cyclist, though that makes it difficult for the person who's cycling to see properly. Another way is to balance like a bird on the handlebars so that your weight is perfectly distributed, but that was very hard to maintain with the bumps and holes in the road surface. And it was sore on your backside! The usual compromise was to mix a bit of both, depending on which way the wind was blowing and whether we had hills to ascend.

That day the stretch of road was flat so I sat perfectly balanced, allowing Duncan to cycle and steer steadily against the breeze.

'I got a letter back from Shaw Savill's this morning,' he said. 'I can start with them next Monday as a deck-boy.'

'Waw!' I shouted against the breeze. 'You don't even have to go for an Aptitude Test or anything?'

'No. I was smart. I got Mùgan to send a reference with my own letter. He was a skipper with them in the old days.'

'Maybe you'll be a Captain too, one day?' I called to him, and I just heard him laughing as we turned the corner into our home-track.

He told Mam and Dad and Fearchar that evening after dinner,

and they were pleased, for Mam said that drifting around an empty airstrip with a mop and bucket was no life for a bonny lad. Dad said it would do Duncan the world of good, to see all those places he'd visited as a young man. After all, things had turned out fine. You could go to Adelaide and still get back home. The dream of the young was to go away, of the old to return.

It was the end of our childhood, for it was the first time that our world was divided. I knew this was different from Dad's days. Duncan would go away and never return, for that was the way of him. He didn't want to be like the other boys who had grown up and become fat and drank too much. He would no longer be restricted by place or time or past conventions. When we went on bike journeys together he always wanted to go further than was allowed, and if Mam and Dad told the three of us to be back by 6pm, Duncan would persuade us that 6.30 would do fine. We'd get a row of course, but we'd always have some kind of reasonable excuse which made everything sound plausible. Freedom seemed to lie beyond what was said or promised.

It was as if words simply meant what they said rather than what people heard. Like rain coming in from the west. It's only now that doubt constantly comes, asking, 'What does this mean?' I suppose too many things have fractured along the way. Then, if we saw a frog hopping across the road, or we opened a book at school, or we saw Niall Cuagach descending the brae of the hill, it was like the sun spilling through the clouds or like Dìleas nuzzling up against me when I came home. It was just the way of things. The strange, marvellous way of things.

The following evening we were out at the end of the barn. I was sitting on the ledge-edge reading a book. Fearchar was chucking a stone at an empty can – the game was to throw a stone ten times and see how many times it landed inside the can. Duncan was putting a patch on the tube of his bicycle. It's what he missed most later on. Just hanging out with us.

'So you're going?' Fearchar said to him.

'Aye.'

'When?'

'Soon.'

'Soon as?'

'Aye. Soon as.'

'Soon as what?'

'Soon as I can get away from here. It's choking me. Leave this boring hole. Everyone knowing what you're doing. And thinking. As if there was anything to do anyway.'

'But there are lots of things to do.'

Duncan laughed. Scoffed.

'Really? Like what? Shear sheep and watch the rain?'

'Play football.'

'What? With that daft Sgliugan?'

'Well, there's also me. And Fatty Morrison. And Annie. So, what are these other things you want to do?'

'Things.'

'Things? Such as?'

'Such as. Such as the things I saw in Inverness. I was there for a night.'

'What things?'

And the word broke out.

'Girls.'

'Girls?'

'Aye, girls. Or women, more precisely.'

'And?'

'And saw things.'

'Things? Did you?'

'Think I'd tell you, eh?'

His tyre was fixed. He jumped on his bike and cycled off down to the machair, past the bonny bleating lambs. As if we didn't know all about it already, surrounded by sheep and rams and lambs and cows and calves and hens and all the rest of it since the day we ourselves were born.

*

His first journey took him to South Africa, then east to Malaysia and Borneo, which was another year. He returned home after two, now a grown man with a fine sailor's beard, though he still had that anxious way about him, as if at any moment he'd be found out and reported for some mistake. I could see him moving his hand a fraction as if to lift it to his mouth so he could suck his thumb as he did when he was a child, but he always stopped himself in time. He'd stopped being a child when he stopped playing football on the machair. His third journey took him over to Melbourne and I still remember the air-mail letter arriving with its beautiful blue stamp of a wallaby crouching in the bushes.

'*Dear Father and Mother and Fearchar and Annie,*' the letter said.

I hope this finds you well as I am well. The voyage out was something of an adventure. We had some very rough weather down the west coast of Africa, but after doing bunkers in Johannesburg we had a good voyage down as far as Australia. This is a lovely country, although very hot at times for a man like me used to the Hebridean wind and gales! The news is that I have got a shore job here in Melbourne at the docks and intend to stay on. The country is short of labourers and my visa has already been cleared so that I can live and work here as long as I wish. And the other very good news is that I have met this lovely girl and that we are just about to become engaged and I thought that you should all be the first to know! Her name is Rachel Wood and she is a born and brought up Aussie, as we say here! I hope you are all keeping well and that I will see you all soon.

With regards,
Your loving son and brother
Duncan

Things were never going to be the same again. He got married the following year and settled in Melbourne. We didn't have enough money to go out to the wedding, though Mam and Dad managed to fly over some years later to see him and Rachel and the grandchildren –James and Kirsteen and Amelie. Goodness – Mam and Dad thought flying was marvellous! They were amazed to be living Duncan's dream. Looking down on the red deserts of Arabia from 40,000 feet up they told me they wondered what all the fuss had been about. Sir Bert and James Campbell may have been asking for so little, after all. Just that we'd become better connected with the world, which would have happened anyway, just as day follows night.

Duncan himself only returned home twice, many years after – the first time for Dad's funeral and then for Mam's. I occasionally ask him if he wants to fly back over to visit the island with me for old times' sake, but he always answers with his stock phrase,

'That was then, this is now.'

As if time was frozen. Which maybe it is. He has become accustomed to the warmth, and gladly took up citizenship decades ago. We belong to our surroundings, even when they wither in front of us. It's like that juniper tree I planted where the old rowan had been. I still see the red berries after all these years!

Lisa and Niall Cuagach lived in their own Australia up on the moor in what was, in effect, a common-law marriage. Everyone on the island believed they lived as man and wife, though it all depends on how you define that. Certainly some disapproved, because they weren't married in church – in fact they had gone through no such official ceremony, as far as anyone knows. Whatever they did they did privately, since love, like everything else, doesn't need to be approved of to be true. Folk watched them working in harness. She digging the earth while he planted the seed. Him leading the horses while she guided the plough over the ridge.

'Neither of us felt the need for that,' Lisa told me. 'We just talked, and shared things – looked after the cattle, grew things and cared for each other. That's not hard to understand, is it, Annie?'

'No. Of course not.'

For once you stop caring you die. Every nurse has seen it; and maybe every human being.

'He respected and trusted me, and I trusted and respected him. It took a while, but even he finally acknowledged that no one owes everything to himself alone.'

Lisa and Niall Cuagach were out of time, which may be the only place to be, though their time has now come. The land itself was their love. They knew that life came from the soil. Hah! The soil. Or the earth. Or the sea. Or the land. Or the rocks. Or the hills, the mountains, the river, the stream, the loch, the potato-patch, the air or the sky. No one ever called it the environment. Just The Loch of the White Swan, or the Red River, or Mairead's Stack, or the Hill of Plenty, or whatever. A place made human. The white frothy line a third of the way up the loch was where the salt and fresh waters met.

Lisa and Niall Cuagach, to the end, basically lived off and for the earth, growing all their own produce, from potatoes to peppers, making their own cheese and crowdie as well as rearing and slaughtering their own pigs and cattle and sheep. Old-fashioned skills that time has caught up with. Mam and Dad would be proud of them. I wonder if the future will envy them.

'We just do the simple things well,' Lisa said the last time I saw her. 'The basic four-year rotation system and making sure that what we take out of the land is always put back, either directly by our pigs and cattle and sheep and horses, or dug in by us from the dung-cart. Good drainage is the key to everything. If you look after things they will look after you. After a while things seem as if they've been there forever. I still have that old bike, Annie. The blue one – remember? Works as well now as it did then. It's something, not nothing.' But then maybe she betrayed herself, adding, as we looked down on to the villages, 'They were the best of times, Annie. Weren't they?'

Lisa's best success was to bring the previously exposed and barren hillside into production with an intelligent mixture of tree cover and irrigation, so that in autumn it resembled the Corsican hillside Eric and I used to walk through on our holidays to collect grapes and mangoes and oranges. Lisa didn't manage such exotic produce, but the more basic cabbages and carrots and turnips and beetroot and rhubarb growing between the teeming patches of wildflowers were equally impressive. What had once been little more than a wasteland gave her everything from bluebells to blaeberries.

'The more colourful the flowers are, the more they attract bees,' she said. 'They like red. And the honey is delicious.'

The irrigation system was both simple and effective. She basically created a high water-meadow where the rain gathered in channels which zigzagged down the brae, eventually trickling into the loch at the bottom. Not an inch of the hillside was wasted.

'The trick,' she told me, 'is to make sure that the first channel gathers enough water not to overflow, and that the lower channels and pools are always kept clear and clean. Once you get them streaming, gravity does the rest. You don't even need a spade. I just walk through the drains now and again, clearing them with my boots. We do very little, Annie, because nature itself does so much. She never breaks her laws. We do. The biggest danger is the simplest thing – some accident. Because most things are never meant. We can plan and sow and nurture and grow, but some things we can't do anything about. Growing older is one of them.'

Lisa and Niall also had a boat from which they supplied themselves, and indeed the neighbourhood, with lobsters and crabs and saithe and mackerel and trout. The last time I saw Lisa she told me that neither of them had been near a shop for years.

'Completely self-sufficient?'

'In everything. From these shoes Niall made out of deer-hide to these ear-rings I'm wearing made out of sea-shells. We live in an oasis, Annie, not in a desert. As long as we have our health and each other and know it. Otherwise…'

She never finished the sentence, but I could see the fear of her isolation out there on the moor in her eyes, for when it comes to what really matters, we need others as they need us.

*

Meantime, James Campbell was one of those guys who would walk out of a crash unscathed. Like the water-horse he was all things to all men, and when the airport went bankrupt, he was the only one to profit from it, because he owned the land and the assets on it, which increased in value whether or not a seagull or a plane ever flew over it again. The cult of the countryside would see to that. I suppose he could only be himself. Like Cuagach and all of us. Fate, they called it.

Sir Bert took the punch, though it wasn't much of a blow to him, for AirFly's assets were registered offshore, which meant that none of the debtors were ever paid. To be fair to Sir Bert, he accepted the public and political criticism with his usual grace, apologising for the failure of the venture, while at the same time making it clear that neither he, nor Campbell, nor Lisa nor Councillor MacPhee nor any of the local workers or contractors were to blame. Failure is part of every performance. Alex's crackly old recorder, the one he brought to the school meeting before the airport ever was, tells it well. It sits there as a working heirloom in the local history museum with a digital button bringing them all back to life. Or at least their words. Which without seeing MacPhee's handkerchief and Campbell's smoke-circles and Sir Bert's childish glances are songs without tunes.

'My dear people, you know yourselves how it works. Investors invest their money, and if they don't get a decent return on it, well they're going to pull out of the operation. That's simply what happened here, and you will all surely appreciate that no one can afford to lose money day after day, week after week, month after month and year after year. Better to return when half-way across an overflowing river than continue all the way and drown, don't you think?'

Sgliugan was a great help to Campbell, for when the airstrip and the café closed down and Duncan had gone off to sea Sgliugan took his place as day and night watchman, making sure the place was wind and watertight and that nothing was damaged or stolen. More importantly, he was Campbell's eyes and ears in the neighbourhood, reporting back on everything that was done and said. Occasional visitors came and looked at the buildings and the airstrip, and all of them were potential buyers for Campbell. Kindness was valuable.

He told Sgliugan to be generous to such visitors and make them tea and make sure they were given a sight of the Piper Cruiser, which Sgliugan still washed and polished to perfection inside the old hangar every day. He used Silvo, which gave such a shine to the plane that it always looked as if had never been touched before. One of those visitors – a Mr Patel from India – came back a few times, and within a year of bankruptcy Campbell sold the plane to him along with a twenty-year lease of the buildings and the land itself.

Campbell moved to the mainland after that, and for a while built houses and offices around Inverness. Some folk say he met an Aboriginal Canadian woman and moved to Ontario and married her, though others said he just sold up and emigrated, seeing better opportunities for himself in Canada where the future was welcomed rather than suspected.

He became a millionaire, helping to develop the successful plans for the Canso Spaceport, and was duly honoured for giving employment and homes to thousands of people across the decades. Brasso polishes brass, Mùgan used to say. Last time I heard, years ago, he had just been appointed to the Senate, and I watched his inaugural speech on television, displaying the same old charm and single-mindedness that he had in the old days. You could almost believe that he believed what he was saying. He spoke about the people's destiny.

'Other nations imagine a past,' he declared, 'but here in Canada we imagine a future.'

His speech brought his fellow Senators to their feet, with no Mùgan to hand to question the meaning of it all. However, Mam always used to say that Mùgan only ever understood what was not said in the first place, so it might not have made much difference.

24

Switched On

IT'S LIKE CYCLING downhill without brakes. Dolina and I did it all the time. The thrill is in knowing that it's all or nothing, resisting the temptation to hold the soles of your shoes to the ground. Things fly by, and the sound of the wind in your face makes you close your eyes, knowing that, if all else fails, the boggy ground to your left will always save you, all wet and squelched and out of breath and glad to be alive. It's inevitable one way or the other.

Strange how quickly we became used to the new world. In a matter of days, we took it for granted that we'd just flick a switch when we came into the house and the kettle would boil, or press another one and within half-an-hour or so we'd have enough hot water for a bath any time instead of boiling the four big pans of water on Saturday night. Within the year we had the miracle of an instant shower.

We tasted speed, and loved it. The immediacy of things: let there be light, and there was light! We could have whatever we wished for. We so hoped the light would get brighter and brighter until there was no darkness at all and we could play all night as well as all day and Dad could shear his sheep whenever he wanted and Mam could visit her friend Morag at any time. But what would the ghosts do then in all that brightness? And Alasdair and Joan, and Sarah and Coinneach, who had just started going out with each other and taking walks down to the shore at twilight? Maybe there would be no more secrets now for Dolina and I.

It took a while, though, for Dad's crackly home-made system

to pass into history. We kept with it for some time, but the constant winds, followed by days of calm, upset the whole thing: when a gale blew, it invariably broke the windmill which Dad and his friend Calum had put up next to the old byre, and when it was dry and airless neither the windmill nor the waterwheel worked as we wanted. Even Mam and Dad quickly became accustomed to the ease of electricity, and before the winter was out they contacted Johnston, who arranged for us also to be connected to the main grid.

'Just because we all wear shoes doesn't mean we're all the same,' Dad said. 'After all – look, I'm size ten, and none of you are.'

'I am,' Duncan said.

'Aye, and soon size eleven,' said Mam.

Dad bought a radiogram, which became his pride and joy. It was a beautiful looking piece of furniture: a large dark wood frame, with the wireless and all its magic stations – you can hardly imagine how exotic names like Berlin and Hilversum and Moscow seemed to us then – and the red dial to the front, and when you opened the top, inside was a record player! At first we had no records, so we just marvelled at the radio, which hissed and crackled from across the wide world. One minute you would hear this beautiful voice from London speaking very slowly and clearly, and the next minute fantastically-fast languages that sounded as if they came from outer space because you couldn't understand a single word or even distinguish one word from the other. Some of them were deep and guttural, the way some of the fishermen sometimes spoke out at the pier, and others were light and airy and sounded like Hazel when she talked about the fairies. Hazel used to see them down on the machair, and sang and danced with them, but when people started laughing at her she didn't see them any more.

The best were the music channels we soon discovered. Mam and Dad liked one that was called Athlone, because the songs they heard there were so like the ones we sang ourselves. Their favourites were 'The Galway Shawl' and 'Danny Boy' and even though Dad had no singing voice he always sang along with Mam when these came on the radio.

At Oranmore in the county Galway
One pleasant evening in the month of May
I spied a damsel, she was young and handsome
Her beauty fairly took my breath away

She wore no jewels, nor costly diamonds
No paint nor powder, no none at all
She wore a bonnet with ribbons on it
And around her shoulders was the Galway shawl

They were too slow for us though, and when Mam and Dad weren't there we played with the dial and went through all the channels, staying for a while on Paris for jazz and Hamburg for orchestras, though our favourite stations were (of course) Luxembourg and Caroline and Radio One because the songs were fast and new all the time, and also because Duncan liked listening to Horace Bachelor who promised lots of money if he wrote to him at Keynsham Bristol, though Radio One was difficult to get because the signal was useless. So we'd just squabble over Luxembourg and Caroline, which often ended up with us listening to neither, at which point Duncan would turn the dial to Leningrad and sit there nodding his head sagely as if he understood, and agreed with, every single strange thing that was being said.

Dad invited Blind Thomas who lived along the road to listen to the news on the radio, for no one hears better than the blind, but Thomas was disappointed that the man inside the box was telling things in a steady regular voice and not like the way he told his stories, going up and down and faster and slower depending on what was happening. Though he couldn't get over the sound of the pips and Big Ben which signalled the hour with a heavy gong, like a funeral. Maybe the Big Ben people didn't have altar-bells which tinkled happily.

'The problem,' he said, 'is that these people are tied to clock-time and not real time. What if the gongs stop working?'

Blind Thomas always shaped things with his hands as he spoke as if that brought the thing he was speaking about into being. When speaking of clock time he beat each hour with his index finger and when he spoke of real time he made circles.

The thing about the stations we liked was that they were for young people just like us – 'The Station of the Stars', as they called it! We became stars, afterwards singing the lyrics as we carted the byre and cleaned the well and cut the turf and stacked the hay on the machair. While old Mùgan in the next field chanted some dirge about Culloden, Fearchar and I danced a duet as we threw the hay to one another: 'it's been a hard day's night', sang Fearchar, 'and I've been working like a dog', I sang, and then we both barked 'woof-woof!' and laughed. We were in Liverpool, where Mam and Dad had met and fallen in love. It seemed that time itself accelerated after that. Duncan left, and we all missed him like you miss the sun when it's not shining, though you know it's there somewhere behind the clouds. Fearchar seemed to have a sudden confidence in himself, or in the future.

Shortly after that we also got a television. It was disappointing, because the picture was just black and white, which seemed lifeless compared to the brown and black and white and speckled cows which grazed outside on the green grass covered with purple orchids and clover! Dad insisted on preserving the electricity we had, so our viewing was restricted anyway. He would occasionally switch it on to see the weather forecast, scoffing as he watched it.

'Uh, uh. That's not what the birds say. Tha an eala a' snàmh; thig frasan blàth roimh fheasgar' ('The swan is swimming; warm showers will come before evening').

I suppose Dad forgot that the forecaster was six hundred miles away in London, where they were in the middle of a heatwave. The only programme Fearchar and I watched was *Blue Peter*, and though I once wrote away for a badge it was never sent, though it may just have got lost in the post because Old Hemingway, who occasionally delivered the local mail when Roddy was on holiday, was known to throw things into the nearest ditch if he took a notion to head off to the pub. And besides, they said he sometimes stole the mail-sacks to make blankets and trousers for himself.

The television pictures paled into insignificance besides my shells, which continued to display all their glory in full technicolour around the house. Fearchar told me I should cement them into the wall, so Dad gave me a small bag of cement which I mixed with water in a bucket, and I began sticking the shells to the top of the garden wall. It was gorgeous, because you could see them shining there as you walked down through the village. They glittered in the sun, reflecting the light like a mirror, and even when it rained you could see them sparkling brightly in the puddles that gathered on top of the wall. They are still there, as if neither elements nor time have happened.

After the initial excitement of the light bulb and the kettle and the radiogram and the black and white telly and the Baby Belling cooker, we returned to normal. Pressing a switch became as customary as lighting a candle, and a well-dressed stranger speaking English out of a box in the corner as normal as seeing the dog snoozing beside the fire. Dìleas was getting old and seemed to sleep most of the day, and was being replaced by another collie, Rover, who got over the initial wonder of strangers and cars and settled in nicely to his work, gathering the sheep when required.

Dad made a shepherd's crook for Duncan and Fearchar and I, and after school, now that Duncan was gone, Fearchar and I took it in turns to move the sheep from one field to the next. It wasn't the same. Without Duncan, it was more like work than a game. It was the first time we had to think about it, rather than the sheep being just there like Mam or Dad or the wind. Rover always wanted to lead, but we taught him the most important thing in the world, which is stillness. To stay at heel so he would begin to trust that the world around him wouldn't disintegrate if he sat there silent and still. We weren't secretly hoarding up anything which might startle him. He learned to trust that there was no sudden danger round the corner. That he could wait.

It was all about slowness and timing: speed and fuss only frightened the sheep, so it was always best to approach calmly and slowly. They'd stop grazing for a moment to look at me, then continue their eternal feed, and when I reached the enclosure gate I whistled softly and Rover glided round them, leading them gently towards the four-barred gate. I think he always hoped that one would go astray so that he could demonstrate his remarkable skills, circling round the lost sheep and bringing her back into the fold.

He could divide and subtract better than I could at school. If I shouted 'Divide!' he separated the sheep into two flocks, and if I called 'Subtract!' he selected a sheep, then took it away from the rest of the flock. When he removed a sheep the field seemed to get bigger, as if subtraction was actually addition, despite what the teacher said. I tried and tried to make him understand the numbers, but failed. It was always my ambition to shout 'Subtract ten' so that he could separate ten sheep from the flock, and 'Subtract twenty' so that he would take twenty to the side, and so forth. Dear daft Rover, and dear old Dìleas, who sometimes sat at the end of the house looking wistfully over to Rover as he worked his youthful dog magic with the flock.

The crook itself was carved from a piece of driftwood I found on the shore, and was best used at the annual shearing up at the fank on the moor. Fearchar and I were employed to hook the crook round the sheep's horns and guide them into the narrow gap where Mam and Dad fleeced them. Duncan was the first to be allowed to shear, but once he left, Fearchar and I were given the clippers, as if Mam and Dad realised that the past was gone and the future was now ours too. Too soon it was mine alone, with Fearchar leaving the following year to start an apprenticeship at Fairfield's on the Clyde.

I spent more and more time with Hazel. In some ways she was a substitute big sister, but at the same time the wee sister I never had. She liked the way I pronounced the z in her name, because everyone else said it like an s, and she told me the z always made her feel stronger. She had tremendous insight and wisdom, but also a terrible innocence which frightened me at times. It was simply that she always thought the very best of people, giving them the very best of motives when I could clearly see that their motives were selfish and vain. Most of them regarded her as a simpleton, so would constantly ask her to do things they were perfectly capable of doing themselves but for their laziness: running errands to the shop, or putting out or taking in their washing, or weeding their gardens or carting their byres. Which might have been fine if they'd given her something for it, though I knew that most folk just took advantage of her and never paid her a single penny. Instead, they'd give her a glass of milk and a biscuit at the end of the task, as if she were a baby. I challenged them and they all said that was all she wanted, and when I asked Hazel herself about it she agreed.

'A glass of milk and a biscuit, what's wrong with that?' she said. And then she'd smile that gorgeous full smile of hers,

'And it's not a Rusk. I don't like them. They give me Rich Tea or Digestives and they're so tasty when dunked in the glass of milk.'

The sweetest thing about Hazel was that she refused to wear shoes. Said they came between her and the earth, and that it was a sin to wear them.

'But you'll hurt your feet,' I told her, and she looked at me with astonishment.

'Nothing hurts me,' she said.

And it seemed true, for she could walk barefoot on any surface without flinching – shingles, stones, seaweed, bog and heather. Maybe because she treated everything like a friend, not an enemy.

'I can even do glass,' she said, and though I tried to persuade her not to, she smashed a lemonade bottle into smithereens and then walked across the broken glass as if it were a soft green meadow and was safe from everything that was ugly. And don't worry – we collected all the broken glass at the end!

'It's the best way to know that spring has come,' she told me. 'When you can put your bare foot on nine daisies, then spring has arrived!'

And she was right, though it was so difficult – but great fun – to find nine daisies sitting that close together, for my feet were so small, unlike hers! I could cover five or six, but eventually we'd always find a small cluster of daisies packed together and once I stepped on them, then winter was definitely over.

When summer came she persuaded me to discard my shoes altogether and it was like being a baby again. How odd things felt! Even though I was still but a child, I had almost completely forgotten how strange and new and exciting different surfaces felt. The grass that Mam kept so well was soft and spongy, and when I put my feet on it they sank into the ground and left perfect marks so that I could look back as I walked and see the pattern of my steps. I'd never realised how near they were to each other – I took such small steps! I then of course tried to lengthen them out but couldn't manage without falling over, so instead I varied them, zigzagging across the lawn so that if anyone saw my footprints they would think some crazy giant had been dancing on the lawn.

I thought I would like to squelch through mud, but I didn't, and never really got used to it, while I had to tiptoe on the gravel path because I couldn't bear the sharp pains the small stones sent through my flesh. But Hazel held my hand, and we persevered and despite squeals and cries and cuts, after a while I became used to it, and could hardly bear to have shoes on, despite Mam insisting that I wear them. I would, but then discarded them and carried them under my arms as soon as I was out of sight so that my feet wouldn't get soft and tender again and be unable to touch all the elements that made our world. The thing is Mam knew it well, for as a child she too had grown up without shoes, though habit and manners had since gotten in the way.

Later on, as a nurse, I learned the true value of pain. How it warns us that something is wrong, and if pain is removed our sense of what's safe and unsafe is destroyed. Do you know that lepers lose their limbs not so much from the disease itself as from breaking them because they have become physically insensitive to pain? The damage is done before pain warns them. And everything has its own pain, so I learned never to compare toothache with earache. Let's be thankful for bumps and bruises and cries and the gift of tears, for they protect us from worse.

I've nursed so many people who couldn't cry, and so I had to weep for them – men who had been brought up to believe that tears were unseemly, and women who had cried so much that they couldn't cry any more. Isn't it true Mary Magdalene gained heaven with her tears? I was privileged over the years with so many secrets I can never share, and as many again as I was asked to tell the world. My cup overflows with their hopes and fears.

Not least from Niall Cuagach and Mùgan and Old Murdo and all the others who shared so much so willingly with me when I did my initial summer placements at home, when home visits were still the norm. As I changed Cuagach's bandage, or took Mùgan or Murdo's temperature, I got to hear their way of thinking, which is everything. I could feel how much it meant to them when I touched their bare arms and felt their heads with my hands. No one had caressed them since they were babies. It's always surprised me how small our heads are once you work your way through the hair. Latterly I used to wash and shampoo and comb Mam's hair which was as soft and white as a lamb's fleece in my hands. I sang softly as I massaged her head and sometimes she would remember the song and sing along with my tears.

Hazel not only taught me to walk barefoot no matter the surface, but also led me eventually into mental health nursing. When my decision time came after two years of general nursing training, I remembered how Hazel walked and jumped over hazards – such as a barbed wire fence – as though they didn't exist, and yet paused and dawdled and stopped at the gentlest and simplest and smallest of things, as if they needed extra care and attention. So that if we were out walking and came across a deep river she'd lift up her skirts and wade through it as if it were a puddle while I walked upstream to cross the bridge, whereas if we came across a butterfly hovering over a flower she'd kneel down and follow its every movement from petal to petal and flower to flower right across the whole machair until it eventually disappeared across the loch. She would never enter anyone's house without carrying in some token of green as a gift, even if it was only just a blade of grass which she'd present to the householder like a communion wafer. She believed that presents always ought to be unexpected things and were forever better than any words.

I think she sensed that fragile things mattered more than dangerous things, and I was always glad I followed her instinct into that frail world of images. Every petal and flower the butterfly landed on, she said, was another year and a day of life, and every time I see a petal or flower or butterfly her life rises and flutters, and then extends. The arrival of electricity was like that. Gradual and instant. The way one day the earth is covered in snow and yet you catch a hint of yellow or purple and next thing the snowdrops and primroses are blossoming and there's no snow and there's warmth in the air, and suddenly it's spring, as if that long dreich winter had never been and all you can think of is summer and the clover bursting through the machair and the way the poppies sway in the breeze and how everything smells so different as if life is bursting through every living thing, and the birds all singing on branches and twigs and poles and house-eaves and the electric wires and aerials that adorn every house.

25

Antoine

THAT WAS THE summer I met Antoine. He was from France, on holiday with his parents at the other end of the island. I met him cycling down on the machair. We arrived at the rickety bridge together. He was heading south and I was cycling north. Well, to tell you the truth he was there a wee bit before me, but must have seen me cycling towards the bridge and stopped to let me cross first. It's a narrow bridge and though two can walk across at the same time, it can really only take one bike. It was kind of him to stop. None of the local boys would have done that. They'd have rushed on.

I could have cycled over and on, but I didn't. Mostly because that was a difficult trick to carry off. The wooden bridge was so shoogly that chances were I'd fall off into the water at any moment. We'd all tried it so many times and failed nine times out of ten. And I didn't want to make a fool of myself. So I came off the bike and he nodded his head as if to let me cross first. But I nodded mine, so he pushed his bike across. It was a lovely bike. Purple with silver wheels.

'Merci,' he said when he reached my side. He was tall with freckles and had fair hair. White sandshoes. I guessed he was seventeen, though he was just fifteen.

'Hi,' he then said. 'My name's Antoine.'

'Annie,' I said. 'Though some call me Annag.'

'Annag,' he said, in that sweet way of his.

'Where you going?'

'To the road end. Then back.'

'Okay.'

He cycled south while I headed off the other way. I was only going as far as the disused fish factory. It had two ramps outside which were great for wheeling up and down. I was just about to finish and return back home when he came back. He was cycling slowly, as if he had all the time in the world. I wheeled up and down the ramp one more time so that he could see what to do. But he just came off his bike, took off his satchel, sat on the sand and unwrapped some bread and cheese with a bottle of juice. I'd seen a picture like that of a boy sitting eating on the sand in the *Sinbad the Sailor* book we'd just read at school.

'Hungry?' he asked.

I nodded. He cut the long loaf into two and gave me half. Cut a big slice of cheese with a knife and handed it to me. The cheese was so different from ours. Sour and sweet. Maybe a bit like the crowdie Mam made with the milk that turned. He poured the juice into a little jar he had in his bag. I sat down opposite him, leaning against my bike.

'Why do you cycle so slowly?' I said.

'To see everything.'

Unlike Duncan and Fearchar and all the local boys, his skin was pale and his hair all clean and newly washed. No acne.

'Whatdya see?'

'Sheeps. Lots of them. And cows.'

I knew what 'merci' meant. 'So what's the French for sheep? And cows?'

'*Brebis*. That's a girl sheep. *Béliers*. Rams. And cows, that's *vaches*.'

'Caoraich. That's what we call sheep in Gaelic.'

'I know,' he said. 'My Mama is from here.'

'But you're French.'

'Oui.'

He offered me a sip of his juice. Wine. It tasted a bit like the blackcurrant juice Dolina and I once bought at the shop out the pier. That was sickly sweet and we poured half of it into the sea.

The wine didn't taste much better.

'You want to go over to the island?' I asked.

'Oui. I've to be back at one though.'

'Me too.'

We cycled across the causeway. Side by side. I had to slow down so he'd keep up with me. We left our bikes and climbed the hill together. There was a big rock at the top. If you climbed it you were on top of the world. I climbed up first and stretched out my hand to help him up. We sat there. He was breathless and pale.

'You not well?' I said.

'No. I've got leukaemia.'

'What's that?'

'My blood isn't right. Leaves me all pale and weak. Means I can't cycle fast. Or run much.'

'You don't need to,' I said. 'That's only for show-offs anyway.'

The sea was nice and blue.

'Can you swim?'

He nodded.

'Wanna?'

'Oui.'

We ran down the hill to the beach.

'Don't look,' I said.

He didn't. We swam in our underwear. Out to the seventh wave then back again. The sea was warm. He had a towel in his satchel.

'I like to swim,' he said.

We lay side-by-side on the sand, drying in the sun. My hands were by my side. His were across his chest. Then his right hand was in my left. We lay there looking up at the sky. Had there been a kayak or a canoe lying about we'd have headed off in it up the coastline.

'Are you going to die?'

'Oui,' he said. 'But not for ages. Not for years and years.'

'That's good. I had a pet frog and she died. That was sad. She was called Flora. Do you have any pets?'

'Oui. A donkey. He's called Louis.'

We stood up. Turned our backs to each other and put all our clothes on. He had a watch with a leather strap.

'I need to go now,' he said.

'Me too,' I said.

And then he kissed me. It was ever so sweet.

It was the first week of his holidays with another three to go. We met every day and though I tried to keep it secret, it was impossible.

'Who's that guy?' Fearchar asked.

'A friend.'

'Never seen him before.'

'He's on holiday.'

'What's his name?'

'Antoine.'

'What kind of name is that?'

'French. Same as Anthony.'

'Tony. He your boyfriend then?'

'Maybe.'

And dear Fearchar left it at that. Mam didn't.

'Is he a nice boy?' she asked.

'Who?'

She laughed.

'Och, Annie!'

'He is. Lovely. Quiet. Kind.'

She squeezed my hand.

'Be careful.'

And we were. We just cycled together and swam and spoke and cuddled and kissed and it was like we were going to spend our whole lives together. Nothing else mattered. Electricity was nothing compared to it. That had come from outside. So had Antoine, but it was different. Like the early summer light which softens everything and wakens you at five in the morning with the promise of a long and sultry day. I had grown up. At home they were all excited about radio programmes and three new standing lamps Dad ordered through the post which had white bulbs that faded if you turned the switch this way or that. Things that came and went.

And then the day came.

'We're going home tomorrow,' he said.

I didn't say anything.

'You should come and visit,' he said. 'And I'll write.'

And he did. Two letters came. The first was full of fun telling me the things we'd done together. How good I was at swimming, and the funny way I refused to take any of that sweet wine, and the day we gathered shells. And I wrote back, posting the letter in the postbox down by the shore. And then Antoine's second letter, saying he was unwell and might have to go into hospital and that we would write as soon as he got out.

The last letter was from his Mama telling me the terrible news. She said that Antoine had been terribly fond of me and that the month we spent together had been the happiest time of his life. She said I could go over to see them in Normandy any time I liked and would be welcome to stay with them as long as I like. She said it was very unlikely they would visit again as the memory would be too painful.

I never visited either, though every time I go home I go down by the shoogly bridge and walk over the causeway to the island. Somehow, it's still a place of joy, where I always see Antoine with that shell to his ear telling me that the sea's singing. In French, of course!

26

Edinburgh

MY WEE FRIEND is here again. Am brù-dearg. The red-breast. *Le rouge-gorge.* Did you know that the robin was once a sparrow who tried to pluck a thorn from the crown placed on Christ's brow, and in doing so got her breast dyed with his blood? He's always the first about, and do you know he has the best eyes of all the birds? So good that he gets to the crumbs even in the dark! The early bird catches the worm! I'd feel lost without his bright puffed-out breast sitting there on the branch in my garden every morning. I try not to think of him as a promise of joy, but his new song always persuades me. I don't know if you have any of the bird-rhymes off by heart, Emily. Do you still learn things off by heart?

> *Little Robin Redbreast sat upon a tree,*
> *Up went pussy cat and down went he;*
> *Down came pussy, and away Robin ran;*
> *Says little Robin Redbreast, 'Catch me if you can'!*

It was your own Mam's favourite rhyme when she was a baby! I'd run my fingers up her face and then all the way down, and she was the robin and I was the pussy-cat, chasing each other. And of course, the cat never ever caught the robin! I think birds and poetry have been my best friends through all my life, maybe because wherever you go they are there. The oystercatchers and peewits of my childhood have become the robins and the goldfinches of the city, but their delight in living now, in this moment, always brightens me. It's as if they have no regret about anything.

All Nature seems at work. Slugs leave their lair –
The bees are stirring – birds are on the wing –
And Winter slumbering in the open air,
Wears on his smiling face a dream of Spring!
And I the while, the sole unbusy thing,
Nor honey make, nor pair, nor build, nor sing.

The world is now so much smaller, but when I was your age so big. I had a choice of places for my nursing training. Inverness, Glasgow, Aberdeen and Edinburgh, though Mam tried to persuade me to go to Liverpool because she had such happy memories of the city. It seemed too far away for me. As I nursed her at the end, she told me about it again and again, and I did go eventually – only for a visit, of course. The Adelphi was still there, and I had afternoon tea with scones and jam for old times' sake. Now I would choose Paris! When you get the chance, go there. I know a wee hotel in one of the rooftops off the Grand-Boulevards that is just perfect! I knew I needed to leave the island to train, but still I wanted to be relatively near home so that I could catch a bus and boat if I had a week off, or the plane from Glasgow for the weekend. Even though I suspected I'd never have enough money as a student for that luxury!

I chose Edinburgh because it was neutral and I knew nothing about it and didn't know anyone there. Maybe after knowing everyone and everyone knowing me I needed to be anonymous. Like having a favourite song which doesn't mean the same to anyone else. Mine is 'Walk Tall' by Val Doonican because it always reminds me of Duncan that day he left to join the Navy. I had friends who had gone to Aberdeen, but they all said it was too cold and windy! Lisa advised me against it.

'As cold as charity,' she said to me. 'And the air as sharp as a scythe!'

*

Edinburgh was bright and sunny the day I arrived, and the warden who showed me to my room in the nurses' home said, 'It's a snell wind.'

The word is forever lodged in my memory as a description of Edinburgh. That, and the sickly sweet smell of hops from the city's breweries. It was just like being at home. Wee villages all stuck together. Stockbridge and Leith and Marchmont and Morningside and Gorgie. Cuagach and Mùgan would have loved it.

The nurses' lodgings were on the south side of the city, looking over towards Blackford Hill and the Braid Hills beyond. It was a big building and at first I got lost in the upstairs corridors, and I still sometimes wake at night fearing that someone will ask me, 'What are you doing here? Don't you stay in the corridor downstairs?'

I felt enclosed and missed the open skies and endless machairs, so as soon as I got my bearings in the city I caught the bus out to East Lothian every weekend to walk by the sea in Dunbar and North Berwick or to walk the endless paths that took you by the edges of the low flat fields of that lovely countryside. I tried to make sure I caught a glimpse of the Forth every day, to feel nearer home.

The rimy weather took me by surprise in Edinburgh. Here, it's some-times like being in a Christmas card, walking across the Meadows on those long cold crisp mornings, the frost clinging onto the railings and the grass and trees, every branch and blade glittering with cobwebs. As if Miss Agnes had newly laid out her best lace tablecloth for me. Just nodding or saying 'Aye, aye' to people as they walked by surprised them. It was the first time I noticed that trees diminished as they went upwards, as if afraid of the sun, the branches widening as the trunk narrowed. I missed the numerous unregulated fields with hollows and fence-posts and rabbit holes and sheep and collie dogs everywhere. I remembered how Mùgan claimed that once upon a time sheep had the gift of speech but had then simplified it to bleating.

The other girls who trained with me were great fun and company. We had some awesome nights out. We were all mad Bay City Rollers fans! 'No matter, no matter what you do, I only want to be with you!' And though a few of the girls fell badly by the wayside, and either gave up or were chucked out of the course, most of us were saved by our sense of vocation. A thing you've wanted to do since you were a child is not easily forsaken. The rewards were never enough at the time, but magnify every time I think of them. I could do whatever I pleased, whenever I wanted. Go into a pub, go skiing, not go to church, smoke, lie in bed all day on my days off if I wanted. Which I didn't. Though no one would have bothered if I had.

The nursing course lasted four years. It was all 'practical'. The days before needing to do a degree course as part of nursing studies. We had lectures and classes and tutorials of course, and read through a whole pile of books which told us everything we needed to know about everything, from ingrowing toenails to cancer treatment. Some of the students, and many of the older matrons, scoffed at what they called 'book-learning', but I found all of it helpful.

The star teacher was Professor Craig. He had a very wide, full-bearded face, like the moor in full heather in autumn. Like Mr Twit, there may have been bits of food stuck in it though we never got too close to check! He always wore his surgeon's gown, even at the lectern, and began and finished every one of his lectures with the sentence, 'Always remember that science is description, not explanation. Be content with that.'

He never claimed that science was infallible. But always tentative

and conditional. Just like the old hocus-pocus poor Gormul
MacLean was said to practice. It was the science of our childhood,
working by trial and error. It was as practical as everything else.
Some camomile here and a blessing there, a twining of the threads
and a cup of spring water from the hill-well. If it worked you knew
soon enough, for the sick person or animal recovered. If not, he or
she or it died. Sometimes things happened at the same time, which
meant they were meant to be. Mùgan's clock stopped unexpectedly
at 2.50am which was the exact moment his Auntie died in Vancouver,
according to the telegram message he got from Fozy, and her own
mirror fell off the wall the same evening the ferry went on the rocks
at the entrance to the harbour. Miraculously, the mirror-glass didn't
break and no lives were lost either, which proved how accurate these
messages were. It was all about harmony. Like making scones. The
balance of the ingredients had to be right, and the oven at the right
temperature, otherwise the scones wouldn't rise or would be too dry
or too crumbly or too hard or too stodgy.

It wasn't even about quantities, but about proportions – six times
the amount of flour to butter and the same amount of sultanas as the
butter. Maybe Cuagach was right after all! Even more important was the
quality of the ingredients. Could anything match the eggs from the hens
freely running about the back door and the ducks waddling about the
pond? And of course the way the eggs were beaten, nice and creamy and
fluffy rather than thin and weak and stretched. It took me ages to learn
to slow down so that the scones were perfect. Give everything time.

The most important thing I learned was to always listen quietly to
the patient. Despite themselves, they would tell you what was really
wrong. Their words might say one thing, but their eyes, faces, feet
and hands told a different story. It was the same mystery as Madame
Petrovna solved.

In reality, we didn't as nurses spend much time on diagnoses. We
were taught that was the doctors' patch. Just on treatment. Though to
say 'just' is to do it a disservice, for treatment is everything. Of course
some of it was connected to giving injections and administering drugs

and stitching people up and covering them with plasters and casts, but the best treatment was listening and empathising.

A lot of my friends thought that mental health nursing was an 'intellectual' activity. That we spent our time giving advice – counselling. As if I were Lady Penelope from Thunderbirds transmitting positive messages, like x-ray signals, to my patients! It was more a matter of wrestling with silence. I tried my best to make our conversations a cèilidh, but we missed the stove and the soft evening light.

The tragedy was that we never had enough time to listen and respond. I'm afraid that I too often resorted to platitudes and pills rather than patience and grace and love and all these other things which I profess to hold dear. Those things which bring Antoine and Mam and Dad and Hazel and Mrs MacPherson and Miss MacLean and Misses Agnes and Peggy and you and Eric and Duncan and Fearchar and Niall Cuagach and all the rest of them back to mind. We were under such pressure in the hospitals that all we could do was to try to make sure that no one died unnecessarily under our watch: that itself was often sufficient care.

I spent three months working in the Pilton and Muirhouse areas, where all the characters I met reminded me of home (these were the days when alcohol rather than drugs was the scourge). What I loved most of all was the eternal optimism and creativity of the children.

I worked with the younger, primary school children in the area, and once I got to know them I realised they shared pretty much the same songs and rhymes and promises and bets and dares and hopes and dreams as Dolina and Morag and Peggy and Katie and all our other pals had back home. It was only the dialect and some of the words that were different.

Goodness, some of them had as many superstitions and ways and means of trying to get good luck as Niall Cuagach himself. Lines on pavements they couldn't cross, seeing a spotted dog on the way to school (lucky), finding a button with one hole (unlucky), crossing forefinger and thumb and so on and so forth. I was especially taken with a group of girls who were collecting and keeping bus tickets, and a couple of them finally told me that their granny said they would get a fortune if they collected a thousand tickets, but the real reason was that they always tried to find a ticket where the numbers added up to twenty-one, which meant that you would be lucky afterwards. So that, for example, if you got Bus Number 27 at 15.15 that meant you'd be lucky and would probably find some money or dancing shoes or jewels or a boyfriend because the numbers added up to twenty-one. Anything was possible.

My favourite adult placement was out in Aberdour where I spent three months helping the community nurses. It was only eighteen miles from the capital city, yet I could well have been back home. The village itself was pretty, but the daily round with Nurses Richmond, MacIntosh and Grant took me out into the surrounding hamlets and farms where, despite the gorgeous rail and road bridges and the functional motorway connecting us all, life continued as it had been over many generations. It was as if nothing could change people. Down dusty and unused tracks to ageing cottars and tenants who had only been to the big city a couple of times in their lives and into farmhouse and smallholding kitchens with haphazard tiled floors where old decorated cast-iron stoves and ranges, with an array of woollen stockings and vests and drawers hanging overhead, still reigned. It may be, after all, that it was not land or religion or poverty or language or anything else that held us together but concern for one another. We talked about odds and ends and they made a similar world. I think our uniforms, especially the little badged hats we wore in those days, reassured them.

When you're young you know you'll grow older, but it's quite an abstract thing, without any real terror. May you stay forever ever young and I pray for your good health. Let that amazing cello-playing of yours be like the balm of Gilead and like the precious oil pouring down Aaron's beard. Like skipping with a rope with your best pal and like running to the ice-cream van and ordering two cones with chocolate and raspberry dripping and a flake for yourselves afterwards. Fill the world with ice-cream and music. I am sending you my favourite shell and you will hear it there.

It's difficult for me now to remember the names of these lovely old people in Fife, though the faces remain with me as if I saw them just yesterday or the day before. No doubt it was the consequence of hard toil and labour out in the fields, but there were fewer old men than women. Though a couple of the women mentioned 'drink' as the reason their husbands had predeceased them. What I remember most are the gnarled hands of the old women and how devilishly difficult it was to find any good veins when I needed to take their blood samples. I think they were thin as a consequence of work rather than because they didn't eat enough. I don't recall any of them being obese, which became such a health issue later on in my career, with the ready availability of sugared drinks and so forth. The thing is, as back home, neither Nurse Richmond nor Nurse MacIntosh nor Nurse Grant nor I were ever allowed to visit without a pot of tea being brewed and home-made bread or farls (what I would call scones) fetched out of some wooden cupboard. A good cup of tea was the answer to most ills.

It was that ancient thing: a mixture of hospitality to the stranger and a curiosity (partially born out of isolation and loneliness) to spend time with a visitor so that they could hear all the news. We learned to speak in general, and never about specific individuals or patients, although we were also wise enough to hear and share safe and interesting information from other farms which would feed their need for external news. Talking, and leaving things as they were, was as good a cure as anything.

'How's Mrs Smith?' they asked, and we said,

'O, she's much better. And her daughter Millie came home yesterday as well, so that will help.'

They were delighted to hear the news, and a bit like the pedlars in the old days, we gave what we could in our travels through that declining countryside. I knew they were comfortable with me when they asked me how the weather was, even though they knew as well as I did how it was. Then we asked each other how we were.

It was the first (and only) time I heard people use the word 'earthly' for someone who was not going to recover from illness.

'Auld Jim is looking a bit earthly,' his wife said when I called to visit. For they knew well the predestined rhythms of the seasons, spring to summer, autumn to winter, seed to harvest, and how you reap what you sow, even though time and chance strikes them all. 'Whit's fur ye'll no go by ye,' they said, giving necessity the grace of fate and desire the spin of fortune. Though we all knew it would never be the same again.

A regular business was finding John, who would take to the bottle now and again and go missing, but would always be located days after sitting on a bollard in Pittenweem Harbour, where he had once, as a child, spent the happiest days of his life on holiday with his grandfather. For we all want to preserve the moments of our joy, which are our life.

'You are better than this. And your family and friends deserve better,' we said to him, but it made no difference. At the end of the day we all do what we really want anyway, so that we are without excuse.

These were still the days when the dead were washed and laid out in their own beds at home, before the whole business of death was completely professionalised and handed over to paid undertakers. It was a real privilege to spend the hours with these widows in their own homes preparing and taking care of the departed in death, perhaps even more than they'd ever done in life. The worst thing in life was to die alone. Mrs Smith said to me that everyone would be resurrected at the ideal age of thirty-three.

The other thing is that these women were forever knitting – little mittens for children who weren't there, and socks and jerseys for men who were absent or long gone. Even if a nuclear bomb dropped I'm sure they would have just carried on knitting. And the more time I spent with them the more I realised that the so-called seven ages of man was a lie, for these women were knitting mittens for children who were not yet born and socks and jerseys for men who had died.

And I remembered how we too back home always dreamt of children yet to be, and how after Mass every Sunday we'd go down to the cemetery to tidy the graves and run down to the machair to collect daisies and orchids and poppies or whatever was growing at the time to lay out for aunties and uncles and friends and neighbours whose angels were looking down on us with a smile. Some folk had urns filled with plastic flowers, which we thought was the saddest thing ever, for there was nothing bonnier than the grass flowers themselves growing where they pleased.

The older men in the farms around Fife who had survived were hard to get to know at first. Most of them lived on their own, though some had children who lived nearby, and they were cautious of strangers. They had forgotten the sounds of their own voices and surprised themselves when they spoke to me. When they did talk they saw me as a nurse rather than a person, but after a while they relaxed and might pour a dram and talk and begin to share things that had long been buried beneath the earth. You almost had to smuggle comfort into their lives, for if they suspected you of charity they'd block you at the door. Habits they'd learned from their parents and grandparents, and ways of thinking which time had eclipsed. They spoke about furlongs and linties and dew-pieces as if time had stood still. They were like shaded fruits which grew and blossomed with a little light and space. It was, in the words of the great physician, the extraction of thought through care, aided by the anaesthetic of whisky and a listening ear. It was at those times that I felt the word became flesh.

Out in those isolated farm cottages I came to know better (more professionally) that life doesn't just begin when you are born to finish when you die, but is part of a much bigger and longer process in which you inherit rituals and procedures that you then retain or discard or change and transform to hand on to the next generation, or – if you are like me – to see fulfilled in paradise. I already knew from my own childhood that isolation gives you a peculiar insight – you see and hear things others don't, and because you are deprived of other people and sounds and sights you fill the vacuum with alternative voices and visions. The flickering will-o'-the-wisp photons on the machair on clear winter nights were angels going about their good business. The wind whistling through the eaves was Beathag Mhòr mourning for her darling lover. If you met a man on a white horse he could name the cure for any illness. Everything was always part of a greater thing.

When I qualified, my first full-time job was in Edinburgh itself, in Leith. (Though the good folk there quickly reminded me that Edinburgh and Leith are two different cities!) We were based at the Health Centre off Albion Place near the Hibs football ground, and when we were doing a late-night midweek shift in winter we could hear the roars of joy and despair rising and falling through the foggy air.

That's where I first met your Grampa. I had just come off shift and was walking down London Road to catch a bus when I stumbled. Eric was walking behind me and held out his hand to steady my elbow. Maybe everything is providential? He was catching the same bus, and we got talking as the bus travelled up Leith Walk. Hibs had won one-nil and I think he was impressed that I was interested in football and could even name some of the players – the advantage of having brothers!

'Best player is Pat Stanton,' I said, and he agreed.

He came off the bus at Balgreen while I continued on to Corstorphine, though by that time he had asked if he could see me again 'to go to the pictures or something?' I agreed, making an arrangement for Saturday night, 8pm beneath the clock at Binns. That store isn't there any more, but the clock is, and when next you come over we'll go up there and take our picture there together! I suppose they were more innocent days, for later on as a mother (and now as a grandmother) I was and am anxious to hear of any young woman making such an arrangement with a stranger!

I suppose it's ironic that Grampa was an electrician. Think of it, Emily, after all that palaver over the arrival of electricity back home! Maybe Gormul MacLean was right all along when she claimed that the future was just a circling of the past. I think in the back of my mind was the fear that Dad would disapprove – which turned out to be nonsense, for they liked each other as soon as they met, and spent many happy times together out fishing the hill lochs every summer we went back home with the children. Just as Duncan and Fearchar and I had done when we were children, Aonghas and Mary, your Mam, made their own bespoke rods – sticks with string and cork and a safety-pin bent back as a hook, while Dad gave Eric an old hazel-rod he'd used as a child.

'Hazel is the magic wood,' he said to Eric. And so it was, for that hazel-rod caught more trout than was reasonable.

Your Mam was always a lovely, quiet child. I know her mental health has troubled you all for several years, but be comforted. It's nothing strange. Like a broken ankle, it heals, even if it continues to ache. We're all fragile. You've been an angel, and what I mostly want to tell you about was the girl and young woman Mary was before you ever knew her as your Mam! She was so like you, sensitive to every growing thing around her, and I have no doubt that sensitivity to her school and college friends' troubles made her carry these with her. Maybe I didn't listen enough either. Didn't give time to hear the billows in between the words. A wee story about your Mam: I used to give her a lunch-box every day for school and then caught her one day putting in two extra sandwiches and an extra orange and apple.

'My darling,' I said to her, 'are you not getting enough to eat?'

'I am,' she said. 'But my two pals Dorothy and Maggie aren't.'

So after that I made three lunch-boxes, and though her bag was heavier, she was so pleased to take them with her. She was, and is, a good and kind woman, which is all that matters.

I've been looking at your map. The one you sent me two Christmases ago. I have it on the kitchen wall so I can see it all when I'm having my breakfast. No doubt one of those apps could instantly tell me where you are, except that I enjoy choosing a coloured pin for you all and then sticking it where you live. All the scattered grandchildren. John and Erica and their green pins in Amsterdam. Gordon's red pin in Rome. Kirsty's blue one in Belgrade, and your bright yellow one in Adelaide.

And did I ever tell you that yellow is one of the great Gaelic colours? It's the colour of the first primrose of the year and of the summer machair and of the gold harvest of autumn. It's the colour of the corn-marigold and the western wagtail and the iris, and the colour of happiness and glory and harmony, and wisdom in China. But most of all it's the colour of singing, and when you next come over, come over in Maytime, when the yellow's on the broom so that we can take a journey up north together and sing as we travel through the Mearns,

When yellow's on the broom,
when yellow's on the broom,
I'll tak you to the road again,
when yellow's on the broom.

27

Returning

INITIALLY ERIC AND I went back home every couple of years, but once Aonghas and your Mam Mary were born our visits became more and more irregular. Visits! What a strange word, as if I was visiting a museum or a foreign country or a patient in hospital or calling by, as we did every fortnight or so, to see Eric's Uncle George who lived in Glasgow and was beginning to suffer from dementia. Our regular visits helped, for he always picked up the story where he had left off as if we'd just popped out of the room for a minute despite the flight of days and weeks and years. We were never sure whether he wanted to remember or forget and it didn't matter anyway. He always smiled when we were kind to him. He'd forget to open his curtains and when I opened them up for him he'd look out smiling as if he was seeing daylight for the first time ever. It was best when we made tea together. While I boiled the kettle he laid our three plates and three cups and three saucers on the little round table by the kitchen door. He always asked Eric to pour the tea, and watched smiling as Eric lifted the pot high so that the tea poured into the cups like a fountain. 'High Tea,' Uncle George always said then, giggling.

When he got restless we'd take him for a walk and even if it was just into the next room it became a new moment for him which fascinated him for a while. He always wanted to go to the same place, his childhood home in Gorgie, though the street had been demolished decades before to make way for the new great western road. I suppose we always want to go back to where we felt most secure. He had nothing else but the present, which never seems sufficient. Thing is, we can only do something, such as opening or closing a door, if we remember how to do it, and it's remarkable how much our bodies remember to do for us. As a musician, you'll know all about muscle-memory yourself. Though I suppose we should never let it get in the way of the unexpected. I'm beginning to forget things myself, but when I come to a door I always know at a glance whether it closes in or out. And ironing clothes, which I do with my eyes closed, yet the collars and sleeves and creases are perfect when I'm folding them away. Like lambs in the April sun.

Mam, Dad and Fearchar came to our wedding, with Mrs MacPherson and Hazel travelling out with them, though Duncan couldn't manage across as he had his own responsibilities out in Melbourne. Dad looked a bit out of sorts in his suit – he had become so accustomed to wearing overalls that it was very strange seeing him dressed up in wool, though he turned down Eric's suggestion that he should hire a kilt for the day! Eric himself was dressed in the full Highland outfit however, along with our best man, his friend Brian, while I asked Dolina to be the bridesmaid and Hazel the flower girl, because she'd always told me that the best thing at any wedding was seeing the confetti and the pennies and the petals being thrown for luck and swirling in the air with all the children running to gather them.

She looked beautiful in the vintage cream dress she bought in a second-hand shop in Stockbridge two days before the wedding. She was all grace. Her hair was the colour of May. Some guests claimed they'd seen an angel. She threw confetti everywhere as we walked down Lauriston Street. The only advice Mam and Dad gave us on our wedding day was to be kind to each other, which was the best present we got.

We received loads of lovely telegrams which I've kept safe in a box and take out now and again to read. Duncan sent one which simply said 'Good wishes to Mr and Mrs Cunningham!' but a good number of ones from the older people contained variations of the old joke 'May all your troubles be little ones!' And truth is, they were no trouble at all when they came along.

When September came, we always made a point of going berry-picking. Initially when the children were small, we just went to the local city and Lothian farms, but once they were in the upper stages of primary school we all went away with a tent for the weekend, sometimes up to the Carse o' Gowrie and other times to Perthshire where we gathered as many wild blaeberries as we wanted from the glens, Aonghas and Mary – and Eric and I at times! – covering our faces with the juice as we (secretly!) ate half of them on the way. The evidence always gave us away. But the berry pies we made in the evening in a pan over the open fire was always the highlight of the weekend. Happy days! Ask your Mam about them. And I wonder if she remembers any of the mad recipes we made up – I remember once we made a blackberry and turnip pie which must have been the worst thing we tasted in our whole life. Though your Grampa loved it!

When we did go back to the island we also enjoyed it, despite the endless questions about how long we were staying and when we were leaving. They were so used to relentless emigrations. Holiday mornings were best. Your Mam and Uncle Aonghas loved playing on the long empty stretches of sand (running around naked most of the time) and Eric enjoyed spending time with Dad, learning the basics of crofting, from sheep-shearing to cutting peats. He liked the precision of the work – branding the owner's initials with hot tar onto the sheep's horns without harming the animal, and how the peat banks needed to be cut in smooth straight lines or they would look wrong and eventually collapse. The best turf for roofing a house came from a bit of earth washed by the salt tide. It was a reassurance for Eric that a natural thing like a lump of turf needed as much care as his electrical wires and cables.

But his favourite time was out on the boat with Dad when they'd sail south in the early morning and spend the whole day fishing the reefs and sheltered waters south of Fiùdaigh, bringing back a good haul of crabs and lobsters and cod. Eric enjoyed both the fishing and the company, even learning some of Dad's stories about Iain Donn, who was said to have sailed from Barra to Iceland on the back of the cionaran-crò (the kraken) guided by the lights of the Milky Way. The clouds that covered the stars at night were just the spray from Iain Donn's open boat surging its way towards Betelgeuse. When he told of Iain Donn, Dad included the names of real stars and islands and constellations to give the story its earthly bearings. It made everything possible because it was rooted in things both of them could see and believe. Eric began to tell stories too.

The most noticeable thing any time we went back home was that people met less and less in each other's homes. Oh, people still called by, and met informally in the pub or in the shops, and increasingly more formally in the newly-built community hall, but Dad said these gatherings 'lacked rhythm', which was an interesting way of putting it.

'What do you mean?' I asked him.

'Och, it's a bit like a song that has no chorus,' he said. 'You just listen rather than sing along. I can't join in. I don't feel so much part of it anymore.'

I know it's such a daft thing, but through time I also began to forget people's sloinneadh (patronymic), and it's as if I didn't know them fully anymore because I could only remember their first or official name. The detail goes, which means the most important thing goes. It's like only knowing the chorus of a song and not the verses. We'd drive past someone in a car and I'd think, 'That's Catriona. Catriona MacIntyre.' And it would take me ages to remember, and sometime I'd have to ask someone who'd tell me. 'That was Catriona, nighean Alasdair 'ic Aonghais Mhòir.' Of course it was! She was two classes ahead of me at school and always used to win the sword dance competition at the annual games. Her father, Alasdair, played the pipes while she danced. I was always placed second when I danced against her, until we both grew old enough to remember that dancing was not a competition.

A good deal of my mental health nursing simply consisted of sitting quietly listening to my patients, making sure that their side of the story was being heard. All those little details which seem so obscure and irrelevant and far-fetched, yet lie at the heart of their joys and troubles. The more noise there is, the more difficult it is to hear or be heard. I don't know if you've ever noticed, but the angrier people get the whiter their faces become, the same way the hotter the sun is the whiter it appears! Real anger, I mean. The one that's not visible. It's remarkable that anyone hears anything anymore. They're forever digging up the roads here, and when us old people try to talk to one another outside it's anyone's guess what we're saying. We just nod and shake our heads in turn and smile, in the hope that one day all the cables and wires and tubes in the world will finally have been laid and nothing more will ever need to be done again and the roads will remain cone-free and silent and quiet and we can finally hear and understand each other. Some hope!

What I missed most when I moved to Edinburgh was space. The wide open skies and the long flat low machair. It wasn't the big view as such, for often in the wind and rain you could hardly see a thing, and even when the sun shone, other, nearer things claimed attention: an oystercatcher sitting on a fence post or a new-born lamb suddenly rising out of a sheltered sandy hollow. It was the best of luck to see the first lamb of the year with its face towards you. And there was a tang in the air which you can never forget or replicate. It's salty air and sand and seaweed, the nearest manufactured taste to it being a malt whisky. The constant wind and rain even made us walk a certain tentative way, as if anything – even an unexpected burst of sunshine – could happen at any moment.

Edinburgh is chilly and ordered in contrast. The hospital was near the Meadows (remember we played with the kites there?), and though I would walk through them some lunch-times and picnic on the grass, it all seemed so *civilised*, I suppose, compared to the wildness of my childhood. It was as if every tree and bush and path and seat and blade of grass had been planned and planted or placed so that you would not be surprised by anything appearing unexpectedly, even though snails and sparrows and squirrels had still never read the rules!

At weekends I climbed Arthur's Seat and looked down on the gorgeous city that was my new home – the lovely spires leading all the way up to the castle and Princes Street Gardens and the beautifully laid-out new town stretching north over to the Forth and the low hills of Fife and the grey sea beyond. Everything rectangular and in order. The cobbled streets shining after a sudden shower, the gardens glistening in the sun. These were the days when coal fires were still allowed, and there was nothing nicer on a crisp winter's morning than to look down on the city with the blue smoke from household chimneys and the grey smoke from the factories weaving patterns in the air. I saw chimney-smoke drifting east on windless days, an old sign of goodness. I missed the gloaming and the stars, however, abolished by the street-lights.

I began to understand Niall Cuagach's obsession with space. It was the need to know that things were in harmony, or at least connected with one another. I think it's the basis of all environmentalism. So that if there is a hill I also want to see a glen or a valley, and if there is a valley I want to see a stream or a river running through it. As a stream runs downhill it becomes bigger and bigger, because it needs to become stronger to cope with everything it meets. And when it comes to a city street, there are a variety of shops rather than just big stores, and there's a green space nearby to ease the eye and for rest. There must be symmetry. Otherwise, things are discordant. The choir has reminded me that counterpoint and dissonance are also important. Nevertheless when things are out of harmony I almost shiver, as if I'm hearing a saw rasping through a nail.

Your dear Grampa's other joy was our allotment at Inverleith. We had to wait some years until one became available, but when it did it was a great blessing. We spent many evenings and weekends there, sometimes pottering about – Eric liked to sit in the shade of the apple tree and read a book! – but mostly working hard, digging and hoeing and weeding and sowing and eventually harvesting. Shallots and onions and carrots and leeks and beetroot and potatoes but also a variety of herbs and even grapes and tomatoes on the vine. We started it basically to get away from our daily jobs, but then the challenge of growing our own food took hold, and though we never grew enough to feed an army we harvested enough through the year not just for ourselves but also for some of our friends and neighbours. There's nothing like taking earth-covered carrots or potatoes out of the ground. I swear by Kerr's Pinks but your Grampa always preferred King Edwards', so we planted both! As time went on we became more adventurous, trying out a variety of specialist potatoes, to the point we were in danger of becoming snobbish about the common ones folk bought in the supermarket. But here's the thing. Increasingly we began to realise we were doing our little bit to save the world, for every tattie from our own earth and every little tomato from our own vine felt like one less air mile and one less plastic bag out there. You reap what you sow, as Peter the Proverb always said!

Your Grampa had his own machair, which was the Leith of his boyhood. We often went down there on Sunday afternoons, when he showed me round all the old haunts he used to play in as a child. Where Tancy Lee used to box, and the Capitol Cinema, where he saw Ivor Novello in *The South Sea Bubble*, at that time turned into a Bingo Hall, and where the French Nougat Van and the Hot Chestnut Van used to be, and then up to Pilrig Park where he saw 'Buffalo Bill' and Elroy the Handless Wonder, who could light a cigarette and open a bottle and shoot the flame off a candle with his toes while painting with the other foot. Hazel would have liked that. Elroy always finished his performance by playing the trumpet. Eric lit up when he told of these places and people and things. The only difference is that he had fewer memories of people like Mùgan and Mrs MacPherson in his neighbourhood. He'd been told to keep clear of older people. He was so proud to be a Leither, though we never stayed there when we were married. He too was an exile. I so wish that you would have known him.

We went out together for two years before we got engaged, then married a year later at the Church of the Sacred Heart in Lauriston Street. It was the nearest Catholic church to the Infirmary, and I would sometimes go there for the early seven or eight o'clock Mass on my way to work and often call in for some peace and quiet and contemplation on my way home after a shift. There are so few places that are totally silent. So few places that reassure me that's it okay to be on my own. Of how I could be.

Eric and I often went to the Orthodox Church of Edinburgh, partly because of the ornate beauty of its liturgy, though laced with such simplicity – 'For temperate weather, abundance of fruits of the earth and for peaceful seasons, let us pray to the Lord.' What better can you ask for? It's what Gormul MacLean and Niall Cuagach asked for too, in their own liturgies. Their sacred petitions in the silence. The Orthodox practices attracted us. Women on their knees here, men kissing icons there, worshippers lighting candles everywhere. It was as if you could worship God in a thousand different ways yet be part of a whole. But mostly we went because of its increased sense of reverence, as if every little gesture and movement had divine content, an outstretched hand meaning more than a thousand words. I always leave their service with a renewed sense of joy that everything matters. The future shines. I've learned that icons are neither mere decorations nor idolatry, but an essential part of the sacred space of worship. For whatever matters is always turned into a ritual. They are like Cuagach's stones and posts in the fields. Words and pictures in the sacristy of grass and earth. Thy will be done on earth. On summer Sunday evenings I sometimes go to the Free Church to sing the psalms of David, but the footpaths are too wet and slippery and dangerous in the wintertime.

We did our best, and it was only afterwards that we discovered it was enough. Even as I write these notes I do so listening to music and singing along. The thing I love most is Gregorian Chant, and my favourite album of all time is the old recording by the choir of the monks of the Abbaye Saint Pierre de Solesmes. I regret that, too often, I've measured things by the golden means of the past – no one ever sings like my mother, no one ever tells a story with the crazy flourish of Mùgan, no one ever played like Dolina, until I remind myself to listen, and when I turn the CD off, I hear the birds in the garden singing as if nothing has ever happened except this moment, with the blackbird echoing its one sole perpetual song over and over and over again.

Sometimes when I can't sleep, I read or shop on my tablet in the middle of the night and I'm always aware of the insistent blue light blinking on the console in the corner of the room. It's the same kind of blue as the sea on the cockle-shell shore after a shower of rain. I don't want to turn it off in case any of you want to get in touch, just as Fearchar and I would tap our fingers against the wall all those years ago to pass secret messages to each other in the night.

But that may just be part of the venial sin of my nostalgia, which is only the desire to be young again and a yearning for what is lost, which is no less real for being imaginary. The golden age is always just over the horizon. It's to do with percentages. I've worked it all out, which probably all sounds a bit sad! The twenty years from my birth to the time I left home were a hundred per cent of my time there. Now it's 29 per cent and reducing by the day. It's like having a cup of tea, isn't it, the cup emptying every sip I take, so I try to make sure I taste and treasure every drop. And then I boil the kettle again and make another pot, though at my age you need to be careful how many cups you have, or otherwise you're up and down to the bathroom all night long!

None of us love enough. But it can be redeemed. We can love backwards as it were, holding that patient's hand we failed to hold, caressing the person we were afraid to hug. It's like that kite

Fearchar and I made once out of Mam's silk shirt remnants and which flew like a multi-coloured bird in the air for ages before we let it go on top of the hill and watched it sail slowly westwards down towards the shore. We raced down to find it was still all in one piece, washed by the surf, and we ran with it all the way along the sand, each of us letting go for a moment, the other one grabbing it before it flew off until we got all the way back home. You can have so much fun running after a kite, flying it this way and that, backwards and forwards, as you learn to catch the wind.

It's as legitimate to live in the grace of the past as much as in that of the present, even though a thing is lost only when you know about it. I never knew so many things mattered until they were gone. It's what a good deal of my nursing has been about. As I nursed my patients I slowly realised that the most important part of my work was to comfort and reassure them that they wouldn't be punished. That their (mostly invisible) illness was legitimate, and not a retribution for some offence, real or delusional, from childhood. Guilt and fear and melancholy were terrible burdens, kindness a sweet relief.

The hardest thing was to convince them that there was nothing to be ashamed of about anything, because we are all in the same boat. Occasionally, a patient was set free, through the vale of tears, by a long close cuddle. There is hardly any border between the mental and the physical, and what exists is fluid. Everyone sees an accident differently. Maybe, after all, the consolation of prayer saves the body as well the soul!

I learned very quickly that it always helped to try and give a reason to people why they were ill, even when the reason was not that clear. When patients were diagnosed with cancer, for example, their first reaction, apart from the horrible shock, was mostly to ask 'Why?' Not even so much 'Why me?' but why at all – what has caused this, what's the reason behind it? Some folk believing they had done nothing wrong to 'deserve' it (had never smoked, for example), others instantly accusing themselves of causing it through smoking or drinking or the wrong diet or eating too much. Still others always looked for a cause from the outside, as if something strange and alien was happening to them, like an invasion from outside their bodies, when the reality is that it's inside us all the time because we are organic living beings and the good comes along with the bad, the tares growing alongside the wheat, if you like. If we didn't live, we wouldn't die.

Stuff happens, and all it takes is a small variation here and there to alter our bodies, and God knows we inhabit and consume enough strange stuff, from chlorinated chickens to shampoo bottles filled with all kinds of chemicals, to cause havoc. It's not always dirt that kills. It's carelessness or indifference. All that packaging which dresses up harm as a treat.

Sometimes, like Old Murdo, I think we've cleansed ourselves into ill health. To have good health and to know it is to possess everything. I nursed so many patients through the valley of the shadow, and nearly all of them – and all the men especially – regretted that they had spent so much time working, or playing golf, or out in the pub with their friends, and so little time with their own families and with their children in particular. All of them said at the end that if they had their lives back they would forsake everything for time with their children.

And fear. Oh, my goodness, fear limits us, my child. It's like having the brakes on as you try to cycle uphill. Remember when we were kids and rode these rickety bikes without brakes or helmets or anything, despite all the adults warning us that we would crash and catapult head over heels? We did, and it was the best thing ever and we loved it and survived. Go on, let's, Emily.

Poor darling Dad. Thankfully, Fearchar was with him the day he collapsed out on the moor while gathering the sheep.

'It was a lovely day too,' he told me afterwards. 'I was up on the high slopes with Rover, and Dad was down nearer the fank with Glen when I heard her barking, which was unusual. Dad was lying down, which was even more unusual, and as Glen continued to bark I knew something was wrong so I ran down the hill as fast as I could, but it was already too late. I just cradled him in my arms for a while and cried. I remember the birds were singing. A heart attack. The only consolation, Annie, is that he died doing what he loved outdoors, in the place that he loved.'

There was so much I meant to ask Dad. About his adventures at sea and what he felt like the first time he held me as a new-born baby in his arms and how he always managed to saw a bit of wood dead straight even without marking it with a pencil and if he ever really expected that bicycle-windmill of his to work miraculously like it did, and oh, a thousand and one other things, not even because I want to know the answers but just because I want to hear his voice and know him better than I ever did, but it never occurred to me as a child, and then I was away and then he was. He always rubbed candle-wax onto the blade of a saw to make it cut smoother. That I do know, because I used to see him do it and though he would not let me rub it onto the saw itself he always allowed me to rub it onto the bit of wood he was cutting, pretending to me that it made all the difference. And his beard stubble smelt of hay and oil.

Fearchar was the only one of us who stayed at home, working the croft and also working part-time for the local council. He finished his apprenticeship at Fairfields and worked in the shipyard for a while, but then returned home to help Mam and Dad. He married a lovely girl from the north end, Sìne, and built a new house next to the road on the croft land, leaving Mam in the old house. He made sure he called in to see her every morning and evening, as did Sìne and their children when they came along. When Mam died, Duncan, as the eldest boy, was given the tenancy, but said that he was unlikely to ever use it, his own family now surrounding him in Australia. I'm so glad you see him now and again.

Sometimes I struggle to find the boys they once were. Though Duncan once said to me as we walked back after a meal and some drinks at that seafood restaurant in Melbourne that he often wakes in the middle of the night hoping I'll tap on the wall or that Fatty Morrison will whistle outside so that they can walk down to the machair to continue the game.

'That last game was very close,' he said. '18-17, and if Fatty hadn't sprained his ankle we'd have continued and made it 18 each. I'm sure of it. And we'd all have been happy, and left it at that.'

The truth is that all these things we might or could have done are as real as those few things we did manage to achieve.

Eventually Fearchar took over the running of the croft land but split the old house between the three of us, so that our families can use it any time we wish. He keeps an eye on it and generally maintains it, and sometimes Aonghas and his partner go there for a week in the summer. At least it's used and still in the family, for the reality is that homes have become houses and crofts have become properties to be bought and sold on the open markets. It's remarkable to see fortunes paid for the ruins of poverty. It's a heartache, and so strange, to see 'For Sale' signs on Misses Agnes and Peggy's and Old Murdo's homes and to see Mùgan's thatched cottage advertised as five-star accommodation without the wayward navigator himself at the helm. And though everyone says it's better to see them occupied than in ruins, I hate to see them as Airbnb equity. Still, a light in them is better than ruin and darkness.

Others now view the setting of the bright moon from the veranda. Someone else hangs his hat and coat on the curved edge of the crescent moon, as Mùgan put it once. It's like a dream where the solid geography of things continuously dissolves. I probably saw the twilight of an ancient way of life that will never be seen again. It faded away like the hissing light of a single tilley-lamp replaced by the universal glow of electricity. Instead of carrying a lamp with you to the different rooms, the light was already there before you. It was only when I went back home as an adult that I fully realised every ditch was a paradise filled with cottongrass and silverweed and marsh marigolds and orchids and all kinds of rare and precious things. Last night I watched a programme about the Aztecs. Seems it wasn't the

Spanish who destroyed them but their own fabulous prophecy that a sun-king carrying thunder and lightning would arrive from over the waters. Miss Peggy's tea-leaves would have been much kinder, predicting soft showers of rain before the harvest hay.

It's the small things that matter. Effie's rose-bushes are paved over, and Peter the Proverb's shoe-making shed a pile of old wood and stone, swept away like dust into a corner. His hand-made stick not there by the gate. 'Every mile is two in winter,' he'd say. And when he walked fast along the road, 'It's too cold to walk slow,' except he said it the other way round so that 'It's too slow to walk cold,' became a new kind of proverb. Despite those boots he made like kettles, he could also make shoes the way people expected them to be when he wanted. I suppose the making mattered to him more than the outcome. He was so proud, for example, of the exact way he could put a nail into a shoe or into a piece of wood, standing back and admiring how the nail sat without leaving any trace of the indent of the hammer on the face of the leather or wood. The nails were neither to protrude nor to disappear altogether, but to be in line with and a visible part of the material they sustained.

'And always use a square nail,' he'd say. 'They hold better.'

An occasional barn with a red tin roof survives, waiting to be bought and architecturally re-imagined. Anyone who didn't know it as it was would call it charming. I'm not sure we can be fully healed from the injury of time. It's like a limp. The things that cry out loudest are the things that are no longer there, though I warn myself against the final tragedy of defining life by its absences. And it's not anger or regret that the future is someone else's not mine. It's the knowledge that so much has been forsaken. Why did no one speak of love? The dreams and problems which made us. How else will we ever understand one another? The silence gets me every time. The ghosts that suddenly speak as I walk along Bruntsfield in the morning sun. Angus Morrison cutting the hay, Bessie Smith hanging out the washing, expecting nothing but a good drying day.

There are things that last. It is not the place that changes, but us. When I return, it's like going to a strange but familiar land. Like Naomi rather than Lot's wife. Or the swallow returning from Africa, the co-ordinates, despite the long and arduous voyage, still sure and certain. Cuagach claimed they always arrived on the evening of the 24th of February. There's East. And that's North. And South and West. And look – that's where Seonag lived, running every morning to the shore with the speckled horses. And see, out there in the garden, is your Mam's tree-house where you swung for ages the last time you were here, resting in that striped hammock the two of us managed to put up! It's still there, waiting for you. Now, don't tell your Mam, but I climb up there sometimes in summer, even if I now use a ladder, and swing on it for a while. I nod off, and waken to the sound of birds and the soft whish of the wind. They sing in Gaelic so that I can join in. Iain Bhig Iain Bhig, thig dhachaigh gud mhàthair, thig dhachaigh gud mhàthair.

It's so sheltered here in Edinburgh, so I forget how exposed and wild it is when storms come back there. Those bare, raw elements. Maybe Duncan was right after all, thinking he was Daniel Boone! For when I go, which is only in the summer now, the gorgeous machair still blooms like memory, carpeted with orchids and daisies and violets and buttercups (Dolina and I still sitting there checking if our chins are turning yellow yet!) and clover and eyebright and corn marigolds and bluebells – I chant them like a hymn to myself sometimes, with the moors covered in cotton-grass and bog-myrtle and autumn heather and the eternal Atlantic still washing itself onto the strands.

Time made and unmade them. We sense the end from the beginning. Just as in a song. They were good people – with all their weaknesses and follies and lapses and hopes and superstitions and stupidities. Good in the proper sense of knowing their smallness in the universe, with the humility and, yes, the grace that comes from that. They wanted so little. All I wanted was for you to meet them. I'm ashamed that I used to laugh at their old-fashionedness. The women with their plastic squares covering their heads when they went to the van, and those strange sisters at school from Linsiadair who wore black clunky sensible shoes their grannies must have given them. We ignored them because they weren't cool like us.

They just seem to have vanished while I wasn't looking. If they were all to rise from their graves and come back tomorrow they would be confused, but then settle down and look for a stove and find one and light a fire. The well at the bottom of the croft is now overgrown with bracken and wild grass, and the old houses filled with crows, with the water-barrels broken and empty, though the old sheep-path to the shore has been widened and marked with clear information for walkers telling you that three kilometres take you to the sea and five kilometres to the ruins of the medieval castle where we were kings and queens and soldiers and vassals. The grassy field behind the school where Dolina and I chased the butterflies is now a car-park. Though when I go near the field where the Annual Fair used to be I still hear the glassy sound and the drovers' voices and the auctioneer's echoing in the air. No one has ever left the Fair. Look – there's Madame Petrovna in her red and yellow caravan, telling the future. Perhaps we spend our lives trying to say what we thought as a child.

It may be after all that the most important things in the world are all the empty spaces. Which is what upset Cuagach – Campbell's desire to fill them up with houses and buildings and planes. As if the cows and sheep and horses didn't need them to feed and graze and wander. Sometimes I want to blink my eyes (or click my heels like Dorothy!) and get a second chance at it all. We were so happy that it was impossible to believe it wouldn't always be like this and that things vanish without trace. And at such speed. The future we longed for has become the sudden past. I have been granted a long life so as to remember them all. For myself. Maybe for you. For Antoine, waiting on the other side of the rickety bridge so that I can cross first.

It's like looking out the front window and seeing them play in the garden in the pouring rain while the back window is catching the sun with a long clear view on the adjoining fields that run on for miles down to the machair. Lord, I cry, why is no one taking care of dear old Mrs MacPherson's garden, gone to rack and ruin simply because she's not there any longer to love it? We wither unloved. If she happened to walk along the road now she would look at it for a minute or two in distress, then go and fetch her hoe and spade and start raking and digging.

I miss seeing Dolina, my friend of eternal promise, but have kept the secret and never told anyone what she told me that day we held hands over the running water. I recover fragments of her whenever I see a river. We used to lie flat on our backs and stare up at the forget-me-not blue sky, and after a while wonder whether we were looking upwards or downwards.

'I'm looking all the way up to heaven,' I said, and Dolina said,

'I'm looking all the way down to Australia. See – there's a kangaroo hopping about!'

It was, of course, a moving cloud, but I never spoilt things by saying so. Nor did she ever say I was merely seeing up into empty space. And I don't think we ever finished the game we always played – the game of 'shops', with those long flat pebbles from the beach for coins and mud and peat mixed with water making the imaginary cakes and scones we sold for tuppence each. If I was given a magic wand I would go daisy-picking down by the stream with Dolina before anything else in the whole world. All you do is tie one little daisy to the next one and then to the next and before you know it you have one long daisy chain that covers the whole world from Dolina's special sitting-place by the school wall all the way down to where the bank runs out by the riverside.

It dawns on me that what connected us all, and will bind us to the grave, is not the place itself, but time, which has stood still and is now non-existent. In the best of times Mam is eternally as she was, Dad lights his pipe, and Duncan and Fearchar and I are running across the machair with Dìleas at our heels. They have become mythic figures, with me all the time, in the same way that some churches illuminate every available space with candle-lights, because even the dark places are still part of the sanctuary. What an empty world it would be if we had nothing to admire or love or worship. If we had nowhere to weep.

I think I was fortunate to somehow know, even as a child, that all these strange older people around were all really children at heart, if only they were permitted to be. Or if only they allowed themselves to be. Since then the pace of change has been so great that my own children, and even Eric, grew up and lived with me as relative strangers. Everything happened so quickly and we didn't have time to slow it down. We all had so many things to do we forgot to sit together on the kitchen stools doing nothing on Saturday mornings. By the time the shopping was done the day was over. It's like when I go to the Borders on holiday in springtime and hear a peewit calling in the fields. It seems strange because he's not crying over the hill loch.

I still see Hazel when I go back, always calling in to see her in her little cottage near the pier. Thankfully she's as free and daft as ever, walking barefoot over the heather to gather her peats, and comfortable enough with me (though not with anyone else) to tell me about the fairies she still sees on her early evening walks out on the old shieling path on their milk-white steeds. You only ever go out of your way for people you really love.

'And the thing is, dear Annie, none of them have grown older. They're the same ones, for I recognise their voices as well as their dress. Even though they've been there years and years their clothes have never worn out. Why would they when they're made to last forever? Their frocks and hats are as green and red as they always were. And they sing the old tunes and dance as well as they ever did. Highland dances. Flings and jigs and reels and waltzes. None of those boring old strathspeys. In other places they'll do ballet and dance on their tiptoes like angels, though not here, Annie. But they bring new tunes. Every time I see them they bring me a new tune, but by the time I get back here I forget it. Why do you think that is, Annie?'

'Age,' I wanted to say, but instead I said, 'Because they want to keep the new things for the moment, Hazel. As a proper secret between you and them.'

She is the best evidence I have that fairies exist.

Eric was a dab hand at building stone walls – our garden was a maze of them as you know – and always said that an object is stable if it tends, after disturbance, to return to its original position. I disagreed, arguing that things always needed to move on and change, though the older I get the less its seems I'm taking my own advice, returning like the mature salmon to the original loch pool. Dad believed the opposite, and abided by the old fishing superstition that it was bad luck to go back into the house for something you'd forgotten. It may be that in the long term Hazel was the most stable of us all. For though she flitted from here to there like a swallow, it was always with perfect airborne balance, as if merely borne by the wind. Happy here and there, then and now.

I think looking back on it she was the only one who always lived for the moment in a sort of present joy. The rest of us didn't. Whether it was baking enough bread to last for days, or cutting enough peats to keep us warm through the whole winter, or studying for exams, we lived for tomorrow. For the result, as it were. It was like the walk from the house down past the fields, on to the shore, down through the villages, past the school and the church and the hall, to the cemetery and from there on to heaven where everyone who was ever good and kind will be sitting on the clover-covered machair singing and making daisy-chains. They will be as delighted to see us as we will be to see them. I hope they won't rise to meet us and accidentally spoil their daisy-chains. Instead, we will kneel down with them, legs tucked under us, and join them in making the loops. Dolina will be there, of course, because she was always so good at making the slit with her fingernails – and sometimes with her teeth – so that I could then slip the daisy stock in to connect. That's what we'll do. It's best when the daisies link together in their natural shape, this way and that, without us having to turn them one way or the other.

Believers ask what heaven will be like, as if it's a single place, like Inverness or Montana. It's zillions of places. A long clover-covered machair here for the people of Barra and Uist and an endless stretch of rocky moorland for the saints of Lewis and Harris and a calm sea for the good folk of Tiree, a mountainous range over there for the people of the Himalayas and Tuscany, a soft swelling and slightly windy sea for all these yachters, wide green perfectly marked out football pitches for Duncan and Fearchar and Sgliugan and Fatty Morrison, and an endless row of stoves for Mam and Misses Peggy and Agnes, and nice cobbled streets for the good folk of Edinburgh! It will be a place of endless activity, like kettles and pots and pans bubbling on the stove and like scythes and harrows and combines cutting the grass and like Fatty Morrison always sticking his leg out and preventing another goal being scored. Gillies will have his forge with Mùgan sitting in the corner smoking his pipe. Rover and Dìleas and Glen will be there, forever gathering the sheep into the pen. Oh, and there will be a choir of angels where, at long last, Eric and I will sing as well as everyone else!

Thank God I still also have strength to climb the brae up to where Lisa stays in the old shack she shared with Niall Cuagach. It's been spruced-up and has solar panels on the roof as witness that the new doesn't have to destroy the old. She grows the most wonderful vegetables, but the best thing is the constant smell of freshly-baking bread that drifts over the moor as you climb to her house. And then she comes out to meet me and we always stand for a while looking down on where the old airstrip used to be and which is now the local football pitch, fenced off to the cattle grazing on all sides. The villages and fields down below look as if they have just been newly washed and put out to dry. It's always the ordinary things that are extraordinary.

'I've no radio or TV or anything so I've no idea now what's going on in the world,' she says. 'Have I missed much?'

Satellite dishes adorn every house and a cavalcade of motor-homes move from north to south, streaming from one ferry to the next, searching for the empty spaces and silence destroyed by the search. Same as you crush a butterfly's wings if you grab it. I don't suppose people will care for things until they have to.

'We'd stand here every morning and Niall used to say the place looked as good as fresh bread,' she says. 'It still does.'

Grey peat smoke still rises from some chimneys, despite the move to oil and now environmentally-friendly wind energy, and the villages all have new houses scattered here and there with children playing outside some of them. Bet they're playing Tig and Chicken and The Ghost in the Well like we did, despite all that cynicism about mobile phones. They will be as familiar with the digital paths of the modern world as I was with the old sheep-path that took me down past the broken plough to the T-junction where the Pictish stone was, and the old churchyard to the machair and the shore. These were tracks and markers that seemed to have been laid out deliberately from the beginning of time to help us navigate. Sometimes I go on the Street View app to walk it digitally from my sitting room, though the camera only takes me as far as the car turning-points. The walking paths remain as yet unmapped.

The strangest success has been Sgliugan, who left school and trained as a mechanic in the local garage where he became an expert in dismantling and re-assembling any engine that was in front of him. He renovated an old lorry and started moving stuff for people. A new road was being built up north and he got the job of transporting material from the cargo boat to the site. He then renovated an old digger and started quarrying, and his business expanded until he had a small fleet of diggers and lorries and stone-crushers and half a dozen workers.

He continued to play in goals for the local football team until he was well into his forties, and those who remember him from the old days still jokingly refer to the brand-new all-weather pitch where the young kids play as Sgliugan's Stadium. He became even more confident and assured of himself as he grew older, suddenly accepting the nickname he couldn't bear to hear as a child as a badge of honour. He took to wearing smart cardigans with coloured leather buttons. Latterly he was elected as local councillor under the splendid banner of A Vote for Sgliugan is a Vote for Sense and Success, though there's no truth in the rumour that the main thing in his manifesto was the offer of free perfumed handkerchiefs! On quiet summer nights they say he wanders down to the machair where the old unmarked pitch was and plays with an invisible ball, scoring endless goals.

The marvellous thing is that when I go home now I see more and more young people return to the old ways of living and working the land. Angela MacCorkindale and her partner and their immediate neighbours, the Coxons, have all gone off-grid and don't use any fossil-consuming machinery on their croft, and it's wonderful to see them ploughing with a horse and cutting the hay with a sickle and scythe. The loveliest looking thing is the hardest thing to do.

'Why?' I asked them.

'Because every little helps,' Angela said. 'And if we let the seasons go we'll have nothing. We can't ask people not to drive or fly off on their holidays if we're not taking care of our small corner of the world. For wide is the road... And besides, everything tastes better when you've sown and grown and harvested it yourself!'

And it does. Their bread is lovely.

The older I get the more I delight in 'little' things. It may be that I just fear unmarked time and need to regulate my day with things to do so that I always have something to look forward to, or look back on, however small it might seem. I divide the day into four, like a cake. Morning, afternoon, evening, night. Sitting in the porch for a while, or – if it's a fine day – out in the garden in the early morning listening to the birds singing in the new day or putting out nuts and bits of bread for them on the little boards and watching them picking up each seed, shelling it and eating the goodness inside. What a contest it is sometimes, with the bigger birds shoving the smaller ones, as is the way of things. But I have enough bird-tables and feeders to keep them all happy, including that ceramic goblet your Mam brought me from Thailand. They do what they want. I want to watch them pecking as they hover in mid-air, but they prefer to eat the fallen seed off the ground, like mere mortals, which is a wee bit disappointing for me, though not for them as they peck away to their hearts' content.

And their dust-baths! Don't they just love them, wriggling about in the soil, then preening themselves in the sun with feathers raised and wings spread out! They're so like us, sheltering and feeding in their little nests in the nooks and crannies, and then hopping on to a swaying branch as if for fun. I leave all the spiders' webs hanging where they are, for they've taken the poor creatures long enough to spin. Who am I to sweep away their life with a duster? Besides, they're sacred creatures, for a spider wove its web over the place where the infant Jesus lay, screening him from his slayers. Sometimes I hear someone whistling in the early morning and I get up to run downstairs to see what Roddy the Postman is bringing in the mail before I realise. The distant sounds become householders cutting the grass with petrol mowers and strimmers and I miss the smell of new-mown hay.

Later on in mid-morning I take my mile long walk down to Bruntsfield to my favourite café for a coffee and croissant and do that old-fashioned thing of either talking to whoever is around or reading a book. We talk about everything from the state of the weather to that of the world. Everyone drinks coffee now, and I have long learned to love the taste as well as the smell. My favourite is the Organic Segafredo Zanetti. Astonishing how we become connoisseurs of the once unknown. When you visit, I will turn into Effie and fetch out my best china cups to drink it from. And you can use that old mallet to crush the beans and I won't give a hoot if you smash them all over the place and make a mess and waken and frighten all the neighbours!

Somehow, I have also managed to avoid the tragedy of old age which – they say – is to have all you need but the taste of it gone. Sometimes I catch a glimpse of a silver-haired woman in a merciless shop mirror and wonder what Mam is doing there. Latterly, Angela used to call in on her once a week to do her hair, and when I sit in the hairdresser's here in Bruntsfield I wonder why I resist having curlers and a shampoo-and-set like she always did, choosing instead to go with the shorter, flatter cut. No one wants to grow old. I'm grateful for what I have. Writing to you has kept me young since that beautiful August evening, months or years ago. Like a child swinging on a branch, it's been all instinct and risk and trust.

Sometimes I get confused. I turn the corner from Bruntsfield into Montpelier Park and the cornfield Mam and Dad were cutting a moment ago is not there. Of course it isn't. And the corncrake I heard first thing this morning was just the man next door whirring his electric bicycle as he set off for work. Of course it was.

One of the benefits of age is that I walk slower and so see more. I'm forever finding ten and twenty pence pieces on the pavement because I look down a lot, and the same when walking past hedges and window-sills and alcoves and walls. I see all kinds of things, from snails to cigarette packets stuck in every second nook and cranny because I'm not rushing by. The other day I untangled a wee sparrow which had somehow ensnared itself in the bowling green fence. I collect any rubbish I find into a small cloth bag I always carry with me so that it doesn't spoil the environment. There's a little stone bridge that crosses the canal and when I reach it Antoine always takes my hand and walks me over to the other side. I know some folk look at me with interest, and a few with a wee bit of pity. Sometimes I walk along Bruntsfield listening only to the birds singing above the constant noise of traffic, and aspire to their perfection by singing quietly to myself, forgetting that everyone is hearing me, 'Praise, my soul, the King of Heaven, to His feet your tribute bring.' They glance at me, wondering. Then I see them think, Ach, it's okay. She's just a daft auld wifie. Lord, have mercy. A Thighearna dèan tròcair oirnn!

Sometimes wee Mrs MacGowan chums me along. Well, when I say chum, I mean she suddenly appears and walks along with me blethering thirteen to the dozen. She lives opposite me. I think she hides inside her porch until she sees me going for my walk, then comes out to tell me things. She's a terrible gossip, but because she talks all the time it doesn't really matter whether I hear or agree or disagree or say anything. I tried at first, but it's best just to smile or tut-tut now and again. Occasionally, I get the bus down into the city to go to the gallery, where the attendants all know me now and give me a seat. I like sitting there looking at the Rembrandts because the red glow in his pictures reminds me of the way our own stove used to shimmer under the light of the oil lamps.

When I get home in the afternoon I read or knit wee things for all of you and listen to Radio Three. I feel like a child then, reassured that some things last. I used to watch *Newsnight* until I got scunnered with their self-importance. As if there were not a million stories. Now and again, I take a journey on the bus and climb the stairs so as to sit at the front upstairs, just so that I can look out at the familiar street names that have so long now been my rod and comfort in this adopted city – Easter Road, and London Road where I first met Eric, and the Royal Mile so that I can feel the youthful rattle of the cobbles, and on up past the King's Theatre and Meggetland and the canal, where Aonghas used to play football before the fields were all turned into houses. The thing I most notice is that every free space is now filled with an advert. The Five Nations tickets already for sale for next year! I'm sure the All Blacks will win again, of course. Why don't you come over for that?

Thank you for the constant encouragement to hang out these fragments, waving like old Mùgan's washing in the breeze. His meal-sacks drying in the wind. I forgot how near and far away everything is when you think about it. At one time, it was like grasping the wind itself. Now it's like handling well-worn and well-used bowls and shoes and wooden spoons. I sometimes lie down in the afternoon in the back room, which is so quiet. Except it's not a silence, but a sort of soft hum, someone clipping the hedge maybe, or a boy or girl wheeling a plastic barrow in the back garden a few doors away. It's the same warm sound I used to hear as a child, something happening near but far away. Roddy cycling by. Morag's dog, Spot, barking far off. Everything that was far away has been brought near. They all call by for a wee cèilidh on their way to the machair every afternoon.

I write this by candle-light, Emily, though reliant on the marvel of electricity. Choice is a wonderful thing. I think of the thousands – the millions – of people who've benefited from electricity. All my patients, the nurses and doctors I worked with, my children, Dad and my darling Mam whose latter days were blessed with the ease of central heating and the warmth of an electric blanket and the consolation and friendship of television and a long hot bath or shower any time she wanted. The delight she took in watching and singing along to Songs of Praise *on TV since she wasn't able to go to church anymore. That and Wimbledon and the Olympics – she loved watching the long distant runners. Her favourite athlete of all time was Kip Keino, who ran as if he was just running down to Donnie's shop for messages, she said. Oh, and Björn Borg. She liked him. Our favourite moments were when I washed her hair. It reminded her of the morning of her wedding, when Marion had done up her hair in that special way. I caressed her beautiful scarred head through the soft fleece that was left. She remembered doing that to me as a child, saying my hair used to fall into curly rings.*

How glad she was that she was liberated from the burden of having to go to the well for buckets of water, and having to rise long before sunrise on cold winter mornings to sit on a freezing bucket before stirring and lighting the fire, and going up the hill to carry home a bag of peats, and from standing all day at those hand-wringers washing clothes and blankets. And the conditions in which previous generations had lived, barely surviving on bread and lard in the cities or on shellfish in the islands. Living to the age of forty if they were lucky, with half of those who were born dying before the age of five. Oh, the blessings of clean running water and warmth and food and memory and health and instant light.

Though nothing is instant. Like the water in the well, which has fought its way through underground cracks and crevices for centuries. So with these memories. As they pushed their way up through the rocks and mud the skies became a bit bluer, and Mùgan a bit wiser and Lisa a bit smarter and Cuagach a bit stranger. But maybe that was only because the nearer they came to the light the brighter and the livelier they became, until they shone like electricity everywhere I looked.

Or like candles flickering in the dark, their fragrance filling the room.

With all my love

Gran x x